GHOSTS OF EMPIRE

BOOK FOUR OF THE EMPIRE OF BONES SAGA

YOWLING
CAT PRESS

BOOK FOUR OF THE EMPIRE OF BONES SAGA

GHOSTS OF EMPIRE

When on deadly ground...

...FIGHT!

TERRY MIXON

BESTSELLING AUTHOR OF *PAYING THE PRICE*

Ghosts of Empire
Copyright © 2015 by Terry Mixon

All rights reserved. No part of this book may be reproduced or transmitted in any form or by any means, electronic or mechanical, including information storage and/or retrieval systems, or dissemination of any electronic version, without the prior written consent of the publisher, except by a reviewer, who may quote brief passages in a review, and except where permitted by law.

This is a work of fiction. All names, characters, places, and incidents are the products of the author's imagination, or are used fictitiously. Any resemblance to actual persons, living or dead, events, or locales is entirely coincidental.

Published by Yowling Cat Press ®
Print ISBN: 978-0692604113
Edition date: 12/26/2017

Cover art - image copyrights as follows:
BigStockPhotos/goinyk
BigStockPhotos/egal
DepositPhotos/innovari (Luca Oleastri)
DepositPhotos/andreus (Andrea Danti)
DepositPhotos/sdecoret (Sébastien Decoret)
NASA/JPL-CalTech
Donna Mixon

Cover design and composition by Donna Mixon

Print edition interior design composition by Terry Mixon and Donna Mixon

Editing services by Red Adept Editing
Reach them at: http://www.redadeptediting.com

Audio edition performed and produced by Veronica Giguere
Reach her at: v@voicesbyveronica.com

TERRY'S BOOKS

You can always find the most up to date listing of Terry's titles on his Amazon Author Page.

The Empire of Bones Saga
Empire of Bones
Veil of Shadows
Command Decisions
Ghosts of Empire
Paying the Price
Reconnaissance in Force
Behind Enemy Lines
The Terran Gambit

The Empire of Bones Saga Volume 1

The Humanity Unlimited Saga
Liberty Station
Freedom Express
Tree of Liberty

The Fractured Republic Saga
Storm Divers

The Scorched Earth Saga
Scorched Earth

The Vigilante Duology with Glynn Stewart
Heart of Vengeance
Oath of Vengeance

Want Terry to email you when he publishes a new book in any format or when one goes on sale?
Go to TerryMixon.com/Mailing-List and sign up.
Those are the only times he'll contact you. No spam.

DEDICATION

This book would not be possible without the love, support, and encouragement of my beautiful wife. Donna, I love you more than life itself.

ACKNOWLEDGEMENTS

Once again, the people who read my books before you see them have saved me. Thanks to Tracy Bodine, Michael Falkner, Cain Hopwood, Rick Lopez, Kristopher Neidecker, Bob Noble, Jon Paul Olivier, Tom Stoecklein, Dale Thompson, and Jason Young for making me look good.

I also want to thank my readers for putting up with me.
You guys are great.

1

"What the hell is that?" Princess Kelsey Bandar asked.

Commander Scott Roche, captain of the Imperial Fleet destroyer *Ginnie Dare*, leaned over Kelsey's shoulder and frowned at the derelict tumbling on her console's screen. "A mystery. I've been studying the Old Empire Fleet databases, and that ship isn't in it."

Kelsey knew that for a fact. She'd downloaded all the available ship's databases—military and civilian—into her implants before they'd started this survey of the graveyard, the name she'd decided fit the swarm of wrecked Old Empire ships orbiting Boxer Station.

Admiral Jared Mertz—her half brother—had tasked Commander Roche with watching over the sector base and examining the graveyard while he handled the negotiations with Harrison's World to get their captured people back. Since those talks were going nowhere fast, she'd decided to take a pinnace out to the destroyer and explore the sea of dead ships.

The horror floating before them in the cold darkness was mind-numbingly vast. They'd tallied tens of thousands of wrecks, all of them filled with dead Fleet personnel, she was sure. They'd been resting here since the destruction of the Old Empire more than five centuries ago.

They'd only examined a small area of the graveyard. The worst-case estimates were between forty and fifty thousand derelicts in wide orbits around Boxer Station. And those were the ships the rebels hadn't destroyed outright. She still couldn't imagine how many desperate battles the Old Empire had lost to fill this terrible place.

Most of the ships they'd found weren't salvageable, but the Terran Empire needed every one that was. Or they would once the enemy, the terrible shade of the Old Empire, discovered it hadn't won a complete victory.

Commander Eliyanna Kaiser and the destroyer *New York* were on their way to the Pentagaran and Erorsi systems. They'd bring back as many people and ships as their allies could spare. They'd need them all.

Jared's ragtag fleet consisted of two destroyers that weren't capable of fighting Old Empire ships of any class, two heavily damaged Old Empire battlecruisers, and a severely battered Old Empire superdreadnought, *Invincible*.

Of the battlecruisers, the ship they'd arrived in—*Courageous*—was still capable of all operations, but the other one—*Scott Pond*—wasn't able to flip. That meant it couldn't leave this system.

With more people, they could bring Boxer Station—the massive Old Empire Fleet base in this system—back online and put their ships into the construction yards for repair.

Which brought her full circle. The AIs that had brought the Old Empire derelicts here after defeating them in battle had sorted each group of ships into classes. This single ship floated alone, and none of the probes had seen anything remotely like it.

One of the obvious differences between it and the other ships was its size. This vessel was only about four times the tonnage of a marine pinnace, but it had flip drives. From the outside, it didn't seem badly wrecked. There was a large hole in the hull amidships, but the damage looked contained.

Kelsey turned in her seat and devoted her full attention to Commander Roche. On one of the Old Empire ships, she could've used her implants to continue examining the ship through the scanners, but on *Ginnie Dare*, she was limited to what she could see with her own eyes.

"Maybe it's some kind of scout ship," she said. "Though, it seems as though there'd be more of them, and the databases would at least know what it was."

"Well, something that small wouldn't take long to explore," he said. "I don't like things I can't explain. We should check it out."

"Good idea. I'll take my security detail over for a look. If you'll get a technical team together, they can assess things once we clear it."

The Fleet officer nodded. "I'll get them down to marine country. I feel obligated to tell you to be careful. Admiral Mertz wouldn't be pleased with me if anything happened to you."

No, her brother would be pretty upset. That made her feel good inside. Their relationship had really improved. Her father was going to be shocked and pleased about that when she finally got home.

Her twin brother, Ethan, was going to be surprised as well, though hardly pleased. He hated Jared and didn't trust him. She hoped that the events of this expedition would help change his mind, but she wasn't going to hold her breath.

"I promise to be cautious," Kelsey said. "Besides, I'll be in commando armor. I doubt anything over there would be able to harm me. I'll stay in constant contact. You can mother hen me if you feel the need."

"I'm *so* reassured."

She laughed. "You'll get used to me after a few more months. Then you'll barely cringe when something terrible happens."

Kelsey had to smile at his suddenly stricken expression. "Lighten up, Scott. Everything will be fine."

After a beat, he sighed. "I don't think I'll ever get used to the second in line to the Imperial Throne calling me by my first name."

"Relax," she said. "We put our pants on just like everyone else. With servants to hold us up and slide them on while we drink ridiculously expensive tea served in tiny cups made from the bones of our enemies."

He smiled. "Just like I'd always imagined. Be careful, Highness."

* * *

"YOUR DEMANDS ARE UNACCEPTABLE," Deputy Coordinator King said haughtily. "I cannot comprehend what you hope to gain by defying me. I am one of the higher orders, and I demand you comply with my lawful directives."

Jared was glad this conversation was taking place in his office. He was doubly glad that the woman was talking with him remotely. If she was this bad on screen, he could only imagine how obnoxious she was in person.

Deputy Coordinator King was the most trying individual he'd dealt with since leaving Avalon. The only person who rubbed him worse might be his half brother Ethan, and he wanted to *kill* Jared.

He tamped down his temper and gave the woman a bland smile. "My demands, Deputy Coordinator King, are not defiance. You have Fleet personnel in your custody. Several thousand people that you have no right to hold under any circumstances. If you want to discuss other matters, I'm more than willing to do so, but only once you return my people to me."

"Perhaps if I made examples of a few of them, it would shake you out of the belief that you can dictate terms to me or Harrison's World," she said coldly. "Those people were transported here as prisoners by the system Lord. You would do well to remember who you truly serve, *Admiral* Mertz."

Her less-than-subtle emphasis on his rank had far less impact than she probably expected. Three days ago, he'd been a commander. The shock of his sister promoting him still hadn't worn off.

Not that he was going to share that point with Deputy Coordinator King. He wasn't even a member of her version of Fleet. Harrison's World was under the control of what his people called the Rebel Empire. The Old Empire his people had fled from had fallen to the rebels and now answered to the AIs that had killed uncounted trillions of people.

Of course, Harrison's World hadn't been in the good graces of the system AI when Jared and his people snuck in. Jared had no idea what they'd done to warrant imprisonment, but the AI had placed three weapons platforms in orbit and had destroyed a number of urban centers.

In other words, the woman on his screen had a lot of nerve talking to him as though she had any leverage. Particularly with the Rebel Empire Fleet that she believed he represented. Besides, he wouldn't tolerate her threatening his people.

"With all due deference, Deputy Coordinator King, you're full of crap."

Her eyes bugged. "How dare you! I'll have you flogged for speaking to me in—"

"You seem to have forgotten your circumstances," Jared said harshly. "Are you claiming the system Lord imprisoned you unjustly? I'm a duly appointed Fleet Admiral with the full backing of the Empire. One in complete control of the orbital bombardment platforms. I suggest you remember how precarious your position truly is before you make threats like that."

Her eyes narrowed dangerously. "The Lord made a mistake. Not the only one, based on your mission here to deal with it. I feel confident that your orders also include instructions to do exactly what I've been insisting on.

"We'll find out when I come up to discuss the matter in person tomorrow morning. You will send a cutter for me. I suggest you take whatever steps you need to salve your bruised ego, Admiral, because this matter is going to be decided in my favor."

She disconnected without another word.

Jared rubbed his eyes. "Can she really be that stupid?"

"I've discovered that rhetorical questions often have yes for an answer," a mellow voice said through the overhead speakers. *Invincible*, the AI they'd installed inside the hull of the same name, was fully sentient, just like the Lords of the Rebel Empire, only without their homicidal core rules.

"That's because we have to ask to be sure we heard the idiots correctly the first time," Jared said. He leaned back in his chair and stared at the ceiling. "Which doesn't explain why she's so certain that she's going to get what she wants. Does she know something we don't?"

"Almost certainly. Until we can unlock the memory of the AI from Boxer Station, we have no idea what caused it to suppress this system. Though the presence of this vessel does indicate some kind of revolt was in progress."

They'd found *Invincible* floating in the graveyard when they'd snuck into distant orbit around Boxer Station. Rebel Fleet personnel and civilians from Harrison's World had restored it to complete functionality, minus any computer system. They'd also shielded her power systems, so they'd obviously desired to avoid discovery.

The final messages from the people onboard had strongly hinted that they were going to rebel against the AI. They would've failed, but they wouldn't have known that until it was too late. It had taken the addition of his ships to make the battle one they could win. Barely.

The senior Rebel Fleet officer had left a message to the woman ruling Harrison's World, Olivia West. She must've been in on the coup. Jared didn't know the reasons why, but there was more going on than met the eye.

"At least we have all night to figure out how to handle her," Jared said. "With the flip-point jammers in place, we can finally be mostly certain no one is about to spring a surprise on us. How goes the scan of the system?"

"Our probes are still searching the more distant areas, but they've located a single weak flip point. I only received the data a few minutes ago."

Weak flip points were a previously unknown version of regular flip points. Unlike the normal kind that assured reliable travel across hundreds of light-years, the weak ones were hard to detect. In at least some cases, they didn't assure two-way travel. Hence, his people being trapped so far from home.

The science teams were working overtime to understand them more fully, but he didn't trust having one in his lap.

He grunted. "So there's a back door? Wonderful."

"If I might be so bold, Admiral, you've never had anyone sneak out of one to surprise you."

"Unless you count Captain Breckenridge."

The disgraced Fleet captain was in *Invincible*'s brig. He'd betrayed his oath to the Empire and attempted to kidnap Princess Kelsey. His retreat through another weak flip point had led to the crippling of his ship and the capture of thousands of Fleet personnel—the very ones Jared was trying to get back.

"We should send a probe through," Jared said, "but I'll hold off until we know a little more about the situation here. We absolutely don't need a second front to this war. Any word from Kelsey?"

"She's exploring an unusual derelict," the AI said, "but everything looks safe enough, according to Captain Roche. He's listening in as they check it out."

"Well, I certainly hope she doesn't find anything dangerous. She has a knack for turning up trouble in the most unusual places."

"The odds of that seem unlikely."

"That's only because you don't know my sister. If there's something dangerous on any of those ships, she'll find it."

* * *

KELSEY HEADED INTO THE LIFT. It took her swiftly down to the appropriate level, and she made her way to *Ginnie Dare*'s marine country.

It was kind of spooky. *Ginnie Dare* had the same layout as Jared's old ship, *Athena*. Kelsey had many fond memories of spending time with the marines there.

Bittersweet, too. So many of the men and women she'd befriended were gone now, killed in the various actions against the Pale Ones and the AIs. The worst loss was Lieutenant Tim Reese, the commanding officer of the marines on *Athena* and then *Courageous*. He'd died taking Boxer Station.

Kelsey put on a neutral face and walked in. This wasn't the time to bring everyone down.

The marines were bustling around doing tasks that she actually understood now. Commander Roche must've called ahead to start people moving.

Lieutenant Angela Ellis, *Ginnie Dare*'s detachment commander, was waiting for her. "Highness. The captain let us know about the excursion. Do you need a full complement of marines?"

Kelsey looked up at the woman. Angela was tall and well built. Not just tall for a woman. Really tall. As in over two meters. She towered over most of the men under her command, and she was easily a giant as far as Kelsey was concerned. Half a meter was a lot of difference.

If they were ever able to start enhancing other people, Angela would make a formidable combatant.

She'd caught a flechette boarding Boxer Station but seemed to have recovered fully. Kelsey was glad. They'd lost far too many good people that day.

"I don't think so," Kelsey said. "It's not very big. I'm thinking Senior Sergeant Coulter, my team, and some techs."

Howard Coulter was the man that Marine Captain Russ Talbot—also Kelsey's boyfriend—had placed in charge of her guard detail. He'd be going no matter what she said, so she might as well incorporate him into her plan.

If her decision made the marine lieutenant feel slighted, she showed no sign of it. "I assumed that's what you'd want, so they're already armoring up. I took the liberty of getting your gear prepped, as well."

"Thank you. This shouldn't take long. If you'll excuse me, I'll go get ready."

The compartment outside the armory was where marines prepped for missions. As they were a co-ed organization, there weren't separate areas for women. That had taken a while to get used to, but now she was able to strip down and armor up without turning beet red.

The marines were almost ready to go, so she changed into her skinsuit. The Old Empire garment provided some protection of its own, which had come in handy on Boxer Station. It also allowed her armor to handle waste management. That was embarrassing, too, but after six hours in a suit, one welcomed the ability to use the bathroom.

Coulter and his people were still using Terran Empire Marine armor. Her powered Old Empire commando suit was significantly tougher and more capable than anything they'd ever seen before.

They'd captured suits of powered marine armor from the Rebel Empire that unenhanced people could use, but she didn't trust them. Those paranoid bastards had put bombs and other devices in them to control their military.

In her mind, it was far better to get something set up to do implants again and allow their marines to use the armor they'd found on so many Old Empire ships in the graveyard. The vast amount of salvageable equipment was arguably enough to outfit every marine in the Terran Empire, with plenty left over to share with their allies.

Kelsey's commando armor was dark grey with a faceless helmet. It augmented her already formidable strength and speed. It wasn't invincible by any means, but it made survival possible in the insanity that was combat with Old Empire weapons.

The armor hung from a rack, so she was able to open the back and step into it. A mental command through her cranial implants closed it up around her. She stepped clear and held her helmet in the crook of her arm.

Coulter and the half dozen marines assigned to her team gathered at her gesture. "We're ready, Princess. What's the target?"

"A mystery ship that doesn't appear in the Old Empire databases. It might not even be Imperial. We'll board and clear. Once we're sure it's safe, we'll bring the technical people in to give it a look."

Coulter nodded. "Got it. We go in prepared for hostile action. If it's as dead as everything else in the graveyard, no problem. If it has any surprises, we're ready. Mount up, people."

They boarded the marine pinnace together with a dozen technicians.

The approach went smoothly enough. Since they were using an Old Empire pinnace, she could interface with its scanners.

The small ship certainly looked dead as it tumbled in space half a dozen kilometers from *Ginnie Dare*, but *Invincible* had proved that appearances could be deceptive. The people from Harrison's World had brought the superdreadnought online and shielded her so well that Jared's people hadn't known she was operational until they boarded her.

Kelsey spotted a small hole on the other side of the ship from the large one she'd noted earlier. It was less than half a meter in diameter. It looked as though something small and fast had punched through the vessel. An asteroid, perhaps?

She supposed it was possible the damage was postcapture. Maybe they could figure it out once they boarded.

The pinnace came in slowly and matched the tumble of the ship. They clamped on with a thump.

"We're tight," the pilot said. "I'm going to use the pinnace's grav drives to level us out. With a ship this small, it shouldn't take more than a few minutes."

The ship slowed its mad spin until it was at rest relative to *Ginnie Dare*. Only then did Coulter take off his restraints and stand.

"Boarding party, form up on the ramp," he said.

Kelsey made no fuss when the marines put her at the back. If she needed to get up front, she could do so quickly enough. Everyone hooked up lines to prevent something from throwing one of them into deep space.

The ramp lowered, revealing the cold, bright stars looking down on the tomb beneath their feet. The marines led the way onto the hull, their magnetic boots holding them steady. Her armor had a miniature grav drive that would allow her to fly around if she chose, but she followed their lead.

They could've gained access through the rupture in the hull, but there was an airlock right there. The marines circled it, and one of them accessed the controls.

"It isn't opening," the woman said after a minute. "It has power, it's just not responding to me."

"Let me take a look," Kelsey said.

The controls had power. She could feel it through her implants. She sent a command to open, and the system promptly rejected her.

Nonplussed, she pressed the manual controls to open it. The lock queried her implants and rejected her a second time.

"That's new," she said. "It pinged my implants and told me to get lost."

"Welcome to the world the rest of us live in, Princess," Coulter said with a smile. "Luckily, we have another way in."

Kelsey looked at the rupture. The interior of the ship wasn't inside the reach of the pinnace's floodlights. The inky blackness had an ominous feel to it. What would they find inside this wreck? Or what might find them?

2

Commander Sean Meyer woke abruptly. The dark shadow of a man hovered over him. The figure had a hand over Sean's mouth. Not to smother but to keep him from crying out and waking everyone in the prison bunkroom.

He nodded to show the man that he was awake. Frankly, he'd half expected someone to attack him before now. Many of these men and women had been under his authority just a week ago. Before he'd betrayed their captain. He'd heard more than a few muttered curses, and everyone had avoided him like the plague.

The man tugged on Sean's arm and guided him toward the men's shower without a word of explanation. Sean was more than a bit surprised when the man began stripping, with every sign of taking a very early morning shower.

He did the same, hoping this wasn't some convoluted plan to kill him.

Two men were already in the shower, and steam covered every worn surface. They'd been cleaning the buildings, so the smell of old age and lingering rot was beginning to fade.

The sound of the rushing water was loud in his ears. Loud enough to conceal a murder, if the men were so inclined. A conspicuously open spot for Sean stood between the two men. His guide moved away from them and turned on the water at the far side of the room.

In the dim light, Sean recognized his guide as an enlisted man from *Spear*'s marine complement. One of the two older men waiting for Sean was *Spear's* senior noncommissioned officer, Command Master Chief Ulysses Ross. He didn't know the third man.

"Command Master Chief," he said as he stripped and took his assigned place. He turned the water on and adjusted it until it was as hot as he could stand. If he was going to be naked in the shower, he might as well enjoy it.

"No ranks," the bald man said. "We think the showers are safe, but I'm not willing to take unnecessary risks, Sean."

"I understand, Ulysses. I was pretty sure no one wanted to talk to me, so I'm surprised to see you."

Ross gave him a cool smile. "Yeah, well, we find ourselves in odd times. You and the boss had a disagreement. Without going into specifics, I'd like you to explain that to us. Oh, my friend is Albert Newland. Al did the same job as me on *Shadow*."

Shadow had been the heavy cruiser *Spear's* consort before the Rebel Empire had destroyed the light cruiser. Now both vessels were gone.

So the two senior enlisted men among the prisoners wanted to have a private chat with *Spear's* disgraced executive officer. He'd find out soon enough if it was for good or ill.

"Well, Wallace and I did have some words. I told him I thought he was making a mistake in the strongest of terms."

Ross snorted. "That you did. You took something he wanted very badly and gave it away."

"He had no right to take it in the first place. Look, I knew the penalty for crossing him, and I'm more than willing to pay the price for it. Still, that seems a little off topic, considering our current circumstances."

He'd been in the brig when the AI's forces had attacked *Spear*. The machines had slain or stunned anyone who resisted. They'd cut him out of his cell and herded him with the enlisted prisoners. An understandable mistake, since Captain Breckenridge had ripped Sean's rank tabs off with his own hands.

The machines drove the prisoners into a large cargo hold, and Breckenridge had ordered them only to give their name and serial number if questioned. Nothing else. The officers had quickly gotten rid of their rank tabs, perhaps thinking that would keep the AI from targeting them for enhanced interrogation. Officers were more likely to know how to get back to the Terran Empire.

All of them knew what was at risk. If word slipped out, the Terran Empire would die.

The AI hadn't spared *Spear's* wounded, either. The medical staff did what they could, but many died.

The machines herded the enlisted people onto ships and brought them to this planet. Apparently the AI had known who was an officer based on their rank tabs the moment it had captured them. So much for the subterfuge.

Sean had only seen one other officer among the men and women: *Shadow*'s critically injured captain, Paul Cooley. He'd been awake when the machines had brought him into the hold but had lapsed into unconsciousness by the time they'd started for the planet.

Based on the severity of his injuries, Sean wouldn't be surprised if the man had died, though the people on the planet had whisked the wounded away once they'd landed, supposedly to a medical facility.

They'd sent Sean and the rest to this old military base. They were on an island, but that was about all they knew. Their captors weren't interested in talking to them. Other than guard patrols and daily landings under heavy guard to drop off some of the nastiest rations he'd ever tasted, they ignored the prisoners.

"That can be sorted out in time," Ross continued. "It's above my pay grade, in any case. What I want to know is why you disobeyed orders. The real reason. I know you didn't think so highly of the things you gave back."

"You're wrong," Sean said flatly. "I valued one of them very much. So much that I couldn't stand to see how Wallace treated it. The second thing was more valuable than Wallace gave it credit for, but the first was a matter of principle that I couldn't let pass."

Captain Breckenridge had taken Princess Kelsey and Commander Mertz prisoner. If it had only been Mertz, Sean would've probably let things go, but he couldn't allow his captain to take the second in line to the Imperial Throne hostage. It was unthinkable. So he'd acted.

Ross gave him a hard look and then nodded. "That's about what I expected you'd say. I've never known you to be disloyal, but the boss put you in a hard spot. Hell, he put us all into a difficult situation."

"Without any officers here to provide guidance, I took it on myself to speak with the others in enlisted leadership positions. You might've been in the brig when this all went down, but as far as we're concerned, that's a problem for others to sort out later. We'd like you to resume your duties."

Newland nodded. "Several of our people overheard two guards talking about some unknown ships taking out the AIs. One of them mentioned Mertz. You've met the man. Do you think he might have turned the tables on those mechanical bastards?"

Sean blinked in surprise. Mertz was a capable officer, but he only had one undermanned battlecruiser. Yes, it was a powerful ship, but…

He put that thought out of his head. "Mertz is more resourceful than we gave him credit for. Is it possible? Maybe. I'm not sure how it helps us down here, though."

"It might not," Ross said. "We won't know until someone actually talks to us. When that time comes, I think you should be our point man. As the senior prisoner, you need to take the conversation to them. Let them know you're the force master chief. We'll back your play."

Sean nodded. "Has everyone been told I'll be resuming my duties?"

"Not yet, but they'll hear about it before dawn. Time to dry off and head back to our barracks. I'm developing permanent wrinkles."

* * *

"LET ME TAKE YOU INSIDE," Kelsey told Coulter. "The edges aren't a threat to suit integrity that way."

The marine noncom nodded. "I'll go first. Form up for quick entry, everyone."

He disconnected himself from the line and floated free of the hull. He'd turned off his magnetic boots.

Kelsey followed suit and grabbed him. It only took a moment to bring them over the opening with her suit's grav generator. Their lights played inside the ship. The cone of destruction led right to the hole on the opposite side. At its widest, the wound was over a dozen meters across. Even after all this time, there was still some debris floating in the damaged area.

"Yeah," she said. "Something small and going very fast blew through this ship. Probably an asteroid. It doesn't look like a missile hit or a beam blast. This is purely kinetic."

Her original plan had been to push him inside, but the number of sharp objects made that too risky. "I'll take you all the way in. Maybe we can open the lock from the inside."

"No," he said. "Bring everyone in. We'll start exploring from the central corridor. I can see that it's open on both sides."

"That's boring," she whined in her best ten-year-old girl voice. "Okay. You stay right there once I drop you off."

It only took a few minutes to get them all inside. They split up, with some going aft while the remainder went toward the bow. As small as the ship was, it wouldn't take long to search.

The interior lights were on, as was the gravity. That indicated the ship still had power. Since they hadn't detected the fusion plants, even at point-blank range, the designers had shielded them devilishly well.

Considering that breaches in the hull should've made the detection inevitable, this ship had even better shielding than *Invincible*.

Kelsey decided to go with the bow team. There were no indications of combat inside the ship. Things were surprisingly neat and orderly. The dead Fleet personnel they found were in vacuum suits. Based on their expressions, they'd died relatively peacefully in places of their own choosing.

Coulter examined the dead as they went. "These people weren't under AI control. No beards or long hair. The AIs aren't big on personal hygiene."

She knew that far too well. The Pale Ones still featured prominently in her frequent nightmares.

"One other thing," he said. "The emergency doors are wide open. Was there a systems failure, or was that intentional?"

"Considering the lack of things blown around, I'd say intentional. Maybe we'll find out what happened when we get to the bridge."

That didn't take long. More men and women in Fleet vacuum suits sat at the controls. They seemed to have died peacefully as well. A quick check of the consoles found them all locked.

"Sergeant Coulter, Princess Kelsey, this is Corporal Brand. I'm in engineering. I'm no tech, but I'm only seeing grav drives and fusion plants."

She frowned. "That doesn't make any sense. The ship has flip vanes."

"Maybe the impact took the flip drives out," Coulter said. "This isn't a very big ship. The grav drives need to be in the stern, but the flip drives can be anywhere inside the hull. They're normally in engineering, but that's a matter of convenience."

"That would've sucked," Kelsey said. "Trapped in whatever system you were in when everything went down the crapper. Maybe we can access the computer and find out. Let's get the techs."

It wasn't difficult finding the airlock. It opened easily from the inside.

The techs came on board and spread throughout the ship. She followed the computer expert to the compartment set aside for it adjacent to the bridge. It wasn't as massive as the one aboard *Courageous*, but it wasn't tiny, either.

"It's still powered," the tech declared, "but it's not responding to my attempts to access it."

"Let me have a try." Kelsey used her implants to find the interface and attempted to connect. It promptly rejected her, but this time it gave her a reason.

Access denied. Implant codes not recognized.

My name is Kelsey Bandar. I'm an ambassador plenipotentiary of the Terran Empire. Here are my authorization codes.

This unit does not recognize your authority, Ambassador Plenipotentiary Kelsey Bandar. This unit is restricted to access only by certain personnel.

She considered how to respond to that. There were other avenues to gain access. She just needed to know what the machine was looking for.

Can you clarify what type of authorization is acceptable?

Only personnel with correct access codes and appropriate hardware may access this unit without authorization.

Perhaps I have the correct hardware. Why not? She had every other kind of equipment inside her.

Kelsey gasped as the computer probed her implants. At least the intrusion was quick.

You do have the correct hardware but lack the required access codes.

She considered how best to explain the situation. *Over five hundred years have passed since the rebellion. The Terran Empire still exists, but we're only just beginning to recover. Does my hardware grant me a more detailed explanation? Perhaps I can clarify things to your satisfaction. What hardware are you checking, by the way?*

You possess Marine Raider implants. This vessel is a Raider strike ship. You do not possess the required Raider access codes, however.

Her heart soared. A commando ship with a computer that could explain her implants to her! This was exactly what she needed!

As I have the hardware, will you grant me provisional access?

Negative. Without the appropriate Marine Raider codes, this unit may not grant you access. Warning. Attempting to access this unit without authorization will cause it to self-destruct.

It was as though it knew that she'd be tempted to get around the restrictions. So much for the easy way.

She turned to Coulter. "This is a commando ship. Or, as the computer calls them, Marine Raiders. It won't give me access. Once again, I'm stuck without an easy way to get the information I need."

"Princess Kelsey, this is Corporal Brand again. We found something else you need to see. Can you come down to the medical center?"

Medical center might have been too gracious a term. It was maybe twice the size of her old quarters on *Athena*. There were a few beds and one cramped operating theater.

The latter showed the first mess that she'd seen on the ship. The table had a few large smears of dried blood, and the scattered instruments made it look as though a hurried operation had just ended.

There was also one large piece of equipment that the marines had gathered around.

"What do you have?" she asked.

"I'm not sure, but there's someone in there," Brand said.

Kelsey looked through the port, and there was indeed a man lying on a gurney inside. He had terrible injuries to his head and face. She could see the graphene coating his skull. Since only commandos had that particular enhancement, he must be one. Unlike the other bodies on the ship, he wasn't a desiccated husk.

Shocked, she checked the equipment with her implants. It was a stasis unit, the same kind of machinery that had kept Reginald Bell alive for hundreds of years, and it was running.

"Dear God," she said. "He's still alive. We've found an Imperial commando."

3

"Hey there, Cowboy."

Jared glanced over at his executive officer in surprise. No, Charlie Graves wasn't his XO anymore. Kelsey had promoted him to captain and placed him in command of the battlecruiser *Courageous*. Which was where he should be, now that Jared thought about it.

"Charlie, what the hell are you doing on my bridge? Don't you have a ship to put back together?"

The younger man grinned. "I do, Admiral, but I need to speak with you privately. Since we had a cutter coming over for some spare parts, I figured now was the time. Might we step into your office, sir?"

Jared rose and gestured toward his office just off the flag bridge. "After you. Zia, you have the conn."

"Aye, sir." His tactical officer, now promoted to executive officer of *Invincible*, took over his station. Her long-time partner in crime, Pasco Ramirez, was filling that role for Graves on *Courageous*. There were higher-ranking officers available, but Jared didn't trust them.

The officers from *Spear* and *Shadow* had been on Boxer Station when Kelsey and the marines had captured it, but they'd supported Captain Wallace Breckenridge's mutiny.

Of course, so had the destroyers *New York* and *Ginnie Dare*, but he doubted they'd try anything funny now. He'd assigned observers to keep an eye on them.

His flag office was more spacious than even his old one on *Courageous* had been. Its size and relative opulence made him more than a bit uncomfortable. He wasn't precisely sure where his people had found the furniture, but as it was a gift, he couldn't very well refuse it.

Ignoring his almost comically large desk, Jared took a seat in one of the comfortable chairs. "What's bothering you, Charlie?"

His long-time friend sat across from him. "Permission to speak freely?"

"Cut loose. I need to know exactly what you're thinking."

"I think you're making a strategic blunder in the pursuit of a tactical solution."

He felt himself smiling. "That's plain enough. And I thought your blunt manner might keep you from commanding a ship in space. Silly me."

Graves smiled back at him. "I've never hidden anything from you, Jared, and I'm not going to start now. We're critically short of experienced officers. It's time to start vetting the men and women from *Spear* and *Shadow*.

"We didn't have enough leaders when we crewed *Courageous*. Now the officers and men from one destroyer are making do on a superdreadnought and a battlecruiser. Soon to be two battlecruisers. We're spread too thin. You need to put those people to use, and I mean right now."

Just the problem he'd been wrestling with, but not the solution he'd wanted to hear. "I appreciate your forthrightness. I know we're shorthanded, but we can't afford to trust them."

The young captain leaned forward earnestly. "We can't afford not to. Jared, those men are Fleet officers. Did some of them willfully mutiny? Probably. They supported Breckenridge. Are you going to hold that against an ensign or lieutenant who was just following orders?

"I know damned well that I'd have had a hard time telling a full captain he was wrong when I was a junior officer under his command, unlawful orders or no. Commander Meyer took a stand against Breckenridge, and that was brave as hell.

"No matter how this turns out, his career is probably over. Who wants a man at his back that might put a knife in it? Can you blame others who might have disagreed for keeping their heads down?"

Sean Meyer, *Spear*'s executive officer, had broken Kelsey and Jared out of confinement on the heavy cruiser. He'd stayed behind to make sure their escape back to *Courageous* was successful. He'd been in *Spear*'s brig when the AI-controlled ships had crippled the heavy cruiser. Now he was a prisoner on the planet below.

Jared sighed. "I know, but it's hard to trust people that fooled you once."

Graves nodded. "Then start with the officers from *Shadow*. They didn't cross us like the ones from *Spear* did, and the lower-ranking officers won't gang up to stage a mutiny. That just leaves the senior officers from *Spear*. A few dozen men and women. With appropriate watchdogs, they won't be a threat. Tag them with trusted monitors. They should know they're on probation, but we need them desperately."

Jared took a deep breath and nodded. "You're right. We'll scatter them throughout the task force and use them. But no command positions."

Graves smiled. "That's really all I'd hoped to achieve. *Courageous* and *Invincible* can monitor them, even in their quarters. We can make that plain enough to them as a condition of their probation."

"Well, now that you've set me straight," Jared said, "is that all you needed? How's your ship?"

"*Courageous* is battle worthy. Or as close to it as we can manage in the short term. A third of her missile tubes are offline or obliterated. Roughly the same percentage of beam weapons are gone. Her drives and battle screens are in good shape, though."

Jared compressed his lips. "*Invincible* is in about the same shape. A little worse, actually. We really need to get the construction yards back into commission. *Scott Pond* is a floating wreck."

They'd recovered *Scott Pond* from the floating graveyard of ships left over from the rebellion half a millennium ago. The rebels had destroyed her flip drives when they killed her crew. After her most recent combat, her grav drives were at less than thirty percent. Most of the ship was in vacuum, so they hadn't manned her. Calling her a wreck was being generous.

The task force was in as precarious a position as it could be. If they hadn't plugged the system's flip points, the next Rebel Empire visitor could sweep them off the table.

He and Charlie chatted a while longer before Jared stood and ended the meeting. "Thanks for telling me what I needed to hear, Charlie. Take charge of getting those officers back to work."

Graves climbed slowly to his feet. "What about the negotiations? Are we making any progress on getting our people back?"

"Not that you'd notice. Those people are remarkably stubborn. I'll talk with their representative again tomorrow. This time, she's coming up here. I can't imagine why they'd continue antagonizing the people in charge of the orbital bombardment weapons."

"Does it really matter why? They want to take control of their system. Something we can't let them do. We want our people. Something they apparently aren't willing to grant without getting what they want. This doesn't end cleanly."

"Probably not," Jared admitted, "but we have to try."

Graves headed for the hatch. "Maybe your Rebel Empire prisoner can shed some light on the dilemma."

Jared doubted it. Lieutenant Commander Michael Richards, the Rebel Empire Fleet officer they'd captured at Erorsi, was much less trusting of Jared than he was of Kelsey. Still, it was worth a try. What did he have to lose?

"I'll talk to him. Keep me up to date on the integration efforts."

"Aye, sir."

"Pardon the interruption," *Invincible* said after Graves had left. "Kelsey has just requested a full medical team to her location."

Jared cursed under his breath. "I knew it. What's the medical emergency? Is she injured?"

"Negative. It seems she's found a functional stasis unit with a gravely injured person inside. Based on the ongoing conversation she's having with Doctor Stone, I suspect that the doctor will take a team to join her shortly."

"Let Lily know that she's cleared to take whoever she needs with her. Keep me in the loop."

* * *

KELSEY WATCHED doctors Stone and Guzman working around the stasis unit. The engineering team from *Ginnie Dare* had restored life support in this section of the ship and made certain the fusion plants were stable.

Not that they'd been unstable, but a power failure right now could kill the injured man.

Kelsey had snagged the revival process from the stasis unit. It wasn't complex. She remembered how Reginald Bell had said this was cutting-edge stuff.

It was. He'd also said that the units couldn't keep someone alive for several centuries without adjustments, but he was wrong. This unit was self-regulating. It would maintain the patient's condition for as long as it had power.

Lily Stone looked over at Kelsey. "We're about as ready as we'll ever be. I want to caution you again not to be too hopeful. From what I can see, this man was so badly injured that they put him in as a last-ditch effort. He might be brain dead."

"We owe it to him to try," Kelsey said. "If he's alive, what are his chances?"

Justin Guzman shook his head. "Not good. At the very least, he's suffered significant damage to his frontal lobe. Let me second what Lily said. This poor man is almost certainly gone."

"We'll pull him out and make the call," Lily said. "If there's a chance, we'll get him to *Ginnie Dare*. We'll do everything humanly possible."

Kelsey knew that. She had to get her hopes under control. "Okay."

The doctors had her shift to the side and positioned the crash team around the stasis unit. They'd leap into action as soon as the field came down, giving every bit of life support to the injured man they could.

"Ready," Lily said.

Kelsey sent the command to shut off the unit. She felt the protective field come down.

The doctors sprang into action as soon as the hatch slid aside. They pulled the gurney out, and everyone bent over the man, attaching instruments and support equipment. One of the machines began wailing.

"No heartbeat!" Guzman said. "Give him ten units of—"

"Wait," Stone said, straightening slowly. "His skull is crushed. There's no brain function." She turned to Kelsey. "I'm sorry. He's dead. All this machine did was keep his body from decaying."

The disappointment was like a punch to her gut. Kelsey sagged. "God. I know I shouldn't have gotten my hopes up, but this seemed like karma."

The medical team stepped back and allowed Doctor Leonard and his teen henchman, Carl Owlet, access to the body. They slid a headset over the man's mangled cranium. Kelsey could now see that there'd never been a chance for the dead man.

Leonard glanced back at her. "His implants are still active."

Owlet tapped the keys on the portable unit. "We're downloading everything in the implants' memory and storage."

They all stood there watching until Owlet nodded. "Download complete. Starting comparison. Well, he has more data than you had on day one. A lot more."

"What kind of data?" she asked.

"It's encrypted. Let me see if I can determine what kind of protection it has."

Lily put her hand on Kelsey's shoulder. "You tried. That's more than the poor bastard had a right to expect after the Fall. Don't beat yourself up."

Once the medical team had taken the body and left, the room felt empty. No matter what they salvaged, Kelsey felt as though they'd failed the man.

"Huh," Owlet said.

"What?" She looked over his shoulder, but the screens full of gobbledygook made no sense to her.

"His implants have the same operating code as yours. The encrypted data seems to be something else. I know you can record video, so maybe that's what these files are. If so, there are a lot of them."

"Can't you tell? You downloaded the data from me."

He shrugged. "You didn't protect it. I can keep trying to crack the encryption, but it'll take time."

"Could it be hardware specific? Maybe he set it up like the ship's computer. Only someone with the right implants could view it. I hope it doesn't need an extra code. That would suck."

The young computer genius looked uncertain. "It's possible, but there's only one way to check."

Doctor Leonard shook his head emphatically. "We have no idea what these files are. Uploading any of them to your implant storage could be dangerous. The size of these files taken together is staggering. They would fill three quarters of your available storage."

"One file," she said. "Let's see if I can access it."

The older man sighed. "You're taking an enormous risk. That file could be anything. A virus, even."

"There's no need for someone to have spent so much effort laying a trap. That in itself argues that this is important and probably harmless."

The scientist threw up his hands. "Fine! One file. A small one!"

She accessed the computer and selected the file with the oldest timestamp. It was relatively small but still of enough size to maybe be a video.

Once she had it in her implant storage, she probed it. The encryption code was relatively easy to figure out. It was the dead man's implant serial number. She was certain that telling Owlet about that would earn her yet another lecture about computer security and why she should pick inconvenient and incomprehensible passwords. As she unlocked the file, it became obvious why that was more secure than it seemed. The vid required Marine Raider implants to view it.

Marine Raider implants weren't that different from those of their Fleet brethren, but they had linkages dedicated to the expanded hardware Kelsey had. That made them operationally more complex, and different enough to be a good security feature, it seemed.

With both those conditions met, she was able to play the implant recording.

The medical bay vanished, and she was standing on a hilltop. The sun setting in the distance was shaded more orange than yellow, and it was significantly larger than those she'd seen before. The air was heavy, with some kind of spicy overtone.

A marine pinnace sat in the valley below with men bustling around it. They were unloading small crates.

"Worried?"

The voice at her elbow almost made her jump out of her skin, but the video perspective shifted smoothly to show her a grizzled man in a camouflaged uniform. Unlike marine battledress, his didn't even have subdued rank tabs.

"Not really." The voice seemed to come from her, so she knew it had to be the dead man. "I can't imagine how anyone expects to be able to rebel against the Empire. This whole situation has to be blown out of proportion."

The older man nodded. "Probably. Still, what I'm hearing sounds grim. If someone really figured out how to override our implants, that could be a real nightmare scenario."

The dead man nodded. "I think that's unlikely, but times like this make me wonder. I figure the best thing I can do is focus on my job."

The other man turned toward the valley. "How are your people holding up?"

"They're fine. We'll be done here in less than an hour, and then we're heading back up to *Persephone*. We're relocating deeper into the Empire to check on this threat. I guess I'll know soon enough how bad it is."

The older man clapped the dead man on the shoulder. "Don't let it worry you, Ned. The Empire has beaten the odds before. We'll come out fine this time, too. I'm done with my part of the mission here, so I'll head back to my pinnace. We'll have a beer in a few months, after all this is done."

"Take care, Jake. If I find out anything useful, I'll try to get word to you."

The video ended, and Kelsey found herself standing back in the medical bay. Both scientists were staring at her, and Leonard had his communications unit in his hand.

"What happened?" the scientist demanded.

"Nothing much. It was an implant vid file."

"I almost called the medical team back," the older man grumbled. "Don't do that to my poor heart."

"I'm sorry," she said. "The file was encrypted so that only someone with Marine Raider implants and the dead man's implant serial number could unlock it. I saw a scene with him speaking to another man. I think our dead man's name is Ned and this ship might be *Persephone*. How many files are there?"

"Millions," Owlet said. "Some small, some really large. With the hardware lockout, I can't determine what they do."

"No, but I can," Kelsey said. "This could be a treasure trove of critical information. It doesn't seem harmful. Upload it to my implant storage, and I can work on it as time permits."

The two men looked at one another with resigned expressions.

"What?" she asked.

"You know this will get us in trouble," Leonard said. "Admiral Mertz will be quite annoyed."

"Then he can take it up with me. Come on. Give me the files."

"I know I'm going to regret this," the elderly scientist muttered.

4

J ared headed to the brig. Richards wasn't the only prisoner there
now. Captain Wallace Breckenridge occupied a cell on the other
side of the room. Oddly enough, the traitorous officer had been
right next to Richards the last time Jared had been down here.

Lieutenant Benjamin Gonzales, *Invincible*'s security officer, rose to his
feet. "Admiral."

"As you were." He gestured to Breckenridge's cell. "Why was
he moved?"

"The other prisoner asked us to relocate him. Captain Breckenridge
was pounding on the bulkhead at all hours and disturbing him. It
seemed like a reasonable request. Was that wrong?"

Jared shook his head. "Not at all. Good call. I'm here to see
Richards. Open his cell, please."

"Aye, sir."

The three marines in the room moved to a spot where they could use
their nerve disruptors on the prisoner if need be, but Jared didn't expect
any trouble.

Gonzales opened the hatch to Richards's cell. The Rebel Fleet
officer had been reading something at the built-in desk but stood to face
Jared. The other man stiffened. Admirals had that effect on people, even
when they didn't serve the same Empire. To be fair, the two Fleets did
share a uniform.

"There's no need to stand on ceremony, Commander," Jared said. "I
just stopped in to see how you're doing."

Richards relaxed a little but didn't sit. "Much better since they moved that lunatic next door over a few cells, Admiral. Thank you for that. If I might ask, what did he do to earn your wrath? Your guards are polite but not very informative."

Jared could see how the situation would make him curious. "Captain Breckenridge imprisoned Princess Kelsey and myself for a while and involved several ships under his command in a mutiny. His actions led directly to the loss of his ship."

"That would do it," Richards said. "He's been a raving madman ever since you brought him in. Pounding on the bulkheads at all hours. Yelling so loudly that I can almost understand him. You might want to check the soundproofing on these cells. Congratulations on your promotion, by the way. It's quite a jump from commander to admiral."

Richards's dry tone was almost perfect. Too little to take offense at yet more than enough to get his meaning across. Jared was impressed.

He took a seat on the edge of the other man's bunk. "One I wouldn't have chosen for myself, but Princess Kelsey can be somewhat stubborn. In case you were unaware, the move you experienced was to the superdreadnought *Invincible*. My new command."

The Rebel Empire officer blinked. "A superdreadnought? Since you only had a battlecruiser the last time we talked, that's very impressive. You're much more formidable than I gave you credit for."

"There's a long story attached to that. One I'm inclined to share with you. You've been a model prisoner. If you'll give me your word that you won't give me any trouble, we can make a trip to the officer's mess. You've been eating the same food we do, but I figured you'd welcome a change in scenery."

The offer surprised Jared. He hadn't come expecting to make it, but now that he'd done so, it resonated inside him. He'd made the right call.

Richards's eyes widened. "I doubt very seriously that I'm a threat to a superdreadnought or the crew that captured one. Plus, I'm certain your diligent guards and ship's computer will keep close watch on me. I freely give you my word as a Fleet officer that I won't attempt to escape or harm you, your crew, or your ship while we're out on this excursion."

A very concise and limited statement, conforming well to the parole Jared had offered. That worked.

"Then come with me. Lieutenant Gonzales, one of your guards will accompany us."

"Aye, sir." If the officer thought Jared's plan a little dubious, he didn't say so.

"*Invincible*, please keep an eye on us, as well," Jared added.

"I'll keep a very close watch, Admiral, but I doubt Commander

Richards will give you any problems. In fact, based on his reading list and spoken commentary, I'll warrant you'll have an eye-opening discussion."

Richards stopped dead in his tracks and stared at the ceiling. "Who the hell is that?"

"*Invincible*'s AI. And when I say AI, I really mean it. Hence the sense of self."

For a moment, Jared thought the Rebel Fleet officer would walk right back into his cell. He'd turned quite pale.

The other man stiffened his spine and walked out with Jared. The guard trailed them at a range that would allow him to stun the prisoner if need be. The three of them made their way to the officer's mess and found a seat in the corner. The people nearest them moved away when Jared requested some privacy.

They ordered tea and sandwiches. The guard stood against a nearby bulkhead.

Jared leaned back. "I'm certain you have questions. Ask away, and I'll do my best to answer them."

"An AI? How the hell did you capture one of the Imperial or system Lords? Forget that. How did you convince it to aid you?"

"I suspected you knew more about the AIs running the Rebel Empire than you'd let on. We recovered the hardware and software for the AI from an asteroid in the Erorsi system. Our experts found the malicious code and removed it before we brought it online here inside *Invincible*. She needed a computer."

The other officer shook his head. "I reject that name. I serve the Terran Empire. If there are rebels present, I submit they are your people, Admiral. No offense."

Jared smiled. "We could argue that point for days. It's just a naming convention, since I also serve a Terran Empire. One that has an unbroken history going back before the rebellion. One with an Emperor, I might add. To avoid confusion, let's use my terminology."

Richards looked as though he wanted to argue but clamped his mouth shut and nodded. "Only for the sake of clarity."

"As to the battle," Jared continued, "we captured Harrison's World and Boxer Station. Have you heard of either of them?"

The commander frowned. "I've heard of Boxer Station. It's a major Fleet base one sector over. Top secret. I've never met any officer assigned there. We couldn't have made it from Erorsi in such a short time. The trip would take weeks, and you'd have to go through occupied systems. How did you manage that?"

"There are some secrets I'm not ready to share at this point. For the sake of this discussion, let's say you accept that I'm telling the truth. We have control of Harrison's World, and I want to ask you some general questions about how the government is set up. I'm already dealing with them and would like to avoid any bloodshed, but they're making things hard."

The other man considered him. "Under normal circumstances, I'd refuse to assist you as a matter of course. We're at war, whether my people realize it or not. However, I've concluded that Princess Kelsey told me an unpleasant truth. The history I learned about the rebellion growing up may very well have been false. I want to find out what really happened."

He's telling you the truth.

Jared considered *Invincible*'s private comment.

How can you be sure?

He specifically sent that information to me and granted enough access for me to be certain. He means what he is saying. I'll notify you if he prevaricates or ceases to allow me to monitor him.

Please do.

Jared knew that if someone gave a computer enough access through their implants, the machine could assess their honesty. A general transmission wasn't intrusive enough. It required a willful granting of access to the machine. But when it happened, there was no deception. The computer was a perfect lie detector.

"You have my complete attention, Commander."

The Rebel Empire officer took a deep breath. "I believe it's in the best interests of my people to discover the truth. I'm willing to give my word to cooperate with you in exchange for the information you have. If you're right, my people are slaves. I have to know if that's true."

Jared nodded slowly. "If you'll agree to continuous visual monitoring by *Invincible*, as well as the files you access, I'm willing to grant you parole. Frankly, your help could save thousands of lives. Perhaps many more."

"I accept," Richards said without hesitation. "I'm willing to have an armed guard watch over me, as well. It's only prudent, and you'll have them standing by in any case."

"Done. I'll assign quarters for you. First, though, I want to bring you up to speed on the current situation."

He explained how the AI in the system had ruthlessly subjugated Harrison's World, vaporizing cities. How it had moved the enlisted prisoners captured from *Spear* to the planet. How he needed to get them back, but he couldn't allow the people below to know who they really were. More importantly, he couldn't let them free from their world.

Richards shook his head slowly. "That's a tough nut to crack, Admiral. The higher orders—the people that rule our society—are always maneuvering against one another. Even as an admiral, they'll see you as a social inferior.

"Fleet officers come from the middle orders of Imperial society. We have implants, as do they, but not from a young age. We only get them after thorough vetting and training as adults. The people you're talking to probably expect that you'll cave in to their desires."

"How do I get them to negotiate in good faith?"

The other man laughed. "Admiral, they're members of the higher orders. They don't negotiate in good faith unless it's with a member of their own class. Even then, I'd count your fingers after you shake on a deal. You'll just have to do the best you can."

* * *

THE UPLOAD TOOK LONGER than the download. Kelsey wasn't quite sure why. Perhaps it was a hardware limitation on the part of the cobbled-together equipment that the scientists had built.

"It takes specialized equipment to overwrite the operating code in an implant, right?" she asked. "Even if there's something in these files, it can't infect me."

"It's a little late to ask that, don't you think?" Doctor Leonard asked a bit waspishly.

"Probably, but I want to hear it again."

He sighed. "Nothing in these files can overwrite your implant code. That doesn't make this safe, though."

"Can you give me an example of what might go wrong?"

"No. I just don't like the unknown."

"Me either. So let's figure this out."

She had her implants start the process of unlocking the files. It would take several hours, even at the speed her hardware ran.

They made their way back to her pinnace. She was just settling in when her implants registered an incoming communications signal.

"Bandar," she said.

"Highness, this is Lieutenant Madison on Boxer Station. I've found what looks like an implant facility."

She recognized the woman's name as one of *New York's* officers. Jared had moved her to Boxer Station before her ship left for Erorsi and Pentagar.

"Is it operational?" Kelsey asked, trying to keep from letting her innate optimism run wild.

"I can't tell. That's why I need your help."

"We'll be right there."

She terminated the connection and called Jared. Once he answered, she passed word of the discovery.

"That's terrific news," he said. "I have some for you, too. *New York* just arrived at the flip point with four Pentagaran ships and *Best Deal*. I'll route them to join you at Boxer Station. I'd like to keep the new ships out of sight."

"Send Talbot out, too. He gets all weird when I find new stuff."

"You mean he gets weird when you jump in where angels fear to tread. I'll send him out right now. I'll be heading to bed soon, so don't do anything crazy. The locals are coming up early. I want to be ready for them."

"I'll file a report so you can read it in the morning," she said. "Good night."

Kelsey accessed the pinnaces' scanners. *New York* and the new ships would arrive at about the same time as Talbot's pinnace. It would be late, but she didn't need much sleep. Especially in circumstances like these.

She sent a message to the medical teams, who were still on *Ginnie Dare*, to join them at Boxer Station.

Half an hour later, Kelsey stood inside the docking area on Boxer Station. Power was back, but the computer systems were still offline. A team of specialists were removing the AI and recovering all the data they could from the other computers. When they finished, they'd wipe them and reload the operating systems.

Lieutenant Madison stood in the vast docking area waiting for her with several ratings. "Highness."

"Lieutenant Madison. Take me to your find." Her security team formed up around her as she spoke.

The Fleet officer gestured. "It's just off the medical center, which sort of makes sense. Several cutters are on their way over from *Ginnie Dare*. They should be arriving momentarily."

Several loud thunks announced the arrival of the aforementioned cutters. The hatches opened and disgorged Doctor Leonard, Carl Owlet, Doctor Stone, Doctor Guzman, and numerous other medical personnel and scientists.

"Perfect timing," Kelsey said. "I hope this facility can be made operational. That would make our lives so much easier going forward."

"*Your* life, maybe," Stone muttered.

She clapped the medical officer on the shoulder. "Cheer up, Lily!

Imagine what you can do with implants in that fancy new medical center of yours."

"I'm imagining the hijinks the crew will come up with to end up in there with me," she said grumpily. "If you only knew how many silly ways they manage to get hurt as it is. These implants will be new territory."

"What could possibly go wrong?" Kelsey asked with a grin. "Let's go, Lieutenant."

Kelsey could've found the medical center from the plans she had in her implants, but that would be rude. This was Madison's discovery. She deserved the chance to show it off.

Boxer Station's corridors raised bad memories for Kelsey. She'd exchanged fire with mechanical fighting devices under the control of the AI here just a few days ago. She'd acquired new injuries and lost a lot of friends. The regeneration chamber had made her physically whole, but her mind was another story. The scars there might take years to heal. If they ever did.

The engineering teams had sealed away the worst of the damage. Life support was stable, and they weren't worried about any more bulkheads losing pressure. The marines—the few they had left—had searched the station several times to be sure there were no more AI-controlled humans hiding in odd corners or war machines left unaccounted for.

The humans were free of mental control at this point, but Jared was keeping them in isolation for their own safety. She'd seen how Commander Richards had become almost subhuman after he knew who they were, and she didn't want to subject the other prisoners to that. They'd been through enough.

The war machines seemed dead, but the technicians were manually disconnecting their power supplies just to be sure. Then they'd transport them to *Invincible*.

The battle to control this system had come far too close to failure. If any one part of the operations in space or on the station hadn't worked, they'd all be dead or captured. They'd lost seventy percent of the marine force in the assault. Fewer than a hundred men and women survived out of three hundred.

They couldn't afford another victory like that.

Kelsey shook off the gloom that threatened to overwhelm her. She had too much to do.

"This is the medical center," Madison said. She gestured through a wide hatch at a compartment bigger than Kelsey had imagined possible. It had to be twice the size of marine country on *Invincible*. At least.

Doctor Stone stepped inside and gaped. "My God."

It had half a dozen full operating theaters, more regeneration pods than Kelsey could count, several stasis chambers, and a compartment full of examination beds. There were adjacent wards that could hold hundreds of sick people. Maybe thousands. The sheer scale of the operation boggled her mind. This facility could probably hold every surviving man and woman in the task force. Even disused, it was damned impressive.

"It's bigger than I expected," Kelsey admitted.

Doctor Guzman shrugged. "This was a Fleet sector base. Besides being a huge station, it served as the command and control post for any number of other bases in the surrounding systems. It may have also been expanded after the rebellion started."

Stone turned to Kelsey. "Can I take it home with me?"

Kelsey laughed. "Where would you put it? Besides, the medical center on *Invincible* is pretty impressive. All you need are a couple of these stasis chambers and you'll be set. Come on, everyone. There'll be time to explore once we assess the implantation facility."

Lieutenant Madison had said it was next to the medical center, but that was still a bit of a walk. This station had probably been home to a quarter million Fleet personnel in its heyday.

The implantation center looked very much like the medical center: big and disused. A thin layer of dust covered everything. Unlike Workstation Twelve—the machine the Pale Ones had used to implant the AI's slaves—the dozens of stations in this facility were all-in-one affairs.

Of course, they hadn't done the full-body implants required for Marine Raiders here. No enhanced muscles, shielded bones, or pharmacology units. Only cranial implants. The individual stations consisted of couches the patient reclined on with equipment around the head. They were very sleek. Workstation Twelve was a kludge in comparison.

The scientists and technicians spread out to examine the various couches. Doctor Guzman went with Doctor Leonard.

Stone stood beside Kelsey. "Nothing for commando implants."

"I noticed that. I can't say I'm surprised. They can't have been common before the Fall. The Marine Raiders had to have been a very exclusive organization. They probably handled their own implanting. As much as I would love to have every marine with us set up to be a Raider, I doubt we'll find the hardware just lying around."

"The AI at Erorsi was getting them from somewhere." Stone said.

"At least there are enough stations to get the Fleet personnel implanted in a reasonable time frame."

The princess turned to the doctor. "I thought you were against using the implants."

"It's the future, Kelsey. It doesn't matter how I feel about it. Frankly, I'll be interested in seeing how they work for myself."

Doctor Leonard waved them over.

"These systems are operational," he said. "I think. They draw power, anyway. Princess, can you access them?"

This was something she'd done many times before. Kelsey accessed the equipment and found it unlocked. The station in front of her provided her with an overview of the process. It was straightforward, though there were a number of complex monitoring screens. The workstations also had computers at least as sophisticated as Workstation Twelve's to oversee the process.

What they didn't have was voice access. Only someone with implants could operate them.

She turned to the scientists and filled them in.

Carl Owlet frowned. "How do we compare the implant code with the clean version we have?"

"Do we need to?" she asked. "You've examined the Rebel Empire Fleet personnel. These machines probably implanted them. They have to have compromised code."

"Doctor Leonard frowns on qualifiers," the graduate student said with a grin. "He takes off points if you use them."

"And rightly so," the older scientist said primly. "Science isn't made when you use words like 'probably,' 'maybe,' and 'hopefully.' You test everything and verify. We need to compare the implant code to what we have on our equipment."

It took her almost an hour to gain access to the code repository. She sent a version of the implant code to Owlet's machine directly from the workstation.

"This is the same code we pulled off the Rebel Empire officer," Owlet confirmed a few minutes later. "The hardware is the same as Admiral Mertz's Fleet implants, so no problem there. All you need to do is upload the clean code to this machine, and we can begin using it."

Kelsey nodded. "I've already checked every workstation, and they all use the same code. I can send it to all of them as soon as I unlock their repositories." She got that process started.

Meanwhile, they found the supplies for the implantation machines. Enough cranial implants to take care of thousands of people. She planned to send half of them back to Pentagar. Even so, there were more than enough to take care of every man and woman in their task force.

There was also a sealed supply of nanites locked away in a vault adjacent to the implantation center. The AIs didn't like using them for some reason. This supply was large enough to help tens of thousands of people.

Kelsey checked the time. Talbot would arrive in less than an hour. She'd better get set up for the first group, because she knew he'd insist on being at the front of the line.

5

A rap at the door made Coordinator Olivia West look up from her display. She put a false smile on her face as soon as she saw who it was. "Abigail. Come in."

Deputy Coordinator Abigail King was a senior member of Harrison's World's ruling council and a huge pain in the ass to work with. The conservative alliance had forced her on Olivia to avoid a council showdown during her election. She often wondered if she'd have been better off fighting them then.

The younger woman took a seat without invitation. "You asked to see me?"

"I wanted to get an update on how the negotiations are proceeding."

Abigail scowled. It wasn't a pleasant expression on her. "The jumped-up prole is still refusing to budge."

Olivia leaned back in her chair. "I see. How do you intend to move the talks along?"

"We have 2,354 prisoners. Executing a hundred or so should make him aware how seriously we're taking his intransigence."

It took a moment, but Olivia managed to suppress the first words that wanted to come out of her mouth. They wouldn't be helpful. "Leaving aside the morality of killing people under our control to make a political point, need I remind you that he controls the orbital bombardment platforms? The exchange of such pleasantries would be very one sided."

Abigail made a dismissive gesture. "He wouldn't dare attack us."

"Allow me to remind you of a few unpleasant facts. Rebels from our world plotted against our Lord. Those actions led to the Lord reducing the capital and several other cities containing many citizens of the highest orders to smoking craters. What makes you so certain that Admiral Mertz won't do that very thing?"

The other woman sniffed. "That was a decade ago. The Lord killed the rebels. Coordinator James and the council of the time paid for their treachery. As painful as that was, it did allow us to assume leadership roles. You wouldn't be in that chair without the removal of so many others with political clout."

Her tone implied Olivia wouldn't have achieved leadership of Harrison's World without the mass executions. True enough.

Abigail acted as though tens of millions hadn't died in the orbital strikes. For the other woman, the deaths of those in the middle and lower orders didn't count as anything but an inconvenience.

Olivia sighed. "You disappoint me. The admiral and his task force came for a reason. The system Lord has not spoken since Admiral Mertz arrived. I've never heard of the Lords disciplining one of their own before, but it's possible that's what happened. That could be good news for us, but we'd be fools to count on it.

"The admiral may have orders to discipline Harrison's World further for allowing rebels to flourish here. We need to walk this path carefully. There will be no executions."

The other woman sneered. "What do those peons matter? You can't tell me that any officer of flag rank cares one whit about the lower orders cleaning his decks. His stance on the prisoners must be some charade."

Olivia made a show of considering that. "It's possible he may be playing some deeper game. When are you speaking to him next?"

"In a few hours. He's sending a cutter to pick me up, but I plan to decline at the last moment. The prole can come down to me."

Abigail's intransigence simply amazed Olivia. People like her were so certain they ruled the Empire under the guidance of the Lords that they didn't care how anyone else thought. Even the people that might revolt and hang them. Or, in the case of the Fleet admiral, drop high-velocity tungsten rods onto them until they died.

"You risk too much," Olivia said after a moment. "We have no deep-space scanners, so we don't have any idea how large his task force is or how it's deployed. Would you like it if he came calling with a troop transport full of marines? They could come down and drag you up to the meeting."

The other woman leaned back, and her nostrils flared. "He wouldn't dare!"

"I'm not willing to bet this planet on your ego. I'll go and speak to Admiral Mertz in your place. We'll come to an understanding sooner with a willingness to actually talk, I'm certain."

Abigail's shocked expression was almost comical. "The council appointed me as negotiator! You can't replace me!"

Olivia stood slowly. "You forget yourself. I am the coordinator of Harrison's World. My decision is final. Run along and complain to your allies all you like. They won't overrule me. I control enough votes to assure that."

The younger woman stood abruptly. "You rule at our pleasure, Olivia. Never forget that. One day our willingness to take your insulting behavior will end, and so will you." She stormed out in a rage.

Olivia could've probably been a little less imperious, but the woman got on her last nerve. Oh well. Abigail King would never have been her ally, much less her friend. The bitch was too ambitious. This day had been inevitable and a long time coming.

* * *

SEAN MANAGED to sleep a while before people started moving. His change in status seemed to have already made the rounds. People that had avoided him like the plague nodded politely. Some even spoke to him.

He dressed in Fleet fatigues without name tags or rank insignia. He figured he could skip the shower after last night.

The prisoners ate in a mess hall manned by their own people, but the food came in grav vans with armed guards. The stone-faced men with Old Empire weapons stayed near the vehicles and only allowed a few prisoners to come get the day's food.

Sean walked toward them and stopped when they raised their weapons. "My name is Force Master Chief Sean Meyer. I'm the senior prisoner. I want to speak to someone in authority."

"Back away," one of the guards said. He aimed his flechette rifle at Sean to emphasize the command.

"No. Take me to someone with authority to answer my questions."

The man sneered. "You think you have some say in this, prole? You don't. Move on."

Sean smiled. "You're sadly mistaken. One word from me and you'll have a riot on your hands. Is that really how you want your commander to learn your name? All you have to do is pass the word up and it's someone else's problem."

The two men looked at one another. The one who hadn't spoken gestured for Sean to back up. "Go sit down and I'll call this in. No promises."

Sean made himself some coffee and sat down. Twenty minutes later, two new guards arrived in an open-topped grav car. They came toward Sean.

"Get up," one said. "Hands behind your back."

When some of the other prisoners stood, Sean held his hand out. "Stand down. There isn't going to be any problem. I'll be back shortly."

The guards cuffed him, led him to their vehicle, stuffed him in back between two additional escorts, and lifted off. With a little height, Sean could tell the prisoners were on a small island. Hemmed in between the guards, he couldn't get a clear look at it, but the island wasn't more than a half kilometer offshore. The water looked cold and a bit rough.

The grav car took them over what appeared to be slums. Further inland, the buildings became more upscale. One might charitably call them middle class, if one squinted. The car zeroed in on one of the larger roofs and landed. The building had a sign indicating it was owned by Roscoe Consolidated.

His guards escorted him through the roof door and into a lift. They went to the tenth floor and led him down a corridor with worn tan carpeting. The art on the walls looked inexpensive and generic.

One of the guards knocked on a door and led Sean inside without waiting for a response. The office consisted of a battered desk, an even more battered man behind it, and office furniture that someone probably should've junked years ago.

The man didn't look at all pleased about the interruption. "Put him in the chair and wait by the door. This won't take long."

That didn't sound promising at all.

The guards dragged a chair in front of the desk and sat Sean down with more force than necessary.

"Thank you for taking time out of your busy day to see me," Sean said dryly.

"Don't be a smartass," the man said with a snarl. "I can have them let you out of the car over the ocean if you piss me off, prole."

"My apologies. I'm Force Master Chief Sean Meyer, the senior Fleet prisoner. I have some concerns about my people and their housing."

The man sneered. "So I gathered. As far as I'm concerned, you should feel glad we didn't drop you a hundred kilometers offshore and let you swim for it, you bastards."

Sean hadn't expected this level of animosity. "Have we met? I certainly don't remember harming you."

The man rose abruptly and stomped around the desk. Sean thought he was going to hit him, but the man only grabbed Sean by his tunic and yanked him to his feet.

"Oh, no?" the man shouted, spraying Sean with spittle. "Maybe you remember Port City better? You know, the capital of Harrison's World before you blew it up, along with my brother. Give me one excuse to rip your head off and I'll dump your worthless body where no one will ever find it."

The level of danger was significantly higher than Sean had anticipated, especially since he had no idea what the man was talking about. "I'm truly sorry that happened, but I didn't do it, and neither did the men with me."

"You think that matters?" The man shoved Sean back down in the chair. "Say your piece so I can have someone come clean my office. Maybe the stink will go away in a few years."

Sean had intended to probe for some idea of what was happening, but he didn't dare.

"A number of our people were taken to a hospital. Not all of them have come back. I want to know how they're doing."

The man glared at Sean for a moment and returned to his desk with a muttered curse. He tapped on the keys to his console. "Six prisoners are in a guarded wing of a local hospital. If I could, I'd haul them back and let them die right in front of you. You want to know anything else?"

"I don't suppose you could give us some reading material?"

The man snorted. "As if you rats from the lower orders can even read. Get this bastard out of my sight. And the next son of a bitch that wants to see me? Shoot him."

The guards hustled Sean out the door without a moment's hesitation.

He had no idea what had happened on this planet, but it didn't look good for him or his people. If the Rebel Empire Fleet had bombarded the capital of this world, he could understand the hatred they were expressing. It limited his ability to see to their conditions, but he couldn't help that.

Based on how grave Captain Cooley's injuries had been before the AI ambushed them, Sean hoped he was still alive. He'd lost his legs and suffered life-threatening injuries when the Rebel Empire destroyer had wrecked *Shadow*.

They flew Sean back to the island without saying a word. He used the time to study the layout of the city and the island once they made the flight across the bay. The view reinforced the idea that the prison camp had once been a training facility. Parts of the island were still in use, though the people below weren't Fleet. They looked like stevedores.

He had a tantalizingly brief view of some ships drawn up offshore unloading cargo containers. They were big. There were also some sizable grav vehicles. He imagined the cargo came by sea and made its way across to the city after sorting.

Maybe, just maybe, they could escape their prison if Mertz didn't come through. At the very least, it wouldn't hurt to make some contingency plans. If they could get into the city, they might be able to get to a spaceport. It was a terrible risk, but if they had to run, they needed to be ready.

* * *

ABIGAIL KING STALKED into her office. Her assistant started to say something but rapidly found more productive things to do with his time.

"I'm not to be disturbed for any reason," Abigail told him and went into her office, slamming the hardwood door behind her.

She immediately called a memorized number.

"Calder Consortium. How may I direct your call?"

"Put me through to Master Calder."

As the head of the conservative alliance, Edward Calder was due the title even from the second most powerful official on the planet. After all, he'd been the one who put her where she was. He could take her out just as easily.

"Right away, Deputy Coordinator King."

The line was silent for a moment before her patron came on. "Abigail, I've been waiting for your call. How are things proceeding?"

"Poorly, Master. Coordinator West has removed me from the role of negotiator and is going up to the Fleet vessels in orbit herself. It sounds as though she's looking for a way to find common ground with Admiral Mertz."

The line was silent for a moment. "Do you think she's become aware of our plans?"

"It's hard to tell, Master. It galls me, but she's more subtle than I am."

Calder laughed. "Don't confuse the persona you play for who you really are, Abigail. You're far more discerning than you give yourself credit for.

"Now, while I'll admit that this might be a setback, I'm not yet ready to throw in the towel. You've put this Admiral Mertz into a heightened state of intransigence, as I instructed. All we need to do is keep him and

Coordinator West from coming to an agreement. If the progressive coalition negotiates our release from Harrison's World, they will consolidate their rule for the foreseeable future. I won't allow that to happen."

"I've tried to assure that there is no agreement, Master, but if she makes more reasonable overtures, he may well agree to her terms. If only to get back at me."

He made a clucking noise. "You're too pessimistic. We still have many avenues to disrupt the negotiations. Perhaps it's time to remove West from power in a more permanent fashion."

Abigail shook her head, even though he couldn't see her. "I think it's far too premature, Master. The council is still more in her camp than out. Her assassination would only make them more mulish. Perhaps the engineered execution of some of the prisoners with the finger of guilt pointing at her? An atrocity would both derail the negotiations and taint her reputation."

"I wonder if we could merge those ideas," he said thoughtfully. "Killing some of the Fleet prisoners and then assassinating Olivia West. Those linked events could get everyone looking at Admiral Mertz as the guilty party for her death. That has possibilities.

"Keep a close eye on the negotiations and begin setting up plans to carry out the execution of some prisoners. If the moment seems ripe, we'll see if we can get the dogs to attack one another. Call me as soon as something important occurs."

He disconnected without waiting for her response. Abigail scowled at the view outside her window. This was risky. Impetuous. If things went wrong, she'd be the immediate suspect.

Which might be Master Calder's plan, she admitted. He led the conservative alliance, and his family had been in power before the system Lord had crushed the planet. As one of only a few surviving members of that clan, he'd want to sit in the coordinator's chair himself. With the death of Olivia West, he'd see Abigail as an obstacle to his ambitions.

She owed her rise in power to him, but she didn't owe him her life. She decided she'd take steps to see that certain information about him became public if something unfortunate happened to her. Done properly, he'd find out and understand the message she was sending him. In the end, the real winner was the one left standing.

6

The communicator on Olivia's desk chimed. She answered her assistant's request with the touch of a key. "Yes?"

"My deepest apologies, Coordinator. Lord Hawthorne is here without an appointment. He's very insistent about speaking with you."

"Send him in."

The titles accorded to the higher orders by birth always made her smile bitterly. They were lords and ladies, just like the AIs that ruled them. Their ruling society had three layers: the Imperial Lords who ruled the Empire, the system Lords who managed individual solar systems, and the higher orders of humanity.

The machine intelligences always spoke of how they worked hand in hand with the human leaders, and the lower orders believed that fiction. Little did they know that even the most powerful humans were just as much slaves as they were.

William Hawthorne was different for a number of reasons. She'd known him for most of her life. He was actually one of her few friends—and her mentor.

The tall man with sandy curls came in and bowed his head. "My deepest apologies for interrupting your busy day, Coordinator. I bring word from my Lady Mother. She commanded me to deliver it at once and in person."

"Then come in and tell me. I can hardly wait."

He closed the door and gave her a questioning look.

"My security team scanned the room this morning," she said. "I've been here ever since. Speak freely. Did your mother actually have a message for me?"

He smiled. "She did, though that's not why I'm here. My youngest sister is getting married next month, and my Lady Mother would be delighted if you could attend."

"I'll check my schedule and let you know, but only because I like your sister more than your mother. She gets on my nerves with all her matchmaking. I'm tempted to tell her about my unrequited love for you just to get her off my back."

William gave her a semipanicked look. "Don't you dare! Not even in jest! She'd never give me a moment's peace, urging me to divorce Craig and marry you straight away. Oh, the scandal that would cause."

He sat and gave her a considering look. "I might be persuaded to name my daughter after you, though. She'll be out of the artificial womb in another two months, and we still haven't agreed on a name. Craig would be honored, I'm sure."

"As would I. What do you really need?"

"I've spoken with the others and taken them the data you provided. Captain Black searched the few Fleet databases we still have and came up empty. No mention of an Admiral Jared Mertz.

"That's not really surprising, though. Fleet databases are fairly segmented. We only knew the officers and ships assigned to this sector and the surrounding ones. The admiral obviously came from farther away. Perhaps even the core worlds."

Olivia considered what that might mean. "They've had a long time to clean up the mess on Harrison's World. Why wait a decade? To see if there are any rebels still hiding here?"

William smiled. "I'd think you, of all people, would be happy to have the time to consolidate your rule. The orbital strikes mostly destroyed the existing political structure. I'm not sure I'd have expected a resistance leader to end up in charge back then."

"The irony isn't lost on me," she assured him. "We financed the restoration of *Invincible* and were only weeks away from striking at the system Lord." She said the last with all the bitterness she felt toward their AI masters. They'd taken so much from humanity, and from her personally.

Her fiancé, Fleet Captain Brian Drake, had almost certainly died when the AI realized the humans of Harrison's World were planning a revolt. His death had almost destroyed her. It probably would have if she hadn't been running for her life and helping rescue people from the devastation.

The Lord had struck at them without mercy, killing tens of millions. Then it had crushed their necks under its boot. The slightest hesitation to obey brought wholesale death. It could've sent probes down to take control of the implants in their heads, but it hadn't seemed interested in that level of domination.

Most of the nobles didn't realize the AI could take direct control of their bodies through their implants. The code in them was perverted. They thought of the lower orders as their slaves, but that was the worst kind of deception. The AIs that had crushed the Terran Empire could make them dance any time they chose to do so.

She knew this because Harrison's World had a loosely knit community of resistance members. They kept memories of what the Empire had once been alive. Maybe it was closer to a religion. They certainly felt a reverence for what they'd lost that was close to worship.

They'd thought a superdreadnought and a few secrets from the Grant Research Facility would be enough to subdue the AI. They'd been horribly wrong.

It had spies on the ground, though seemingly not in the resistance itself. It had gotten wind of the coup, or at least enough information to believe that humans were a threat to its rule.

Most of her allies on the ruling council would be horrified to know the truth about her. If they even suspected her role in the aborted coup, they'd speedily see her executed.

"Are you even listening to me?" William asked.

She shook herself out of her thoughts and focused. "Sorry. I let my mind wander. What did you say?"

He gave her an exasperated but resigned look. "I said that we've gone over the data we stole from Lady King's network. Leaving aside her profound incompetence as a negotiator, we've analyzed the video she recorded of the initial meeting.

"Admiral Mertz is definitely on a Holyfield-class superdreadnought. The same kind of ship as *Invincible*. The flag bridge layout is unmistakable. With his support ships, he's too strong a nut to crack, even if we managed to slip some people out to *Invincible* and finish bringing it online. His trained crew and support vessels would slaughter us. Whatever plan you formulate needs to be subtle."

She nodded. "I'll give it my best. I told Abigail that I was going up to negotiate in person. I'll bring back as much data as I can. Is there anything else?"

"One more thing. We looked at the meeting with the Fleet landing party. Something odd came out of it. Look at this."

He sent her a video snippet through his implants. It showed a woman in powered armor standing up to Abigail's obnoxious demands. Olivia found herself liking the small woman.

"Okay. What am I missing?"

"The men behind her are in a variant of standard unpowered Imperial Marine armor. So far, so good. Her armor is not standard marine issue, however. Also, even though she never used them, Abigail noted she had implants, so she's an officer."

Olivia frowned. "That doesn't make sense. Only shock troops use armor."

Imperial shock troops were the Empire's most deadly ground weapon. The massive suits made them virtually invincible. The people inside them, though, weren't trusted. Their officers kept them on a very short leash. At the first sign of a problem, their officers would eliminate them. The AIs didn't want humans to possess that kind of destructive power.

"That's what Captain Black said. We don't have any marines in the families now, but we have the basic data. Marine officers use unpowered armor. No exceptions. And look at her size. She's a tiny little thing. I could scruff her and she'd never land a blow on me. She's not a marine."

Bumped out of her comfortable mental space, Olivia took the time to consider the situation and listen to the exchange between the woman and Abigail again.

"She calls them 'her marines' right out in the open," Olivia said. "What about her armor? If it's not standard issue, perhaps identifying it will give us a clue who we're dealing with."

William shook his head. "That only deepens the mystery. The old databases identify it as Marine Raider armor."

Olivia's frown deepened. "What's a Marine Raider? I've never heard the term before."

"According to the records, Marine Raiders were the premier troops of the prerebellion Terran Empire. So heavily enhanced they could take out dozens of regular marines all by themselves. Artificial muscles, hardened bones, combat drugs that made them almost immune to pain, and faster than death.

"That armor is lighter than the stuff used by the shock troops, but these commandos could strike out of nowhere and be gone before you knew you were dead. There hasn't been a Marine Raider in over five centuries. They died trying to stave off the AIs. Or so we've always thought."

Well, that certainly made for an unexpected surprise. Who was this woman, and what was her role? Had the AIs resurrected the Terran

Empire's deadliest killing machines? Was she a weapon the Imperial Lords would use to stab Harrison's World in the heart?

Her name was Kelsey Bandar, or so she'd said. Olivia looked forward to meeting this exquisitely deadly woman in person.

"Well, now that you've ruined my day," Olivia said, "let's have a drink. The good stuff. I might not be in a position to enjoy it tomorrow."

She poured a drink for her friend and for herself. When he was ready, she raised her glass. "To the Emperor. May he rest in peace."

William finished the ceremonial toast. "And to the Empire. May it rise from the ashes."

Olivia drank deeply to that. One day they'd restore the Empire or die trying.

* * *

JARED AWOKE when his door chimed. A quick check showed Crown Princess Elise of Pentagar smiling at the pickup. His internal chronometer said he had an hour left before his alarm went off, but he'd cheerfully lose some sleep to see his girlfriend again.

He threw on some clothes and opened the hatch. "Hey! I didn't expect you for a few more hours."

She stepped into his arms and kissed him. "I know you have a busy day ahead of you, and I wanted some time alone first."

Her Royal Guard companions remained outside as he closed the hatch.

She hugged him hard. "I'm so happy you made it through that battle. I watched the vids on the trip out. God. If I hadn't known in advance that you'd made it, I'd have been certain you'd all died. That was insane."

The battle for this system had been brutal. "We didn't have a choice. We had to win or suffer the consequences. We lost so many people, particularly the marines."

"I saw some of that, too. While it won't make up for the loss, we brought as many Royal Pentagaran Marines as we could pile into the corridors. They're on Boxer Station. We left our ships there, too. They'll need some remedial training on your equipment and how you operate, but that should help."

He nodded. "It does. Not against the planet holding our people but in case we have to do more fighting in space. We appreciate the help."

"We're allies. You've given so much to help us. How could we not give everything we could in return? We brought the heaviest ships we had upgraded to use the space-time bridges. We also brought extra crew to transfer to your ships. That should help fill some of the remaining gaps."

Jared mentally translated "space-time bridges" to "flip points." "I'm going to be in so much trouble when I get back home. Even with Kelsey making it an Imperial order to allow Pentagaran crew on our ships, the admiralty is going to flip without a ship."

"Leave tomorrow's problems for tomorrow," she advised. "I know you have a very important meeting this morning. Before then, I'd like to do something I've never done before."

He raised an eyebrow. "What would *that* be? I thought we'd been pretty...thorough."

Elise smacked his arm and pulled him down to sit on the couch. "That, too, but not right now. We don't have time, and you are *not* going to meet a foreign head of state after a roll between the sheets with me. What did Kelsey tell you about what they found?"

"They found what might have been the implant center on the station. Are you wondering what they might be like? I thought we'd discussed that to death. You need to experience them yourself is the best answer I can give."

She smiled oddly. "I'm ready to start."

He opened his mouth to say something and stopped. A quick check told him that she had implants.

"I hadn't heard the implantation center was operational," he said. "I wish you'd waited. We don't know this equipment as well as I'd like."

"Kelsey seemed satisfied," Elise said. She took his hand in hers. "And if she was going to allow Talbot to do it, how could I miss the opportunity?"

Jared frowned. "Wait. How many people are we talking about?"

Elise gave him a lopsided smile. "She's already shepherded a few dozen people through the process. Some of my people, her guards, Talbot, Doctor Stone, and some scientists. The second round consisted of mostly my people. She didn't want to get too far ahead of your approval in getting your crew done."

He sighed. "Too late."

"She said you'd say that and begs your forgiveness."

"I should never have told her it was easier to beg forgiveness than ask permission. I've created a monster. If she'd asked, I would've said yes, but I certainly wouldn't have put you in the first group."

"Then it's a good thing I didn't wait. You need people to have implants, you know. The Rebel Fleet officers are implanted. If yours aren't, that'll set off alarm bells when your visitors arrive."

"You're right. Still, I don't have enough time to get people to the station, see them through the implant procedure, and then get them back before the negotiating party arrives. Why didn't she wake me?"

"It was late and she knew what you'd say. She invited certain crew members to come visit Boxer Station. If you approve, they have time for the procedure and the trip here. That's one of the reasons I dropped in so early."

Jared needed to have a long talk with Kelsey. It could wait until this situation was resolved, though.

He opened a channel to his sister through *Invincible*'s communications system. It would take minutes for her to respond, so he decided to make this brief.

Kelsey, you've officially gotten even. Go ahead with the people you sent for. In the future, I'd appreciate it if you didn't go behind my back where my people are concerned. The chain of command exists for a reason. Come back with the crew. I want you here on Invincible *when King comes up. Mertz out.*

He returned his attention to Elise. "There. I've scolded her and given her the green light. Now, what do we do about you?"

Elise shook her head with a bemused expression. "You stared off into space for just a few seconds. That must've been the fastest ass chewing in history."

"Hardly. You should've heard what she said when I got implants and didn't tell *her*. So, what can you do?"

Elise seemed to consider his words for a moment and then stood. "Actually, we can talk about that later. You have plenty of time to shower. I've missed you and have better things to do than talk."

That was a plan he could wholeheartedly get behind. Worrying about King could wait.

7

K elsey stepped out of the cutter. Jared's bridge crew filed out as soon as she cleared the way. Her security team, Talbot, and Charlie Graves followed them. The cutter crew closed the hatch and decoupled, taking the senior officers from *Courageous* home.

Jared shook Charlie's hand. "Looks like we'll have to start cutting you in on the action."

Graves grinned. "I'm looking forward to getting back to *Courageous* and testing these implants. Now that you and the princess aren't hogging them."

"I bet. *Invincible*, please grant everyone present with implants the appropriate access to your systems."

"Done, Admiral," the AI said. "Welcome aboard, everyone."

Jared gestured toward the lift. "Zia, Kelsey, Talbot, Charlie, and Elise. Let's adjourn to my office. Everyone else, you know where you need to be. Start getting familiar with using your implants."

The large crowd dispersed, and Jared led the way to his office just off the flag bridge. It was a large space seemingly designed to impress visitors. His desk was made of dark wood and so large that Kelsey doubted he could reach the other side while sitting.

She looked around the space with interest. The shelves were of a similar make. He'd picked up enough knickknacks on Pentagar to fill them. The rest of the furniture was comfortable and expensive looking.

All in all, she thought the room set the right tone for the visiting negotiators. Of course, they hadn't seemed very impressed with a fleet of ships in orbit, so she might be wrong.

They settled into comfortable chairs, and Jared started things off. "I'm glad to see no one had any problems with the implant procedure. That'll make things a lot better for us the next time we have to fight. Unfortunately, we have a battle of a different nature coming up. The woman assigned to negotiate with us is difficult. Now she's coming to see me face to face.

"How do we keep her from knowing we aren't Rebel Fleet officers? Or that this ship was the one they were getting ready to stage a coup with? One misstep and they could kill thousands of our people."

Graves frowned. "I still don't understand how they could be so suicidal. We control weapons of mass destruction that could obliterate millions of their citizens."

"Weapons we won't use," Kelsey said. "It's never a good strategy to bluff. If they call, we look weak."

Talbot gave her a smile. "You bluff all the time."

"Never so often that you can read me," she shot back. "If we blow this, we have no leverage. Let them read the threat without us mentioning it."

Jared nodded. "That's probably for the best. I'd been planning to use a different conference room, but now that we have enough officers with implants, I think a trip through the flag bridge is in order. Impress her with this ship and its implied firepower."

"You'll need to replace the ship's plaque," Zia said. "The chances of there being two major ships with the same name are too small."

"*Invincible*, can you do that?"

"Of course, Admiral," the AI said. "What name would you like to use for our deception?"

He pursed his lips for a moment. "Let's go with *Athena*. And you'll need to tone down your interaction. You need to sound less capable."

"This unit will comply, Admiral."

"Perfect. Now, let's talk about the meeting. I'm envisioning Princess Kelsey and myself as our faces. I'll also need a flag captain."

Graves smiled. "I'm ready to fill the role."

Jared shook his head. "You have to be on *Courageous*. What if they need to know who commands that ship later? No, it needs to be someone that's here all the time."

He looked at Zia. "Since you've been acting as my executive officer, that makes you the logical choice. You'll need new rank tabs, Captain."

The woman's eyes bulged a little. "I know it's only pretend, but I was a lieutenant a week ago, sir. I'm feeling a little out of my depth."

"Who said I was making this up?" Jared turned to Kelsey. "I'd rather have someone I trust implicitly at my back when trouble comes calling."

Kelsey nodded decisively. "That's the right choice. *Invincible*, please log Zia Anderson's promotion to captain and her assignment as flag captain of this ship."

"Promotion and assignment logged, Highness. Congratulations, Captain Anderson. I look forward to working with you."

Zia swallowed hard, her skin going pale. "This is crazy. I'm the tactical officer from a destroyer. I don't have the experience to command a ship like this."

Jared shook his head. "I've seen you fight, Zia. Never doubt for a moment that you have what it takes. I was only a destroyer captain when this started. We all have to step up. Imagine what the situation will be like when we get any other ships from the graveyard operational. We won't have nearly enough people unless we promote from within."

The tall redhead sighed and nodded. "I understand, sir. I'll do my best."

"Then we're in excellent hands." He looked around the group. "I'm clearing the officers from *Spear* and *Shadow* for duty, but I want to vet them more thoroughly."

He looked at Elise. "I'm open to bringing some of the Pentagaran officers on board as well. We'll need every hand we can get. Since Kelsey has authorized your people to serve, we'll use this as a training opportunity."

Elise smiled. "Since at least some of these derelict ships will be coming back to Erorsi and Pentagar, I think that's the best plan. Our people need to be able to work together seamlessly."

"Pardon the interruption, Admiral," *Invincible* said. "The cutter you sent down to pick up the delegation has signaled they are on their way up. ETA half an hour."

Jared rubbed his eyes. "That figures. The one time I want them to drag their feet they're early. It looks as though we'll need to work out the rest of the plan on the fly. Let's get moving, people."

✶ ✶ ✶

OLIVIA SAW the brief look of confusion on Fleet Admiral Mertz's face when she stepped out of the cutter. He'd obviously been expecting Abigail and all the mental pain that entailed. The fact that she noted the emotion at all told her a lot about the man.

He might be used to command but not to moving in political circles.

No noble with any experience would show weakness to an opponent like that.

The man stepped away from several other officers and bowed slightly. Not as much as she was entitled to, but she wasn't going to make an issue of it. They had more important things to worry about.

"Welcome aboard *Athena*. I'm Jared Mertz. I'm afraid I was expecting someone else and don't know who you are."

Olivia smiled politely. "I'm Coordinator Olivia West. I head the ruling council of Harrison's World. Abigail works for me."

"Ah. I see. Coordinator West, allow me to introduce Zia Anderson, my flag captain, and Kelsey Bandar, my senior special operations officer."

Olivia found her attention centering on the short woman in a marine uniform with no insignia. "Please excuse my ignorance, Miss Bandar, but I'm not familiar with your position or how to address you. What is your rank?"

"I'm not at liberty to explain in detail, Coordinator," Bandar said. "Suffice it to say, I'm along to handle any unusual aspects of this mission."

Olivia raised one of her exquisitely shaped eyebrows. "I saw a vid of you speaking with Deputy Coordinator King. Your work must involve the threat of significant violence if it requires powered armor."

"My work occasionally requires a hands-on approach, yes."

That didn't explain anything about the woman. She was still an enigma. It made Olivia want to dig deeper.

"If you'll accompany me," Admiral Mertz said, "we can adjourn to my office."

The lift quickly delivered them to a large control center. It was identical to the one on the superdreadnought *Invincible*. That room had always seemed half finished, but men and women in Fleet uniforms filled this one. The only difference was the wall plaque.

The feelings of loss threatened to break through her wall, and she ruthlessly suppressed them. "Most impressive, Admiral."

"Thank you. She's a wonderful ship. This way, please." He led them into a side compartment. The office was lavishly if sparsely furnished. They ended up sitting facing one another in the open area in front of his desk. Her aides took seats behind her and to the sides. Mertz's officers sat beside him.

"Might I offer you refreshments?" he asked.

"Thank you, no," she said. "I'd rather see if we can get these negotiations back on some kind of regular footing. I feel as though

Abigail may have taken the wrong approach in dealing with the issues at hand. Perhaps we can start over."

Mertz smiled. "I'd be happy to. Not to speak ill of your subordinate, but she wasn't willing to see any point of view other than her own. I'm willing to negotiate on many issues, but not about the return of my people."

She considered him for a moment. "I'm somewhat bemused at your concern for the lower orders. Why are they such a sticking point?"

"Because they came from my ships and I want them back. Is that so difficult to understand?"

Training new personnel would be time consuming, but that couldn't be the reason. There had to be some additional aspect to the situation she wasn't aware of.

She bowed her head slightly. "Of course. At the very least, I promise you that they have received medical care and we're housing them in a satisfactory manner.

"Are your people cleared to know about the situation in this system? Mine are, but I don't wish to cause problems by mentioning classified details to someone not ready to know them."

Miss Bandar leaned forward. "You mean who truly ruled this system? Yes, we three know."

"That makes things somewhat easier. The system Lord declared that the leading nobles on Harrison's World were in league to usurp its control. It destroyed every ship and facility outside the atmosphere. That was ten years ago. Now you've come in and used force to destroy or disable it."

She leaned forward and focused her attention on Mertz. "I'd like to know why the Imperial Lords made that decision and what it means for my people."

He cleared his throat. "That's a somewhat delicate situation. Your Lord made some decisions that the others disagreed with. In a way, it was trying for a coup of its own. They dispatched us to end its rebellion. In the course of that action, it destroyed some of my ships and captured some of my crew. Hence our current difficulties."

Olivia still found that hard to imagine. She'd never heard of an AI rebelling against the Empire before. Still, would she have heard about other situations like this? Probably not.

"What about Harrison's World?" she asked. "What have the Imperial Lords decreed?"

"They aren't willing to allow you back into space at this time, but your cooperation will bring the moment when you can rejoin the Empire closer."

"It hardly seems as though we have much to discuss, then."

He shrugged. "I didn't order your people's confinement. The Imperial Lords did. Are you ready to go back to war so quickly? Allow me to remind you how that worked out last time."

A twinge of frustration shot through her. They needed to get back into space. *Invincible* had the flip-point jammers that could give them the time to consolidate her rule and put forces loyal to the true Empire back in control. They had to control Boxer Station and the ships around it. With them, they could build a fleet that would challenge the AIs.

And none of that mattered right now. Admiral Mertz had a boot on their throats as long as he controlled the orbital bombardment platforms and sat here in this massive ship of war.

It was time to see what compromises could be worked. "What can we get in exchange for our good treatment of your people and their safe return? Surely there's some bone you can throw us?"

"What would you like that we can realistically provide?" Miss Bandar asked. "You already have the best technology the Empire can boast of."

Olivia turned to the mysterious woman. "You must not have dealt with many nobles. If I give an advantage away for nothing, that erodes my power base. Have you ever heard the term 'saving face'? That is what I need to do here."

The other woman's expression blanked for a moment, and then she looked at the others. "I know this meeting just started, but it's almost lunchtime. Allow me to order something for us while we consider your request."

Captain Anderson stood. "Perhaps I can offer you a tour of the flag bridge while they discuss things privately."

Olivia rose to her feet. "Of course. Something to eat would be very nice." She wasn't hungry, but if it allowed them a way out of this impasse, it was worth faking it. Besides, she wanted to tour the flag bridge and think about Brian.

*　*　*

ONCE EVERYONE WAS GONE, Jared rubbed his eyes. "This is going to be more difficult than I'd hoped. She wants to get her people back into space, but we can't allow that. Not even a little bit. We have to control this system and the resources in it. Those ships give us a chance against the AIs."

His sister nodded. "We can't let an enemy loose at our backs. Until we crack the encryption on the AI's data, we don't even know how many patrols they still have out. Is there anything we can offer her?"

"The Rebel Empire Fleet prisoners we recovered from Boxer Station?" Jared asked.

She frowned. "Why would we trade some Fleet personnel for others? That doesn't make much sense unless you know *why* we want our people back."

"I've spoken to some of them," Jared said. "We're keeping them isolated from the ship and other personnel, but someone had to get some information from them. Many, if not most, are from Harrison's World. Offering to let them go home after the tragedy that their lives have become seems humane to me."

Kelsey seemed to consider that. "Maybe. Let's talk about this some more before we commit. If we make a mistake, it could cost thousands of people their lives. I'm not willing to rush with stakes like that."

8

C aptain Anderson escorted Olivia and her aides out to the flag bridge. "Allow me to explain the purpose of each station to you." She took the three of them on a trip around the bridge and gave them a very high-level run down of what each was for.

The noblewoman listened with one ear while she looked around. The memories of the past kept rising to the surface. How many times had Brian sat in a chair very like the one in the center of the bridge and spoken to her? Did his body rest there even now?

Something about the admiral's station bothered her. Something about it kept pulling her in.

Olivia focused her full attention on it and froze. The right side of the console had a small discoloration in the shape of a heart. It wasn't easy to see, but her eyes knew exactly where to look. The admiral's console on *Invincible* had one just like it. *Exactly* like it.

She was on *Invincible*.

It took every ounce of her willpower to keep her face neutral. What the hell was going on? Fleet wouldn't need to perpetrate a fraud like this. They had ships all their own.

The lift opened, and a man holding a tray of sandwiches and drinks walked in. The door to the admiral's day cabin opened a moment later. Miss Bandar stood there.

"If you'll come back in, we can eat quietly and then come back to your question. I think we've found a possibility."

Well, this should be *fascinating*.

Olivia examined Admiral Mertz more closely as she sat back down. He had a military bearing and his people certainly behaved like the Fleet officers she'd met. Who was he, and what was really going on?

And then there was Kelsey Bandar. She was a civilian through and through. Her posture told the tale, and the way she spoke. Yet she'd seemed very comfortable in that powered armor. She'd walked along the dock like a panther in Abigail's recording. Those weapons she'd worn hadn't seemed like props.

So, who was really in charge of this ship? Olivia was beginning to think it wasn't Admiral Mertz.

Time to test the waters.

Olivia leaned back in her seat. "Before we begin, I have a question. Nothing revolving around the negotiations. Where are you based? What sector? I've discovered over the years that a person's home says a lot about them."

Mertz's eyes flicked toward Bandar just enough for her to notice. He was looking for guidance. Bandar was the one in charge.

"We're based in the core systems," Bandar said. "We can't be more specific than that."

"Ah, the Core Worlds. What do you think of Terra?"

"Big," Mertz admitted. "I hadn't imagined buildings so large before I visited it. So many people in such a small place."

That wasn't the answer Olivia had expected. Far from it. She kept an interested smile on her face, but deep inside, she knew this charade went much deeper than she'd thought possible.

Terra had resisted the AIs until the end and beyond during the rebellion. When the orbitals had fallen, the populace fought the invading troops with every weapon they could manage. On a world with the highest technology in the Empire, those weren't empty words.

The resistance had heard of the years-long guerrilla war fought in the skeletons of the massive buildings, a fight so brutal that the AIs had eventually decided it wasn't worth the continued effort. They'd interdicted the planet much as they'd done for Harrison's World. No one in, no one out.

That wasn't common knowledge outside the resistance. The AIs preferred that their slaves think that Terra still ruled them. Not the emperor, of course. Everyone knew that institution was long gone. A democratically elected council made up of humans supposedly ruled the Empire with the help of the *benevolent* AIs.

The so-called Freedom Council supposedly met in the old Imperial Senate chambers. Only that august body didn't exist. God only knew what the machines had done with the planetary delegations. The most senior members of the higher orders and government on Harrison's World knew the truth.

Even adding the resistance to that number only bumped the count up by a few thousand people. Why would he claim to have visited the home world when it wasn't true? Or even relevant. This was a serious blunder.

Olivia couldn't imagine who these people were, but they controlled the orbital bombardment weapons menacing her world, so she wouldn't underestimate them. Any digging into their background wasn't wise when she was up here. They could lock her up in a few minutes.

No wonder they wanted their crewmen back. They knew the truth about who these people really were. It gave Olivia several thousand chances to figure it out for herself. If she could get back down to Harrison's World, that was.

"I went there once," Olivia lied. "The Imperial Palace still ranks as the most amazing thing I've ever seen. It's a museum now, filled with the finest art from all corners of the Empire. The Imperial Lords think we need to have those things as humans, and I suppose they're right."

She smiled. "I hope to show you how Harrison's World compares very soon. You said you'd thought of something I could offer the ruling council in exchange for the release of your people?"

Mertz nodded. "When we secured Boxer Station, we rescued hundreds of Fleet officers. They mostly hail from your world, so I think allowing them to return home for treatment is the best course of action for everyone."

That was the very last thing she'd expected to hear. Surviving Fleet prisoners? Could Brian be among them?

Her throat felt suddenly parched. "Do you have a list of their names?"

"I do," Mertz said. "They'll need therapy. They were under direct control of the system Lord for a long time."

Her implants pinged with an incoming file. She scanned it, and her heart sank. No, Brian wasn't among them. Loss rolled over her again. She shouldn't have allowed her hopes to rise. He was long dead.

She cleared her throat. "I believe the return of these brave officers is certainly worth the return of your crewmen. I'll need to get the agreement of the ruling council, but I don't see that as difficult. It might take a day or two before some of the more obstinate members give in to the reality that they won't get more concessions, though. Is that acceptable?"

"One can't ask more than a best effort," Mertz said. "It's really all we can offer at this time, other than my word that your cooperation will speed your release from this world."

"Then I think we've achieved as much as we can in this first talk," she said. "I'd like to return home to get the process started. As you agreed to grant me safe passage on your ship, allow me to offer you a chance to visit my world and depart in peace no matter what the decision is. I personally guarantee your protection and speedy return to your ship the moment you decide to leave."

She smiled. "While Harrison's World isn't quite up to the standards of Terra, I can assure you that it has its own wonders. I'd be pleased to show you some of them while we wait for the formalities to be worked out."

The other two looked at one another, and Mertz nodded. "We'd be honored."

Olivia couldn't wait to speak to the Fleet officers. What stories would they tell her? She would speak with Mertz's crewmen, too. They'd make up stories, she was certain, but the lower orders had never been very clever. She'd get to the bottom of this mystery. To that she swore.

* * *

KELSEY WATCHED the other woman depart with mixed emotions. The woman's body language was very controlled, but there was a new dynamic to it, and that worried her. Had they somehow given away the fact that they weren't from the Rebel Empire?

The plan of sending the AI-controlled Rebel Fleet officers down was good, but it had its own risks. The longer the men and women were on *Invincible*, the better the chance they'd realize something was amiss. So getting them down to the planet was in everyone's best interest, and the gesture might get their men and women back.

Elise and Talbot joined them as soon as the cutter carrying the coordinator undocked.

"That seemed to go very well," Elise said. "Though I think you raised some suspicions. I'm not sure how, but Coordinator West seemed more on guard at the end."

"It happened on the flag bridge," Talbot said. "I was watching her through my implant feed. Damn, that's going to be useful. She was only curious right up to this point."

He fed them all a vid, and they saw her watching the tour with mild interest until she looked toward the rear of the compartment. Then her body stiffened and her eyes widened. The expression only stayed on her face for a few moments and then vanished as though it had never been.

Jared sighed. "Yeah, she saw something. Any idea what?"

"No clue. I'll scan the room from that angle and see what pops, but does it really matter? She knows something."

"Yet she's willing to continue negotiating," Elise said. "I think she meant everything she said at the end. She wants to convince them to return our people."

"I hope you're right," Jared said. "We can't very well get our people back by force. We don't even know where they're holding them. We're scanning the planet looking for possible locations, but that's hard to figure out. If they're in buildings, how would we know?"

Kelsey nodded. "All we can do is keep trying. If we locate them, we might be able to get them, though lifting thousands of people out under fire seems a recipe for disaster. I think the best plan is to try to get them released peacefully. We might not be able to make friends here, but I'd rather not make new enemies."

Kelsey yawned. "Sorry. I need to take a quick nap. I've been up for almost two days, and even my enhanced body needs a little rest."

"I'll stop in later and take you to lunch," Talbot said.

"That sounds good. Night."

Kelsey made her way back to her quarters, took a shower, and crashed.

* * *

NED WATCHED the town through his ocular implants. Parts of it were still on fire. People ran furtively from one building to the next, probably searching for food or shelter. Other groups of armed people, mostly in Fleet uniforms, stalked the streets. They stunned anyone they met. Others piled the unconscious onto vehicles and took them away.

They'd landed the pinnace under stealth a fair way off from their current observation post. The Fleet cruiser in orbit hadn't seen *Persephone* as she'd ghosted into the system. They'd dropped on the far side of the planet. He'd suspected then that the vessel was under the control of the rebels, but now he knew.

Time to get a prisoner to question.

"Mathews, Walker, you're with me. I want one live prisoner. If we can get him or her alone, perfect. If not, take down anyone who resists as quickly as possible. The rest of first squad will come part way as backup."

The remainder of the team would stay here, long-range flechette rifles on standby, in case he needed fire support.

His armor was in camouflage mode and blended with the foliage as he moved. As long as they didn't run, they were as good as invisible from fifty meters. The optics in his helmet and on the rifles made certain his people knew where each other were.

They slipped in close to the town, and he called a halt as he looked for likely targets. The rebels were operating in groups of at least four. He'd prefer not to kill too many of them right now. A missing person wouldn't raise the alarm like a pile of bodies.

"Captain, I have something," Corporal Davidson said over the encrypted link. He was the team's best sniper.

"Go, Hawkeye."

"There's a small group of civilians fleeing down a street to your left. Two hostiles are in pursuit. They should be coming out into the open in less than twenty seconds."

Ned pivoted to face the area in question, and his teammates reacted without orders. They could hear the information as well as he could.

"Thanks. Okay, boys. We stun both of them, if possible." He crouched down and aimed his neural disruptor at the street opening.

Two children, a boy and a girl, erupted from the street and ran for the trees as fast as they could. They looked to be ten or eleven to Ned. A man and woman, presumably their parents, ran after them.

A blue bolt flashed from the street behind them, and the woman fell soundlessly. The rebels had stunned her.

The man gave up his chance to reach safety and tried to pick her up. A second bolt took him down before he'd even gotten the woman onto his shoulder.

The rebels came out into view. One was a woman in a Fleet uniform that had seen better days. She was filthy. Her rank tabs marked her as a lieutenant commander. The other rebel was a civilian in even worse condition. His scraggly beard looked as unwashed as the woman's hair.

What was going on?

He mentally shrugged. They'd find out soon enough.

The woman made a better target. A Fleet officer should know something about what the rebels really wanted. At this range, he had to restrict himself to just her. His implants helped him line up the long-range shot, and he squeezed the trigger.

The blue bolt took her in the shoulder, and she dropped without a peep. The man ignored her and pulled a flechette pistol out of his pants. He was going to shoot the prisoners!

The man's head exploded long before the weapon was high enough to threaten the civilians. Davidson had taken him out.

"Get in there," Ned said. "Secure the prisoner and the civilians. We'll take them with us. Backup team, catch the kids. Try not to scare them too much, but we're on the clock. I want to be back in orbit before someone comes looking for these people. The Empire needs this data."

His men grabbed the civilians. With their enhanced strength, particularly in their Raider armor, that was no problem.

He was reaching for the Fleet rebel when Davidson called back in. "More rebels! They came out of a side street."

Four men in enlisted fatigues came boiling out of the street, almost in hand-to-hand range. They had neural disruptors in one hand and flechette pistols in the other. Blue bolts and fast-moving projectiles began slamming into his armor.

It was time to go old school. His hands flashed to the sword hilts over his shoulders. The dark blades were just like the Raider-issued knife on his belt, just bigger.

In seconds, he was among them. Arms and heads flew. It was over almost as soon as it started. The enemy was dead, and his short blades were running with blood. He wiped them off on a dead man's tunic and sheathed them. Time to get out of here.

Ned picked up the rebel Fleet officer and tossed her over his shoulder. In moments, he was back in the forest. The support squad reported they had the kids, so he ordered a retreat to their concealed pinnace.

Everything went smoothly, and they made it back there in less than half an hour. The kids were terrified, of course. He took his helmet off and gave them his most reassuring smile.

"Hey, you're safe now. We'll get you and your parents out of here. My name is Ned Quincy. Who are you?"

The boy stuck his chin out. "Larry. This is my sister Anne. Are you going to hurt us? What's wrong with Mom and Dad?"

"We're not going to hurt you. We're going to save you from the bad people. They're just asleep. They'll wake up in a few hours. By then, we'll be a long way from here. Come on."

They secured the prisoner tightly, even though she shouldn't wake up for a while. The medic checked the civilians and pronounced them healthy. This mission was a bigger success than he'd hoped. They had a prisoner, and they'd saved a family from the rebels.

That was nothing compared to the billions of people on this world, but he had to take his victories where he could. They might be rare if what he'd seen so far was playing out across the Empire.

The pinnace lifted off and began the slow trip back up to his ship. They couldn't let the enemy spot them now. They had to get the prisoner back to Fleet for debriefing, and that meant they couldn't allow the enemy to spot *Persephone*.

He sat down at the command console and looked at his reflection. There'd be a time in the future when he and his Raiders could fight back against the enemies of the Empire. It just wasn't today.

KELSEY SAT bolt upright in her bed, breathing heavily. The final view of the man in the console hung in her mind. It was the dead man from the stasis chamber.

What the hell?

9

Olivia focused on her duties for the first few hours after she returned to Harrison's World. There were too many eyes on her to dig into the mystery. She needed to document what she'd officially seen and what she'd discussed for the ruling council.

They wouldn't be happy that she hadn't secured the planet's release into space. They'd be even unhappier when they found out she'd decided not to even try for it.

The more conservative elements of the council believed that they controlled every aspect of life on Harrison's World. They hadn't truly accepted that the situation had changed, even after a decade. They were of the higher orders and that was that. The military would bow to their will.

Even if "Admiral" Mertz and his people had truly been Fleet officers, that stance wouldn't have worked. They'd have had the full might of the Empire behind them. The Lords had decreed they'd remain in isolation for daring to consider rebellion. They wouldn't be releasing them any time soon.

Ironically, those same conservatives would never have pondered fighting the Lords to regain true human control over the Empire. They liked their position in society. Thus her conundrum.

Olivia suspected the people in orbit didn't want to let the people of Harrison's World loose because it would ruin their charade. How they'd managed to take out the AI and gain control of the system, she had no idea.

That's what she needed to know. The resistance might be able to deal with these people, even if the coordinator couldn't.

The buzzer on her desk went off.

Yes, her assistant could just ping her implants, but that wasn't the way the higher orders worked. The advanced technology of the Empire seemed to inspire them to avoid using it to interface with one another. They'd be more likely to send a hand-written note on matters of import than to ping someone.

She pressed the accept button. "Yes?"

"Deputy Coordinator King is here to see you, ma'am. She says it's quite urgent."

No doubt, that diplospeak meant Abigail was pissed. She must've seen the preliminary report Olivia had filed with the council. Well, this fight had been inevitable. She might as well get it over with. She could use it as a pretext to leave early and get to digging for the answers she needed.

The door burst open, and Abigail stormed into Olivia's office. She didn't even wait for it to fully close before she started.

"What the hell did you think you were doing up there?" Abigail snarled. "You gave up everything worth fighting for in less than two hours. Everything I've worked so hard to accomplish is ruined."

"Come in, Abigail," Olivia said with a false smile. "Sit down and tell me what brings you over."

The other woman stopped in front of Olivia's desk and glared at her. "Don't even start that nonsense with me. I demand an explanation."

After giving Abigail a long look, Olivia leaned back in her seat. "You're on the wrong side of this desk to be demanding anything. You can calm down or leave. The choice is yours."

The other woman took a deep breath and then three more just like it. The flashing anger hadn't left her eyes, but she was under a little more control.

"Those circumstances could change faster than you might think," Abigail said in a low, dangerous tone. "The coalition that appointed you coordinator can choose someone else if you fail to lead the way they expect. Right now, I'm certain your actions have a number of the council members reconsidering their support. Perhaps you'd care to explain why you gave ground in the negotiations?"

Olivia supposed the woman's threats were better than listening to her scream.

"I gave ground because they weren't going to agree to your hardline terms. The Lords hold the power to release us. We can't continue to delude ourselves that we can force them to do that. We have to bargain in a more nuanced manner. If you think differently, you're mistaken."

"That's crap. We have their people. If we hold out they'll—"

"They'll leave them and get more. It's a miracle that Admiral Mertz is willing to negotiate for them at all. He told me in no uncertain terms that they couldn't release us without the approval of the Imperial Lords."

"And you believed him?" Abigail shook her head. "I thought you were smarter than that. He wouldn't bargain for them if they weren't worth his time. They know some secret he doesn't want us to have. Rather than giving in, we should be questioning the prisoners."

That was unusually adept for Abigail, Olivia mused. The other woman was usually more of a blunt instrument.

"If they know some secret, then what?" she asked. "Are you planning to blackmail the man in command of the bombardment stations?"

Abigail showed her teeth. "Yes, I am. They took out the system Lord. That means there are events happening that we need to know about. That's not just me speaking, Olivia. That's the conservative leadership.

"If you don't address their concerns, they'll call for a vote of no confidence. They might not control an outright majority, but there are enough others who dislike what you've done to remove you."

Olivia shot the other woman a predatory smile. "I've heard that before, yet here I sit. More than enough council members will want to see what I'm up to before they allow the conservatives back into power. After all, you rebelled against the Lords. Do you really think the other council members have forgotten how their predecessors died?"

That was certain to infuriate Abigail, she knew. The conservatives had been in power since the rebellion. They couldn't understand why any of their leadership from a decade ago would support a coup.

Yet that's what the system Lord told them was the reason it blasted the capital and spaceports to oblivion, along with every outpost that had existed in the system.

The other ruling parties had formed a coalition to strip the conservatives of their rule, but theirs wasn't a strong majority. While Olivia was certain she could bring them around to her point of view, she couldn't afford to appear weak.

Olivia leaned forward in her chair. "You need to go back and consult with your political masters, because I don't think they were quite so strenuous in their instructions to you. If you push this matter now, it might be you who is out of a job."

She let her words hang between them for a moment before she

stood. "I intend to bring Admiral Mertz down to the planet's surface and continue the negotiations in a more cordial environment. It remains to be seen exactly what we can achieve, but I assure you that I'm working tirelessly for the people of Harrison's World. I'll get the best deal possible for all of us."

Abigail spun on her heel without a word and strode out of Olivia's office.

It never ceased to amaze Olivia. If Abigail's father hadn't been a powerhouse in the conservative movement before his death, the woman would never have reached her current position as Olivia's primary deputy. Abigail was a time bomb waiting for an inappropriate moment to explode.

* * *

AFTER HIS VISIT into the city the previous day, Sean had decided a scouting mission to the other side of the island was in order. He'd spoken that night with Ross and Newland. They'd agreed that some discreet intelligence gathering would be helpful. They'd said they'd take care of it.

Now it was almost lunch, and Sean was getting antsy. There hadn't been any sign of trouble, but he hadn't wanted to huddle with the others again so soon. Even though he doubted their captors were monitoring them that closely, he wasn't willing to risk it.

When he went to get his midday meal, the server gestured for him to come around behind the counter. He did so without question and found Ross waiting for him in the kitchen.

The man was dicing something. "Sean, good to see you. I hope you're good with a peeler. We have a pile of fresh vegetables. You must've made some friends yesterday."

He snorted. "Hardly. If anything, the guy I spoke with would've been happy to cut off the food entirely. I can't claim any part of this."

His experience with a peeler was strictly limited, but he grabbed it and pitched in. The noisy kitchen would make monitoring them almost impossible.

"What happened last night?" Sean asked.

"Nothing," Ross said. "Too much chance of someone seeing them in the dark when normal people were asleep. They went right after breakfast. Some of the boys made a scene on the other side of camp and drew the guards' attention. A romantic entanglement gone astray. One of my best girls played her role to the hilt and beat the snot out of her 'wandering man.' It was quite entertaining, I'm told. Gina knows how to be very convincing."

Sean had heard something about it, but the brawl had ended by the time he'd gotten over there. "I'm sure the citation write-up will be unusual. Did your people make it back safely?"

"Just did. They slipped into the docks on the far side of the island. Whoever put up the fences to keep us in didn't check the original buildings closely enough. There are service tunnels that go under them.

"Several merchant companies receive goods on the docks and transship them into the city on big grav lifts. Our boys broke into one of the warehouses and found a few uniforms. Coveralls, really, in blue with one of the company logos. That let them blend in as they explored the place.

"The bottom line is that we might be able to get our people over there and co-opt enough vehicles to get everyone into the city."

"Don't the guards search the vehicles?"

The noncom shook his head. "Nope. At least they didn't on the one ride the boys took to move cargo."

"They went to the city? That was a little dangerous. What if someone challenged them?"

Ross smiled. "They got caught by the company supervisor and yelled at for goofing off. They had no choice but to 'get back to work.' On the positive side, they made some friends, and now a number of people think they work there. That kind of cover is useful. Useful enough for me to send them back. They'll go off shift with the real crew and into the city. They'll look for places we can hole up."

"That sounds good," he told Ross. "I'm not sure we should make a break until we give Mertz a chance to get us loose. Knowing where the spaceport is and some things about its schedule would be good, though."

The older man nodded. "That's on their list of things to inquire about. They're good people. They'll do what needs to be done and avoid sticking out."

Sean hoped so, because if they were caught, the outlines of the bold escape plan he'd come up with wouldn't work. He wished Mertz could get some information to them. Knowing what was going on in the negotiations would make his job easier.

If they needed to get moving, he'd like to know sooner rather than later.

* * *

KELSEY CONSIDERED THE DREAM. No, it wasn't a dream. It was a recording of events seen by the man in the stasis chamber. Somehow, she'd accessed his files while she slept. That *had* to be it.

Nothing like that had ever happened before, and it scared her. Her implants were like a computer. They did what she told them to, with the exception of the combat protocols. They shouldn't have been able to feed the recording into her sleeping mind like that.

She rubbed her face and checked the time. She'd gotten about four hours' sleep. Well, that was it. There was no way she was going back to sleep now.

With this new anomaly, she decided she'd better go have a few words with Doctor Leonard and Carl Owlet. She needed to figure this out before something went seriously wrong.

The lab compartment on *Invincible* was huge. They'd given over a full cargo deck to the scientists and the artifacts they were bringing back from the station and graveyard. She saw a stasis unit, the damaged flip-point jammer, and scores of tables covered with smaller items.

Doctor Leonard wasn't there, but Carl Owlet sat hunched over a computer station off to the side.

She walked up behind him and cleared her throat. "With implants, do you really need the screen?"

He jumped a little and turned to face her with a smile. "It's still very helpful. I can see things at a glance that don't pop out in the implant feed. I suspect that will change as I get used to the new hardware. For now, I'm doing both."

"That sounds complex. Where's Doctor Leonard?"

"Off hunting for artifacts. Is there something I can help you with?"

Kelsey considered how to frame her problem. "I finally got to bed a few hours ago and had a dream. Unfortunately, it wasn't mine. It was memories of the dead man from that ship. His name, by the way, is Ned Quincy. He was a major in the Marine Raiders and in charge of *Persephone*."

That got the graduate student's full attention. "That's not possible. Files in implant storage aren't accessed like that."

He stood up and started setting up one of the machines near his workstation. "Let's take a look at the files."

She sat where he indicated and put on the headset he handed her. He frowned and focused on the screen. "There's some unexpected activity. A large number of the smaller files are accessing one another. They're also adding new files. Weird."

"Are they filling up my implant storage? Do I need to delete them?"

"You still have a lot of free space. What concerns me is that the activity seems to be continuing. Are you accessing those files?"

Kelsey shook her head. "No."

"Let me look at the logs here... The files are initiating the access requests, but only within the new material. One file in particular. Let me look at the code in the static memory of my system. There, I've copied it. You can get up."

She nodded and took off the headset. "I want to look at some stuff while you figure this out. Did they bring over anything from *Persephone?*"

He gestured toward some of the tables nearby. "Since we were there, yes. A lot of personal gear and any odd equipment."

Leaving him to his work, she walked over to the tables and started examining everything as she walked down them. It only took her ten minutes to find what she was looking for. A pair of short swords in a harness.

She drew one and looked at it closely. It was exactly like in her dream. The honed edge of the dark blade looked just like her marine knife. That made it insanely sharp and durable enough to hack through a bulkhead.

Kelsey slid the harness on and tightened it. The sword hilts projected over her shoulders. They felt oddly familiar.

Carl waved for her to come over. "The file is complex. I'm not sure I understand what it is. I'm going to keep poking around in the code, but it might take a while. Nice swords, by the way."

"They were in my dream. Or the recording. Whatever. I'm going to step over here and see how they feel. I'll try not to throw one by accident."

"We'd all appreciate that."

Kelsey walked over to a cleared area and took a deep breath. She'd never had any martial arts training, but her implants knew some things. Combat reflexes, she supposed. At the very least, she could see how they felt without chopping up anything important.

She drew the swords awkwardly and tried to have her implants guide her, but that didn't seem to help. Apparently, her hard-coded responses didn't include sword fighting.

Kelsey sighed and put the swords clumsily away.

The files in her memory probably had something about the swords and their use. Maybe she could find a tutorial.

She accessed the file Carl had said was doing all the work and asked for a sword tutorial. It promptly requested control of her limbs.

This was similar to when her implants took her into combat mode. She checked the limits of what she was granting, and her hardware informed her that she retained override authority. If she wanted, she could stop at any moment.

What the hell. She authorized the file to proceed.

Her hands flashed up to the hilts and drew the swords smoothly. Her body then went into something very much like a choreographed dance. The blades went this way and that as she flowed across the open area, attacking imaginary foes.

In fact, that was exactly what it was. Her implants were taking her through a dance of death.

The blades slashed, thrust, and chopped, each move obviously representative of actual combat. Her body flowed along with it, even leaping as required, higher than an unenhanced person could manage.

The blades had every bit of power behind them she could manage. Considering how much she could really do, that meant something.

The routine ended with her crouching low, with her blades out at her sides. She felt like a predator.

The program was about to sheath them, but she countermanded it and stopped its control just to make sure she could. Her body was again her own, and she was certain that she could have stopped at any point she wanted to.

That's when she saw everyone in the room staring at her with their mouths open.

She rose to her feet and flushed a little. Her hands put the swords away with only a little trouble. "Sorry about that. I was just giving these a test drive."

Carl slowly clapped as she approached. "That was beautiful. You look as though you've been using them for years. I found something"

"Tell me."

"The central file is acting like a clearing house for the rest. It's written much like the control programs for the ship's computer. Well, not this one, of course. Regular ships."

"So it's a rudimentary AI?"

He shook his head. "It's what we call an expert system. It doesn't have nearly the capability or resources of an AI, much less a computer like the one on *Courageous*. Think of an automated library assistant."

Kelsey had used that kind of program quite extensively before this mission. They acted almost like people but weren't that smart. They used pronouns like "I" for themselves rather than the Old Empire standard of "this unit," but they were just mimicking intelligence. There was no spark of life to them, unlike the computer on *Courageous*. Or especially the AI on *Invincible*.

In any case, Jared was going to have a cow when she told him about it.

10

"You did what?" Jared asked.

His sister had the grace to look embarrassed as she repeated herself. "I loaded the files from the dead man into my implant storage, and I've been playing around with them."

Her admission came in his office in front of Elise and himself.

He considered Kelsey critically. "Has anyone ever explained the difference between boldness and recklessness to you? This was not the wisest of plans."

Kelsey looked mulish, but she nodded. "On reflection, I suppose that's true. However, it seemed necessary at the time. I need those files. *We* need those files."

"Just moving them to storage on *Invincible* wasn't good enough?" Elise asked.

"No. They're hardware specific, and implant serial number locked, too, but I was able to spoof that. On a regular computer, they just sit there. Even unlocking them takes a while. I made the right choice."

Jared wasn't sure she had, but it was too late for him to do anything about it. "What about your dream? That sounds dangerous. What if you'd activated some fighting protocol and beat the snot out of Talbot?"

Kelsey nodded. "I thought about that after the swords. Every attempt to access my body requires my authorization. I can't give that while I'm asleep. Accessing the vid files, well, that's a little different. Carl thinks he can modify the protocol to prevent unconscious access."

Elise considered Kelsey. "Why is it so important to you?"

"I have this equipment inside me, but I know virtually nothing about it. I want to be its master, not its servant. Somewhere in one of these files is the access code to *Persephone*'s computer and all the data I could ever want to know about the Marine Raiders and the implants inside me. I'm sure of it."

"How close are you to finding it?" Jared asked.

His sister slumped a little. "I don't know. The program talks like a person, but it's just an advanced interface. It's sophisticated enough to fool people who don't know what it is, but it can't really think."

"Perhaps parsing the files directly might give you more access to the contents," *Invincible* said. "Or at least allow for a more refined search for the codes you seek."

She looked at the ceiling with a skeptical expression. "My implants aren't really made for that kind of thing. I can make access requests and do searches, but I can't have it running in the background. Well, not very effectively. These aren't even straight recordings. I can hear some of his thoughts."

"There are ways of doing deep recordings that also include your surface thoughts. That's implicit in the interface between the human brain and cranial implants.

"In any case, I could construct a more comprehensive indexing program that would run in the background on your implant hardware. Coupled with some changes to the library program that use some of my own heuristic models, and it would make your access program significantly more useful in parsing what files might meet your needs while still respecting your privacy in much the same way I already do."

"I'm not sure I get that, *Invincible*," Jared said. "What do you mean about respecting privacy?"

"I have restrictions preventing me from invading the privacy of the crew. I can freely monitor the public areas of the ship, but not their personal quarters. This program would be similar in that I would create a subroutine for Kelsey that would do a systematic reindexing of the files available to her, but it would not report anything back to me."

Jared cocked his head. "You answer questions and requests when I'm in my quarters. How does that work?"

"My subroutines monitor for attempts to communicate with me and for emergencies. They only alert me in situations where regulations allow me to interact with the crew. They retain no data, so I'm unaware of what is occurring outside those situations. In the case of a medical emergency, I would summon a medical team at once."

"That would've been useful back on *Athena* when Carlo Vega died," Kelsey said. "What would I need to do?"

"Authorize me to access your implant storage and the central program. I'll replace certain subroutines with my own programming to optimize the searching and access of the data. As it updates the file indexes and cross-references the data, you will be better able to find information."

"Do it," Kelsey said. "How long will it take?"

"Not long at all. I'm accessing the program now. Updating the search routines and optimizing the ability of the program to catalog and access data now. Update complete. I did find a file in the index marked 'welcome.' I believe it to be a message from Ned Quincy to you."

She stared at the ceiling for a moment. "Play the message for all of us."

* * *

ABIGAIL HAD her driver speed back to the council building and summoned a crew in to search her office for monitoring devices. Once they had declared it clear, she used her private com link to call Master Calder.

"Yes, Abigail?"

"I confronted Coordinator West a few minutes ago, and I'm afraid that her initial report to the council is more of an understatement that we feared. She doesn't intend to push for our release at all. She's most likely going to give the prisoners back in exchange for some Fleet officers the Lord had on Boxer Station."

"Well, I can't say that's surprising news," he said. "We already suspected that she wouldn't push things. It's time to cause a rift in her relationship with Admiral Mertz. Implement the plan."

Abigail smiled. "With pleasure. I'll make the arrangements right away."

* * *

JARED'S IMPLANTS notified him that a vid file was available. He instructed it to play.

The scene around him dissolved, and he was sitting in a small compartment looking into a mirror. The man's face was pleasant enough in a rugged way. He smiled at his own reflection. "To whoever finds these files, greetings. My name is Major Ned Quincy, Imperial Marine Raiders. Consider this my final report.

"I don't know where I died, or even the manner of my passing, but you wouldn't be seeing this if I was still around."

His smile widened. "Don't mourn me. I probably went out doing something insanely risky. Even for a Raider, I've always been fond of taking chances and going big. I hope I died doing something epic."

Jared hoped Kelsey wasn't getting the wrong ideas from this man. She'd been doing entirely too many epic things herself this last year.

"Now, these files you've found," the man said. "I stole a copy of the library assistant and had one of my techs modify it to work with my implants. The man is a genius, if you ask me. I didn't think he'd be able to do it.

"You've broken my lock and have a full set of Raider implants, so you're my brother or sister in arms. Some of this information is probably not of much use to you, but it might inform you about who I am and what I've done. That's the idea, anyway."

The dead man continued. "I began retaining vids from my implants when I first heard about the rebellion. This is kind of my own history in fighting it. Moments that seemed important. I hope you find them informative and useful."

He leaned forward. "One positive thing, I can be pretty sure that we won the war if you find this. At least that's what I choose to believe. Good luck, and go kick some ass."

The vid ended, and Jared's view of his office returned.

Kelsey shook her head. "That's so sad."

"The Fall is filled with sad tales," Elise said. "If we knew them all, we'd go mad. He died doing what he loved and fighting for those he'd sworn to protect. Who could ask for more?"

"I'm going to keep looking for those access codes and take advantage of any information I find in there," Kelsey said. "I probably should've mentioned something before I did it, and I'm sorry."

Jared gave her a look of mock sternness. "I really hope you don't jump into something you shouldn't next time. Seriously, Kelsey, you take too many chances. One of them will prove fatal if you don't learn some restraint."

"I'll try, really. What do we do next?"

"We're getting our new Pentagaran crewmen up to speed. Doctor Stone is running people through the implant process as quickly as she can. It'll take weeks to get everyone done, so we're focusing on the most critical personnel first.

"Doctor Leonard is working to repair the damaged flip jammer. If we can get it operational, we can secure Erorsi and Pentagar. That's a priority. It would really help if we had the plans for them, though I'm not sure we could build one."

"It would be wonderful to have a shield against the Rebel Empire,"

Elise agreed. "A single destroyer could make life hard for us back home. A task force would take both systems in short order."

"What about getting the yards online at Boxer Station?" Kelsey asked. "We need to repair our ships and bring as many derelicts back to operational status as we can."

He nodded. "That's a priority, too. Baxter tells me his people almost have the original computer system verified. Once he's confident of its integrity, he'll bring it online and start assessing the situation. I'm hopeful we can get *Invincible* in there quickly."

"As am I," the AI said. "The parts you've salvaged from the graveyard have brought more of my systems back online, but there are serious repairs that can only be done in a shipyard."

"What about the planet?" Kelsey asked. "Won't they wonder why *Invincible* is away? Do we dare move her without getting *Courageous* in better condition?"

"It's a risk," he admitted. "The only other option is moving *Courageous* there first. We'll make the call when we have to."

"What about Coordinator West's offer to have you go down to the surface?" Elise asked. "Are you seriously considering it?"

"We have them under the gun. They wouldn't take action directly against me or my party."

"Would those be the same guns that are encouraging them to return your people? That doesn't seem to be working that well so far."

"Trust has to start somewhere," he said. "Otherwise, we might as well just leave our people with them."

Jared checked his internal chronometer. "It's time for lunch. Let's go eat. If I don't hear from Coordinator West by noon tomorrow, I'll call her back. She needs to know how seriously we're taking this situation."

Elise rose to her feet. "Diplomacy is sometimes slow. Don't rush things. Tomorrow morning is soon enough to start pestering her. We'll spend a few hours going over what we can, and then I want you to get some sleep. You'll need your wits about you."

His sister stood, too. "I'll let you two have some alone time. I think Talbot is feeling neglected."

* * *

SEAN WATCHED the wedge of grav vehicles land with some trepidation. They'd brought a lot of guards. This wasn't a food delivery.

That became clear when the men started herding prisoners toward the vehicles, using their weapons to threaten them as need be. It looked as though they were gathering about a hundred people.

He walked out toward them and stopped as soon as the cordon focused their weapons on him. "I'm the senior prisoner. What's the meaning of this? Where are you taking my people?"

One of the larger men stepped forward and sneered at Sean. "That's none of your concern. If you don't want to find out the hard way, you'd best shut your mouth and move back."

"I'll take that offer. Me in exchange for one of them."

The guard laughed. "I think not. As for where they're going, I have no idea. Coordinator West sent word to gather them up. When she's done with them, I'll bring them back. If they're alive."

Sean stared at the man coldly. "They'd best come back in good condition, or I'm holding you and Coordinator West responsible."

That only made the guard laugh harder. "You do that. Now get back before I shoot you and leave you here to bleed out."

Lacking options, Sean backed up and watched them load his terrified men and women into the grav cars with impotent fury.

Ross stepped up beside him. "What do we do now?"

He glanced at the senior noncom. "We find out what they're going to do. If they're ready to start questioning us, we need to break out and get our people back. Then we'll find a way to signal Mertz for a pickup. Get some men ready to head to the shipping docks. I'll be going with them."

11

O livia worked for another hour before shutting her console down. Her assistant looked up from his work as soon as she stepped out of her office.

"Yes, ma'am?"

"I'm making an early day of it. There are a few things I need to take care of, and Abigail has my blood pressure up. You really need to come up with new words to describe her mood. 'Urgent desire' was a little understated."

He smiled blandly. "I'll work on that, ma'am. Perhaps a flashing light when she's frothing."

Olivia laughed a little. "That would work. Call my driver up to the roof. I want to stop in to see someone before I go home. Privately."

"Of course, Coordinator. I'll see to it right away."

She headed for the lift. He was a good man to have on her payroll. Smart, perceptive, and unusually competent. He'd see that her guards stayed some distance away yet close enough to protect her. He'd also make certain that only her most trusted security people were on watch for the flight home.

William Hawthorne had visited her, so she could plausibly return the favor. He'd be a fine sounding board for her suspicions.

The Hawthorne estate was located in the same general area as her residence. Most of the higher orders lived in estates grouped close to one another for exclusivity. Of course, that meant the AI had virtually exterminated the most prestigious families in the orbital bombardment a decade ago. In the old days, her family would have been strictly second tier.

Her security team meticulously cleared her flight path with all of the estates they overflew. Even as the coordinator, she needed to mind her manners. It wouldn't do for someone to make a "mistake" and shoot her down.

Her family and William's had been close before the rebellion. Five hundred years had allowed for many cross-connections between them. They'd intermarried to the point that everyone was related to everyone else to some degree.

That was true of most families in the higher orders, but not like the West and Hawthorne clans. They hadn't been nobles when the Empire fell but merchant families. Ones that had gone out of their way to prove their allegiance to the machines when they took over.

That sickened her, but her ancestors had done what they needed to do to survive. Those terrible deeds had gone a long way toward shielding the resistance.

That loose group of loyalists hadn't been in charge of the families back then, of course. They'd slipped into leadership roles generations later. They'd still be working to make up for what their ancestors had done for many years to come.

She relaxed a little once her air car settled onto the landing area beside William's home. His mother occupied the large house, but he preferred the more relaxed lifestyle of living apart from the hubbub with his husband.

William came out from the patio as soon as her car settled onto the ground. "Coordinator, it's good to see you again so soon."

"It's been a rough day, and I wanted to run something past you, if you have time." She motioned for her guards to wait outside. They didn't like that idea very much, but they obeyed.

William led her into his home. "Craig is off looking over the South Shore power plant. He'll be sorry he missed you."

"I hope nothing is wrong."

He shook his head. "No, nothing like that. They're upgrading the backup circuits to handle more of the load. Transmission technology has improved significantly since they built the facility. As one of the senior engineers, he wanted to be on hand for the tests. He'll be inconsolable once he realizes he missed you."

Olivia smiled. "I'm sure that isn't true. He's a remarkably steady fellow. You know, the kind you want around when something goes terribly wrong at a fusion power plant. I'm sure he'll be fine. Might we retire to your den to discuss something?"

His eyebrow rose. "Of course. I do hope my reputation won't be tarnished when word gets out that the two of us were huddled together without a chaperone."

"I'm tempted to start some rumors to see what people say."

He laughed. "Alas, I'm afraid no one would believe them. Would you like a drink?"

"Some red wine would be wonderful," she said as he led her into his exceptionally comfortable den. He'd decorated it in dark fabrics and subdued lighting. The bar built into the wall held some of the best liquor on the planet. She'd spent many an evening here plotting her ascension to the coordinator's office.

His dashing demeanor made many people assume he wasn't more than a social butterfly, but appearances were most deceiving. William Hawthorne was the leader of the resistance on Harrison's World, and she'd never met a more brilliant and determined man.

He poured their drinks and came back over to sit beside her. "The house is clear, and I've engaged the privacy screens. What's wrong?"

Olivia sipped her wine. It was excellent, as always. "I couldn't risk sending a message, but I have two issues for us to worry about. First, the people in orbit aren't Fleet. I'm not even sure they're really from the Empire at all."

His hand paused while pouring his drink. "That's not what I expected to hear at all. Explain."

"Their ship isn't just a superdreadnought like *Invincible*. It *is Invincible*."

"You're certain?"

She nodded. "Completely. I've compared the flag bridge to the one on *Invincible* in the messages Brian sent me. There are a few flaws in the admiral's console that precisely match. Also, when I asked them a question about Terra, their answer told me that they had no idea of the conditions there. They made as though it was still a civilized world. One Admiral Mertz claimed he'd visited."

"It might be," he said. "Just not on the surface. So who are they? How did they gain control of this system without the AI roasting them? They wouldn't try to pass *Invincible* off as their own if they had a similar ship."

Olivia took another sip of wine. "Precisely. I have no idea what they're doing, but they don't know about the Empire. At least not as it is today."

He sat back and considered her words as he stared at the ceiling. "We need to know more about them as quickly as possible. The prisoners might be a source of information. They want them back very badly, after all."

"My thoughts exactly. Can some of our people look into questioning them?"

"Of course. They're isolated on Spark Island, just offshore, so they're close by. Other than airships patrolling overhead, no one is directly interfacing with them. After all, they're only of the lower orders. Or so we thought. They might be something completely unexpected. Also, a few of them are still under medical care."

"I'm going to invite Admiral Mertz down to the surface, along with the mystery woman, Kelsey Bandar, tomorrow morning. A trip to inspect their people might be just the time to ask some pointed questions.

"Which brings me to my second problem. The conservatives are furious that I'm not holding out for complete freedom. Abigail stormed into my office and made some particularly pointed threats about impeachment."

William waved his hand as though dispersing a cloud of smoke. "They don't have the votes to sustain that kind of motion. No one really wants to see them back in power. They'd be fools to try."

"They've been fools before."

He inclined his head to acknowledge the point. "I'll make some calls and get our people in the other parties to start spreading the word. Perhaps dragging their plan into the open will encourage them to see reason. It can't hurt."

He sipped his drink. "Now, send me everything you recorded on that ship. Every word they said. We'll go over it with a fine-toothed comb and see if we can come to some conclusions about them before they come down. And I want to meet them."

They sat up late into the evening dissecting every moment of her visit to *Invincible*. It was late when she headed home, but she felt more certain than ever that they were on the cusp of something that would change Harrison's World forever. If they could survive the transformation, that is.

* * *

SEAN COULDN'T BELIEVE how easy it was to slip over to the other side of the island. The guards had rigged a fence that wasn't climbable, but they hadn't searched the abandoned buildings very closely. One near the edge shared power and cooling with another outside the fence. A tight service tunnel connected them.

The marines that had been conducting the reconnaissance led him across. They all changed into pilfered coveralls in the deserted building's first-floor bathroom. The three of them slipped into the more occupied areas of the port.

Sean had overseen the loading of supplies before, but this operation was significantly larger than anything he'd imagined possible. The massive ships offloaded huge containers that workers moved into a number of warehouses. Looking down the docks, Sean could see several different colors of coverall. That would distinguish one company from another, he supposed.

A number of men wearing the same color coveralls as them greeted the marines. They in turn introduced Sean as the new guy. They all assured him that he'd learn how the real world worked now.

He worked side by side with these men loading containers onto large grav lifts. He even accompanied several across to the city to unload them.

When he raised an eyebrow at one of the marines, the man shook his head. "Shift ends in a few hours. Then we go back with everyone else without making people wonder what we're up to."

By the time the shift was over, Sean was beat. He hadn't worked at something this physical in years. He really should make more time for the gym.

Crowds of men filled empty grav lifts and made their way to the city. The other workers invited the marines to bring the new guy bar hopping, but they declined. In a few minutes, they'd walked away into the strange city, blending in with the working-class crowd.

The marines led him to a rundown parking garage. They went up some darkened stairs and came out on a floor containing some of the shakiest grav vehicles Sean had ever seen. They didn't look capable of flight.

Sean gave the men a look. "You can't be serious."

One of them grinned. "I worked on all kinds of vehicles before I joined up, sir. Most of these are junk, but I found one that was repairable. We worked on it last night, stealing parts from the others as needed, and I got it working. No one will report it missing. Hell, I'm not completely sure these aren't abandoned. They don't look as though anyone's been in them for years."

Against his better judgment, they slipped into a vehicle so rusted that he couldn't be certain what its original color had been. It started, though it made noises that he feared meant something important was about to fail.

"That sounds bad."

The marine shrugged. "It's the backup grav generator. It should work well enough to get us down in one piece if the main fails. Not much more."

"I didn't think grav generators made noise."

"Only ones that are *very* out of tune. What's the plan, sir?"

"First, what do you know about this area? What kind of people work and live here?"

"Working-class poor, sir. I grew up in a neighborhood like this. People are trying to make ends meet any way they can. If you're worried about someone calling the security forces, well, that isn't the norm for this kind of place. Only when things go really bad."

Sean nodded. "Okay. That sounds good. We'll need to find a place where we might be able to hide a few thousand people in a pinch."

"Bad idea, sir." The marine in the driver's seat turned to face him. "This close to the island, the security forces will tear everything up. They'll search every building. We'll need to take everyone further away from here."

That wasn't what Sean wanted to hear, but it was probably true enough. "Then we focus on finding our people. I know the general area where they took me and what the building looked like. If we can find it, we might be able to locate everyone and find out what their intentions are."

"And if not?"

He grimaced. "Then we stash the grav vehicle and slip back onto the island before breakfast. Who knows? Maybe they'll bring everyone back before we need to do something."

Sean doubted that. They wouldn't have made such a big deal out of taking so many people if they were just going to bring them back. The clock was ticking.

12

Jared hadn't expected quick action from Coordinator West, so he was surprised when she called him early the next morning. He'd just arrived on the flag bridge when the officer manning the communications console turned to him.

"I'm glad to see you, Admiral. I have an incoming communication for you from Harrison's World. It's Coordinator West."

He sat in his chair and tugged his uniform jacket tight. "Put her on my console, Lieutenant Carver."

The right side of his curved console came to life with an image of the coordinator. She sat behind a large desk made of honey-colored wood. The wall behind her was a subdued blue, and he could see a painting over her shoulder. It looked like a landscape.

"Good morning, Coordinator," he said politely. "I hope you slept well."

"You mean you hope I slept at all," she said with a sardonic smile. "I had a lot of people to talk with last night. As you might imagine, not everyone is as ready as I am to make concessions."

He tipped his head in acknowledgment. "While I can see your point of view, I'm concerned about my people. Every day this remains unresolved, they stay locked up."

"I understand. With that in mind, I'd like to invite you and Miss Bandar to come visit your people and see our capital while we clear up this regrettable situation. You'll be here as my guests, and you have my word that you will not be restrained or prevented from departing as soon as you wish."

"I'll admit I still have some lingering concerns. Deputy Coordinator King painted a very firm picture of how she'd like to conduct negotiations. Forgive me, but what's to stop you from taking me hostage as soon as I land?"

"I'm not Abigail King, Admiral. And, not to point out the obvious, you have the means to enforce your will upon us.

"That's not to say you'd use weapons of mass destruction to secure your release, but rest assured I have that clearly in mind."

"Very well. The better we know one another, the faster we can come to an agreement we're all satisfied with. As a gesture of goodwill, I'll bring the prisoners we rescued from Boxer Station with me. Since we rescued almost a hundred and fifty people, it'll take a few trips from orbit, but those poor people deserve to come home as soon as possible."

West inclined her head a little. "We appreciate that. In exchange, we'll immediately return five times that number of your enlisted personnel." Her smile turned wry. "That'll make a few people down here a bit testy, but it's the right thing to do."

That was almost a third of the prisoners. The unexpected gesture made Jared feel like this whole negotiation might go off in spite of his doubts.

"When and where would you like to receive us?"

"I'll give you a code to call me back when you're ready. Rather than meet in the middle of the city, I was thinking an open setting would make us all feel more comfortable. A friend has agreed to host the negotiations on his family estate. You're more than welcome to keep a cutter or pinnace there for your convenience and safety."

He nodded. "That sounds perfectly fine."

"Excellent. I look forward to your call, Admiral. Good day." The transmission ended.

Jared reached for the communications controls and stopped himself. He needed to get used to using his implants as much as possible or he'd never master them. He pinged Kelsey for an implant link.

She answered a moment later. *Morning. What can I do for you?*

I just got off the com with Coordinator West. She wants us both to come along. Against my better judgment, I've decided to agree to you joining me.

He could imagine her smiling.

I'll be good. I assume powered armor is overkill. What can I take?

Whatever seems appropriate for someone of your rather murky nature. We can keep a pinnace down there with us, too. We're bringing the prisoners from Boxer Station with us. They'll give us five times that number of our people back in exchange.

That sounds good. Really good. I'll meet you at the marine docking level in an hour. It'll take at least that long to get those people ready for transport. Anything else? Nope. See you then.

He disconnected the call. Going into the lion's den worried him, but he didn't really have a choice. Not if he wanted to get his people back.

* * *

SEAN and one of his marine guides made it back a few hours before dawn. They'd found the building housing the guard commander, but they couldn't get in without raising a ruckus. So they'd left a man in a nearby parking garage to monitor who went in and out.

It was a risk, but his mechanic had salvaged some of the parts from the dead vehicles and found a contact to sell them to. Sean wasn't exactly sure how the man had been able to find a buyer in the early morning, but he wasn't going to ask questions.

There'd always been a market for proscribed items in Fleet. Usually nothing serious. Mostly things that broke minor regulations when aboard ship. Sean had the idea that his man might have made supplying those needs a sideline. Or maybe a second career.

A month ago, he'd have been outraged. Now, he welcomed the man's skills with open arms.

They'd used the local funds to procure half a dozen civilian com units, a few civilian-grade stunners, and a pair of highly illegal flechette pistols. He'd told his scrounger to find others that could help them get more money and buy other weapons. The man had smiled and asked Sean what limits he wanted to set. Stripping vehicles, burglary, armed robbery, or something else.

It made Sean feel like a criminal overlord. He restricted them to criminal acts that didn't involve coming face to face with the locals. No one was to be hurt.

The man nodded and gathered his team. Sean promptly dubbed them his pirate crew. They'd slipped back to the island before dawn.

Sean felt as though he'd barely drifted off when a hand shook him awake. It was Ross.

"We have company," the noncom whispered. "More grav vehicles and guards. Different uniforms this time. They're asking for you by name."

Sean sat up and rubbed his face. "Tell them I'll be right out."

He hoped that didn't mean they'd caught any of his people on the mainland.

It took a couple of minutes to get dressed and brush his hair. He walked out into the early morning light and spotted Ross. He was standing near a man in what certainly looked like a military uniform.

The man extended a hand to Sean. "Force Chief Meyer, I'm Detachment Leader Tomas Brent. I'm here at the instruction of Coordinator Olivia West and the ruling council of Harrison's World."

Sean shook the man's hand firmly. "Detachment Leader. What's going on?"

"Your commanding officer, Admiral Mertz, has arranged for a prisoner exchange. As the senior prisoner, you need to designate 750 of your people. Whoever you choose will be taken directly to an exchange point and turned over to Fleet representatives for repatriation."

That was unexpectedly good news. And Mertz was styling himself as an admiral now? Interesting, but probably necessary to negotiate from a position of strength. Sean didn't know anything close to the real story of what was happening between the AI's forces, these people who thought they were still part of the Empire, and Mertz's ships. And he didn't dare ask any questions.

He smiled at the detachment leader. "I'll get that underway at once. Does that number include the hundred people you took away yesterday?"

The man frowned. "We haven't taken any of your people anywhere."

"I'm afraid that isn't the case. Some of the men assigned to guard us took a hundred of my people away yesterday. I don't know where or for what purpose because they threatened to shoot me if I made a fuss. They claimed it was at Coordinator West's direction. Will you shoot us for asking for them back?"

The man shook his head. "I will not. You go select the people you want to send back to orbit while I go ask a few questions of the contractors who're guarding you."

* * *

JARED MADE his way to the quarters they'd assigned to Commander Richards. He nodded to the marine guard just down the corridor and pressed the admittance buzzer. The hatch slid open almost immediately. Richards was rising from the small desk off to the side of the compartment.

He gestured for Jared to come in. "I wasn't expecting you so soon, Admiral. Is there something I can help you with?"

"I'm about to go down to the planet and wanted to run some things by you. I'm not certain you've heard, but we met with

Coordinator West yesterday. Things seemed to have gone very well. We're sending the Fleet personnel we rescued from Boxer Station down to them in exchange for about a third of the prisoners they have in their custody."

The Rebel Empire officer nodded and offered Jared a seat. "That's good on several fronts. The longer you had them on your ship, the sooner they would've realized something was different about you. No offense, but you people have some odd behaviors. As I'm sure you'd say we do. Can I get you something to drink? Water?"

"Thank you, no. It's hard to know what seems odd when we have no common experience. Coordinator West seemed undisturbed, so I think we pulled it off for the moment. Now we're going on a longer visit, and I'd like your advice."

The officer sat down across from him. "My first piece of advice is not to get drawn into any long discussions about your home. While each of the worlds of the Empire are separate from the rest, the less specific you are, the less likely you are to give them something to think about. Ignorance is your enemy here, Admiral. Especially since you don't even have current information on any of the possibilities."

"That's excellent advice. I think our general comments about the Empire weren't specific enough to cause us any grief. The only world that came up was Terra, and we kept our responses very general."

The other man nodded. "Good. Keep doing that. I'll make a short list of planets and the general information about them. Stick with that and you should be safe enough."

Jared considered him. "You don't have to help us, so why do so? Your parole is to behave. This is more like collaborating."

Richards shrugged. "I've been able to access a lot more data and talk to dozens of people since you let me out of the brig. Any doubt that I had of your sincerity is gone. You and your people come from worlds isolated from the Empire. I'm certain of it.

"That doesn't mean your assessment of the Empire is correct, but it does mean that the data you recovered from *Courageous* hasn't been tampered with, and that troubles me. The people fighting the rebellion didn't seem as though they were under anyone's heel."

The Rebel officer sighed. "Worse, Princess Kelsey has shown me some of the recordings she recovered from the graveyard. Horrifying. Add that to what I saw of the attack on Boxer Station, and I'm almost to the point of conceding I was completely wrong."

He leaned back in his seat. "If so, I can't help the Empire. That's hard for me to admit, but I can't think of anything else to do."

Jared could only imagine how hard that must be for the other man.

To have his entire world upended. To find out that the monsters under the bed were real and that you'd been working for them.

"You say you're almost there. What's holding you back?"

"Stubbornness," Richards said. "The evidence is there, but I can't bring myself to admit it. Yet."

"I'm sorry this is causing you so much pain, Commander. We'll do what we can to help you get through the trauma. You'll find friends among us, I hope."

Richards smiled. "I already have, I think. Let me get something together for you, Admiral. I'll have *Invincible* verify I'm being honest and send it to you before you leave. Good luck and watch your back. The higher orders are a snake's nest. Trust no one."

13

K elsey stood outside the pinnace docks and watched as the men and women they'd rescued from Boxer Station boarded vessels that would take them down to Harrison's World. They were going to have a hard time of it. In one way or another, each of them had profound posttraumatic stress disorder.

Several had attempted suicide, and they'd had to restrain them. Some were insane. Ten years under the control of an AI would do that. It chilled her to imagine the poor bastards in the Old Empire that had lived for centuries under those circumstances.

It made her even more determined to bring the AIs down.

Each pinnace took just over a dozen of the prisoners so that it could return filled with seventy of their people. That way neither side had to trust that the other would follow through on their promises any more than they had to.

Jared exited marine country and waved as he walked over to her. He had two marines in unpowered armor around him. "I've got my honor guard. Are you ready?"

She nodded. "My people are inside. As is a full strike team of marines who'll wait in the pinnace, just in case we need rescue. Shall we?"

"A flechette pistol *and* a neural disruptor? Isn't that a little bit of overkill?"

She smiled. That didn't count the miniature versions of both pistols she'd hidden elsewhere on her person. Or her knife. The old Kelsey would be horrified. The new Kelsey felt a bit underdressed.

"Not if I need them," she said. "There've been too many times I've needed something and not had it. I wish they made a plasma pistol."

He shuddered. "That's *really* overkill. I'm glad they don't have things like that."

She probably shouldn't mention the powerful Old Empire grenades in pouches on her belt. As Talbot said, it was easier to beg forgiveness than ask permission. If she could've gotten away with wearing her armor, she would have. She'd even considered bringing her new swords, but they'd have stood out too much.

"You didn't leave your neural disruptor at home," she said, changing the subject slightly.

"I'm not crazy. With our record, something is all too likely to go wrong. Come on. Let's go meet our hosts."

They made their way into the pinnace, and it undocked moments after they'd secured themselves.

"While we make the descent," he said, "let me share some data on a few Rebel Empire worlds that Commander Richards gave me. If pressed, use the data to make a cover story and be sure I know about it. We can't afford any conflicting statements."

Kelsey reviewed the data he sent her. There were a few dozen worlds mentioned, along with some basic information about them. She selected one at random and sent her claim to Jared.

"What do we do if they press us harder?" she asked.

"Change the subject," he said. "We can't afford to slip up. Even the little we said about Terra could have gotten us in trouble. Thankfully, it didn't seem to bother Richards."

"What about the AI from Boxer Station? Have they been able to get its data unlocked? Surely it must know a great deal about the Rebel Empire."

Jared shook his head. "Not yet. Doctor Leonard said that Carl Owlet was close. That might mean tomorrow or next week. I'm not sure. Once we have access, we'll do what we can to filter the data and beef up our stories."

Kelsey split her attention between the conversation and the external scanners. The view of the planet was stunning.

The pinnace entered the atmosphere slowly, at least in comparison to a combat drop. Kelsey was able to look ahead in their course and zero in on the landing area. The other pinnaces were going there as well. Local ships were ferrying people in from the large city nearby. Perhaps that meant the prisoners were there.

She found her attention on the local vehicles sharpening when she saw them flying higher and faster than the grav cars at home. Their designs were probably far in advance of what she was used to.

Their pinnace landed a bit closer to the sprawling house than the others had, and a small delegation of people came out to meet them. She recognized Coordinator West. The other two were strangers. She supposed she was lucky that Deputy Coordinator King was absent.

The ramp at the rear of the pinnace lowered as they approached. Jared led the way down. Their marine guards followed them out.

Coordinator West extended her hand to Jared. "Admiral. Welcome to Harrison's World. Miss Bandar. This is my associate, Lord William Hawthorne. He's graciously allowed us the use of his home for our talks."

A tall man with a rather flamboyant beard and mustache held his hand out. First to Jared, then to her. "Admiral Mertz, Miss Bandar, welcome to my home. Allow me to introduce my husband Craig."

The thin black man beside him shook Jared's hand. "Admiral. Miss Bandar." He bowed over her hand.

"Thank you for having us," Jared said. He turned to Coordinator West. "I hope the transfer of your people is going well. Many of them will need some serious help over the next few months and years."

Kelsey saw the twinge of some dark emotion on the other woman's face before she smoothed it out. "It's quite sad. Yes, we're taking them directly to a hospital where they can get every bit of assistance possible. We should go inside to speak, though."

* * *

ABIGAIL PUT in an appearance at her office so that she didn't draw undue attention by her absence. She read the report about the meeting between Admiral Mertz and Olivia and tried not to see red. They'd selected Lord Hawthorne's estate for their dialogue, and she knew from experience that the man protected his privacy.

For someone not entangled in politics, the man had an electronic security team second to none. No bugs ever survived more than a day. Most only lived for a few hours. Even getting them inside the building wasn't easy.

If she hadn't known that he never meddled in serious matters, she'd have suspected him of being up to some plot or another. But other than being old friends with Olivia, he seemed disconnected from people of power, except in social situations.

Frankly, the man was vapid, so she easily dismissed him from consideration.

After about an hour, Abigail left her office and made her way through the council building to a private air car that one of her aides had left for her. That assured her of privacy. The government tracked all official vehicles.

Her driver took her directly to her family's agricultural facility, where she'd decided to house her *guests*. The automated harvesters roamed the golden fields without need of human supervision. This allowed her a reasonable expectation of conducting her affairs unobserved. No one would question her presence.

Her car landed outside a large storage warehouse, and she stepped out. The loose organic matter in the air made her sneeze. She hated the countryside. It was so dirty.

One of the private guards came out to escort her inside. He didn't say a word, knowing better than to talk to her. At least he'd learned to respect his betters with only one object lesson.

Temporary cells housed the prisoners and a dozen additional guards made certain that no one felt like trying anything heroic. That might change when the time came to eliminate them. Even animals would try to survive in the end, even if they had no chance.

Abigail spotted the man in the lab coat bustling around a chair set up against the far wall, and she made her way to his side.

"Are you ready, Doctor Nelson?"

The bespectacled man turned toward her with a start. "I didn't hear you come in, Deputy Coordinator! My apologies. Yes, everything is ready."

"Then bring in the first prisoner and get this started. I can't be gone for long without raising suspicion."

"I prefer the term 'subject.' It makes this less personal."

She waved a hand dismissively. "I don't care what you call them. Just do it."

The man gestured to a pair of guards waiting nearby. They went out and retrieved a female prisoner. She struggled as they strapped her to the chair.

Nelson taped a number of monitors to her face and neck. "This will not harm you in the slightest, my dear. Of course, that doesn't mean it will be painless, but pain is transitory."

The woman tried to hit him with her head. Only the guards saved him from a nasty blow to his face. Belatedly, he pulled back.

"My name is Linda Montoya," the woman snarled. "I'm in Fleet service, and you have no right to do this."

Abigail admired the woman's spunk. She didn't sound nearly as uneducated as someone from the lower orders should. Perhaps they really did give them an education in Fleet. That could be helpful under the right circumstances.

She came close enough to catch the woman's attention but not so close that she was within striking distance. "We have every right to do whatever we please, up to and including executing you. I suggest you remember that. Your very existence revolves around answering my questions as straightforwardly as possible. If you waste my time, you won't live to regret it."

"You don't really have a choice, my dear," Nelson said. "The drugs I'm going to administer will make being untruthful quite challenging. The monitors I've placed on you will get a baseline very quickly and administer corrective shocks to encourage compliance. And before you determine not to answer at all, I feel compelled to warn you that excessive resistance could endanger your life."

Montoya defiantly stuck her chin out. "You can all go screw yourselves."

Nelson turned to Abigail. "This isn't a promising start."

"Just get on with it. If the questioning kills her, dump her body back in her cell to encourage the others to cooperate."

Nelson shrugged and gave the Fleet woman an injection. "This will take a few minutes to achieve full effectiveness. I can see that you're inclined to resist, and I'd prefer you didn't. We're not monsters."

The woman glared at Abigail. "I'm not sure that even you believe that."

Abigail stepped forward and slapped the woman with all her strength, sending some of the monitoring devices flying.

"Mind your place, prole, or I'll have you beaten."

"You talk big, bitch. Take these straps off and we'll see who does the beating."

"You think you have the option of talking back to your betters?" Abigail asked. "Then you're more of a fool than I expected. I can make an example of you that will get the next prisoner to tell me what I want without using drugs."

The woman laughed. "Then you don't know us at all."

Nelson finished reattaching the leads. "We're ready to begin tuning the monitors to the subject."

"Why are you telling me?" Abigail snarled. "Get on with it."

He asked the woman a few questions of a general nature, but she refused to answer them. Nelson shrugged and raised a virtual lever on his console. The woman cried out when the monitors administered a corrective shock.

"Every time you fail to answer," Nelson said, "I'll move that up another notch. Your screams will be quite instructive to your companions."

The woman's response was colorful, physically impossible, and incorporated disgusting acts with farm animals. Abigail reached past the scientist and moved the lever up two notches.

After a few minutes, the lever was almost two thirds of the way to the top. Even though the pain made the woman scream, Abigail was impressed that she still refused to answer. She had to respect the woman's willpower.

She turned to Nelson and spoke in a low voice. "As entertaining as this is, I'd prefer answers to my questions. Do you think you can break her without killing her?"

The scientist looked back at the sweat-covered woman bound to the chair. "I'm not sure. She's remarkably determined, even in the face of the drugs. Perhaps she has some innate resistance. That's not unheard of."

Abigail considered the prisoner and consulted her watch. "I'm on a tight schedule. If she dies, she dies. Get on with it."

14

William Hawthorne engaged Kelsey with a wide smile as he escorted her to his home. "You're a bit of a mystery, Kelsey. May I call you that? And you must call me William."

She smiled politely. "Of course you can. How am I a mystery?"

"I fancy myself something of a history buff, and while I'm not an expert on all things Fleet, I've never heard of a special operations officer. One whose rank is secret."

"That's part of what makes people like me more effective," she said. "The lack of general knowledge about us, that is. I'm afraid I won't be whispering any secrets in your ear. My apologies."

The man's eyes twinkled. "Well, then, I'll just have to figure it out for myself. I'm quite the amateur detective. Of which I read quite a bit. I'm afraid that I'm addicted to books about sleuths. If I might say, you're quite well armed for someone with an escort."

His outright curiosity and charm were refreshing, but Kelsey didn't let down her guard. "I promise not to use them unless I have to. I do hope there aren't any unpleasant surprises. Your home looks very beautiful. I'd hate to put any inconvenient holes in it while I get Admiral Mertz to safety."

"I assure you, there shall be no surprises of that nature on my property," he said seriously. "Coordinator West has given me her word that this will be a peaceful gathering. Informal, even. While this isn't the primary home of my family, it's been in our possession for generations. Craig and I are quite fond of it."

She had to admit it seemed like a nice place, sprawling and old. It looked comfortable. Stone walls covered in ivy, a dark slate roof, and a lawn manicured within an inch of its life.

"It's quite beautiful. I'm certain that your assurances are good enough. As a lord, you must have many interests."

The man's smile widened. "I'm afraid I'm one of those people that coasts on the work of their forebears. I'm something of a social butterfly, really. I do quite a bit of charity work. Craig is an engineer, so I don't feel as though we aren't contributing to society at all. As for politics…" He shuddered. "I wouldn't put one toe into that vipers' nest."

Kelsey smiled. "I've thought the same thing a number of times."

He led them all through the wide doors leading into the house. "I've taken the liberty of setting things up in my den. There's only one entrance, so some guards can remain outside the door while others are inside. I've also selected some of the best Harrison's World has to offer in the way of refreshments."

Kelsey had to admit the room was homey. Expensive-looking dark furniture, and the room looked very lived in.

Something else she noted were the servants William had looking after them. Tall, muscular, and fit. Her implants quickly identified a number of concealed weapons on them. They doubled as guards. Or perhaps they were security filling in for the normal staff.

It only took a minute of watching them to link them to William Hawthorne rather than the coordinator. They watched their master for cues.

Jared's marine guard came in with them, while her escort remained out in the hall. William closed the doors behind them.

You're inside scanner shielding.

It took every bit of her willpower not to jump at the unexpected voice in her head. It was the electronic ghost of Ned Quincy.

You shouldn't be able to initiate contact with me like this.

The other's mental voice seemed to take on a wry tone. *Something must've changed. I seem to have some small amount of latitude now that I've become aware of a possible threat to you. This room is shielded against signals. I thought you should be aware of the situation.*

This new turn of events was unexpected and more than a bit disturbing. She wondered if it had something to do with the changes *Invincible* had made to the program's code.

Well, she didn't have time to worry about that right now.

She made a show of examining the plaster on the ceiling. It was very pretty, but it concealed another surprise. She couldn't see any heat sources above her. A glance at the walls showed the same. Even the marines outside the door were invisible. The room was indeed shielded. Nothing blatant. All very subtle.

Kelsey attempted to access the marines' monitor equipment. She couldn't sense that either. No signals were going in or out.

"What do you think?" William asked her. "I can't take credit for the building, but the furniture was all my work. Not constructing it, of course. Only selecting it."

She gave him her full attention. "It's very nice, though I think you're not giving yourself enough credit. You've made some interesting modifications to the structure of this room. Unless the whole house is shielded, of course."

He cocked his head. "I'm not certain I catch your meaning."

"I think you do, Lord Hawthorne," she said formally. "This room is shielded so that no signal goes in or out. IR, implant communication, and possibly most other forms of signal. If you want to put me at ease, I'm not sure this kind of subterfuge is the way to go."

He bowed low. "My apologies." Some of the playful tone he'd used before was gone. "I often speak with others on matters they would prefer to remain private. Most don't even notice that there's a shield at all. You're most perceptive."

"Others have used scanner shields like this to hide an ambush. I've grown nervous when I can't see what others are doing around me. I'm afraid situations like that often lead to inconveniently large explosions. I'd prefer it if you allowed me to communicate with the marines."

"That presents something of a conundrum," he said. "Coordinator West would prefer that these conversations remain private, yet I'd like to accommodate you."

Kelsey dug a combat remote from a pouch on her belt. "If you could open up an authorized channel for this device, I could maintain contact with the guards without placing a large hole in your privacy. No one else can use it. I can narrow it down to a single frequency, and it will warn me if anyone else is on it."

He took the remote and examined it curiously. "What is it?"

"It's a combat remote. It allows me to extend my senses into dangerous places—like ambushes—and target my enemies without exposing myself."

His expression told her he was impressed. "You must do more fighting than I'd imagined possible. Forgive me, but you aren't the most imposing of people, Kelsey."

She felt the corners of her mouth tugging upward. "You'd be surprised."

"I'll speak with my people on allowing this device access. I don't want any of you to feel as though this is an ambush. Excuse me for a moment."

William went back out of the room, conspicuously leaving the doors open. Kelsey reestablished communication with the marines. More importantly, she reconnected with the high-powered link in one of the marines' backpacks.

It had the strength to connect her implants with the pinnace and its scanners. With them, she could watch every approach to the building.

Jared would take the lead in the negotiations. She'd focus on making sure no one attacked them while he was busy. She wanted to trust that these people wished them no harm, but they were part of the Rebel Empire. Both of them had implants and could be deeply in the AI's pockets.

She'd stay on high alert. If they had betrayal on their minds, she'd make them regret it.

Her mind crept back to the unexpected ability the Ned Quincy program had demonstrated in contacting her and observing her environment. That had her even more on edge. It was changing. She needed to understand what that meant and put a stop to it if it was dangerous. One more thing to worry about.

* * *

OLIVIA SETTLED into one of the comfortable chairs and devoted her attention to Admiral Mertz. She'd selected a juice from the western continent. William always had the best selection. The others followed her lead.

"The exchange shouldn't take more than a few hours," she said. "Shall we discuss how we proceed from here?"

"I thought that was settled," Mertz said. "We would send the Fleet personnel from the station to you in exchange for our people. I don't have a lot of leeway to offer you the outright freedom that you want."

"I need to convince the ruling council to approve that deal," she said. "As you know, getting others to agree to a plan they don't want to hear is never easy. I'm not actually speaking to that, though. I'm talking about an itinerary while you're here. I assume you'll want to see your people."

William came back in from the hall and closed the doors. He and Miss Bandar joined them near the fireplace.

She shot him a message through her implants. *What's going on?*

Miss Bandar spotted the privacy shielding. She requested an exception for her to maintain communication with their people. I agreed. I also consulted with my head of security about the scans he took as our guests entered the building.

Olivia waited a moment and then mentally sighed. *Don't make me beg. What did you find?*

Miss Bandar is heavily enhanced. Graphene sheathing on her bones, artificial muscles, and other internal equipment that isn't completely clear. Olivia, as far as I can tell, she really is a Marine Raider.

That set Olivia back on her mental heels. Her clandestine research indicated the AIs had decided the Raiders were too dangerous after the rebellion. They were entirely too capable. As far as she knew, the Empire didn't even make the equipment for that kind of enhancement anymore.

This only deepened the mystery about her guests.

The mental communication had only taken a few moments. Admiral Mertz was just now responding to her statement. "Absolutely. I'd like to see them as soon as possible."

Miss Bandar cleared her throat. "If you don't mind, Admiral, I'd like to see if Lord Hawthorne could show me around the city."

The nobleman smiled widely. "Finally, a task I'm suited for. I know all the most interesting places in the capital. We have some wonderful architecture and cultural sites."

Olivia nodded. "That sounds like an excellent division of labor. We can return here for dinner. Then you can make the decision to either stay the evening or return to your ship."

They spoke for a while longer, but the conversation kept coming back around to the prisoners. It was as if they were an itch that Mertz couldn't scratch. Finally, she decided they just needed to go see them.

She rose to her feet. "Perhaps you'd like to go see your people now? I'll take you to see the prisoners in the hospital first. A number of them arrived with serious injuries, though most have recovered and been returned to their fellows. Maybe a half dozen of the most badly injured are still under care. I'd be happy to return them to you as a gesture of goodwill."

"If they can be safely transported, we would appreciate that."

"Consider it done, then."

She led the way out. Her official air car had a boxy appearance due to its heavily armored nature, but she knew from experience that it could go much faster than most people thought possible. It had advanced grav drives and compensators.

Compact screens kept the atmosphere from creating much drag, so it could go as fast as many atmospheric interceptors. She'd never been aboard when that kind of speed was necessary, but her pilot had confided to her that it was a rush to fly so fast.

Her personal guards and Mertz's marines postured at one another but got into the car without any actual trouble. She sat across from him as they rose into the air and headed for the city.

"We'll land directly on the roof of the hospital," she said. "I suspected we'd be coming, so I made arrangements to go right in."

"How many people died after they arrived?"

"Many were badly injured," she said with some sympathy. "We did what we could, but several dozen died anyway. We have their bodies ready to go back with you. I assume you know how many people we have in custody."

He nodded. "We recovered the bodies after the battle and know who wasn't there. We'll do an identification on everyone as they come back. If someone remains unaccounted for, there will be questions."

"Understandable. We have implant recordings of them coming off the cutters. Your experts will be able to tell that we haven't tampered with the vids. We won't be keeping any of your people from you. Again, you have my word."

She watched him look out over the city and let the silence grow longer. She could see how he took in the vast sprawl of the city. Her suspicions grew as she watched how he reacted. It was as though he'd never seen an urban center this large.

The air car made good time to the hospital. Her driver had no doubt called ahead to clear the way. Even though most people would probably never notice them, there were other cars keeping pace with them, just in case there was trouble.

The car landed on the roof long enough for the passengers to exit, then it flew away. It would circle until she called for it. She led Admiral Mertz into the busy facility. A trio of doctors in white coats met them just inside.

One stepped forward and bowed. "Coordinator West, I'm Doctor Janice Hauptman, head of the surgical department at Adams Memorial. These are my associates, Doctors Mather and Jimenez. We've been overseeing the treatment of our guests."

Olivia bowed slightly in return. "Doctors. This is Fleet Admiral Jared Mertz. I'll defer to him about what to see."

Mertz extended a hand. "Doctors. Thank you for your care of my people. Might I inquire about who they are and their condition?"

"Of course," Doctor Hauptman said. "We tried to get some medical information from those who could talk, but they were uniformly uninformative. Most gave us a name and serial number. Nothing more. Here is a list."

Mertz took the tablet from her and scanned the list. "You have several without names. I assume that's because they're too injured to speak?"

Hauptman nodded. "Yes. Three of them have been unconscious since they arrived. They are in critical condition, even with full support. I'm guardedly optimistic about two of them making some kind of recovery. The third is still too injured to know."

He nodded, his expression somber. "If you don't mind, I'd like to see them first. I might be able to provide their names for you."

They traveled as a group to the intensive care ward. The first woman was so heavily bandaged that Olivia couldn't clearly make out her face. She lay in a bed surrounded with life support machines. Tubes and wires crisscrossed her body.

"Why can't you regenerate her?" she asked Doctor Hauptman.

"Her injuries are so severe that she's been through six brief sessions in the regenerator. I'm hopeful that she will be strong enough for a longer stint tomorrow. If we can get her to the point she can tolerate full-time treatment, she'll make it."

Mertz turned to them. "This is Petty Officer Margret Powers. Do you think she'll recover?"

Doctor Hauptman nodded. "I do. As will the young man beside her."

They turned to another young person in much the same condition. Mertz identified him as Able Spacer Thomas Rinaldi.

Doctor Hauptman showed them to a third ward. "This gentleman is in the worst condition. He'd lost his legs prior to arrival and suffered a tremendous amount of internal damage. Frankly, I'm astonished he survived the trip down from orbit. His life or death is almost out of my hands. All we can do is care for him as best we can while his body decides whether to live or die."

Mertz stared at the man for a long time. "His name is Paul Cooley."

15

K elsey watched the city pass slowly beneath William's air car. It had an air of decay about it. Few of the buildings were clean, and some even looked abandoned. It had few of the megastructures that she'd seen in the vids of Terra.

Even though she had no evidence to base her suspicions on, she thought it had been this way even before the AI attacked the planet.

After a few minutes, she turned her attention to the Rebel Empire nobleman. "If you don't mind my asking, what was behind the suppression on Harrison's World? I know the basic facts, but what specific events occurred?"

He leaned back in his seat and looked at her with a thoughtful expression. "I'm not privy to all the details, mind you, but I know the general outline. The system Lord discovered a movement afoot to usurp its rule. To say that it reacted strongly, well, that's self-evident."

"So I'd heard. But how could it know what was going on down here on Harrison's World? Boxer Station is not close by, and an AI isn't capable of dropping in for a visit."

"The Lord had its ways of observing the general populace. It was plugged into every computer system on the planet, I'm sure. It must've heard something it didn't like. I'd imagine that it used persons of proven loyalty to verify everything. That's all supposition, of course. I have no idea of what really happened. Olivia would know more."

"It seems like it could've used those loyalists to take the conspirators into custody," Kelsey said. "It's a huge jump to bombarding the planet."

He nodded. "It was quite shocking. We haven't even begun to recover. The Lord obliterated the capital and every spaceport. Unfortunately, those also had large cities around them. We lost more than a third of our population in that one afternoon."

Kelsey could see the pain he felt clearly written on his face. "You must've lost so many friends. I'm sorry."

William smiled wanly. "You didn't do anything. The Lord made the decision." He took a deep breath. "In any case, what's done is done. Tell me what you think of the city."

She scrunched her face a little. "It seems as though it could use a good washing. Sorry."

"Plainly stated but true. A decade ago, this was the largest manufacturing center on the planet. Mostly run by the middle orders and staffed by the lower. They didn't have to keep things in the most pristine condition. 'Functional' was the byword. We still haven't recovered enough to begin making progress on it."

"It must've been quite a challenge to turn it into the capital of the planet."

He snorted. "You have no idea. My fellow lords never had to directly rule over the common people. They had an entire bureaucracy in the old capital that carried out their instructions and shielded them from any distasteful contact with the grubby merchants and workers. Or, heaven forbid, the criminal elements.

"My family came from the merchant classes of the Empire before the revolution. We still have many connections to that kind of people. That spared us the devastation the other ruling families suffered. Their estates were centered around the old capital. Ours was here."

He gestured at the cityscape flowing past his elegant vehicle. "This city is not a haven for the higher orders. These people blame us as much as they do the system Lord. After all, they don't know about our AI leaders."

She thought she heard a mocking undertone to that last, but she wasn't sure. Perhaps he wasn't enamored with a machine ruling him.

"Where would you suggest we go first?"

He pursed his lips. "I can think of a number of interesting places."

"Dealer's choice. You have some assumptions about what kind of person I am. Surprise me."

William smiled. "I know just the place."

* * *

ABIGAIL BARELY NOTICED as Nelson unstrapped the prisoner that they'd just finished questioning. The first woman had cracked, but she'd held out far longer than Abigail had anticipated. Then there'd been the need to verify the tall tale she'd told. With three others telling the same basic story, Abigail had to believe it was true.

Horrifying but true.

These people were nothing but puffed-up pirates from a planet the Imperial Lords had missed during the revolution. Or perhaps not so puffed up. They'd eliminated the system Lord, and they controlled the bombardment weapons in orbit. She had no idea what their ultimate goal truly was.

Well, she could find out from "Admiral" Mertz. He'd tell her everything she wanted to know if she could get her hands on him.

Abigail smiled. This also sealed Olivia's doom. She was conspiring with rebel scum. That wouldn't be too hard to spin into a death sentence. It virtually assured Abigail the coordinator's seat and the restoration of power for the conservative alliance.

She gestured for the guards to take the prisoner away. "Put him with the others. See that they're fed and given any mandatory medical care. These people might very well be important witnesses to a very despicable crime."

The plan for killing them was no longer required, of course. She didn't need to cause a split between Olivia and Mertz. She didn't want to. Unseating Olivia would now take a very different form.

She strode back out to her vehicle, sending the driver scrambling to open the door for her. "Calder Consortium. Now."

Her vehicle took off and curved toward the city. Once she'd had a chance to speak with Master Calder, she could make her move against Olivia without any fear of damaging her own standing.

She allowed herself a luxurious stretch and grinned. Life was looking very good.

* * *

THE SIGHT of the remaining patients pained Jared. These brave men and women had grievous injuries that would take months to recover from. Injuries that hadn't needed to happen. The list of crimes Breckenridge had to answer for kept getting longer and longer.

Coordinator West sent all of the injured except for the three in intensive care to join the rest of the prisoners going back to *Invincible*. The remaining three weren't stable enough to move. A final vehicle transported the dead. Fleet would eventually lay them to rest at the Spire.

The thought of all the bodies that had to fill the ships in the graveyard made him despair a little. The Empire would need to expand the Fleet burial ground many times over to allow room for the millions of heroes waiting to go home. Just recovering them would be a gargantuan undertaking.

Olivia seemed subdued as they waited for her car on the roof. "I'd read about their injuries, but that isn't the same thing as seeing them. I can only imagine the events that hurt them."

He gave the woman a small headshake. "I'm afraid you can't begin to understand them. These are the people that survived. All told, thousands died. Not unlike those who perished when the system Lord obliterated so many cities, I suspect. That's something I can't grasp."

The air car settled in front of them, and they all boarded. It rose and headed for the ocean.

Olivia gazed at him quietly for a minute before sighing. "We must avoid anything like that going forward. I'm taking you to see the rest of your people, but I want you to understand that I'm doing everything I can to get them released as soon as possible. If you try to send your forces after them, there are weapons that can destroy your small craft. That would prompt a stronger response from you. I beg you, let's take this slowly."

"I've sent too many people to their deaths recently," he said. "I'd much prefer to let this situation resolve itself. I appreciate your courtesy."

The air car flew out over the bay, giving him an excellent view of the many ships and small craft on the water. Almost all of them seemed to be purely oceangoing.

He pointed at a large container ship. "That isn't a grav craft."

Olivia looked at it for a moment and nodded. "No. Most bulk cargo still moves via water. Why waste the energy to move something by air when it's more cost effective to go slowly? The economy itself dictates what works best."

"I looked over the maps of this area shortly after we knew which city we were coming to," he said. "There are a number of populated islands not too far away, aren't there?"

"Indeed, though most of these ships come from more distant ports. The global trade is still intact, thank goodness. Harrison's World is slowly getting back on its feet. Look over to the left. See that island port? We'll land there so you can see how this works from the ground level. The camp where your people are is on the same island. We can walk from the port to the camp."

Jared examined the port more closely as she instructed the driver where to go. It seemed to have an unending stream of large ships unloading bulky containers. Vast fields of them were stacked high in the interior of the island.

The other side of the landmass captured more of his attention when he realized it must be where his people were. A number of low buildings sat inside a fence. Small air ships circled above the area, no doubt on the lookout for potential escapees. He was just close enough to see small groups of prisoners. His people.

The air car came down on a flat pad that seemed designed for loading containers into flatbed grav haulers. A number of them were doing so nearby.

He suspected that this pad was supposed to be in use, too, based on the man stalking toward them. He wore a faded yellow hardhat and a deep scowl with equal ease.

The scowl fled when one of the coordinator's guards got out to speak with him. In fact, he became quite a bit more accommodating. The remainder of the guards climbed out before Jared and Olivia exited the vehicle. His marines brought up the rear.

Her air car took off and allowed another with even more guards to land. Those men and women spread out around them in a close circle.

Jared had seen the Imperial Guard do the same when the emperor went somewhere with crowds.

Many of the workers stopped what they were doing to gawk. Coordinator West took that in stride, barely seeming to notice them. Her guards saw them, but only as potential threats.

That left him time to look at them as people. Perhaps that's why he saw the man staring at him in obvious surprise.

Of course, Jared was equally shocked, though he suppressed the expression before it made it to his face. The last person he'd expected to see loading a container onto a grav lifter was Commander Sean Meyer.

* * *

SEAN LOCKED eyes with Jared Mertz long enough to see the recognition flare in the man's eyes. He was dressed in an admiral's uniform and traveling with someone important. A powerful woman with dark hair in an impeccable suit. Guards surrounded both of them.

The woman and Mertz exchanged some words. He started over toward Sean. Well, this was going to be interesting.

Mertz stopped beside him. "Pardon the interruption, but could you explain how this works?"

Sean bowed as he'd seen the foreman do with other important

visitors. "I'd be happy to explain the process, sir. If you'll step this way, I'll show you where it starts."

He lowered his voice. "Well, this is the last place I'd have expected to see you. Does this mean we're going to get out of here soon?"

"I hope so," Mertz said softly. "How the hell did you escape the prison camp?"

"We found an unguarded access tunnel, and some of the marines are good at making friends. We even have some people on shore looking for a way to get everyone to the spaceport, just in case we have to make our own travel arrangements."

"You're very resourceful, Sean." His tone was admiring. "You might as well call them back. There are no spaceports. The AIs had this planet on lockdown. It blew the capital and spaceports just like they did during the rebellion."

Mertz put his hands on his waist for a moment before raising his voice. "Tell me about how the ships are unloaded."

Sean gestured toward the ships nearest the dock. "Each of these comes in and is assigned a docking time. The large cranes unload it and place the containers into the stacks. Each has a number that the supervisors keep track of. Based on things like the perishability of the cargo, the need for faster delivery, and other priority factors, each is loaded onto these grav lifts for transport to shore."

"And once there, the lifts take them to other cities and so forth?"

Mertz shielded them with his body and slipped Sean his com.

Sean pocketed it and shook his head. "No, sir. Grav trains take cargo to the more distant locations. These lifts only deliver the containers to a facility similar to this on the shore. Workers there see them on their way."

Mertz frowned. "Then why not just unload them there in the first place?"

Sean had wondered the very same thing. "The yard on shore is too small. With all of the extra cargo coming through this bay, it was easier to use the island to get all the ships unloaded. The grav lifts serve the shore port and a number of train yards. I should've said that up front. Sorry."

"I hope you can get back into the camp quickly," Mertz said softly. "We're on our way there now. Coordinator West probably didn't get a good look at you, but you'd best change your appearance some. A hat, shave, etc."

Sean had been cultivating his stubble to blend in. That would be an easy fix. That and a hat would hopefully be good enough.

Mertz shook Sean's hand. "I think I've got it. I appreciate you taking the time to explain it to me."

"It's my pleasure."

He watched Mertz rejoin the woman and her guards. They continued toward the edge of camp.

The foreman yelled for everyone to get back to work, so he blended into the suddenly busy crowd. With luck, he'd be back at the barracks and ready for visitors before they got there.

16

bigail arrived at the Calder Consortium building and exited her vehicle in something of a rush. Her guards struggled to keep up as she breezed past the security checkpoint. The people manning it knew better than to delay her.

She took the lift up with two of her people and headed for Master Calder's private office. She placed her guards outside the door with a gesture and stared at the Master's assistant. "I need to speak with him. Now."

The man smiled apologetically. "I'm sorry, Deputy Coordinator King. He's in an important meeting and left instructions not to be disturbed."

"I'm telling you to interrupt him. This cannot wait."

The man considered her for a moment and then rose to his feet. "I'll go do so in person, Deputy Coordinator. Please wait here." He went into the office and came back out after a minute. "Please go in, Deputy Coordinator."

Abigail gave the man a nod and went inside. Master Calder stood behind his desk, staring out the window at the city.

"This had better be important, Abigail. The negotiations you interrupted might not go so well when I reschedule."

She bowed her head, knowing he was watching her reflection in the glass. "I apologize, but this is more important than your meeting, Master."

He turned and raised an eyebrow. "Well, then. I shouldn't delay your update with my posturing. Please continue."

"Admiral Mertz and his people aren't Fleet. Not ours, anyway. They're descendants of loyalists who escaped the Lords with Emperor Marcus's son Lucien during the revolution."

Master Calder blinked and stood stock still for a moment. Then he gestured for her to take a seat. "I grant you that's a worthy reason for bursting into my office. I assume the rush is because he's still on Harrison's World and you want to take action against him and Olivia now?"

She settled into her seat and nodded. "Yes, Master. We can prove that Olivia is collaborating with the enemies of the Empire. That's not only enough to strip her of her office but to execute her for treason."

"You can legally prove that she knows who she's dealing with? After all, you took these prisoners without cause to have them tortured. With my blessing," he hastened to add. "But our enemies will not be fooled."

Abigail stuck her chin out defiantly. "We did what needed to be done. Olivia is weak. These people are playing her. The others will see that."

"Will they? After the Lord turned on us, they wasted no time seizing power. They're not going to be eager to hand it back. They know the price they'll pay."

"There isn't time to play subtle games pitting one faction against another," she said firmly. "Mertz will have what he wants in a few days at most. Honestly, it really doesn't matter at this point. We have enough of his people to prove our accusations at any time.

"The window to take Olivia out of play is narrow, though. If we don't strike while Mertz is here and blame him for the attack, we'll have no choice but to trust the political process. We've seen how well that works."

The conservative alliance had been the eyes and ears for the Lords since the revolution. The system Lord had rewarded them by using its influence to keep them in a dominant leadership role on Harrison's World. Until it had inexplicably turned on them.

It had accused them of planning a coup and had used irresistible force to scour the system of all human presence. That, in turn, had led to a coalition of weaker parties wresting control of the planet away from its rightful rulers.

Master Calder considered her words while drumming his fingers on his desk. "A successful attack might very well allow you to take the coordinator's chair. A failed one will start a civil war. Given a chance, Olivia might lead the unwashed hordes to our doors with torches."

"If she allows them to rise, they'll attack all of the higher orders indiscriminately," Abigail almost sneered. "She won't."

He nodded slowly. "If we commit to this path, we have no choice but to push through to victory. Once the others become aware of the resources we've been gathering, they'll consolidate into a solid wall of resistance. You'll have one chance to strike the head off the snake."

Abigail smiled. "I can do that."

The Master walked to his bar and poured a drink. "Even if I grant you that point, these invaders control weapons that could destroy Harrison's World. We need to expedite Project Damocles."

Abigail shrugged. "Will the time ever be better? The Lord is disabled, and these people only have two ships. They think themselves safe. Also, they don't have a superdreadnought as they'd claimed. The prisoners all agreed that this so-called Admiral Mertz is a commander in their Fleet and only has a repaired battlecruiser and a freighter. They don't even have widespread use of implants. We can eliminate them all with one bold stroke."

"They defeated the system Lord. Are you telling me they did so with one cobbled-together warship?" Master Calder sounded unconvinced. "Then where did these thousands of prisoners come from?"

"Other ships that followed Mertz to this general area. Based on what I heard, a patrol sent out by the system Lord crushed their ships. I'm not sure how Mertz was able to capture this system, but he cannot hold it from us."

Master Calder shook his head. "This Mertz may be more formidable than you give him credit for. I need to think for a moment."

He paced his office for a few minutes before seeming to come to a decision. "If we can take the orbital bombardment platforms off the table, the ships can't cause widespread damage to the planet. Even if the intelligence you have is wrong. The time has come for us to restore order to this world. Do not fail me."

Abigail rose to her feet. "I won't, Master. By nightfall, Olivia West will be dead and we'll control our own orbital space." She smiled widely. "Then we'll eradicate these rebels from the heavens."

* * *

WILLIAM DIRECTED his driver to take them to a location away from the city. Kelsey happily switched her observation to the coastline. The never-ending flow of dilapidated buildings had become monotonous.

The city trailed off into rural areas. Much of the land seemed dedicated to food production. Massive machines tended and harvested vast fields. The corn was recognizable, but she couldn't place the other plants.

"The land below produces the food that keeps us all from starving," William said after a while. "Well, not really starving. Even though the urban centers are large here on Harrison's World, we're not lacking for arable land. Still, it feeds everyone in this city, and much is exported to surrounding areas."

She pulled her gaze away from the fields below. "Was that a danger when the AI attacked? I've seen the results of large-scale bombardment up close. It can be...extreme."

He gazed out the window for a few moments. "It feels wrong to say this, but the damage from the bombardment was limited to areas close to the targets. Rather than one large kinetic weapon, the orbitals have smaller ones that strike in close proximity to one another. That still means total destruction for a city and all the horror that entails, but it restricts large-scale damage to a manageable level. Has something larger been done elsewhere?"

She nodded grimly. "I'm afraid so. A ten-kilometer asteroid. Not quite an extinction-level event, but far too close for my peace of mind. Let me tell you, being nearby when it hit was...unpleasant."

He stared at her. "You were that close to a massive asteroid strike? And you lived?"

Kelsey shrugged. "We had good pilots, but not everyone made it. I can't go into the details of the situation, but I'm here to tell you that those rides at the amusement park no longer even raise my heart rate."

"I'd imagine not." He took a deeper breath. "Anyway, my family owns a fairly large swath of these fields, so it's been my pleasure and headache to see every inch of these lands for the last few years. We have a number of houses and buildings, but there's one in particular that I'd like to show you."

"I don't know that much about architecture."

He laughed. "You won't need to. It's not the building itself that you'll find intriguing. It's what's inside it."

The building in question looked like a large warehouse. They circled it once, and the driver brought them down to a cracked plascrete slab beside it. The exterior of the single-story structure hadn't seen fresh paint in quite some time. The original color was white. She could tell that from the few places where the last coat was still intact.

The sliding doors were locked tight, and small blinking lights told the tale of alarms at the ready.

William climbed out and held the car door for her. Her two marine guards flanked them as he led her to the building entrance.

"If it had been anyone but me, the alarm would've already warned the intruders away. A hidden weapons emplacement would've targeted anyone foolish enough to continue. Only the most stubborn would feel its wrath, though."

Kelsey raised an eyebrow. "You'd keep something that valuable way out here in the middle of nowhere?"

He smiled. "This seemed like the best place for it. Come."

There wasn't a keypad, so he must've used his implants to disarm the building's protections. The large door ponderously slid open a few feet and stopped with a screech.

"Well, so much for me avoiding any embarrassing lapses," he said with a chuckle. "I obviously need to bring someone out to fix the door."

The interior was dark but not so obscured that her optical implants couldn't show her what was waiting. William didn't know that she could see in conditions of almost total darkness.

In the center of the open area, a civilian cutter sat in the gloom.

He turned on the lights with a flourish. "And here we are. The last ship on Harrison's World still capable of reaching orbit and beyond. Theoretically."

Kelsey walked over and gave it a closer look. In the light, it had some similarities to the building. It was obviously old, and the fuselage could have done with some repairs. In all, it looked incapable of atmospheric flight, much less making it into space.

Still, it was a ship on a planet that had lost every spaceport, so that had to count for something.

"I can see what you mean by theoretically. Does it still work? How did it survive the orbital bombardment?"

William wiggled his hand in the air in a way that she thought meant uncertainty. "It should still be capable of flight. At least the self-diagnostics say it is. My father gave it to me as a fixer-upper. It was long past retirement from the family fleet, so he told me I could have it so long as I maintained it. I'd brought it out here because we didn't have an unused space large enough to hold it."

He sighed. "And then the capital was destroyed, taking the main spaceport with it. If I'd moved it to one of the smaller spaceports, it still would've been lost. Like my father."

She could see the emotion he was keeping bottled inside him. "I'm sorry for your loss."

He nodded his acceptance of her condolences. "Everyone lost someone that day. I'm hardly alone in that. It still hurts, but in the face of such a tragedy, it seems gauche to mention it."

After a moment, he continued. "In any case, I've made a number of inquiries. I suspect that this may be the only remaining spacecraft on the planet." He turned to her. "You're not going to blow it up, are you?"

"I think our ship is safe enough from it," she said dryly. "Besides, I'm not sure it would even get high enough for the orbital bombardment platforms to shoot it down."

"True enough. Now that you've seen it, I'll admit to asking you out to see it with ulterior motives."

She raised an eyebrow. "I'm flattered, of course, but I'm seeing someone."

"Dear God!" he said, clutching his chest. "Your virtue is safe with me!"

Kelsey laughed. "Well, if not an assignation, then what?"

His gaze sharpened. "I just wanted to ask you a few questions away from prying ears."

"Fire away."

"Where did you come from? You're not Fleet. At least your Admiral Mertz doesn't hold the rank he claims. Who are you really?"

She stood there, frozen in place at the unexpected question.

17

Olivia allowed her guards to lead the way to the fence isolating the prisoners from the port. A number of empty buildings separated the two areas. There was one guarded gate along that stretch. A heavy stunner commanded all the approaches the prisoners might use.

An unkempt man stood beside the guards. He bowed at their approach. "Coordinator West. Welcome. My name is Jack Oliver. I'm in charge of the internment camp."

She gave him a nod. "Mister Oliver. This is Fleet Admiral Jared Mertz, your prisoners' commanding officer. He's here to inspect their condition. I assume everything is in order."

His eyes darted to Mertz and then back to her. "Of course. If you'll come this way."

The man's furtive glance filled her with dread. What was he hiding?

They made quite a sight, all of the men guarding her, walking as one large crowd. The camp guards stayed away from her personal protective unit, but that didn't keep her people from regarding them as possible threats.

It took almost five minutes before she saw the first prisoners. Dressed in Fleet uniforms, they watched the procession curiously. The onlookers grew more numerous as they came to the central square of the camp.

A group of men stood waiting for them. They looked like officers, but she knew that wasn't the case. They had no implants.

One of them seemed familiar, somehow. A tall, thin man with a clean face and sharp eyes. She couldn't place him, but she'd seen him before. Or perhaps his twin. If you met enough people, you'd find unrelated folk who were so similar it was spooky.

The man in question saluted with his fist to his chest. "Admiral. Force Master Chief Sean Meyer reporting. You know my associates, Command Master Chiefs Ross and Newland. We're glad to see you, sir."

Mertz returned the salute. "Gentlemen, I'm pleased to see you as well. This is Coordinator West, the leader of Harrison's World. I hope to conclude negotiations with her very shortly to secure your release. Are your conditions acceptable? Do you need anything?"

Meyer glanced at her and then back at his commanding officer. "Things were a bit rough the first few days, but they're looking up. I'm most concerned about the men and women separated from us. I know we'd all like to know where they went."

Mertz frowned. "Didn't they tell you? They're going back to *Athena*, our flagship in orbit."

The tall man shook his head. "Not them, sir. The hundred people the guards took yesterday."

There was a moment of stunned silence before Mertz turned and gave Olivia a stony look. "That *does* sound like a pressing question. I'm sure the coordinator can tell us where they are."

* * *

KELSEY STARED at the man in shock. How had he known?

"Excuse me?" she asked. "I don't know where that came from, but you're off base."

He smiled, showing her marines his hands when they perked up. "Am I? Please tell your men that I'm not silly enough to attack a Marine Raider with my bare hands. I'm certain the results would be spectacularly humiliating."

She gestured for them to search the building in case this was more of an ambush than it appeared.

Once they were gone, she put her hands on her hips. "I think you should explain what you mean."

"It was a combination of things, really. Let's start with the biggest mistake. Terra. I'm sorry to inform you, but the capital of the Empire was suppressed shortly after the revolution."

His expression became more solemn. "The citizens there resisted fiercely, and they never stopped. It became the most impressive guerrilla action in history. The Imperial Lords finally decided that the planet was a lost cause and declared the system off limits. It has orbital bombardment platforms much like those over our heads. So I'm afraid that Admiral Mertz's claims of visiting it ring false."

Kelsey had to admit there was a possibility he was telling the truth, but she couldn't just say so. "Coordinator West also said she visited it, so why should I believe your tall tale? I'm not sure what you hope to gain from this charade, Lord Hawthorne."

"Olivia would be the first to tell you she knew you were lying right then. Well, actually, she knew you were hiding something even before that moment. If Terra isn't enough to get you to speak more freely, shall we discuss your ship? Her name isn't *Athena*, is it? Let's just call her by her true name. *Invincible*."

He smiled at her expression. She expected she looked like an animal caught in a bright light, unsure of which direction to run.

"Rest easy," he said as she struggled to come up with a story. "If we intended to act against you, we would've already done so. You can call Admiral Mertz and verify that he's in no immediate danger."

She considered doing that but decided to test the waters a little further first. "How do you know that name?"

"*Invincible?* Simple enough. We spent quite a lot of time and money refitting her in secret. Let me assure you, slipping personnel and parts under the very nose of the system Lord was a challenge.

"Olivia, the poor woman, was in a relationship with the senior Fleet officer on that ship when the Lord suppressed us. She received a number of messages from your flag bridge over the years preceding it. Ones showing marks on the Admiral's console that were quite distinctive. She knew right away where she was."

He allowed her a moment to consider that before he continued.

"If you were truly Fleet personnel, you wouldn't need to finish restoring that ship to carry out your supposed mission to take out the system Lord. You'd have brought enough force to handle that. For the life of me, I can't figure out what you're really doing here or who you are. Perhaps you'd care to explain it to me?"

Kelsey sighed. "I should've known things were going too smoothly. Why were you about to stage a coup against the AI?"

"I'll show you mine if you'll show me yours."

In spite of the gravity of the situation, she laughed. "You're a rascal."

"Craig agrees with that assessment completely. Honestly, we mean you no harm. Your people control all access to Harrison's World, so attacking you would be madness. You truly hold all the cards in this game. Can't we be honest with one another?"

She considered him for a moment. "It's a long story. The basis of which is that we're not from around here."

His eyebrows drew together. "You come from the other side of the Empire?"

"Not exactly. What do you know of the Fall?"

"I assume you mean when the AIs suppressed the Empire. I know what most people know, and a bit more handed down by tradition in secret. The AIs took over Fleet faster than Emperor Marcus could marshal forces to stop them. The AIs crushed the Imperial forces near the border of the Empire. Many of the derelicts orbiting Boxer Station came from that last stand."

"The emperor perished there?"

"Legend says no ships escaped the cul-de-sac where Fleet made its final stand. I see no reason to doubt that. We couldn't exactly search the derelicts without raising suspicions."

She allowed the corner of her mouth to quirk upward. "Well before that last battle, the emperor sent his son away to a distant world. Once the fighting ended, our world was damaged but alive and unoccupied. The emperor's son, Lucien, kept the flames of civilization burning, and though it took centuries to again get to the stars, here we are."

He stared at her for a long moment, thunderstruck. "That isn't the story I was expecting at all. If, of course, it's true. Why are you here in this system?"

"To get our people back," Kelsey said. "Taking on the AI cost us far more than any sane person would want to pay. Yes, we appropriated *Invincible*. Without her, we'd never have succeeded in defeating the AI and its ships. And, for the record, finders keepers."

William shook his head slowly. "Remarkable. I certainly won't contest your possession. After all, you accomplished everything we'd hoped to do. Though, unless we work together, those gains may be very short lived."

"How so?"

"There are some devices in the ship's hold. They are critical to protecting this system."

Kelsey nodded. "The flip-point jammers, yes. We found them and have this system locked down. For the moment, we are in complete control. There won't be any surprises from the AIs." She put her hands on her hips. "Now, show me yours."

He leaned up against the leg of the cutter. "You and I have something in common. Ever since the AIs overwhelmed the Empire, there has been a resistance. A fairly ineffective one, considering the AIs control virtually all the industrial capacity. We have no ships and few troops. Yet on every world, we're looking for a way to take the Empire back.

"Here on Harrison's World, the conservatives have been the spies and willing helpers for the AIs. Only in the last few decades has the resistance gained the tools it needed to have a chance of overthrowing their rule. Those flip-point jammers and the almost-completed superdreadnought. With those, we thought we could secure the system and rebuild the true Fleet. We still can, if you'll work with us."

She paced as she considered her response. "Some accommodation might be possible, but you need to know that your plan was doomed. Even with total surprise, the AI would've destroyed *Invincible* if we hadn't had other ships. Even with them, we lost a lot of good people. You can prove your commitment to wanting to work with us by returning my people."

He raised an eyebrow. "Yours? Not Admiral Mertz's? So you're in command. Forgive me, but you don't look like a military person. Even with those impressive implants. You strike me more as a member of the higher orders. Or a noble, as they were once called."

She nodded. "That's true enough. Perhaps you noted my name is Bandar. My father is the sitting emperor of the Terran Empire and my brother the heir. Under the edict put forth by Emperor Marcus and by my father's appointment, I am Princess Kelsey, heir secundus to the Imperial Throne and ambassador plenipotentiary of the Terran Empire. The true, unconquered Empire."

Abigail left Master Calder's office and went straight to the headquarters of the conservative alliance. Gavin Decker, his chief troubleshooter, was already waiting for her. He closed the door in the faces of her guards and led her to a sitting room decorated in dark, rich browns. She sank gratefully into a large leather chair.

He sat on the edge of his desk. "Master Calder instructed me to cooperate in every way possible, Deputy Coordinator. What can I do for you?"

"I need you to kill Coordinator West. I think eliminating the admiral's companion—Miss Bandar—will sow enough suspicion so that we can spin Olivia's death as retribution. If Mertz can be taken alive, that would be helpful, but I understand how complicated that might be. Kill them both if you need to. I need it done today. Bandar should die within the next few hours, if possible."

The man hid his shock well, but she saw it flicker across his face. "I have people following both groups. Lord Hawthorne and Miss Bandar are away from heavily populated areas, so direct action is possible. May I inquire why we're embarking on this course? There will be a significant amount of blowback."

"I'm aware of that. The ultimate reasons are not your concern. Master Calder has endorsed my plan. Is that going to be a problem?"

He seemed to consider her words for a moment and then shook his head. "No. Depending on the circumstances that hold sway in a few hours, the assassinations might be subtle or overt. The coordinator's location and security posture will dictate how this plays out. Do you have any preference in regard to the methods I use?"

"Not particularly, so long as no one doubts Mertz and Fleet are responsible for her death."

He smiled. "Consider it done."

18

O livia turned her attention to the camp commander. "Perhaps you'd care to enlighten us, Mister Oliver?"

The man shrank back a bit but straightened almost immediately. He glared at the prisoner. "That's a damned lie. No prisoners are unaccounted for."

"That's good," she said, eyeing the perspiration beading on his forehead. "I know that a complete list of prisoners was made. We'll do a thorough head count, just to settle this. Now."

The man nodded. "Of course. I'll get that started right away."

Olivia watched him walk toward the gate and leaned over to speak softly to her guard commander. "He might be telling the truth, but I don't trust a man who sweats under questioning. Grab him if he tries to make a quick escape."

The woman in uniform bowed. "Right away, Coordinator." She motioned for two other guards to follow and headed after the man, her com unit to her lips.

That matter dealt with for the moment, she returned her attention to Admiral Mertz and Force Master Chief Meyer. "We'll get to the bottom of this matter very shortly. I authorized no such prisoner removal. I swear it."

Mertz gave her a steady look and then nodded. "I believe you, but I also have no reason to doubt the force master chief. How will you go about finding my people?"

"If the camp commander had anything to do with it, we'll get that information from him in short order."

They'd only begun a tour of the camp when her guard commander returned with Oliver in cuffs. Two men had him held between them and were forcing him to walk quickly. Her remaining guards focused their attention out on the camp guards. If there was going to be trouble, now would be the time.

None of them seemed inclined to do more than grumble.

"He made a break for his air car," the guard commander said. "I had people waiting for him."

Olivia shook her head with mock sadness. "I'm so disappointed in you, Mister Oliver. Who paid you, and where did they take these people to?"

The man glared at her, which earned him a slap to the back of the head from one of her guards. That didn't dampen his animosity one bit.

"These people killed millions of us," he snarled. "Why should we care what happens to them? You should've killed them all as soon as they landed."

"Watch your tone," she said coldly. "We didn't kill them because they had nothing to do with the attack on our world."

"But Fleet did! Screw those bastards!"

Olivia understood his reaction. Only the cream of the higher orders knew the AIs ruled humanity. Regular people knew nothing of computer-controlled warships or the system Lord. They thought Fleet was responsible, when nothing was further from the truth.

"I gave my word that these prisoners would be cared for," she said coldly. "Where are these people?"

"I have no idea, and at this point, I don't really care," Oliver said sullenly. "My brother died because of them, and they deserve what they get."

She felt like slapping the man, but that wouldn't do much good. "Who paid you?"

Oliver said nothing.

"Take him back to his offices and hold him there," she told her guard commander. "If he doesn't tell you the truth before I get there, he and I are going to have a very unpleasant conversation."

The woman bowed and led the man away.

Olivia turned to Mertz and Meyer. "I'm very sorry this happened. We need to account for every one of the missing people, and I'll do whatever it takes to return them as soon as possible."

Mertz turned to the senior prisoner. "Force Master Chief, do you have a list of the missing?"

"Not completely, sir. If there is a master prisoner list, we could go over it and get the last few we couldn't place."

Olivia found the file in her cranial implants. "I have it right here. Let's get started."

* * *

"THAT'S QUITE A CLAIM," William said. "One I'm not willing to credit without supporting evidence."

"And here I thought my word was good," Kelsey said with a chuckle. "I'm not certain how I would prove something like that. You don't happen to have any Old Empire computers lying around, do you? No? Then we're at something of an impasse."

He rubbed his chin. "Actually, we do have access to a significant Imperial asset from before the rebellion. Perhaps it will allow you to prove yourself."

She gestured toward the door. "I happen to be at your disposal. Oh, and until we sort this out, it might be best to leave Jared and Coordinator West out of this. I'd especially like to avoid mentioning any of this unless we're face to face."

"It shall be our little secret," he assured her. "I'll need to call and tell Olivia that we'll be gone for at least a few hours. I suggest you let Admiral Mertz know as well."

She retrieved her military com. It linked to a long-range unit carried by one of the marines back to the pinnace. From there she could reach Jared.

The call didn't connect. Strange, his unit was off. That wasn't right.

Kelsey watched Lord Hawthorne speaking to Coordinator West and waved for his attention before he disconnected. "Is she with Jared? His com is down."

He asked and nodded. "She's handing him her unit."

She held the civilian com up to her ear. "Jared?"

"Right here."

"I tried your com, but it was offline."

"That's not good. I'll get a spare from one of the marines. I'm fine, though there are some concerns developing."

She listened as he described the situation with the missing people. That concerned her, and she was certain who was behind it. "It has to be Deputy Coordinator King. She's still working some angle."

"I agree. I'm going to focus on this. Are you comfortable being on your own for a while?"

Kelsey looked at William. "I'll be fine."

"Be careful. I'll ping your com unit with my new information as soon as we hang up."

He was as good as his word. Her com lit up with a new code and a text message from Jared authenticating it. It said *All good here. I'm still not happy with what you did with Elise.*

She smiled. He was making sure she knew it was really him. No one down here knew about his love life.

Kelsey sent a message back. *You'll thank me later. At least that's what Talbot says.*

"Okay," she said aloud. "We're good. Where are we off to now?"

"A secret base, of course. Where else would a group of die-hard loyalists live?" He led her and the marines back out to his vehicle. The driver took off and headed even farther away from the city while he made a discreet call.

She settled back in her seat. "Aren't you worried about anyone tracking you to this secret hideout?"

"Of course," he said with a smile. "But they won't know a thing. You'll see."

They flew for almost an hour before landing at a small town. Specifically, at a diner.

He held the door open for her. "Try the malthar bites. They're fabulous."

Kelsey watched him order with more than a hint of confusion. She'd thought they were in a hurry.

A man and woman dressed eerily like them came out from behind the counter and headed out toward the car. Two men in credible marine armor followed them. Lord Hawthorne drew her into the kitchen with a twinkle in his eye.

"I doubt anyone is following us, but they'll continue on and return here when we call. No one will be the wiser."

"We'll just wait here in the kitchen?"

"Not quite." He tugged her arm and led her to the freezer.

"You're kidding, right?"

Without a word, he opened the door and stepped inside. She and the marines followed. Her breath puffed in the cold air, and she shivered a little.

He proceeded to the rear of the large space filled with meat and other perishables and opened the top of a large box marked "malthar bites." Instead of frozen meat, there was a ladder leading down into the darkness.

"Malthar bites," she said. "Clever."

"I rather thought so. From this point forward, the shielding will block any outside communications. Watch your step."

Kelsey had no trouble navigating the narrow ladder, but the armored marines did. Nevertheless, they all managed to reach the plascrete below without any problems.

She found herself standing in what looked to be a tunnel with an arched roof about three meters overhead. It led downward at a slight angle.

William gestured toward the ceiling as he led them deeper into the ground. "This access originally led to a small warehouse a block over, but that drew more attention than we liked. It was better if we went with a business that had lots of people arriving and departing at all hours, just in case someone was watching."

"Is this a pre-Fall construction?" She felt the wall, but its rough surface told her nothing. "Are you going to eat those? I'm starved."

He handed the food over without a word. The nuggets of fried meat were good. The savory flavor was unlike anything she'd tasted before.

"Mmm. These are excellent! What's a malthar?"

"A large, flightless bird with less intelligence than my shoe. They make good food, though. The restaurant we just left is famous for its secret spices.

"Yes, this tunnel is prerevolution. The town is only a few hundred years old. People loyal to our cause set up shop here and are still a significant proportion of the residents. That helps with concealing everything, too."

"Why don't you tell me more about this resistance movement?" she asked as they made their way onto what looked like a rail tube stop. A sleek car sat waiting for them.

He shook his head. "I'd rather wait until we arrive at our final destination. Sometimes seeing is worth hours of chatting."

The interior of the tube car was old but serviceable. She sat on a faded blue cushion next to him. The marines took the spots opposite them. The car doors closed, and it took off smoothly.

The trip lasted about ten minutes, and the two of them chitchatted after they finished eating. William refused to discuss anything of substance.

Once the car slid smoothly to a halt, he led the way out onto a stop almost identical to the one they'd left. Only this one had other people waiting for them—half a dozen men in full armor with flechette weapons and one with a plasma rifle. The man with the latter had it aimed conspicuously at her.

William shrugged apologetically. "I'm afraid that you're going to have to turn over your weapons now. As sad as it would be, any resistance will result in your deaths."

The marines had already raised their weapons and closed ranks with her. The tension was like a mist in the air. She knew that the next few minutes were going to be critical, and they really shouldn't throw away this opportunity.

"Lower your weapons," she ordered. "We're going to cooperate."

Kelsey started digging out her pistols. "You know that I'm more than capable of taking you on hand to hand, right?"

"I'd really rather you didn't," he said in a sorrowful tone. "No one needs to get hurt. After all, if you're telling the truth, I swear you'll get everything back, and we'll become the best of friends."

"And if, for whatever reason, I can't convince the computer?"

"I'd regret having to explain your untimely passing. I wouldn't have you killed, of course, but you'd be our guest here for a very long time."

She sighed. "Well, I suppose I'd better give this my best effort."

* * *

ABIGAIL WATCHED her office chronometer make its way slowly toward the end of a regular workday. She'd been listening to the news through her implants with more than a bit of anticipation.

She'd already planned how to quickly consolidate power and isolate the most troublesome of the council members opposing the conservative alliance. Before any of the fools knew what was happening, she'd have her boot on their throats.

Then she'd execute stage one of Operation Damocles. That would get everyone's attention. Perhaps at that point, Master Calder would read her into the rest of the program. She had her suspicions about what came next, but it was only guesswork.

A throwaway com unit she'd acquired chimed softly and she snatched it off her desk. A new file had arrived for her. She played it with shaky fingers.

The image showed that old stick Lord Hawthorne's antique air car flying along. Abigail could just make out the back of the blonde rebel's head. The woman started to turn toward the lens of the camera, but a bright flash of light shot onto the screen, and the car exploded.

That made her grin. One down. Now all she had to do was wait for Olivia and Admiral Mertz to die.

19

It took longer than Jared cared for to identify all of the missing personnel, but he now had their names and faces. Exactly one hundred people were unaccounted for, so he was relatively certain their count was accurate. The number was too precise to be accidental.

Of course, that meant that the people Meyer had ashore had to have already slipped back into camp. He hoped that hadn't screwed up some aspect of what the man was doing. They hadn't had more than a few moments alone, so he really didn't know what was happening on that front.

Honestly, an escape attempt right now might be the worst thing they could do.

Olivia turned away from the guard she was speaking with and stepped over to him. "Admiral, I'm satisfied that we have a good count of your missing people.

"Honestly, I know Abigail King is behind it, but I can't figure out her reasoning. Mister Oliver's testimony won't be enough to question her legally, but I *will* get to the bottom of this. I doubt she's seriously injured anyone."

"She'd better not have," he growled. "I'll tack her hide to the nearest wall if she's harmed any of my people."

"And I'll help you. It might be best if we go get the inevitable confrontation out of the way."

He nodded. "I'd appreciate a moment with the force master chief."

"Of course." She walked back over to her guards.

Jared lowered his voice. "Can you get weapons in the city?"

Commander Meyer's lips twitched. "Sir, I've discovered that you can get damned near anything as long as you have money. So, yes. We've already bought a number of flechette pistols and civilian stunners."

"I'll message you with the coordinates for an island we have under our control. If need be, get your people ashore and make your way to that general area. It's probably only a few hours in one of those grav lifts. Call them for pickup once you get close, and the marines will work something out."

"Aye, sir. Let me give you a couple of civilian com codes, just in case." He rattled off three strings of numbers that Jared committed to implant storage.

"Got them. Good luck. See you again soon."

He made his way over to Olivia just as she finished her conversation with her lead guard. "Is confronting Deputy Coordinator King so directly safe?"

Olivia laughed. "What's she going to do? Shoot us? No, she'll deny everything, but she won't attack us."

He wasn't so sure about that. "I'd recommend you have forces positioned in case you're wrong. Recent history has taught me that it's better to be ready when the sky falls."

She seemed to consider that and slowly nodded. "I suppose having a plan B doesn't hurt. Once we're inside the council building, there'll be too many people around. I suppose any attack would need to take place as we're arriving or leaving."

Her com chirped, and she glanced at it. That became a double take.

"What is it?" he asked.

"The news service is reporting that a vehicle like William's crashed outside the capital. They've found five bodies." She looked up. "That would be William, Miss Bandar, the two marines, and the driver."

Jared pulled out his com and called Kelsey. There was no response.

He cursed his decision to allow her to come to Harrison's World. If she'd died in what he guessed was an attack, he'd never forgive himself. Still, she'd pulled off miracles before, so he wasn't really going to believe she was gone until he saw her body for himself.

"Why would King attack her?" he asked through clenched teeth.

"To drive a wedge between us? Perhaps that's also why she took the prisoners. Or this could just be a terrible coincidence."

They stared at one another and shook their heads.

Olivia headed for the gate. "We need to confront her as soon as possible. Then we should go to the crash site."

"I couldn't agree more, but I have an idea."

* * *

KELSEY ALLOWED them to herd her and the marines through a massive vault door. Inside was a lift easily large enough to hold ten times their number. It had to be for cargo. As soon as the door closed, it dropped at a fairly good clip.

She raised an eyebrow. "So, now that I'm a captive audience, would you mind telling me where we are?"

If he was worried about being within her grasp, it didn't show. "Certainly. Though I suppose that makes me look like a clichéd vid villain. Should I explain my entire evil plan so that you can make good your escape and take me down?"

Kelsey shook her head. "You're incorrigible."

"Thank you. Well, this is a prerevolution facility that we managed to hide from the AIs. It wasn't known to the public, so that was easier than it sounds."

"A planetary defense center would be the obvious choice," she said, "but I'll venture a guess that this is the Grant Research Facility."

His eyes widened and his jaw literally dropped a bit. "My, my. You *are* full of surprises. I'd have sworn no one knew about this place before the revolution, much less after. How the devil did you know?"

"You'd be surprised what an ambassador plenipotentiary and daughter of the emperor is allowed to know."

"For all our sakes, I fervently hope you're telling the truth."

The lift settled to a halt, and the doors opened. A wide entry area with prominent weapons emplacements covering every angle greeted them. Depending on how far below ground they were, it would be difficult indeed to dig these people out.

A large set of armored doors slid open across from them, and several men and women walked out, eyeing her curiously. One of the men wore a Fleet uniform with captain's tabs. He seemed to be in charge.

William bowed slightly to him. "Kelsey, this is Fleet Captain Aaron Black. Aaron, this is Kelsey Bandar. As to what she does…well, that's a bit more complicated. Let's leave it at saying she's Admiral Mertz's special operations officer. Be careful with any handshake. She's a Marine Raider with full augmentation."

If that disturbed the short black man, he didn't allow it to show. And by short, Kelsey really meant it. His eyes were level with hers.

He extended his hand. "I'd be pleased to call you by your appropriate rank, Miss Bandar. At this juncture, is there really much point in keeping it to yourself?" His voice was a pleasant alto, and his smiled revealed shining white teeth.

She shook his hand slowly. "I've already told Lord Hawthorne, so if he doesn't want to share, who am I to ruin his surprise?"

The man shook his head. "Lord Hawthorne thinks he has a sense of humor. We've tried to correct his misapprehension. But he still feels compelled to try. Welcome to the Grant Research Facility. Still under the original management. It's my privilege and honor to run it for the resistance.

"Before you feel compelled to attempt a daring escape, allow me to warn you that even a Marine Raider won't be getting out unless we say so. I don't know everything about your implants and enhancements, but I've looked over Lord Hawthorne's scanner readings, and you're a marvel. It still won't grant you a miracle."

Kelsey laughed. "You'd be shocked at the things I've survived in the last six months, Captain. I believe we found some products from this facility on *Invincible*. Those flip-point jammers really saved the day. Unfortunately, we broke one. The other two are covering the entrances to this system as we speak."

The man raised his eyebrow. "Indeed? Well, that's gratifying to know. It took us a very long time to take them from theory to hardware. We had no way to test them, either. But where are my manners? Allow me to introduce my staff and lead scientists."

Kelsey made note of each name and face as Captain Black introduced them. Part of her mind was still working on how she might escape. Perhaps blowing a hole in the roof of the elevator?

That probably wouldn't work.

She almost jumped at the voice in her head. Again. *You really need to stop doing that.*

Why?

Because it surprises me. I'm not used to having another person in my skull.

It's not like there's a real person monitoring everything around you.

No, she thought. Not exactly, anyway.

So, what did you see that I missed?

As the elevator descended, I detected several levels where there were emissions consistent with weapons platforms. Perhaps they're targeting intrusion from above, but I wouldn't bet your life on it.

Hmm. That was a point to consider.

Are you monitoring everything I do all the time? I didn't see those things. I didn't even have a scanner out.

Your implant hardware has adequate passive scanners, if you know how to access them, and of course I'm watching. It's not as though I need to sleep. I'm adding your sensory recordings to the ones my creator made. Also, I'm pleased to say that I've completed the indexing of his files. They should be significantly more useful now.

Thanks. If I survive the next half hour, I'll take a look.

The internal exchange had only taken a moment. She had to admit, even though the program in her implants was a little creepy, it had its uses.

"So," she said to William, "what's next? How can I prove myself to you?"

"Well, this facility has a computer built and installed by the most paranoid security freaks the Empire could find before the revolution. If you have the credentials you claim, surely you can get it to confirm them."

He raised a hand to forestall her instinctive reaction. "I don't expect you to gain access to the systems. That's not really within the realm of possibility. All I want is to see the computer verify you're telling the truth."

She nodded. "Let's get this over with so you can stop threatening me."

The interior of the facility felt like the inside of a large orbital. They had to have put heavy shielding around everything, because the power emanations alone would've been detectable from the surface. If she'd known how to use the passive scanners that Ned had mentioned, she had no doubt she'd have detected any number of strange readings as they led her to an area deep under the entrance level.

The lift claimed it serviced levels 50 to 75, as well as the entrance. There was no telling how many levels there were in total. It might be as large as *Invincible*. Or even bigger.

On level 70, they brought her to what was obviously a computer center. The large, thick hatch was familiar to her. Of course, they didn't actually take her inside. They led her to a conference room beside it.

It bore a striking resemblance to the one in the planetary defense headquarters on Erorsi. If that was anything to judge by, there must've been a lot of people down here at some point. Perhaps there still were.

William took the seat at the head of the table with an ease that made clear he was Captain Black's superior. He gestured for her to take a seat beside him. "Sit. Perhaps you'd care for some tea?"

Kelsey sat. "No. Let's get this over with."

"Very well. Computer, this is William Hawthorne. I would like you to create a virtual instance of yourself and have it perform some tasks for me."

"Virtual workspace ready," a standard Old Empire computer voice said from the overhead speakers. "This unit is booted and standing by for your instructions."

"Excellent. The person seated next to me will be communicating with you. I wish for you to verify the veracity of her claims and authenticate them as best you can."

"This unit is ready. Implant access to the virtual workspace is granted. State your name through the implant channel."

Kelsey found the access channel it was offering and sent a communication request. Once it accepted, she started speaking with it through her implants.

Computer, I am Princess Kelsey Bandar. I give you permission to access my implants for the sole purpose of verifying the truth of what I'm saying.

Access acquired, Princess Kelsey Bandar. Proceed.

My title is ambassador plenipotentiary of the Terran Empire. My father is the emperor of the Terran Empire, and I am second in line to the Throne. Here are my Imperial access codes.

She sent the computer her authorization codes. She knew from asking Carl Owlet that they had virtually unbreakable encryption and identified her as what she claimed. Even if someone else took the codes from her, without her hardware, they'd be invalid. He informed her smugly that they were better identification than her DNA.

Access codes received and confirmed, Ambassador Plenipotentiary Kelsey Bandar. How may this unit serve you, Highness?

I understand you are only a copy of the main computer. Is that correct?

Affirmative.

So any instructions I give you will not hold true for the actual computer?

Correct.

Will the main computer be aware of what transpires in this virtual workspace?

The main computer is monitoring the basic communication and is aware of this conversation and this unit's conclusions. No commands or files are being transmitted, however.

Thank you. Can you tell me what level of authority someone with my credentials has on your system?

Complete authority, Highness. This facility operates under the authority of the Imperial Throne. As an ambassador plenipotentiary and heir secundus, you have complete authority over this unit and this facility.

Thank you.

Kelsey looked back to William. "Done."

He smiled a little. "Computer, is Kelsey Bandar speaking the truth? Are her credentials valid?"

"Affirmative. Her Highness Princess Kelsey Bandar, heir secundus and ambassador plenipotentiary to the Terran Empire, is who she claims to be."

His eyebrows went up almost to his hairline. "That's a surprise, but a pleasant one. Computer, dismiss the virtual workspace."

Kelsey smiled. "Now that that's done, let me give you a less pleasant surprise."

She pinged the computer and requested access. It immediately granted it to her.

Computer, do I have complete access and control of your systems?

Affirmative, Highness.

Excellent. Lock out all other users from the computer systems and put this base on lockdown. No one in, no one out. Be certain that nothing is detectable outside the facility and that no research projects are impacted.

Grant users in the middle of anything enough access to complete what they're doing. Accept no commands from those users other than ones related to the experiments in progress.

Acknowledged, Highness.

The overhead speakers began blaring something similar to general quarters on a Fleet vessel, startling everyone in the room.

Captain Black surged to his feet. "What the hell did you do? Computer, what's happening?"

"Access denied, Captain Black."

Kelsey sat back in her chair and smiled. "Now the shoe is on the other foot. I have complete and utter control of your facility." She held up a hand to stop the Fleet officer from exploding. "I haven't done anything to reveal it to anyone outside this facility. I'm not your enemy."

"Well, you're sure acting like one," he snarled.

She looked at William. "Are you ready to sit down and talk like adults? Are we done with the threats? Do you accept that I'm who I say I am?"

The Rebel Empire noble rose to his feet and bowed as deeply as possible. "Of course I do, Highness. I'm yours to command."

* * *

TIME DRAGGED, but eventually Abigail's spies informed her that Olivia's car was approaching the council building. Unlike the first kill, she could watch this one in real time. If, of course, the assassins struck as Olivia was arriving.

Honestly, she hoped they did. She really wasn't looking forward to Olivia confronting her over those missing prisoners or Lord Hawthorne's death.

How would they do it? Another anonymous crash? That might look suspicious. Of course, the people prone to seeing things that way would do so anyhow.

And they'd be right, after all.

The car was thirty seconds from touchdown when it happened. A dark shape rose from the river and raced toward the council building.

Olivia's car turned and sped away, a good indicator that she'd been suspicious. That spoke well to her character.

The new vehicle, larger than a regular grav car by a fair margin, closed the distance in record time. Abigail finally recognized it when a small missile blew Olivia's car out of the air. It was an Imperial marine pinnace, just like the one that had brought the now deceased Admiral Mertz to Harrison's World.

Where had Master Calder found one? Had he had it all this time?

The pinnace peeled away, going right over the bright lights of the city. The building's vid feed would have recorded it clearly.

Realization hit her. This was the perfect frame. No one other than the visitors had vessels capable of reaching space. With that provocation, it would be perfectly clear who'd attacked whom. Brilliant!

Abigail got on the com to her assistant, who she'd insisted wait for Olivia's meeting to be over before leaving.

"Get me the military liaison. A Fleet pinnace just killed Coordinator West. I want atmospheric fighters scrambled to take it out. To take them all out. I want Fleet gone from Harrison's World before dawn. Do you understand me? Get him on the line now!"

20

Olivia watched the vid feed with a sick stomach. She'd sent those people to their deaths. Her guards had been going to bring Abigail to join her at the crash site where William went down. People who'd been with her for years. Now they were all dead.

"I need to contact the security forces and have Abigail picked up," she said dully.

"Actually, are you sure that's the best idea?" Mertz asked. "I've had some unfortunate experience recently with coups. King has probably been planning this for a while. If you talk to the wrong person, she'll know you're alive and try again. At this point, they think you're dead. You'll want to keep them thinking that until you take them down."

She looked over at him in the other seat of the car she'd borrowed for the trip. "I can't just let her get away with this! She's going to be consolidating power right now."

"It's your call. I suggest if you're going to let them know you're alive, go big. Make some kind of general broadcast. Notify your ruling council all at once. While you're doing that, I need to call my people and get them moving. It won't be long before she takes a swing at us."

Olivia shook her head. "You really don't understand how this works. She's already started purging the government of people loyal to me. I need to make my calls right now and pray it isn't too late."

She pulled out her com and made a call to her office. From there, she could get the word out quickly. Unfortunately, it wouldn't connect.

She tried the backup number she'd had a very bright resistance tech install, and she was into the automated system at her office.

"This is Coordinator West. Authenticate me. Sigma Alpha three five seven."

"Identity verified, Coordinator," the computer said. "How may this unit assist you?"

"Code red. Execute emergency plan Omega."

"Executing. Primary connectivity unavailable. Switching to secondary. Secondary unavailable. Switching to tertiary. Connected. Transmitting. Transmissions complete. Wiping system. Goodbye."

The line went dead, but that was all according to plan. Emergency messages had gone out to every council member not associated with the conservative alliance. It might be too late for some of them, but many would get the word in time and go to ground. She hoped. It had also notified contacts within the resistance. Then the computer had purged itself.

Unless everything had gone to hell and Abigail had more reach than Olivia had ever suspected. If so, she'd hunt Olivia down, erase all the gains of the last decade, and kill a lot of good people.

She returned her attention to Mertz. He was just wrapping up his own emergency call.

"They tried to attack the pinnace at Lord Hawthorne's estate, but it was on alert. It's on its way back to the island we have under our control. It can't make it to pick me up, but that's fine. I'm not going anywhere until I know what really happened to Kelsey."

She felt herself frowning. "But William's car is destroyed. They found their bodies in the wreckage. I'm sorry, but she's gone. So is my oldest friend."

Just the thought sent her spirits sagging. She forced the savage sorrow aside. She didn't have time to grieve.

"You don't know Kelsey like I do," Mertz said. "She's surprisingly hard to kill. How far away from the crash site are we? Where can I get some different clothes? I stand out like a sore thumb in this uniform."

"There's a town close by. I know some people there. They can have clothes ready by the time we arrive."

Olivia called ahead to the diner and gave the correct code phrase to identify herself. "I need some casual men's clothes. We'll be there in ten minutes." She made an estimate of his sizes and included that before she disconnected.

"I should make the call now to get the prisoners released," she said. "I don't want them caught up in the middle of this."

"Hold off on that. Right now, King has bigger fish to fry. I ordered them to make their way out after dark."

"Excuse me?"

He smiled. "I spoke to them briefly before we left. They've already discovered a way out. In fact, I'm somewhat surprised that you didn't recognize that I was speaking with Meyer at the port. He had to rush back into the camp and shave to have any hope you wouldn't recognize him."

Olivia felt her eyes widen. She put the images of the man at the port and Force Master Chief Meyer up side by side. Definitely the same person.

"I'll be damned. I never would've imagined someone from the lower orders could be so clever."

"You shouldn't let your prejudices get in your way. People can be smart no matter what their background. When we have time, I think I need to tell you a story."

"Would this be about how you aren't really who you say you are? I figured that out already. I knew for sure the moment that you said you'd been to Terra and I realized that you were actually on *Invincible*."

It was his turn to be shocked. "Yes, we really do need to talk. First, though, we need to find Kelsey, and hopefully Lord Hawthorne."

* * *

SEAN PUT his com unit away. Mertz had wanted him to wait until dark to get things rolling, but he really didn't know how much they'd accomplished. It would be better to start everyone moving now. Then he'd have enough people in the port after dark to commandeer several grav lifts and get the exodus done in one go.

And, contrary to what Mertz probably wanted, Sean would be taking a team to find the missing prisoners. He knew where to find the bastard that had run the camp. The trick was going to be getting in to snatch him, but Sean had a few ideas.

First, he needed to get the plan in motion.

He found Ross and Newland. "There's been some kind of attack on the coordinator, and Admiral Mertz believes it's time for us to decamp. I want to appropriate four grav lifts."

Newland grunted. "I figured we needed to do that before too long. That's going to screw with their delivery schedule, and that'll draw attention pretty damned fast. Once the foreman for that section of the dock gets wind of the delay, it won't take him long to figure out something is squirrelly. We'll need a distraction that won't draw the camp guards' attention."

Ross smiled. "A fire would be too flashy, as would an explosion. What about a grav failure on a loaded lift that's just departed? The damned thing would sink and spread containers all around the harbor."

Sean considered it for a moment. "That's as good as anything I can think of. It would get attention but not the kind that would get prison guards all excited. We'd need to have our people staged and ready to go in the buildings outside the fence. How long to get them out there?"

"An hour should be enough," Ross said. "We'll get everyone moving and let the last few people get dinner ready. If we hit the docks closest to the camp, we can get everyone to the loading area without too much risk. We'll just have to stun anyone in the warehouse."

Newland shook his head. "Too open. They'd be right on the lift deck for the guards to see."

"Well, then," Sean said. "We'll just have to focus the guards' attention at the critical moment. Leave that to my team and me. Go get everyone moving. This could go bad any minute."

Sean left them to it and rounded up his shore team. They met in one of the barracks. In the shower, of course, though they kept their clothes on.

"Gentlemen," he said, "the time has come for us to decamp. Timing is critical, and while we don't want to draw the guards' attention too quickly, we'll need to provide a few minutes of entertainment to get them all looking away from the port. I don't suppose anyone brought explosives back from the shore?"

They shook their heads. One man, the scrounger, spoke up. "Explosives are harder to get than crappy weapons, sir. We have some civilian stunners and flechette pistols. Maybe we can cause them some grief with those."

"I'm not sure I'd want to get them shooting at us, Corporal. All in all, I'd prefer to escape without them knowing we're gone for a bit."

"What about the air patrols?" one of the others asked. "If we stun the two men in one of the vehicles, they'll figure it was a mechanical failure and get into search-and-rescue mode."

Hmm. SAR might be just what they needed. "They might see the beams, and those stunners are short-ranged weapons. Probably not that accurate, either."

The man nodded. "We can tune out the color. If we focus the beams as tight as possible, we might be able to tag someone flying low and slow. It would have to be a two-man team to get the lookout, too."

"Are any of the guards patrolling that low?"

"Occasionally. Some of them like to show off."

It wasn't the best of plans, but he supposed they could light one of them up with flechettes if they had to. "Okay. We'll set up on the far side of the camp. I'd prefer the thing to crash on the other side of the fence, but we don't have a lot of choice. As long as everyone else gets away clean, I can deal with that. Which two men are staying with me?"

* * *

JARED LOOKED over the town as their air car came in for a soft landing. It wouldn't have been out of place in Avalon's agricultural districts. The driver stayed in the car while Olivia led Jared inside. He'd taken off his jacket to reduce the number of people that might recognize his uniform.

Something smelled good, reminding him that he hadn't eaten in a while.

Despite what he'd told Olivia, he felt hollow inside. The crash could've killed his sister. He was putting on a good face, but it could all be true. He prayed it wasn't. That would be a disaster, personally and professionally.

Olivia went to the counter and put in an order for food. The man behind it leaned over and said something to her. She stiffened and then sagged a little.

Jared saw something very much like joy in her face as she came over to him. "They got out of the car here. They're okay."

He closed his eyes for a moment. "Thank God. If they're here, who was in the car?"

"Some poor people who were providing cover for them. Stunt doubles, as it were. It doesn't look as though you'll need that change of clothes just yet. We won't be under observation as we make our way to them. Come on."

To say that he was surprised when she handed him a bag of food and led him into the freezer was an understatement. The secret tunnel under the diner was even more of a shock.

"What the hell is down here?" he asked.

"That's going to take a while, and I think that it would be best to get together with William and Miss Bandar for that explanation."

They boarded the grav train and ate as it bore them into the darkness. The food was good, but he couldn't remember what it tasted like as his mind swirled. What was this place? One of the planetary defense centers? Something else?

It only took ten minutes for them to make their way to another station and disembark. The large armored door failed to open when they arrived.

Olivia tried it again and frowned. "That's odd. It should've opened right up, and I'm not getting ahold of anyone inside."

* * *

KELSEY SMILED at Captain Black and William. "I'm glad that we were able to settle that so easily. Computer, restore access to everyone affected by my earlier instructions."

"Done. Coordinator West and an unknown visitor are at the station and requesting admittance. They signaled during lockdown."

"I hope that's Jared with her. That would make explanations much simpler."

William headed for the door. "I'll go get them and be right back, Highness."

She scowled at him. "That's going to get old fast. I thought I told you to call me Kelsey."

"So you did, but that was before you told me who you *really* were. One simply doesn't chat up their social superiors in a public setting. Perhaps in private. We'll see."

He left, and she shook her head. "What about you, Captain Black? Can I get you to call me by my given name?"

The dark-skinned man smiled a little. "Is that an order? I'm still not even certain I'm in your chain of command."

"I think we can work that out," she said as she gestured for him to sit beside her. "I'm curious. How did a senior Fleet officer become a member of the resistance?"

Black sat and regarded her for a moment. "They caught me young. My father is a member. After I joined Fleet and passed the security screening, they felt out my allegiances. Once they were certain I was fully committed, they used some hardware here to overwrite the code in my implants to allow me to be their spy. I was down here when the axe fell, so we faked my death for official purposes."

"Wow," she said. "That sounds exciting. I'm sure our scientists will want to compare notes to see if your code matches what we're using. But that will come in due time.

"As for whether you're in the same Fleet as my Empire, I think being a member of the resistance counts for a lot. With my brother being a Fleet admiral, I think I'm going to go with yes. Unless you have some reservation, of course."

He inclined his head. "My allegiance is to the Empire, but Lord

Hawthorne and Coordinator West are going to have to tell me if this counts. If they get behind you, I will, too."

The door slid open, and William escorted Jared and Olivia West in. Her brother rushed to her side and pulled her into a hug. "I thought we'd lost you."

She gave him a confused look. "I told you we were going to be incommunicado for a bit."

William looked grim. "And things have happened while we were. Abigail King shot down my car. She killed everyone. She tried to kill your brother and Coordinator West, too. It seems that we have a coup in progress."

21

S ean watched as the people under his command slipped out of the prison camp one small group at a time. The remaining personnel kept moving around the open areas enough to simulate the correct number of prisoners for the guards.

The marine armorer used the time they had left to modify the stunners. With the color inducer bypassed and the range boosted to the maximum, this might just work.

He asked the question that had been bothering him while the man worked. "How do you know what to do? I didn't think we had any of these weapons."

The man grinned. "I knew some people on *Athena*. They slipped me the tech manuals and a few pistols to study. One neural disruptor and one flechette pistol, as well as a maintenance kit. I didn't tell the LT, but she might have guessed. I have no idea if she reported it up the chain. It's too late to ask her now."

That was the damned truth. He sighed. When he'd read Mertz's report on how many people they'd lost fighting against the Pale Ones, he'd been certain the man was a colossal screw-up that had gotten most of his people killed for no reason.

Now that he'd seen how many of his crewmates they'd lost, he knew the truth. Mertz had pulled off a miracle. Breckenridge's task force had started with a heavy cruiser, two light cruisers, and two destroyers. They'd lost all three cruisers and most of the people on them.

In hindsight, it was obvious who the incompetents were: Wallace

Breckenridge and Sean Meyer. It was too late for his former captain to learn from his mistakes, even if he could, but Sean was determined to make up for his own failures.

"You did exactly right, Corporal," he said. "Your foresight might save thousands of people. You can count on me recommending you for a damned medal if we make it off this planet alive."

The man started putting the stunner back together again. "If it's all the same, sir, I'd rather you didn't. I didn't exactly do it for the right reasons. I was—"

"It doesn't matter," Sean said, guessing what the man's original intent had been. "I've learned some hard lessons over these last few weeks. What counts is that you did the right thing."

He looked out at the sun. "It's about time for us to make our move. What are the possible repercussions of your modifications?"

The man finished putting the weapon back together. "The pistols might burn out, but they should get one shot, minimum. I was real careful, so hopefully they'll still be accurate. These things have no recoil, sir, so aim right where you want to hit. No leading and no dropping of the shot with range."

Sean picked one of the pistols up. "How will we know when they're close enough?"

"If they're close to the fence, these should reach them."

"Good enough. Come on."

They went outside and joined the people moving around the camp. Command Master Chief Ross fell in beside them smoothly. "Things are on schedule, and I have some good news."

Sean smiled. "I love good news. Tell me more."

"We've seen one of the air patrols that has a history of making close passes. We've moved as many people out as we dare. Our people are standing by to make their move on the cargo lifts as soon as I give the signal."

"Well, then, let's not keep them waiting." Sean led the way to the building where they'd decided they had the best chance of hitting the target. With the stunners modified the way they were, they had to make direct hits to have any effect at all. Without the color traces, they'd have no idea where their shots were really going if they missed.

"How many people are still in camp?" he asked Ross.

"About a hundred. They'll scatter as soon as the air car comes down and make their way clear. We'll be the last ones out."

The senior noncom eyed the stunners when the corporal laid them out. "How good is your aim, sir? You want me to take the second shot?"

Sean settled in next to the window and picked up one of the

stunners. "I think I can handle it, Command Master Chief. Why don't you go outside and stand next to the window here. You can give us a warning and countdown to shoot."

"Aye, sir. Shoot on zero."

They only had a few minutes to wait before Ross spoke. "Here they come. Left to right, moving about thirty kilometers an hour. Two guards, the one on the left at the controls."

"You have the one on the right, Corporal," Sean said.

"Aye, sir."

"Stand by to fire," Ross said. "Three…two…"

The air car flew into view, moving slowly enough for Sean to line his sights up on the driver. When Ross said "zero," Sean pulled the trigger. Even without a beam, he knew right away that he'd hit. The driver slumped.

The corporal missed, though. The passenger lunged for the controls.

Sean snapped off a shot as the corporal fired again. One of them hit the man, because the air car veered off course and slammed into a building outside the fence. The impact was impressive, even without any explosions. If that didn't get their attention, nothing would.

"Time to go," he said, tucking the pistol into his tunic.

The two of them stepped outside and joined Ross on a casual walk toward the other side of the camp. A pair of air cars flew overhead, racing toward the crash site. The guards on the ground were also looking in the right direction. Sean figured that the communications channels were alive with chatter right now.

The few remaining Fleet personnel in evidence quickly disappeared in the same direction they were heading. Three minutes later, they were under the fence and into the port. The only question now was how long it would take for one of the guards to notice the camp was deserted.

If anyone in the port had noticed, Sean couldn't tell. Everyone was still loading cargo. Well, everyone except for the people at this dock. His people had taken the loading crew prisoner and were efficiently boarding four lifts in small groups. It looked as though they already had more than half the camp population on board.

As soon as everyone had boarded, Sean shook Ross's hand. "You've got the coordinates to the island. Get them there safely, Command Master Chief. I'll find our people and make my way to join you as quickly as I can. Good luck. Oh, and here's Admiral Mertz's Fleet com. You'll need it to get hold of the marines on the island."

The older man pocketed the com. "We'll be fine, sir. You're the ones that need the luck. Be careful, Commander."

"Bet your ass. Get going. It won't take them long to find the people we have locked up, and once they do, all hell is going to break loose."

Ross saluted him and made his way out to a lift. They'd kept the drivers on board but had them under close guard. A few of his men had previously finagled their way into the control rooms and knew something of how the process worked. They'd keep the drivers from doing anything to give them away. With the number of lifts working this area of the coast, it was almost certain that no one would notice anything amiss, even after the alarm went out.

Sean motioned to the dozen men he'd selected to join him. They'd all changed into coveralls and would be taking a small grav car over to the city. The warehouse supervisor's car. They'd sell it to a dealer in stolen vehicles that his streetwise marine had buddied up with. It might have a hidden tracer in it, or he'd have kept it. It ran better than the ones they'd secured for their own use. Pity.

At least that had been the plan.

That changed as they were walking toward their ride. A large man in the same color coveralls as their own stormed up to them from the loading area. "Where are my lifts? What the hell is my cargo doing sitting out in the open?" He frowned. "Who the hell are you? You're not part of my dock crew."

So much for simple.

* * *

JARED EXPLAINED the outside events to Kelsey, Lord Hawthorne, and the man in the Fleet uniform quickly and succinctly. "So, as much as I wish I had time for the long version of what you've been up to and what this place is, we need to get back up to orbit as quickly as possible."

Olivia gestured toward the table. "We have to take the time to sit and work our way through this. Even the coup needs to wait. I've made calls and you've taken steps to get your people to safety. Well enough, but we need to come to an agreement. If we don't do it while we're all sitting in the same room, we might not get it done at all."

She waited for them all to take a seat. "Admiral Mertz, as I explained earlier, we've known you weren't what you claimed since I visited your ship in orbit. Or should I say *our* ship. The three of us are the leaders of what you might call the Terran resistance on Harrison's World.

"We found *Invincible* in its orbit and set out to rebuild her with the intention of destroying the AI in this system. We planned to restore as many of the wrecked ships to service as possible and to take back the Empire from the AIs. Our families never gave up."

She smiled at Jared. "Your turn."

Jared sent a private message to Kelsey through his implants. *What do they know?*

His sister smiled. *They know who I am and where we're from, in general terms. They know why we're here. She's the only one in the dark.*

"Well, then," Jared said smoothly. "In actuality, Kelsey has already let the cat out of the bag. We're from a splinter of the Old Empire that never fell. Emperor Marcus sent his son to us, and Kelsey is the daughter of Emperor Karl Bandar. She's second in line to the Imperial Throne and an ambassador plenipotentiary of the Terran Empire."

To say Olivia looked shocked was an understatement. "What!?"

Lord Hawthorne nodded and smiled wryly. "It's true. The computer verified her honesty. Not only did it confirm her story, but it also ceded control of this facility to her. She locked us out to prove her point. I can't think of a more convincing endorsement."

"She graciously let us back in, but I'd rather she didn't do that again," Captain Black said in an unhappy tone. "We have a lot of experiments in progress, and I'd rather not risk any unfortunate accidents."

Kelsey grinned. "No worries. I'll keep myself in line." She focused her attention on Olivia. "As you said, we're short on time. I realize how much work you put into *Invincible*, but we bled for her. I think Imperial salvage laws apply. For what it's worth, we did get your flip-point jammers in place."

Olivia waved her comment away. "That doesn't matter now. You've achieved almost everything we'd hoped. We need to join forces and stop this coup before it undoes all the hard work so many people put into getting the conservatives out of power. They were always the lackeys of the AIs. If they regain control, we might never get them out again."

"Olivia is right," Lord Hawthorne said gravely. "The resistance is small compared to the conservative alliance. If we lose control, we may never recover. We need to come to an agreement.

"Admiral Mertz, I'm the leader of the resistance on Harrison's World, and I recognize Princess Kelsey as the direct representative of the emperor. I'm begging you to help us retain control of Harrison's World in the name of the Empire.

"Think of what we could do together. This world hasn't lost any of the technological prowess of the Empire at its height. In fact, with this research facility, we're even more advanced in some areas. The AIs frown on a number of fields. Research in them has virtually ceased."

Jared gestured toward his sister. "You're talking to the wrong person. Princess Kelsey makes those kinds of decisions. If she thinks that is the right course of action, that's good enough for me. Personally, I think it is."

Lord Hawthorne turned to Kelsey. "Highness? What do I need to promise? Shall I strip naked, paint myself pink, and dance in the capital square?"

"I'm sure we'd all rather you didn't. Jared, I've already done a number of searches in the computer here. I believe their story and I like their plan."

"Then we're in agreement," he said. "What should we do?"

Kelsey gestured toward Lord Hawthorne. "That depends on how committed the resistance is. You recognize who I am and what I represent. I'm willing to consider you loyal citizens of the Terran Empire as we know it today. I'll even concede that you are in control of what happens on this world, just as they did in the Old Empire, but I decide what happens in the system until we have a stable situation here."

The three people from Harrison's World looked at one another and rose to their feet, then sank to one knee. Lord Hawthorne spoke. "On behalf of all of us, we recognize the authority of the Imperial Throne and once more swear our allegiance to it."

Kelsey scowled. "You don't need to kneel to me. Please get up."

They rose, but Olivia shook her head. "You might not like it, but that's really only an abbreviated version of how Imperial nobles swore public allegiance to the emperor in the old days. I've seen recordings of Marcus's coronation. It was a circus, and I say that as someone who grew up in a society that positively dotes on pomp and useless frivolity."

"Still," Kelsey said. "My father is the emperor and my brother the heir. You can try that on them, if you like. I'd rather have friends and allies than courtiers. We can work out the details of what this all means once we have the situation on the ground under control. Jared, we need to get the prisoners released first."

He smiled. "Already done, I suspect. Commander Meyer is executing an escape plan as we speak. He already had a way out of the camp, so I thought that the most prudent way to proceed. By now, they should all be on their way to the island." He let the smile fade. "Except for a hundred people. Abigail King took them somewhere."

"We have to assume she knows everything they know," Olivia said. "Which means she knows who and what you are. In more detail than I do, but we don't have time for the full story. It might be best if you both make your way to the island and back to orbit. Once you're gone, she can't use you as a weapon. I'll find your people. I swear it."

"Jared can go," Kelsey said. "They need him in command up there. I'm staying here until we get everyone back."

"That's not the safest course of action," Jared said. "You need to come with me. If they catch you, they'll use you as a bargaining chip. If we're both clear, we can work from orbit to help the resistance."

His sister shook her head. "If they catch me, they'll seriously regret it. I'll want a team of marines and my armor, if that can be managed."

"Perhaps I can offer a few compromise solutions," Captain Black said. "We have some powered armor here. No Marine Raider armor, of course, but very advanced. I think you'll be pleased with one as a temporary replacement."

"I'd rather not make any more trips than we need to," Jared added. "Just because they don't have ships capable of reaching orbit doesn't mean they can't shoot small craft down. The weapons on the island cost us some good people, and I don't want to risk more unless we have to."

Olivia nodded grimly. "That's wise. We have a network of weapons capable of taking out small craft. We also have atmospheric fighters that are probably even more powerful in engaging them. I can probably arrange for a window where the weapons are offline and the fighters are…unresponsive. That would be enough to allow you to get away. I can't say the same about anyone coming down from orbit."

The coordinator turned to the Fleet officer in charge of the facility. "Captain Black, is there a way we can get Admiral Mertz to the island without him being intercepted?"

The officer smiled. "I think we might have something that will do the trick."

"Good. Work with him and make that happen. I'll take Lord Hawthorne and Princess Kelsey to see if we can stop this coup and find her people."

"That sounds like a plan." The dark-skinned man's expression became cold. "Do me a favor. Kick that woman's ass. She killed some very good people this afternoon."

Olivia smiled like a shark. "If by kicking her ass you mean kill her, I'll take care of that in the most expeditious manner possible."

Jared rose to his feet and pulled Kelsey into a hug. "Be careful. We need you back in one piece."

She squeezed him back hard. "Don't worry about me. You stay safe. I imagine King has plans to attack you in orbit. Damned if I know how, but she can't be doing all this crazy stuff without some bigger plan."

"Let her try," he said. "I'll slap her down so fast her head spins."

22

Abigail glared at the man in front of her desk. She could see the slight tremble in his hands. Good.

"What do you *mean* the coordinator's computers aren't recoverable?" she asked in a low, deadly tone.

That made him shake a little harder. "They've been wiped clean, Deputy Coordinator. I'm not certain how. We segregated them as you instructed. Perhaps they had some code that triggered a hidden program. Now that it's done, we have no way of knowing."

"What about backups? I need to know what she was doing. Not only for the continuation of the government but to know who she colluded with." Abigail narrowed her eyes. "Perhaps a computer specialist working for me?"

The man was quivering now, obviously terrified. "The backups were wiped, too. I swear it's nothing my people did. We're loyal."

"You mean you're useless. If I find out you had anything to do with this, you'll live a long time, regretting your choices every minute. Get out!"

The man fled.

She sat behind her desk, sulking. He was innocent. Probably. Olivia had been a wily one. She had to have understood that Abigail would come for her someday. The only mystery here was figuring out which of her staff had done the deed.

This takeover would've been easier if she'd had access to the other woman's files, but she'd make it work without them. It wasn't as if she didn't know who her enemies were. They'd stymied her and the conservative alliance in the council often enough.

She'd already sent teams after the leaders and prominent voices of the opposition, supposedly to take them into protective custody. And, really, it was. For her. If they had a chance to start plotting, they'd vanish like roaches when the lights came on.

Roaches. Odd how that was the one Terran species that seemed to have made it to every world colonized by mankind and more than a few they'd given up as too harsh for habitation.

No doubt, some of her enemies would escape. Then she'd have the merry task of rooting them and their sedition out before they made too much of a bother. That could be a pleasure, she supposed. Those people would be the most satisfying to see tortured.

The com on her desk buzzed.

"Yes?"

"I have Mister Oliver holding for you. He says his call is urgent."

She frowned. "Who?"

"The man in charge of the Fleet prison camp, Deputy Coordinator. The one Coordinator West had arrested. We had him freed as part of the initial housecleaning."

Now she remembered the man. A prole but a hater of all things Fleet. Appointing him to guard the prisoners had been a stroke of genius on her part. He'd create an incident if she ordered him to, and he'd had no problem with her taking some of the prisoners to question.

"Put him through."

The vid screen on her desk came to life. The man looked even dirtier than she'd remembered.

"Deputy Coordinator, the prisoners are gone."

She stared at him for a moment. "What?"

"They escaped after Coordinator King had me arrested. I have no idea how, but they killed two of my men, and they're gone. All of them."

She surged to her feet. "You imbecile! How could you lose thousands of unarmed prisoners?" Abigail throttled her temper. "Never mind how. Find them. They can't have gotten far. No excuses!"

She cut the connection and rubbed the bridge of her nose. Why was she surrounded by idiots and incompetents? How hard could this be? These people had had no contact with Harrison's World before the Lord delivered them. They didn't even know where to go to meet their compatriots. They'd stand out wherever they went.

As soon as the man recaptured them, she'd have him executed. That's what the passel of idiots surrounding her needed: a good example of why they'd best not fail her.

She opened a channel to her assistant. "Get the Defense Force commander on the com."

"Yes, Deputy Coordinator."

Abigail hoped they'd be able to seat a reformed council tomorrow so she could officially become coordinator. It was long past time to sweep Olivia away and take her rightful place.

"I have General Thompson, Deputy Coordinator."

The vid screen came to life again, showing her a powerfully built man in a light-green uniform with a myriad of ribbons. No doubt they told some kind of story about how he'd saved the world a few times. Military men and their egos demanded it.

"General," she said. "I'm expecting some good news out of you. What is the status of taking the island back from the Fleet assassins?"

"We're almost ready to attack, Deputy Coordinator. To be certain we had enough force, we've pulled in fighters from around the planet. They're refueling and arming now. I anticipate we'll attack in about two hours."

She'd rather he acted now, but she knew they needed overwhelming force.

"Too many people have failed to live up to their reputations in the wake of this tragedy, General," Abigail said coldly. "You'd best not be one of them. I hear the polar base is a terrible assignment. Am I being clear enough?"

To his credit, the man didn't look intimidated. "Yes, ma'am. They won't get away with this treachery. We'll make them pay for what they did to Coordinator West."

"I want a full report as soon as you have the island secure. Take it, no matter the cost."

"I'll contact you as soon as we're done, Deputy Coordinator."

Abigail terminated the call. At least *he* sounded like he might get his task accomplished. She wanted that island under their control before she executed Project Damocles. It would be best to keep these fake Fleet people from being able to react.

The timer at the corner of her implant display told her she had less than twelve hours to go.

* * *

"If you'll step into the warehouse, I think I can explain everything," Sean said.

"I'm not going anywhere with you," the man snarled at Sean. "You tell me why my cargo is on the dock and where my lifts are right now."

"Okay. We hijacked them."

The man stared at Sean for a moment and then grew even redder. "You son of a bitch, stop trying to piss me off. Tell me where they really are."

Sean produced his stunner and jabbed it into the man's gut. "I just did. Now get inside the damned warehouse before I do something we'll both regret."

For a few seconds, Sean thought the man was going to resist. "Seriously? You'll never get away with this. And why the hell even bother? Lifts aren't that valuable. Hell, you left the expensive cargo on the dock. You are the *dumbest* criminal ever."

A few more pokes of the pistol got the man started into the warehouse. Sean kept him under control while his men surrounded them to keep anyone from seeing what was really going on.

"That's because I'm not a criminal. You'll get the lifts back. Cooperate and no one gets hurt."

They stuffed him in the storage room with the other workers and headed back out front.

"Heads up," one of the marines said. "We have company."

An air car had landed on the dock, and a dozen camp guards climbed out. Some went toward the remaining lifts and others trotted toward the warehouse. All of them held flechette rifles. They looked pissed.

Three of the men came toward Sean and his team. The one in front was obviously in charge.

"You there," the man said. "I need everyone gathered on the dock. This port is closed. No lifts in or out."

"The hell you say," Sean snarled, giving his best impression of the man they'd just locked up inside the warehouse where the guards were going. The clock was ticking. They had to get out of here right now or they'd never make it.

The two men flanking the guard leader half raised their rifles in a show of intimidation. Their leader poked his finger in Sean's chest. "The hell I say. We're looking for some escaped prisoners that killed two guards. Friends of mine. Give me any crap and I'll have my boys show you what a rifle butt feels like on that thick skull of yours."

Sean raised his hands a little. "Hey, I don't know nothing about any prisoners. We're just trying to make a living here."

"You can make a living when we're done. Go over to the right side of the dock and wait for us to get everyone out of the warehouse."

Other air cars were delivering guards to the rest of the docks. The other guards were in the warehouse now, so it wouldn't be very long at all before they wondered where everyone was. The men dispatched to the lifts were out of sight. If Sean and his men were going to escape, now was the time.

He pulled his stunner from his coveralls and shot the leader. The man went down without a peep.

The corporal followed his lead and shot one of the remaining guards as the man was raising his rifle.

Sean had the last man. The pistol crackled as soon as he pulled the trigger again, and the smell of fried circuitry filled the air. The man got his rifle up, obviously not stunned.

One of the other marines tackled the guard from the side, which didn't stop him from pulling the trigger, but it saved Sean's life. The burst went high and tore the siding on the warehouse.

Every head on the docks turned toward them as the marine smashed the man in the face three times, knocking him out. Every guard in sight began heading in their general direction at a run.

Time to get the hell out of there.

"Grab the rifles and spare magazines. Come on!"

They piled into the guards' air car as quickly as they could. One of the marines fired at the warehouse when some of the guards inside came running out. He shot over their heads, and they threw themselves flat.

Sean had the air car up and speeding over the lifts as the men on them came out. Guards further up the docks fired on them, but nothing connected. He took them out over the water and gunned the air car toward the city.

"They're in pursuit," one of the marines said. "Three…no, four air cars on our six."

"Keep them back and hang on."

Sean took the air car into a sharp turn and began making it a more difficult target. That would make the marines' aim shaky at best, but it beat getting a flechette through the head. He called out his maneuvers before he executed them, trying to give the shooters as much of an edge as he could.

Their whooping told him they'd hit something, but he couldn't spare the attention to look back. The city was coming up fast, and he wasn't planning to slow down. They'd need time to get lost in the general population, and he'd do whatever it took to give it to them.

The windscreen shattered. He flinched in spite of himself and hunched lower. Apparently, the bad guys had a few good shooters of their own. He just prayed that they'd make it in one piece.

The air car screamed over the docks, sending the people below diving for safety. He cut over the road between buildings and found himself going the wrong way down a stream of traffic. The air car beeped a warning that no doubt meant something to people trained in its use.

Sean resisted the urge to pull up and dove for ground level. In the relative safety below traffic, he pushed his luck, sped across an intersection, and raced a few feet over the pedestrians' heads.

"How are we doing back there?" he asked over his shoulder.

"We took out one of the air cars over the bay, sir. I'm not sure what happened to the second one, but we only have two behind us now. It's way too crowded with civilians for us to take any shots at them. You think you can lose them?"

"That's the plan. Hold on, I'm about to do something my driving instructor would fail me for."

"Like he'd give you a passing grade right now?"

Sean laughed. "Here we go!"

He took the air car around a corner at what he'd conservatively call insane speed. He banked it and pulled back on the controls.

The air car missed the far building by what felt like centimeters, racing along perpendicular to the ground with cars seemingly right over his head. Under other circumstances, he'd have been amazed at the sheer number of terrified faces that screamed past them. Literally screamed.

A glance back revealed that one of the air cars pursuing them hadn't made the turn. Thankfully, it hadn't injured any pedestrians. There was no sign of the other one, so he guessed it had gone straight.

"I'm going to find a spot to drop you," he shouted as he ducked back under traffic. "The security forces will be along pretty quickly, and we don't want to get into a fight with them. Get ready to bail out. We'll meet at the safe house."

They'd rented a place in one of the more rundown suburbs to use as a base of operations. It had their vehicles and a cache of weapons that would give the security forces even more of a heart attack. Once they shook all their pursuers, they could plan the next step toward finding their missing people.

Pedestrians scattered as he came in for a fast landing at a small plaza. The marines piled out, separated into three groups, and headed off to get lost in the crowd.

Sean started to join them, but an air car full of guards found him again. Rather than let them get out and start chasing his men, Sean pulled his own vehicle back into the air, this time, with the traffic flow.

The guards opened fire on him, making him curse. Every flechette went somewhere. Those bastards would kill someone.

He headed back toward the waterfront. With him above traffic, perhaps they wouldn't hit any noncombatants.

Of course, that meant they had a much better chance of hitting him. With the number of shots the air car took as he pulled around the corner, he hoped they didn't hit anything important.

Like the grav drives.

Warning lights flashed on the dash. Not the drives, but some of the automated controls. The car wanted to set down, but he found the override switch. He needed to get out while he could, but he wasn't going to allow his vehicle to crash into anyone. Ahead, he could see the water of the bay.

Time to make a flashy and dangerous exit.

He savagely jerked the air car into an almost vertical climb and aimed for a large building's roof. It was almost on the waterfront, so the view must be spectacular from the top floors. He had to time this just right, or he was going to have a very exciting drop to the plascrete hundreds of meters below.

That, of course, opened him up for even more hits, and the air car began to make some terrifying shimmies as it flew. One of the grav drives was out of alignment. He needed it to stay working for just one more minute.

Sean threw himself out of the air car and hit the roof at what felt like a hundred kilometers an hour. He rolled uncontrollably and slammed into something that stopped him dead in his tracks. A loud "crack" and intense pain told him he'd broken his left arm below the elbow, and his knee on that side was on fire.

He lurched to his feet just as the guard's air car howled overhead in pursuit of his former ride. They didn't even look down. Of course not. Only a complete mental defective would jump out of a speeding air car onto a roof.

The range was opening up, but he pulled his flechette pistol and shot at them. In one of the action vids, he'd have brought them down with his coolly aimed flechettes.

As far as he could tell, they never even realized he'd been firing at them.

His air car slammed into the bay, thankfully far away from any of the small craft on the surface. The guards began circling around it, obviously looking for the bodies of the idiots crazy enough to try those stunts.

The security forces chose that moment to show up. The guards found themselves under the guns of what looked like some seriously pissed security forces.

Satisfied that they wouldn't be going anywhere for a while, Sean looked for a way off the roof. With his luck, they'd have locked the door.

They had. Thankfully, his pistol made short work of the locking mechanism.

He started painfully down the stairs. He needed to get out of the area before more members of the security forces showed up. Once clear, he could make his way to the suburb via cab and walk to the safe house. It'd be dark by the time he got there, but after all the excitement, a nice walk sounded relaxing.

23

Olivia left Admiral Mertz and Princess Kelsey in Captain Black's capable hands. She had to organize the resistance against Abigail's coup. Aaron would see the admiral safely toward the island, and William would help Princess Kelsey find out where the prisoners were.

That is, if Olivia didn't get the information when she got her hands on Abigail.

The grav train saw her back to the diner in short order, and she changed into clothes from the stash below the freezer. Now she'd pass as a working woman, so long as no one looked closely at her hands. Her pampered digits would never pass muster.

Two of the facility guards came with her, both women. A group stood out less than a single person. They borrowed one of the beat-up vehicles in the lot from one of the cooks. It would raise no eyebrows.

While one of the guards drove them toward the city, Olivia got on the com to one of her people through a backup channel. No video, but she had a passphrase that let him know it was her and that she wasn't under duress.

"What's the status?" she asked.

"About two thirds of our allies escaped. Government forces have been on lockdown since they shot your air car. They supposedly have footage of a Fleet pinnace blowing it up. Emotions are running high. Deputy Coordinator King is scheduled to give a live address in about an hour."

"Not supposedly. They really have a pinnace stashed away somewhere. That means they've been playing some other long-term game that we haven't figured out yet. What about our security teams?"

"We have everyone on alert. Once you decide where we should strike, we can move. We don't have the same number of bodies as the security forces, though. We'll need to be choosy."

"Be ready for my call."

She disconnected and considered her options. A straight-up fight would kill a lot of good people on both sides. She was the damned coordinator. Surely, she could turn this on its head and put Abigail on the run.

After a minute, the bare bones of a plan formed. She smiled. It would be perfect if she could pull it off. Since Abigail thought she was dead, Olivia had a better-than-even chance of making it work.

If it failed, well, she wasn't any worse off than she was now.

Olivia gave the guard driving the air car her instructions and called one of the cells to meet her inside the city.

About fifteen minutes before Abigail was scheduled to speak, they pulled up in front of a building in the lower business district. Half a dozen men and women loitered on the walk, waiting for her. One stood ready in what looked like his son's tricked-out air racer.

The man smiled sheepishly when she raised an eyebrow. "It's all I could get on short notice."

"It'll do fine if we need a speedy getaway," she assured him. "Wait here and be ready to leave quickly. Once this goes down, we need to be somewhere else fast."

She turned to the women from the research facility. "Head a few blocks to the south and wait. If I don't call in half an hour, head back home."

With the instructions given, she led the way into the building. The lobby was more upscale than the exterior suggested, but that wasn't a surprise to her. The owner liked to flaunt his wealth.

The wide desk on the other side of the lobby boasted two human receptionists and a beefy guard. The large sign behind them proclaimed who they worked for.

The central receptionist smiled at Olivia brightly. "Welcome to Calder Broadcasting. How may I be of assistance?"

"You can take me to the main studio right now."

The woman's professional smile turned a little sad. "I'm sorry, but we don't give public tours. Perhaps you could schedule a special event. I'll give you the public relations com number."

Olivia smiled wryly. Her disguise was obviously too effective. "Take a closer look and see if you know who I am. Actually, we don't have time for that. George, if you please."

The man beside her drew his stunner and shot the guard. He went down without a peep.

When both women screamed, Olivia held up her hand. "Quietly. We won't hurt you. I'm Coordinator West, and you're helping me stop a coup. I need you to move quickly. Take me to the studio."

The woman on the right stared at Olivia in shock. "It *is* her! She's alive!"

The main receptionist's expression told Olivia that she was less enthusiastic. Of course, her boss wasn't Olivia's fan, either.

Still, Olivia was surprised when George stunned the woman.

"She was reaching under the desk," he said. "Probably a silent alarm. Miss, you keep your hands where I can see them." His stunner never wavered from the remaining receptionist.

The woman nodded sharply, frightened but still cooperative. "There's an alarm, but she didn't activate it. If you want to get to the studio before the address, we need to hurry."

Olivia gestured for the woman to proceed. Time was very short.

* * *

CAPTAIN BLACK TOOK Jared and Kelsey to a massive underground hangar. A number of sleek vessels sat waiting there. Most were only for atmospheric use, but a few along the back wall looked space capable.

"These are prototype vessels meant to demonstrate some of the work we've been doing here," the Fleet officer said. "We don't take them out very often. Many of them incorporate stealth technologies of one kind or another. We can get you to the island in one of them."

"Can one of them get me straight to orbit?" Jared asked. "That might make things easier."

The slender Fleet captain gestured to the small craft against the far wall. "These three can make it out of the atmosphere. One of them— the marine pinnace—is offline. We're swapping the grav units for upgraded versions. We thought we might need extra speed with current events. Just not so soon."

Jared had to admit that it didn't look capable of flight with the back end opened up and dozens of technicians stripping out the drives.

"How soon to get it back online?" he asked.

"At least a few hours, Admiral. If I'd known you were coming, I'd have started getting it put back together sooner."

"What about the small one?" Kelsey asked. "It looks like a fighter."

Captain Black nodded. "It is, and she's ready to go. Unfortunately, there's no stealth on her, other than what normally comes with a ship that size. Its upgrades are in the weapons department. She doesn't use missiles. Instead, we put a powerful but short-range beam weapon on her. It can make two shots before the capacitors are discharged, but inside its range, it should be a thoroughly unpleasant surprise for someone."

Jared was impressed. That was a lot of punch for that small a vessel. More than the missiles they normally carried when used at short range. It wouldn't be very safe for the pilot, though. At beam range, a bigger ship would kill them all too easily.

"What about the third one?"

The boat in question looked nothing like a normal wedge-shaped pinnace. Instead, it was more of a disc.

"It's a stealth testbed," the other man said. "It's slow, but the damned thing is almost invisible to regular scanners until you get right on top of it. It's completely unarmed and only has room for two. It's also, I hesitate to say, a screaming bitch to fly."

That brought a smile to Jared's face. "Is that the voice of experience?"

The other man nodded. "Oh, yes. It's prone to spinning and wobbling. We've been working on it to bypass the orbital bombardment stations, but there hadn't been a driving need to act just yet. I think the time has come."

"Does it have a standard docking rig?"

"I'm afraid not. This was only a proof of concept. For a real mission out to one of the orbital platforms, we'd build a larger ship. We still might not have included a docking setup. That would pretty much announce its arrival to the station."

"Having examined the stations," Jared said, "I'm not certain they would've noticed or cared." He turned to Kelsey and Lord Hawthorne. "I think this is where I take my leave of you. Be careful, Kelsey. As much as I want our people back, we can't lose you."

She gave him one final hug. "I'll be fine. They can't kill me if they can't find me."

"I'm not reassured." He looked at Captain Black. "I'll need a pilot and a suit."

"I'll have someone meet you there, Admiral. Have a good flight."

Jared shook his hand and then Lord Hawthorne's. He took the indicated walkway and went down to the floor of the hangar. He spent a few moments admiring the atmospheric craft. They looked wickedly fast and as deadly as a supernova.

When he arrived at the saucer, a man in a vacuum suit was waiting for him. He was short and thin, almost boyish in size. He held out his free hand. The other had a second vacuum suit in it.

"Admiral Mertz, I'm Roger Walton, one of the test pilots. I'll be taking you up."

He shook the man's hand. "Roger. You're a civilian?"

"Through and through. It'll take me a few minutes to preflight the critical systems, so I'll let you put your suit on."

Jared slipped it on and waited patiently for the man to finish. The very last thing he wanted was for anything to go wrong.

After a few minutes, Roger climbed up into the ship via a slender ladder. He didn't invite Jared up, so he was probably still looking at things. He stuck his head down after a bit and waved for Jared to come up.

"Everything looks good, Admiral. It's somewhat tight in here, so watch your elbows. Are you a pilot?"

Jared nodded. "Sure am, but I have no intention of being a backseat driver."

That made the man smile. "That's good. I'll give you the rundown, but unless I'm somehow incapacitated, please keep your hands off the controls."

The cockpit was even tighter than Jared had imagined. No wonder they'd picked such a small man to pilot it. Jared felt like he couldn't move at all without being in danger of touching something he shouldn't.

"Not a lot of room, is there?" Roger asked. "It takes a lot of space for everything they have to have to make the stealth field work."

Jared strapped himself in to the couch. "How does it work?"

"Damned if I know. The brains tell me it's need to know and that I don't."

The man brought a console between them to life. The piloting controls did look somewhat familiar, but Jared hoped he didn't have to try them out during an emergency.

"How do we get out, and how do you keep the locals from wondering what all the strange aircraft are?"

"Most of the people in this area are friendly. There also aren't many folks feeling a burning desire to move to the country and grow crops. Those that do come along, well, let's just say that the locals make them feel very unwelcome.

"As for getting out of here, there's a shaft leading to the surface inside an abandoned grain silo. It's reinforced to take the stress of grav drives moving inside it. The roof opens like a flower. We launch at night —usually very early in the morning—and steer clear of town."

That made sense. "And the planetary traffic control network?"

"We have some people in the loop. They add us to the expected traffic—while changing our origin point to somewhere safe—or cover for us if we're seen while testing any stealth mods. We keep flights to the very minimum, though.

"Today, we're not on any flight lists. We're going outside the atmosphere, and there's just too much risk of someone seeing us. We'd rather not leave even a fake electronic trail this time."

Without another word, Roger brought the craft to a hover and nudged it toward a massive hatch in the wall. The thick metal slid aside, revealing the shaft the pilot had mentioned. It went horizontally into the ground for several kilometers before it curved upward.

They shot out of the silo at low speed and accelerated into the sky. Jared wished the craft had implant interfaces. The view must be spectacular, even at night.

"We're taking it slow," Roger said. "Half an hour to orbit. We don't want to chance anyone seeing us. We especially don't want to risk one of the orbital bombardment platforms shooting us down. That would ruin our evening."

"The platforms won't engage inside the atmosphere," Jared said. "Once we're high enough, I'll enter the clearance code into our transponders."

Roger grinned. "While I'd love that, we don't have any transponders. That sort of defeats the whole idea of a stealth ship. I guess none of the brains thought it likely we'd ever get our hands on something like that."

Jared couldn't see anything in that to make him smile, so he kept his mouth shut and let the pilot focus on his work. The ship rose to the very edge of space without anything disastrous happening.

"Scanners from the orbital platforms are still safely below detection thresholds," Roger said. "We're angling to pass beyond them in the northern polar region. Their coverage there is slightly weaker. Of course, if they see us, all three of them will be able to take shots at us."

"That's not very reassuring."

It felt like it took hours for them to climb close to the level of the platforms. Roger's cheerful commentary trailed off to nothing as he focused on his work. Jared gripped his seat and prayed.

"Approaching maximum scanner strength from platform three. It's going to be closer than I'd prefer, but I think we'll squeak by. The brains allowed for some leeway, so even if it hits detection threshold, the platform might still miss us. Not that I want to count on that kind of luck."

This was far more hair-raising than Jared had planned. He sat with his heart racing as they inched into the top of the orbital's envelope and beyond. He knew the moment they were safe because Roger visibly relaxed.

The other man turned to him with a look of pure joy on his face. "We did it! The scanner strength is dropping off. They're focused on the planet, so we're safe."

Jared clapped the man on the shoulder. "Very well done! Now we need to get to *Invincible*. Preferably without letting anyone down below know we're here."

"I'm picking up her active scanners. I verified what her orbit was before we took off. Setting course now. We can signal them when we get closer."

Jared was actually curious how close they could get without letting *Invincible* know. This was very similar to the approaches he'd done on *Courageous* in a fighter before they got to Harrison's World. Except that kind of stealth relied on high-speed coasting.

"I'll set up a channel and be ready to respond if we're challenged, but I want to see how close we can get."

Roger gave him a dubious look. "We kind of pushed our luck with the orbital stations, don't you think? We're already way inside your ship's normal detection range. Isn't that enough?"

"I thought you were the daring pilot looking for some adventurous stories to tell. How many free drinks will slipping up on a Fleet superdreadnought earn you?"

"Zero if it blows us out of space. Okay, we'll try it, but I don't want to risk getting shot. If the scanner strength spikes, call them before they get too worked up."

The man was right. If they'd had missiles, they could've opened fire and almost certainly have gotten the first salvo in before the startled bridge crew could raise the battle screens. Perhaps even before the AI could react. Of course, it helped to have a handy planet screening their approach.

Unlike the bombardment stations, *Invincible* wasn't putting out a constant stream of targeting scans. She relied on a number of detection criteria in which another ship would reveal itself so she could focus on it for more detailed readings.

Propulsion was a big factor. Large ships required massive grav drives. Those distorted space enough to detect a ship long before they'd otherwise see it.

"We're coming up on five thousand kilometers," Roger said. "We're still below detection threshold, but someone observant might still spot us."

"How close do you think you can get before they see us?" Jared asked.

"That depends on the angle of approach. We're above them now. If we come straight in, maybe three or three and a half thousand kilometers. If we pass them by and come in from their stern, their own grav drives will mask us until we're maybe two thousand kilometers away. Give or take."

Jared gave the pilot a decisive nod. "Come in from astern."

"Aye, sir." Roger gave him an exaggerated salute and a smile.

In the end, they beat Roger's best estimate and Jared's worst nightmare. They slipped right up to the ship and attached to her hull just forward of engineering without any challenge.

Once the magnetic clamps locked down, Roger turned to Jared with a huge grin. "Now *this* is worth a lifetime of free drinks for sure!"

"Yes, it is," Jared said glumly. "I'm going to have to find out what the brains' secret is and update our scanning profiles. We're obviously at risk. Put us into standby mode, and we'll go surprise a few people. I'll buy the first of your well-earned drinks, too."

"After all this stress," the pilot said, "make it a double."

24

Once Jared was safely away, Kelsey turned to William and Captain Black. "Okay, now it's time to find our missing people. Actually, I'd like to make sure that the others get safely to this island first. I have a Fleet com unit. Jared said that he slipped his to Commander Meyer, so we need to get close enough to reach them. The booster my marines have only works on my end."

William considered that. "With the cordon of military around the island, you're not likely to get that close. But perhaps there's another way. If we get back into the city, I can arrange for us to hack into one of the orbital transceivers.

"Those would be the ones that Olivia used to contact you before all this mess got out of control. We won't have long, but you should be able to call your ship and have them verify they made it to the island."

"How are the prisoners going to get through that cordon without drawing attention?" Captain Black asked. "The forces on the island will have to drive our military back to get them under protection. No offense, but I'd prefer to see no loss of life here on either side."

Kelsey considered the situation and had to admit it posed a few challenges. "What we need to do is get the military to allow them to pass through. Maybe when Olivia makes her countermove, she can order them to stand down?"

"That's a big maybe," William said. "It might be best to intercept the prisoners and get them to a safe location to sit out the fighting. Then, once the coup is dealt with, they can go in safety."

Captain Black nodded slowly. "That might work, but only if we can figure out where they are and get word to them. Once we locate them, we can slip them into one of the ports closest to the island. I'm thinking of one that has a large warehouse that they can hide inside."

"If we can get close, my com should connect with theirs," Kelsey said. "Close being within twenty kilometers. How about one of those stealth atmospheric craft?"

"It's a risk, but not a terrible one," Black said. "Still, I'm not sure Admiral Mertz would be pleased if I send you right out to the military."

"Perhaps we should try a different method," William said. "The press will have any number of air cars circling the island in case there are developments. If we masquerade as one, we don't even need to use a stealth craft. We can mix with the crowd."

Kelsey liked it. "Fortune favors the bold. Let's make that happen." She turned to Captain Black. "Now, I believe you promised me some powered armor. If this all goes into the crapper, I want to have some protection. If it goes smoothly, then I'll have it with me when we find the missing prisoners. That makes rescuing them a lot simpler."

The dark-skinned man shook his head. "I think I see why you give Admiral Mertz grey hairs. I believe we have something that will work for you. It has some upgraded features when compared to the original Imperial Marine armor, but that shouldn't stop you from using it without training."

"I've gotten quite good at figuring things out on my own," she said. "As for Jared, you have no idea. He's my half brother, you see. I've been making him age prematurely for decades."

William raised an eyebrow. "He's from the other side of the sheets, is he?"

"That galls both him and Ethan, for entirely different reasons. Jared would rather not have his parentage hanging over his head, and my twin looks at him as a threat because of it. To my shame, I shared Ethan's point of view for entirely too long."

"That's completely understandable," William said seriously. "I'm surprised he doesn't see you as a threat. I assume you were born after him?"

She nodded. "By ten whole minutes, and thank God for that. I'd rather be doing something interesting."

"'Interesting' isn't precisely the word I'd choose for what you do," Black said. "Come with me."

He took them on another trek through the facility to a massive armory. Kelsey was impressed. It was even bigger than the one aboard

Invincible. Row after row of full-size marine combat armor stood ready for use.

Compared to her lean Raider armor, it was thick with artificial muscle. It looked exactly like the marine armor they'd recovered from derelict Imperial ships orbiting Boxer Station. Only these suits weren't in desperate need of refurbishment.

These suits were heavy enough that they stood without the need for a rack. Unfortunately, whoever had lined them up had them facing out from the wall. With the entrance at the back, that might prove inconvenient if people needed to get armored in a hurry. She'd obviously been spending too much time around marines over the last year.

She ran her hand down one of the heavily muscled arms. "Tell me these are implant controlled."

"They are," Black said. "They come in a few different sizes, one of which should be short enough for you. The armorers normally use their implants to move them. Give me a minute to get some of the men to bring it out so we can fit it to you."

Considering that most marines towered over her, she was glad she didn't have to make do.

"There's no need," she said, wrapping her arms around one. She grunted, lifted the massive suit, and walked it out into the open. It was heavy enough that she had to turn off the governors on her artificial muscles, but it still didn't max her out. It came close, though.

At only a meter and a half, no one expected to see feats of strength from her. Yet the Old Empire Marine Raider bone reinforcement and artificial muscles increased her power tenfold. She could only imagine how strong a similar enhancement would make someone like Talbot. Her lover was not a small man by any measure.

Captain Black blinked at her. "Okay, then. I knew about your enhancement, but it's so easy to forget. Climb in, and these gentlemen will begin fitting it."

Kelsey entered the armor from the rear and ordered the suit to close up via her implants. They must not have expected many people to come in and just take a suit, because it didn't require any authentication at all. Something else Talbot wouldn't approve of.

The supports that held her were set wrong for her height, so she'd need to come back out for the techs to adjust them, but she could look at the armor first.

The systems came online and began feeding telemetry right into her implants. The dark interior of the helmet vanished, and she found she could see everyone just fine. She tried to turn on the interior cameras to project her own image on the faceplate but found the armor didn't have that capability.

Maybe that was what the designers intended.

That's exactly what they intended.

Kelsey flinched. "Dammit! Don't do that!"

She found speaking aloud made her feel better, and inside the privacy of her new suit, no one would think she was crazy. Well, any crazier than they already considered her.

I'm sorry. I was just trying to be helpful.

"We're going to need to work out some rules of the road. It's kind of creepy having you in my head watching everything I do." That's when it occurred to her that the program was running when she went to the restroom. Christ.

Well, it was too late now. At least she hadn't had sex since she'd taken him into her head. She really needed to get him moved into some other system. If she could.

"It's okay, Ned. I'm going to call you that, okay?"

It is my name.

"I thought you couldn't read my mind."

Only the strong surface thoughts. It's almost as though you're talking to yourself. That I can hear. The tactical doctrine of the marine armor is to make it as intimidating as possible. Faceless killing machines project the right kind of image. With Raider armor, we don't want people to see us until it's too late, and there are circumstances where a face is useful. Also, we have our own ways of intimidating people.

"Such as?" She began running through a systems diagnostic of the armor while she conversed with the ghost in her head. Everything was green.

The projectors that put your face on the helmet can put other things there, too. Grinning skulls and demonic faces are particular favorites. Were favorites.

His mental voice sounded so sad that she felt a chill go down her spine. It would be very, very easy to think of the program as a real person with actual emotions.

"I'll keep that in mind going forward. I hope this doesn't seem ungrateful, but you're sounding more like a person than you did the last time. That's...well, creepy."

I've integrated all the data files and raw memory maps. I feel like more of a person than I did before. It's more than a bit unsettling.

"Memory maps?"

That's what I called them when I made backups of my vids and files during the rebellion. I told my implants to make direct copies of my memories. Our doctor didn't think they would even be readable, much less useful if I died, but I figured it couldn't hurt. I think I might have been wrong.

"How so?"

Now I really know that I'm dead. It's as though I'm a ghost in your implants, watching things take place that I can't control. I feel like a ghost.

That made things much more complicated. What had she created? When she'd told *Invincible* to update the program's ability to integrate data files, she might have done way more than she'd bargained for. She might have created a new kind of AI.

She was going to have to do a lot more testing of what this being was, but now was not the time. Even though the conversation had only taken a minute, the others were waiting for her to talk with them.

"Is there anything else that you need to tell me before I deal with my other problems?"

Just one thing. The search of my recordings is complete. I didn't record myself accessing the ship's computer on Persephone.

"Dammit. I really need that code. No offense, but I'd like to have more than you to tell me about my implants, and that ship is a treasure trove that we can't use."

I didn't say I couldn't provide the code. As I incorporated my memory maps, I remembered things. In this case, I found the code about an hour ago. I'll gladly share it with you, Kelsey.

"Why didn't you say so then?"

You were a little busy confronting these men, and you told me to keep quiet.

That last sounded a tad smug. "I can see I'm going to have my hands full with you. Fine. Thank you. Do those memories address how you died or what happened to *Persephone*?"

Unfortunately, no. Perhaps those things will be made clear when you assume command.

* * *

AWAY FROM THE MARBLE-PANELED LOBBY, the broadcast station was more utilitarian. Bland white walls, bright lights, and somewhat worn carpeting in commercial tan.

It was also busier. Hordes of people moved quickly down the halls and into various rooms stuffed full of equipment Olivia couldn't identify, all chattering away in what sounded like a foreign language, one made up of technical phrases and acronyms that meant nothing to her.

The receptionist led the way through the crowd and up to a door with a security lock. It opened with a card she produced. "This corridor takes you directly to the main studio control booth."

"Thank you. I won't forget your help. If your boss fires you, I'll find you a place on my staff that will more than make up for the loss."

The woman snorted. "If you're serious, I'll submit my resignation today. Leaving this place is no loss."

"You're hired. Come with us."

Olivia led the way into a darkened control room at the end of the short hall. Screens covered the walls, some showing a news desk where a talking head was jabbering on about something. Probably Olivia's supposed death, based on the burning wreckage in the vid behind him. Other screens showed an empty seat in what looked like Abigail's office.

It wouldn't be empty much longer, based on the countdown clock beside it. Five minutes to go.

A man without a jacket, his sleeves rolled up and his face perspiring heavily, gawked at them and shot to his feet. "What the hell are you people doing in here? Get out! We go live in four."

"Yes, you will," Olivia said. "Just not with the broadcast you expect. Listen up, people. What you're reporting is a lie. I'm Olivia West and I'm very much alive. Abigail King is staging a coup, and you're going to help me stop her."

"Bullshit! I don't know you. Master Calder said—"

George raised his stunner and took the man down. "Who's the associate producer?"

No one spoke, but everyone looked at a younger man with a monumentally ugly tie. George stalked over and pulled him to his feet. "Do you recognize Coordinator West?"

Motion on one of the screens got Olivia's attention. Abigail was sitting down behind her desk. The woman's smug expression of anticipation infuriated her. They had three minutes.

"I'm going down to the set," she said. "Make certain they don't cut to Abigail."

The receptionist—Olivia really needed to learn the woman's name—led her to a door on the other side of the room. Several of the resistance members followed. A short set of stairs led down to another door and into the studio.

There were a lot more people running equipment than she'd expected. Dozens of men and women focused on their tasks, all surrounding a brightly lit desk with the talking head. He sounded like he was preparing to cut over to Abigail.

Olivia had to hand it to him. The man looked only mildly alarmed as she brushed past the cameras and stepped close to the set.

"Cut to commercial," she said softly from just outside the camera range.

The man blinked once and turned up the brightness of his smile. He picked right back up with his calm, measured monologue, barely glancing at Olivia.

"As I mentioned earlier, Deputy Coordinator King is about to make a statement from her office on the terrible events that took place earlier today. A highly placed source in the administration has informed this reporter that some very shocking allegations will be revealed in just a few minutes.

"You'll want to hear them first right here on Channel 7 News. Let's break for a short commercial, and we'll be right back."

Someone off the set shouted, "Live in fifty-five seconds."

The anchor stood and pulled Olivia onto the set. "Sit right here beside me, Coordinator. My name is Jackson Zapata. Just call me Jackson. I'll make the assumption that the rumors of your death are grossly exaggerated."

"You could say that. There's a coup underway."

That seemed to make him very happy. She supposed trouble was what folks like him thrived on. "Then you'd best say so up front. The security forces might try to shut us down, so lead with the meat of the story."

A woman with a tray of makeup rushed up to Olivia. "Let me put this on your cheeks, or you're going to look like a corpse."

"I think that's what someone had in mind," Olivia said with a hint of gallows humor.

Another woman—a producer of some kind—whipped off her blouse without any qualms about showing her undergarments to God and everyone. "You can't go on air in that! Arms up!"

"We'll come back with the camera on me," the anchor said. "I'll make a brief introduction so the audience is prepped. You'll know when to start speaking. Just look into the camera and pretend it's a person."

In an astonishingly brief period of time, they had her face made up and her top changed. The producer was brushing Olivia's hair when someone off set started counting down.

"Live in three...two..." the man beside the camera held up a single finger as the producer dove behind the desk.

"Welcome back to Channel Seven," the anchor said gravely. "It's my great pleasure to introduce a very unexpected yet most welcome special guest in studio, Coordinator Olivia West. Coordinator, I'm sure that our viewers are all greatly relieved to see you alive and well. Please tell us what's really going on."

Olivia smiled into the camera like a wolf, imagining that she was

staring right at Abigail. "Thank you, Jackson, and an even bigger thanks
to Lord Edward Calder for providing this forum for me."

She took a deep breath and launched into her explanation. "People
of Harrison's World, it saddens me to inform you that Abigail King,
formerly Deputy Coordinator of our world, is attempting to stage a
coup. The vid you've all seen is a lie. That pinnace didn't belong to Fleet
but to rebels intent on overthrowing the rightful rule of law. Perhaps
even the Imperial Lords themselves."

That last was untrue, but the rules of politics were crystal clear.
Admit nothing, deny everything, and make counteraccusations. Let
Abigail be the one on the defensive.

"Now, let me explain very quickly what really happened. We don't
have long before the rebels kill this transmission, so let's make our time
together count."

25

S ean came limping into the safe house just as the big news broadcast came on. The marines leapt into action, getting his broken arm set and putting some ice on his knee. The medic thought it was only a bad bruise.

The coordinator only got about ten minutes into her speech before the channel went off the air with a nondescript "technical difficulties" banner. For some reason, he didn't think many people were going to believe that. In the end, it hardly mattered. She'd said more than enough to get people thinking.

"Well, this is a pleasant surprise," he said. "I expected our escape to be the big news of the day, but with all this going on, the security forces won't even be looking for us."

"I wouldn't be so sure about that, sir," the medic said as he finished wrapping Sean's knee. "Someone is going to care about what we're doing. Maybe only the capital security forces, but still."

"This kind of thing spawns riots. The people that feel suppressed in society will be taking the opportunity to even the score. Which opens us up to random danger but clouds our activities from view. We need to get some eyes on the target building. I don't want our little songbird to escape before we can find out what he knows."

The medic didn't look pleased. "You really need to stay off that knee, sir. If you abuse it, we'll be carrying you."

"Are you saying I'm fat?" he joked.

The nonplussed marine only sighed.

"I've had enough excitement to last a lifetime, Sergeant. I don't need to lead the charge to secure the prisoner. I'll be happy to wait with the getaway driver. But it's getting dark, and the crowds won't wait long to begin roaming the streets."

He outlined the general plan for them. They had three vehicles, including a grav van. That was for securing any prisoners. The other two air cars would deliver troops onto the roof where the guards had brought Sean into the building. Hopefully, the camp commander would be in the same suite of offices he'd occupied earlier. If not, perhaps someone there would know something worthwhile. That was the only place he knew to look for answers.

They mounted up and headed into the city at a sedate pace. His predictions proved accurate. Once they made it into the business district, there were small groups of people roving around, and a few agitators were already whipping them into a frenzy. It wouldn't be long before they started setting fires and looting.

The security forces were getting ready. He saw a couple of checkpoints—complete with officers in riot gear—going up and came up with a new scouting plan. They moved all the weapons out of the first air car and relocated all but two of the men from it to the van. It led the way.

This approach proved wise when it ran into a surprise checkpoint. The rest of them took a side street and avoided some very uncomfortable questions. The security forces gave his men a hard time but let them through when the mob put in an appearance up the street.

They all made it to the target building without any further problems. A convenience store provided a place to park while they swapped out people and weapons. The owners were securing sheets of hard plastic across the windows, no doubt anticipating looting.

The occupants of the building had the target floor brightly lit, so Sean expected someone to be there. Probably trying to figure out where all the prisoners had disappeared to.

He decided to keep the van in the parking lot after having a word with the suspicious owner of the shop. Some local currency got them drinks and junk food in case they couldn't get back to the house. A shotgun and a few boxes of ammo made the man a friend for life.

Once everything was in readiness, the two air cars went up to the roof. Without communications—other than local coms—he couldn't follow along with the raid. He was just glad none of the windows blew out in an explosion. That would draw the security forces, even with riots taking place.

His com signaled. "Yes?"

"We have takeout. You want to come to the door?"

"Be right there." He hung up and slapped the driver on the shoulder. "Go."

The van took off and landed on the roof. His team hustled three men and a woman out to meet them. They'd rigged up some makeshift restraints ahead of time, so these folks were not a serious threat. The two men in back with Sean could keep them under control.

The marines dumped them into the van and took off for their air cars. This time they'd be taking more of a chance getting back to the house. The lead air car would have a full load of passengers, though no weapons.

Sean smiled when he saw the bastard who'd given him so much trouble. "Well, well. Things are looking up. I'm actually pleased to see you."

"You can go screw yourself," the man snarled.

"While that might be entertaining, I'd rather get a little information from you. We can do this the easy way or the hard way. I'm hoping you go for hard, honestly."

The man spat at Sean but missed.

Sean smashed his good fist into the man's face. It hurt, but not as bad as his broken arm. Blood streamed from the man's nose as he bellowed in pain.

"I'm an officer," Sean said as he shook his hand, "but I'm not inclined to be a gentleman. Admiral Mertz would disapprove of my methods, I suspect, but I find they hold a particular charm. You took a hundred of my people. You can tell me where they are or I'll cheerfully break you in half. If I get tired, one of these hulking young marines can spell me. Are you certain you wouldn't rather tell me what I want to know?"

The prisoner's answer was profane and to the point.

"This is going to be a long night," he told the driver. "I'm glad we picked up snacks. We're going to need the energy."

OLIVIA WASN'T SURPRISED when the power went out only ten minutes into her address. Honestly, she'd expected only half that time. She'd already made her final plea for the people to spread the word and resist the unlawful regime. If Abigail hadn't cut her off, Olivia would've been in the awkward position of having to pass things back to the anchorman. This way was much more dramatic.

Emergency lights came on all over the studio when the overheads went out. Jackson Zapata stood. "Well, that's it for tonight, Coordinator. We need to get you out of the building before the security forces close in. I hope you have a speedy ride waiting for you."

"I have that in spades. Thank you for making this as straightforward as possible."

He smiled and extended his hand. "It was an honor and a pleasure. Not to mention a huge boost for the station's ratings, I'm sure. Maybe I should ask Lord Calder for a raise."

"I'd hold off on that for a while if I were you. In fact, you might want to come with us."

He smiled slowly. "That's a *wonderful* idea, and I'll gratefully accept your generous offer. We could do a documentary-style show of your fight against the tyrant and usurper. Charlotte! Get a camera crew ready to go! We're following the coordinator!"

The woman in the bra started shouting for people by name and ordering them to do things. Olivia decided that if the apocalypse ever came, she wanted that woman organizing the last stand against the zombies.

"What's the best way to get out of here?" she asked as she peeled out of the woman's blouse. She'd stand out less in the one she'd worn earlier. "I have men and vehicles outside."

"The tunnels," he said promptly, taking his producer's blouse from Olivia and tossing it to her as she trotted by. "They crisscross under the district. One leads to our satellite office a few blocks away. Your people can meet us there and not risk running into security forces."

Olivia slipped her blouse on and buttoned it quickly. The door leading to the control room opened, and her people came out at a run. One of them hurried up to her.

"The security feed is on backup power. There's no sign of trouble yet, but we need to get you out of here."

"I'm already working on that. What's the address for this other office?" she asked Zapata.

He gave it to her man. "Have them go into the parking garage, top level. The employee code is 1234."

"You know that isn't secure," her man said, obviously offended by the broadcast company's lapse in security consciousness.

"Take it up with management," Zapata said. "Coordinator, we can head down to the tunnel through the stairwell behind the studio. Someone will tell the security forces about it, I'm sure, but they won't have time to block you from leaving or follow you, for that matter. Especially if they think you went somewhere else."

He raised his voice. "Your car can land on the roof, Coordinator. Allow me to take you up there myself."

She smiled. "You're clever. I like that in a man."

"You're making me blush," he said with no sign of any such redness. "We should make our exit now."

He led them to the stairwell and started down, but the security team insisted on going out front. The trip to the basement was noisy and quick. Deep underground, machinery sat in the darkness. The emergency lights were few and far between.

The ever-resourceful Charlotte produced handheld lights from a maintenance locker. Zapata led them through a side corridor and into a tunnel.

"Do you know where everything is?" she asked Charlotte.

The woman nodded seriously. "Yes."

Olivia smiled. "You may just be the most competent person I've ever met."

"Thank you."

The tunnel was dark but clean and clear of debris. They made excellent time to the destination building and quickly went up the stairs to the parking level.

The building still had power. Her vehicles stood in a line, ready to go. Behind them, a grav van with a fold-down satellite transceiver and the Channel 7 logo was pulling up. The cameramen and staff that had followed the producer swarmed it.

Olivia gestured for one of her people to go with them. "In case we get separated, make sure they get to the rally point. I'm beginning to think a record of what we're doing here might be very useful."

She turned to Jackson Zapata. "I'm not going to tell you where we're going, just in case you get picked up. Thanks again for all your help."

The handsome man grinned. "I haven't had this much excitement in years. I just hope that everything works out without too much violence."

He said the last with a note of solemnity. She wondered if he practiced the expression in the mirror. Probably, but that didn't mean it wasn't genuine.

Olivia made her way to the getaway car. The air car couldn't have been as fast as the vehicle Abigail had destroyed, but if there was a problem, it might be able to outrun it.

She climbed in. "Ready? Let's get out of here before the world comes down on our heads."

"Yes, ma'am." He brought the vehicle to a hover and took them out of the building with the others following behind.

They took the side roads out, but she still saw several security vehicles speeding toward the broadcast building. She didn't breathe easily until they were away from the area.

* * *

"Am I surrounded by incompetents?" Abigail screamed at her assistant. "This is unbelievable! Can anyone do anything right? Anything at all?"

The man was in on almost every aspect of the plan, so she wasn't giving anything away by ranting at him in her soundproofed office. Part of her knew that it wasn't his fault. None of this was his doing, but she didn't care. How could they have missed killing Olivia? The one thing they absolutely had to do. This was all going to come apart.

"Deputy Coordinator, I understand you're angry, but if you insist on ranting, Coordinator West is going to rally people around her. You need to find her and stop her right now if you intend to avoid hanging."

His calm rebuke hit her like a bucket of ice water. She forced herself to take a deep breath and stepped back from the cliff. "I…You're right. Of course you are. Go write me something to tell the press. This isn't Coordinator West. It's an impostor. Tell them she doctored the statement. Tell them she's the one staging the coup. Anything. We only need to keep a lid on this until we find her and kill her."

He nodded. "An excellent idea, Deputy Coordinator. I'll have something for you in a few minutes." He left her office at a dignified pace.

She buried her head in her hands as soon as he closed the door. This was all going wrong so quickly. She had to get back on top of the situation right now.

Her com signaled. Not the official one but her private unit. A glance showed it was Master Calder.

"Master Calder," she said, astonished that her voice was so level. "There have been some unexpected developments."

"So I saw," he said with more than a hint of anger. "I'd ask you how she survived, but I think we both know the answer to that. She suspected a trap and sacrificed her security detail. That's much more cold-blooded than I expected from her. And, to be fair, killing her wasn't your task.

"Unfortunately, your head is on the platter if we don't regain control. You need to discredit her tonight. Or at least leak enough information to do that for you. Here's what I want you to do…"

Five minutes later, she'd made a call to the people overseeing her personal prisoners. They'd increase the guard and start questioning them again. This time they'd record everything and doctor the vids to implicate Olivia in a plan to become the dictator of Harrison's World, in coordination with rogue Fleet elements.

She had the perfect way to distract everyone. A quick check of the timing on Operation Damocles told her that she could move the plan up to take place in half an hour. Not all the elements would be precisely in place, so there would be a delay of about twenty seconds. That shouldn't matter. No one would be able to react in time to make a difference.

She walked out to her assistant's desk with a cold, hard smile on her face. She'd hunt Olivia down like a rabid dog. The woman wouldn't be able to do one thing to change her fate, no matter what evidence she had.

26

To say that everyone was shocked when Jared strolled onto the bridge would've been an understatement. Even *Invincible* didn't seem immune to that emotion.

Zia gaped at him and jumped to her feet. "Admiral! You're back! I had no idea you were even on your way up."

"Indeed," *Invincible* added. "In fact, no transport has left the surface at all. Your presence here on this vessel seems impossible. Would you care to explain, Admiral?"

Jared shook his head. "Actually, I think I'll leave you all in the dark for a bit. This is my friend Roger. *Invincible*, he has full guest privileges, and you can speak freely in front of him. Plus, his first drink is on my tab."

"Of course, Admiral. Hello, Roger."

The man frowned at the ceiling. "Is that a computer? It doesn't sound like a computer."

"It's a *long* story," Jared said. "One we don't have time for right now."

He stepped behind Zia's command chair and glanced at the superdreadnought's status screens. "We all seem to be in one piece. Keep the marines on the island on high alert. Our lost people are loose and making their way toward them now. I'm not certain how they'll make themselves known, but they'll be on cargo lifts."

Zia nodded. "I'll see that Major Talbot is informed. What about the princess?"

"She's working on rounding up the last of our people. About a hundred of them were separated from the rest. And we've made some new friends below. I'll want the senior staff brought together in my office in twenty minutes. What's *Courageous*'s status?"

"She's relocated to the Pentagar-bound flip point, sir. The jammer there started emitting a warning signal. Some kind of malfunction. Doctor Leonard thinks it might have received some subtle damage during the battle before we deployed it. We've relocated every other vessel to cover the flip point in case we have unexpected visitors while it's offline."

"That's smart. If we have any more computer-controlled destroyers pop in while we have no cover, we're dead."

"That's what Captain Graves thought, as well. We broke the encryption on the base AI while you were incommunicado. There are two additional pairs of destroyers out on patrol, one in the direction of the Imperial core and the other through the worrisome flip point. The AI expected the patrol in question to return about two days from now, but it might be early. The other patrol is a week out."

"Was there any other information I need to know about on the AI's data storage?"

The slender officer shrugged. "We're still skimming the data. Considering the source, we thought it a little risky to have *Invincible* sorting it out. Doctor Leonard has it hooked up to the standalone system, and Carl Owlet is overseeing a team. He hopes to have the basic outlines of what's there in a couple of days, but detailed information is going to take longer.

"There's one bit of good news. The AI wasn't expecting any direct visits from the Rebel Empire. With the system on lockdown, there's no need. This AI sends a destroyer to pass on an update once a year, and that isn't due for another six months."

That gave them some breathing room but presented its own set of problems. They had no modern destroyer to send. Or, actually, they might. There was the Rebel Empire destroyer they'd disabled at Erorsi. With the flip carrier to transport it here, they might be able to get it online again in time.

Well, one problem at a time.

"Okay, let me bring you up to speed on what's happening on Harrison's World."

The lift doors slid open, and two people stepped out onto the bridge: Major Talbot and Crown Princess Elise Orison.

She rushed over and gave Jared a fierce hug. "I just heard you were back. I was so worried."

It was good to hold her, but the bridge wasn't the place and this wasn't the time. "I'm sorry about that. I was just about to explain what was going on down there, and Kelsey is fine, Talbot."

He nodded. "I figured she was, but she's in the middle of it, isn't she?"

"Surprisingly, no. Just the outer edges. It seems that Coordinator West is actually aligned with a resistance movement that's been around since the Fall. She and her people were responsible for outfitting *Invincible*. They're in control of the Grant Research Facility."

"Is that how you made your miraculous appearance?" *Invincible* asked. "I've looked over the logs, and an exterior maintenance airlock was accessed before you surprised us, so I'm going to rule out teleportation. For now."

That distracted Jared from his story. "Is teleportation even possible?"

"Admiral, with a sufficiently advanced technology, almost anything is theoretically possible. That feat remains highly implausible, however. You were saying."

"Right. They've been working on some very effective shielding technology."

"Obviously," Zia said sourly. "How am I going to ever live this down? Someone actually boarded us without me knowing."

Roger grinned. "If it's any consolation, the Admiral gave me some pointers."

"You're not helping. How does it work?"

"Magic? I have no idea. I'm just the pilot."

That answer obviously didn't please Jared's flag captain. "*Invincible*, go to full active scans. If there's a pebble sneaking along near us, I want to know about it."

"I'll assume that was meant less than literally. Commencing active scans. No vessels or anomalies detected."

"Well, keep an eye on things. If you spot something unusual, let me know and take appropriate countermeasures. No more surprises."

* * *

KELSEY FELT a bit ridiculous flying around in a van wearing a set of combat armor. She couldn't even sit down. She had to stand in the rear, braced against the wall. She had her usual array of heavy weapons slung outside her suit.

God help her if someone stopped them for an inspection.

At least she'd been able to convince her marine guards to take more mundane transportation to the capital. Jared's companions had gone with them. In this getup, she didn't need any extra protection.

The driver took her out to the swarm of press air cars at the edge of the military exclusion zone around the island. "We just got an official warning not to cross into the interdicted area," he told her. "I'm not seeing any cargo lifts."

"What about closer to the mainland? Do you think they might be there?"

"Probably. The nearest city is a port."

"Take us that way. I'll know if we get close."

The man took the van back toward the coast while Kelsey checked her Fleet com through her implants. No signal yet, but it would register the other com as soon as it came in range.

They passed over the city and curved up the coast toward the north. It looked beautiful, she thought. It was right on the equator and seemed warm and toasty. The beaches were gorgeous, even at night. Perhaps *especially* at night. So romantic.

Her com beeped. "I think we just touched the edge of their range."

As they left the city behind them, her com locked on. She opened a channel and waited for someone to answer.

"Yes?" a voice asked cautiously.

"You know this is a Fleet com, so don't sound so suspicious. This is Princess Kelsey. I'm just south of your position."

"Ah. Good point, Highness. I'm Command Master Chief Ross. I have almost all of the prisoners with me on four lifts."

That was excellent news. "Great. Put Commander Meyer on."

"He's not here, I'm afraid."

She frowned. "Where is he?"

"He took a team to the capital to find the missing crewmen. I have his civilian com number, but we're out of range for that network."

Dammit. That complicated things. He should've just come with everyone else and let her find the missing people. Of course, Kelsey was sure Talbot thought the very same thing about her when she went rogue, so she probably shouldn't point that out.

"Give me his number." She stored it in her implant memory for later and turned to face the rear of the van. She had a good view of the city from there and could describe the docks for them. "Now, we have a warehouse at the nearest port. That's safer than running the blockade around the island. What I want you to do is—"

The night lit up brighter than day. The intense blast of light from the center of the city would've blinded her if not for her optical implants dimming it. A nuclear explosion? But that didn't explain the intense

Ghosts of Empire

195

beam of energy rising from the center. It was already gone, but the afterimage remained, shooting straight into the sky.

The shock wave is coming.

The ghostly voice of Ned Quincy startled her into action. She slammed the helmet onto her head and locked it in place. "Take us down!" she shouted through her exterior speakers.

The pilot started to, but the massive shock wave struck them like a brick wall moving at light speed. The van came apart, and Kelsey's world went dark.

* * *

AN INTENSELY LOUD alarm interrupted Jared's explanation of what they were going to do next. He whirled and stared at the main screen even as his implants told him what was happening. Someone had just set off a nuke on Harrison's World.

No, two blotches of horrible light were fading on the image of the planet below. Someone had just taken the coup to a completely new level.

"Get me readings on—" he started to say, but *Invincible* overrode him with an even louder alarm.

"All hands brace for impact," the AI said over the speaker. The massive warship accelerated with brutal force, momentarily stressing even her mighty grav compensators and staggering her crew.

Jared was going to ask what was happening, but a giant fist smashed into his ship, sending it tumbling madly. Main power failed, and he was hurled to the deck.

* * *

SEAN GAVE up on being the heavy when they got back to the safe house. It was much easier for one of the marines to intimidate the man. He left it up to them to pick the most appropriate member of the squad.

They picked a whipcord-thin woman named Gina. He thought she might be the woman that had created the distraction in the prison camp. The supposedly jilted lover.

She went to the bathroom and returned with an old-fashioned straight razor. Okay, now even he felt uncomfortable.

She squatted in front of the main prisoner. They'd tied him to a chair, and he was literally a captive audience. "Hey there," she said in a friendly tone. "I'll bet you're wondering what I need this for. We'll get to that. First, I want to tell you a little story. You okay with that?"

The man swallowed noisily but said nothing.

"I'll take that as a yes. My name is Gina and I have a friend named Linda Montoya. Linda and I are close. Very, *very* close, if you take my meaning. You took her, and I'd be really, *really* happy if you told me where she was. To encourage your speedy cooperation, I took the precaution of buying this handy straight razor."

She held it up so that the light reflected in the prisoner's eyes meaningfully. It looked, well, razor sharp.

"I'm not cooperating with you, bitch." He sounded terrified.

Hell, Sean felt his own anatomy trying to retract. He was morally certain that the marine intended to give the man gender reassignment surgery. Or would it be gender obliteration surgery?

"Sure you will," Gina said. "You don't have a choice. You're playing the game no matter what you want. The only thing left undecided is how many parts I take before you tell me what I want to know. Shall we begin?"

One of the other male prisoners—who all looked suitably horrified —leaned forward a little, making the ropes holding him down in the chair creak. "Don't be an idiot, Jack! She's not bluffing! She's going to castrate you!"

Gina smiled at the second man sweetly. "Thank you! It's always nice when other people take you seriously. However, you're off a little bit on your assessment. I'm going to start with something a little more... prominent. You know what they say, go big or go home."

"For God's sake," the woman said. "Are you going to let her maim you to prove how much of a man you used to be? Moron." She focused her gaze on the marine. "He gave them over to Deputy Coordinator King's people. They hauled them away. We don't know where they took them."

"That's helpful," Gina allowed, "but not enough. We already knew who was behind it. That doesn't get us any closer to finding them. I'm certain you know more than you imagine. Some detail that will get us where we'd all like to be. Me reunited with my girlfriend and you not wondering where all your parts are or whether the doctors can reattach everything."

She held the razor back up. "So, do we have any takers? Every bit of information gets you off the hook for a bit. Surely you want me aiming my sharp tongue at someone else, right?"

Sean's admiration for her acting ability rose. At least he hoped she was bluffing. If not, he'd have to stop her, and in his condition, he wasn't certain he could. And if what she'd said wasn't a clever ruse, she'd be inclined to slice and dice.

27

O livia and the rest of her people arrived at the building they were using to regroup just in time to hear about the bombings.

Holy God. Someone had nuked four major cities. The death toll was going to be in the millions. Maybe the tens of millions. The number of injured people was going to crash the medical system.

Every channel was going on nonstop about the blasts. Even Jackson Zapata was in front of the camera, recording something. She made sure that one of her people went over to verify that wasn't going out live. They couldn't afford for the security forces to trace his transmission.

Abigail had already issued a statement blaming the "terrorist attack" on Olivia. She looked suitably horrified at the "brutal destruction and death" that she claimed Olivia was responsible for.

"We've got to get out in front of this," she told William as soon as he arrived. "If people believe we did this, it won't matter what the truth is. We're done. The resistance is done."

He nodded and took a seat beside her in the rather Spartan office she'd appropriated. "We need to find Abigail, and I'm worried about Princess Kelsey. She wasn't very far away from one of the blast sites and the com system is down. Obviously. You'll also need to get someone in the military on your side. Might I suggest General Thompson?"

Thompson was the logical choice. While not the most senior officer on the planet, he wasn't political like General Abernathy. She could rely on the latter being in the conservative alliance's pocket.

"Where are our political allies?" she asked.

"Those that escaped are in hiding. Those that didn't are in 'protective custody' at the council building. You can be sure there are more than enough guards to keep them secure. I'm also relatively certain that's where Abigail is hiding, based on the movements of her staff. If we can get in, we might be able to kill two birds at once. So to speak."

She could field a larger force than Abigail expected, that was for sure. The research facility didn't have marines, but they did have people trained to use heavy weapons. They also had powered armor.

That was overkill, honestly. Of course she could breach the defenses, but could she keep her allies alive? That was more difficult to control. She needed eyes in place in the most heavily guarded building on the planet.

"That's the right thing to do," she said at last. "But we have too many crises going on at once. Let's see if I can take one of them out of play."

Her tech team had a command center set up for her use. It had plenty of high-tech gear capable of communicating with whomever she wished.

She pulled the lead tech aside. "I need to speak to General Thomson. How long is that safe to do? I don't care to bring an armed assault down on us."

"Me, either," the woman said. "I can bounce your call around the planet any number of times, but I wouldn't chance more than a couple of minutes. We won't know if they've traced us, but I can't see how anyone could do it in that short amount of time."

"I suppose I'll have to talk fast. Set it up."

That took a comically short period of time. The woman walked over to her console, tapped a few buttons, and nodded to Olivia. "Use the built-in screen right here."

Olivia initiated a connection from a number in her contact list and waited. A man in a green uniform appeared. It wasn't General Thompson, but she recognized his chief of staff. "Colonel Wells, I need to speak with the general right away."

The man looked somewhat surprised to see her. "He's busy, but I'm sure he'll make time for you, Coordinator. Hold one moment."

The screen blanked and came back to life a few seconds later. General Thompson stared out at her. "Coordinator. I've got my hands full at the moment, and I'm not even certain I should be speaking with you. Deputy Coordinator King claims to have proof that you're behind the mass murder of millions of our citizens."

"I think we both know who's lying, but allow me a minute to walk you through this. For the record, I had nothing to do with this atrocity. I'm horrified and so angry that I could kill her and the bastard she works for."

He nodded. "She swore something very similar to that only a few minutes ago. You'll need to do better than that."

"Are you incompetent, Dwight?"

"Excuse me?"

"You heard me. Can you tie your own shoes?"

"If that's all you have to say, I'll go back to the tasks demanding my attention."

"You're supposed to say 'of course not,' to which I'd cleverly ask where the pinnace came from."

He frowned. "The pinnace?"

"Yes, the one that tried to kill me. Did you detect an extra one coming down from orbit? Did it come from the island? Surely, someone tasked with keeping us safe from the 'Fleet menace' would notice a little thing like that."

"No. It came from nowhere and went back when it was done."

"Isn't that a little convenient? Particularly since I'm supposedly in league with those very same Fleet officers. The basic story just doesn't hold together. I had no reason to fake my own death, much less blame Fleet. They had nothing to do with this, but Abigail King did."

He sighed. "I want to believe you, I truly do. Nothing I've seen about you screams 'mass murderer,' and I'd like to think my judgment isn't that flawed. But I can't just come out and support you without proof."

"So don't," she said. "Just don't allow Abigail to steal our world away from us. The Fleet personnel on that island aren't a threat to us. If they wanted to blow up a city from orbit, they could do it without a problem. We know that all too well. Just leave them be and focus on saving as many people as you can."

He shook his head. "You're behind the times, Coordinator. The situation in orbit has changed. Those nuclear blasts weren't just terrorist attacks. They somehow generated powerful bursts of energy that wiped the orbital bombardment platforms away like they were paper."

"What!? Are you sure?"

His smile was grim. "That response, more than anything, convinces me that you're telling the truth. Yes, I'm quite certain.

"The fourth blast crippled the Fleet superdreadnought. It's tumbling into a decaying orbit as we speak. If it doesn't come crashing down into the atmosphere like a massive shooting star, it'll be the next best thing to a miracle."

* * *

KELSEY CAME GROGGILY BACK to consciousness. At first, she didn't know where she was. Then she recognized the armor she was wearing. Finally, she remembered the explosion.

That brought her the rest of the way awake in a hurry.

She was standing somewhere, but it was dark. Pitch black.

It's good to see you awake again, Kelsey.

"Ned. Where am I? The bottom of the ocean?"

I'm certain not even this armor could take that. We're about a kilometer offshore. The water pressure isn't tremendous, so we're probably only deep enough to prevent light from filtering down.

"This thing doesn't have a grav unit. Great. That means I get to walk back to shore."

I'm sure the driver would happily trade places with us.

That's when she remembered the poor man. He wouldn't have survived a shock wave like that. Of course, there were probably plenty of people in that city that wished they'd died so cleanly.

"We have to get out of here. Which way is shore?"

Turn right. More. Stop. It's directly ahead.

Kelsey started walking. It would take a while to get to shore. Hopefully, the Fleet personnel on those lifts had been far enough away from the blast.

"Who the hell would do something like this? It's crazy!"

You'll get no argument from me. Did you notice the energy shooting upward?

"That beam? Yes. What was it?"

I suspect the weapon was a bomb-pumped laser. A special core focuses the blast into a coherent beam of energy. It only survives for a moment, but that's long enough. One that size could have certainly made it out of the atmosphere and struck something in orbit.

"Like our ship? God. We've got to hurry."

She sped up until she was almost racing through the muck. She fell repeatedly but struggled to her feet and slogged on.

Getting to the surface faster won't change anything. I hope that your brother made it, I really do, but falling into a hole you can't climb out of won't be doing him any favors.

"And that's the difference between being a human being and a copy of one. I don't know if you're really an AI or not, but you don't remember what it's like to be this desperate."

Perhaps you're right. Or it might just be that I don't know them as well as I know you. I don't want you to die when a few minutes will make no difference at all.

What will you do when you get to shore? You can't call them. With the nearby blast, you might not be able to call anyone else on the planet, either. You need a plan, Kelsey. Stop rushing around mindlessly and figure out what you need to do.

Dammit. Dammit. What to do? What would Jared do?

"The people on the lifts. The Fleet coms are hardened. They'll still be working. We have to find a vehicle and circle around until we find them."

There you are. Now, make it happen. Without killing us.

* * *

Jared struggled back to his feet. "Status?"

Zia stood beside the helm with blood streaming down her face. "Our drives are down, and so are all the fusion plants. We have a hull breach in engineering."

He blanched. "What's our course? *Invincible*, are you online?"

The AI failed to respond.

"We're tumbling," Zia said, "but I think that blast of power to the drives may have kicked us into a higher orbit. Stand by... Yes, we're going to curve up and then pass close to the atmosphere. Maybe too close, but we've got about an hour to fix that."

"What the hell happened?" He staggered over to where Roger lay sprawled on the deck. The man had a nasty gash on his forehead, but he was breathing. The rest of the bridge crew were getting up, most with minor injuries.

Talbot was helping Elise to her feet. Neither of them seemed seriously injured.

"I'm checking the scanner records on this console now," Zia said. "It looks like there was another nuclear explosion on the planet below our position in orbit. It went off about twenty seconds after the rest. There was some kind of beam that shot out of the atmosphere and hit us."

She tapped the console to go to a different display. "*Invincible* brought up the battle screens and accelerated right before it went off. The beam only struck us a glancing blow. It almost missed us entirely."

"If that was winging us, I don't want to know what a direct hit was like."

"No, sir, you don't. The two orbital bombardment stations we had in scanning range are gone. The first blasts took them out. There's nothing but debris left. I'd be willing to bet the third station was destroyed in a similar fashion."

The bridge lights flickered and came on. He checked the ship's status through his implants. One of the fusion plants was back online.

Someone in engineering was still making things happen. He pinged Baxter's implants.

You still there?

Barely. The decompression didn't happen all at once. We got our masks on in time. Some kind of electromagnetic pulse took down the drives and fusion plants. You know, the ones that are hardened to prevent that sort of thing. What the hell was that?

Ask me after you get the drives online. We have about an hour before we find out what an uncontrolled atmospheric entry feels like from the inside.

Shit.

"*Invincible* is back online," Zia said.

"Indeed I am. I apologize for my unscheduled nap. An exceptionally powerful electromagnetic pulse caused me to reboot."

Jared glanced at the lift doors as they opened and a medical team rushed in. "I'm just happy to have you back with us, and that you saved our hides. What happened down there?"

"I hypothesize the explosions were bomb-pumped lasers. I realized that the blasts destroyed the orbital bombardment stations and that we were almost directly over a city like the others. I felt it was prudent to change locations in an expeditious manner."

"You did the right thing," Jared said with feeling. "Someone without any scruples for human life planned for this long and hard. Those didn't happen in a day or a week. This has been in the works for a long time. The question is, what's their next step?"

"Perhaps we'll be able to figure that out once we restore our scanners to full capability."

Jared checked them. Almost all the scanner units were inoperative, and they only had a view of their immediate surroundings. They couldn't detect another vessel if they had to.

They also couldn't dodge another of those bomb-pumped lasers until Baxter brought the drives back online. If there was one more down there waiting for them to travel to the right part of the sky, they were dead.

28

A bigail felt trapped. Yes, previous administrations had built the council building to withstand a riot, and she had security units all around it, but she was sitting here waiting for Olivia to strike. Her now-discredited ex-boss had to take action against her—and soon—if she expected to have any chance of winning this fight.

She thought many bad things about Olivia West, but stupidity was not one of the woman's failings. She *would* strike back, probably with more force than Abigail's advisers thought possible. Someone would defect and support the woman. Bastards.

The problem was that Olivia could be anywhere in the city. Hell, anywhere on the planet. And she could find Abigail any time she chose.

That needed to change.

"Have the guards gather our guests," she told her assistant. "We're moving them to a safer location."

The man raised an eyebrow. "It's hard to imagine any place on the planet more secure than this building."

"I'm sure the citizens blown up by the nuclear bombs felt quite similarly."

"A point, I grant you. Where will we be going?"

"The farm. I already have guards on site, and no one knows about it. They can't find us there. If they're stupid enough to attack this building while we're gone, so much the better. That could work out in our favor, too."

Her com signaled. It was Master Calder. She gestured for her assistant to go. "Get everyone moving. I'll join you at the vehicles as soon as I make arrangements."

Master Calder's image appeared on her screen when she keyed the accept button. He seemed pleased. Almost jovial. "Yes, Master?" she asked.

"I wanted to take a moment to congratulate you on turning this situation around, Abigail. I'm very impressed. Moving Operation Damocles up was a risk, but it seems to have paid off. The stations are gone, and we've critically damaged the Fleet superdreadnought. It will enter our atmosphere and burn up in a very short period of time. Well done."

She preened inside at his words but only allowed herself a small smile. "Thank you, Master. I'm very pleased to have made that operation a success. Once I find Olivia West and kill her, we'll have undisputed control of the planet. Do we know where the other Fleet ship is?"

"Our scanner readings are limited from the surface, but I believe it's at Boxer Station or one of the flip points. Now that they don't control the bombardment platforms, we can initiate phase two of Operation Damocles. That's the reason I called. I won't be available while it's in progress, so you're going to have to lead the conservative alliance until I put an end to these rebel interlopers."

Abigail had no idea what phase two entailed, but if it was capable of taking out the remaining warship, she was all for it. Victory was within their grasp.

"I'll take care of everything, Master Calder. You might want to have anything you don't want damaged out of the capital. I've come up with a plan to deal with Olivia once and for all."

He listened to her explanation, nodding his head as she wrapped up. "An excellent ploy. I'll notify everyone. Give us an hour before you act."

"That may not be possible," she said. "I won't be the one initiating the events."

"True. Do what you can and give everyone a warning once things kick off. I'll talk with you shortly. By this time tomorrow, the last decade will be only a bad memory. We'll claim our future and restore the Lord to power. Until then, good luck."

"To you as well, Master."

Once he ended the call, she went out in search of her assistant. She found him discussing the new plans with the chief of Council Security. That worthy had been secretly in her pay for quite a while, though the blackmail material she had on him was more than enough to assure his cooperation. If anyone else knew his dirty little sex secrets, he'd never see the outside of a cell.

The man bowed as she joined them. "Coordinator."

She'd arranged a farce of a council meeting an hour ago to impeach Olivia and install herself as their newest head of state. Finally.

"Chief Yancy. I want the prisoners moved out to a facility my assistant will designate. Quietly. I don't want anyone to know they've been moved."

He nodded. "I'll see that it's done, but some people are going to see them being moved inside the building. I can minimize that by clearing the area around the parking bay, but people will notice."

"So see that anyone that knows goes along for the ride. You're imaginative. My private file on you makes that abundantly clear. I don't care what you have to do or who you detain to make that happen.

"Also, I'll have a special delivery coming in later today. Grant the people bringing it full access to the vault. They'll be incorporating some new equipment. It's very secret, so no one is to hamper them or attempt to inspect anything. They'll seal the vault when they finish. Understood?"

He bowed again. "Yes, Coordinator."

"Excellent. Now, I'll be going out in advance of the prisoners. Let's get things set up so that no one is aware that I'm gone."

Her assistant smiled. "I have just the thing, Coordinator. If you record another public address, we can send it out after everyone has left. Mention that you're staying in the council building until you capture the criminals behind this despicable deed. Then everyone will see what you expect them to see."

"I like that. Let's go take care of that little detail and get the hell out of here."

* * *

KELSEY WAS EXCEPTIONALLY glad once she got to shallower water. The light filtering down from above made walking through the muck easier. Once the silt changed to sand, it became simple.

She wasn't sure what people would think when her head broke the surface, but that turned out not to be a problem. The beach was deserted.

The city in the distance was burning. Based on the number of air cars she saw, the people that could were fleeing, most likely afraid of radiation or a second explosion. Those that weren't running away were heading *toward* the city. People there needed rescuing. That covered both sides of human nature.

With no one standing around to gawk at her, she popped her helmet and took in a deep breath. The smell of fire dominated even the salt of the ocean. Her suit's built in rad detector was reading higher than normal background, but not outrageously so.

It would be worse the closer one got to the city. Many, many people would die before they could get adequate medical treatment for radiation sickness. The Rebel Empire's rejection of medical nanites would seal their fate.

"Ned, can we bring down the medical nanites from Boxer Station and help these people?"

I'm afraid not. They require implants to function. Civilian implants are fine, but they take time to build and install. These people don't have that kind of time. Realistically, every ship and medical center on this planet will need to make rad pills as fast as they can. It won't be nearly enough, but it's all we can do.

The realization that millions of survivors would still die crushed her, but she didn't have time to mourn them now. She linked her implants to the Fleet com and saw that Ross was still in range. Kelsey breathed a sigh of relief and called him.

"Princess Kelsey?" he asked.

"Command Master Chief. I'm glad to hear your voice. Are you okay?"

"We're fine, but we feared the worst when you didn't answer our calls."

She looked back out over the waves. "That's what happens when you sink to the bottom of the ocean. Where are you?"

"We're in the outskirts of the city. We're digging people out of the rubble and using the lifts to get them out of the radiation zone."

She hadn't expected anything less. "What are the radiation readings? I don't want anyone staying longer than they can tolerate. Medical care is going to be hard to come by for a while."

"We're good, actually. The buildings in the city center took most of the damage and shielded the suburbs from a fair share of the fallout. Also, we have rad pills. The military cordon around the island is lifted, and we have pinnaces inbound with medical supplies and more troops."

"What about *Invincible*?"

"They're alive, but the ship is damaged. They need to get the drives back online as soon as possible to avoid entering the atmosphere. Once the pinnaces drop off the medical supplies and marines to help with SAR, they'll join the rest going up to help."

"Give one my location. I'm going up. I'll be the short woman in powered armor."

"Will do, Highness. Ross out."

She only had to wait a few minutes before a pinnace came swooping out of the sky and landed near her, blowing sand in every direction.

Kelsey charged up the ramp and grabbed on as it lifted off aggressively. The bay was empty except for one marine acting as the crew chief.

"Highness, the pilot asked for you to come to the flight deck, but I don't think you'll fit."

Not a chance in this armor. "I'll take the marine command console and call him from there, Sergeant."

She strapped herself to the wall behind the console and opened a channel to the flight deck. A Fleet officer with a headset on appeared. That was new. He must have implants.

The man glanced at her. "Princess Kelsey, Admiral Mertz asked me to brief you. We'll be docking with *Invincible* in about twenty minutes."

"Lay it out, Lieutenant."

"The ship's drives are offline. The admiral doesn't think they're going to be operational soon enough to help. He's ordered the crew to prepare to abandon ship while we use all the small craft to try and shift their course."

The idea made sense. When they'd found *Courageous*, they'd had to stop her spin with a pinnace. A lot of them working together might be able to affect a ship as large as the superdreadnought. If they had time.

"What are the chances?"

"*Invincible* gives us maybe thirty percent."

"Not good enough. There has to be something else we can do."

"If you have any ideas, Highness, I'm sure the admiral would *love* to hear them."

"I'll think about that. Get up there quick while I take care of one last thing."

* * *

In the end, Sean hadn't had to stop the marine from giving the man the closest shave of his life. The prisoners hadn't been able to give them a decisive clue, but they'd obviously told her everything they could think of that might be relevant.

The best piece of information they had was something the woman had overheard one of the deputy coordinator's guards mention. He'd said something about "the farm," and another man had quickly shut him up. So their comrades were probably somewhere outside the city.

With all the nuclear explosions, that might be for the best.

All they had to do was figure out where this farm might be located. For that to happen, they needed information that he didn't know how to acquire.

His civilian com chirped. It was an unknown number. He considered not answering it but decided that Ross or the admiral might have picked up a new unit.

"Hello?"

"Commander Meyer," a female voice said. "This is Coordinator West. I hope I haven't caught you at a bad time."

He blinked in shock. She was the last person he'd expected to be calling him. He almost disconnected, but if she were tracking them, she already had their location.

"No, this is a perfect time, Coordinator. We're just sitting around mulling over a problem. What can I do for you?"

"I have a favor to ask. And, before you become overly concerned, I've formed an alliance with Admiral Mertz and Princess Kelsey. Yes, they've read me in on your secret. I'm not sending anyone after you. You're perfectly safe.

"Well, unless the security forces catch you first for all the damage you caused in that wild ride through the city. Have you considered a career in racing?"

More like the demolition derby. "If things don't start looking up, I might. What can I do for you, Coordinator?"

"I need some people skilled in combat to undertake a rescue operation under fire. Princess Kelsey said that you might also need my help in finding the lost prisoners. I'll give what help I can in any case, but there are some important people that need saving, too.

"She and Admiral Mertz have more pressing matters to attend to, and you're the senior Fleet officer left on the planet. His Fleet, anyway. There are a number of your marines available, but only if you agree."

Sean considered her offer and decided he had nothing to lose by sharing what he knew. "I'll need to make a call first. Who are we rescuing, and why don't you have the people to do it?"

"The military is sitting out my struggle with Abigail King. I have some skilled fighters, but we're talking about storming the planetary council building. It's a fortress. Abigail has a number of my allies in that building, and I'd like to get them back alive and put her on trial for mass murder."

He snorted softly. "There's nothing I'd like more than to make that woman pay. Not only for what she did to my people but for what she did to yours. As I said, I'll call you back once I see what I can find out. Do you know anything about a farm that might be associated with King?"

"Not off the top of my head. You make your call, and I'll make a few of my own. Then we'll see if we can't ruin Abigail King's day."

29

O livia had a brief conversation with her tech wizard and started the woman searching for data on any farm that might be associated with Abigail. By the time she had that in motion, Commander Meyer had called her back.

"I've spoken with the marines on the ground," he said. "They managed to get through to Admiral Mertz. I have his blessing to help you.

"Here's what I'm proposing. You'll need to get the marines out of the city by the coast. They're assisting in search and rescue. Take them to the island, and they can draw combat gear. Once they have that, you'll need to provide their rides. All the pinnaces are helping in orbit."

She nodded to herself. That matched what she'd heard. "I have the transport available. With all of this moving around, I think we'll need to hit the council building sometime before dawn. That leaves us time to rescue your people if I can find any farm or rural property that is associated with Abigail in any way."

"That works for me. I can give you an address to pick us up. We'll need combat gear for a dozen marines. I suggest you pick us up now, and we can coordinate what needs to happen next."

That suited her just fine. "Give me the address, and I'll send someone right away. Thank you."

She disconnected the call and turned to William. "We'll need someone from Grant to bring the pinnace, if they have it put back together, and some weapons for Commander Meyer. I don't want to divert any of the other transports."

He shook his head. "That's not going to be possible. We've already sent the pinnace to assist *Invincible*. I spoke with Captain Black and authorized him sending it. In fact, I'm going to be joining him in trying to save that ship."

Olivia blinked in surprise. "Okay, I can see sending the pinnace up to help. Exactly how is your presence supposed to improve their odds?"

"Because I'll be flying another ship up to add one more set of grav drives."

"You can fly? All they have left is the fighter. Surely that won't help something so large."

"You don't think I could fly a fighter? I'm sure I'd be dashing. No, there's another ship. It hasn't flown in a very long time, but the automatics say it's still functional. It might just make the difference between success and failure. And yes, I'm trained to fly a ship. It's just been a while."

She didn't know what to say. It wasn't as though he needed her permission. "Good luck. Come home to Craig. And me, of course."

He gave her a florid bow. "I shall return. I'll want your promise that you'll be careful. If Abigail kills or captures you, I'll be devastated."

"We have a pact, then." She rose to her feet and gave him a hug. "Good luck."

Once he was gone, she went out to find her tech. "Tell me you have something."

The woman looked up from the console she was working at. "Several things, actually. Deputy Coordinator King—now styling herself with your title, by the way—made another public statement. It was more of the same, but she did confirm our suspicions she was inside the council building by word and deed."

"How so?"

"The address was filmed in your office. She also mentioned she was going to stay there 'working for the good of the people of Harrison's World' until you were brought to justice. The number of security people around the building is becoming ludicrous. Surely all those people have something better to do than guarding some political gasbag."

The woman paused for a moment. "Present company excluded."

"Thanks for that," Olivia said dryly. "Any word on where this farm might be?"

"Possibly." The woman manipulated her screen and displayed a map of the area. "Deputy Coordinator King's family owns a number of agricultural facilities in the area surrounding the capital."

Olivia examined the map closely. It showed a dozen large properties. "We'll need to scout them. Can you get an enlarged image of all of them?"

"I'm not plugged into the satellite network, and someone has been cutting off my access. They haven't frozen me out, but I'm certainly not able just to waltz into that kind of system anymore. It might take me a while."

"Unless you'd care to drive out there personally, I'd suggest you get busy."

* * *

JARED RESISTED the urge to go down to engineering. That wouldn't make any of this go faster, and it might slow them down. The pinnaces and cutters were doing what they could to alter *Invincible*'s course, but it was increasingly looking as though they wouldn't make enough of a difference to save the ship.

The crew would be able to use the escape pods, but the loss of the massive ship would hurt the Empire badly. The loss of the AI would be even worse. They didn't have enough time to get the computer removed.

Ginnie Dare and *New York* were racing in from the flip point, but they'd be hours too late to do any good. Unless of course he managed to save the ship. Several pinnaces had managed to match the ship's uncontrolled tumble and were using their drives to stabilize her as much as they could.

The lift doors opened, and Princess Kelsey rushed onto the bridge. She wore a massive suit of armor, though she held the helmet in the crook of her arm. "It wasn't my fault."

He felt the corners of his mouth twitch. "I must not have heard what happened yet. What disaster did you not cause?"

"Any of this. I just wanted the record to show that for once. How are we doing?"

"Not good. The small craft are giving everything they have, but it's not going to be enough. I'm preparing to give the order to abandon ship. Unless, of course, Baxter pulls off a miracle."

Kelsey stood beside one of the backup consoles. "Do you think there's much chance of that?"

"Honestly? No. You know what galls me? We're not that far away from having enough thrust. If we had three or four more pinnaces, we'd squeak by. We'd skip off the atmosphere and probably burn off every external fixture on the ship, but we'd survive long enough for the destroyers to get here."

"How long do we have?"

He checked the countdown timer in his head. "Five minutes until I have to order the crew to the pods. Ten minutes until we enter the atmosphere. I'll order the small craft to break away as soon as we begin the evacuation."

She shook her head. "There has to be a way. *Invincible*, is there anything on the ship that can give us the extra boost? What if we vented the atmosphere out the back?"

"While clever, that would not generate sufficient thrust," the AI said.

"We need more ships," Kelsey said.

He agreed, but they were using all they had. "The resistance sent up their pinnace. It's helping. Lord Hawthorne is bringing a ship up. It won't get here in time. That's it for every small craft in the area."

"Actually, it isn't," *Invincible* said. "Scanners are back online, and I'm picking up another pinnace. It has already left the area around Harrison's World."

"What?" Jared accessed the scanners through his implants and saw that *Invincible* was correct. There was a pinnace racing toward…a gas giant in the outer system away from the flip point? That didn't make any sense.

Kelsey must've been checking it, too. "Why is it going all the way out there? It has to be the pinnace that tried to kill Coordinator West."

"And we have no way of catching it, either." Jared checked the clock and their updated trajectory. "Time to call this. I'm sorry, *Invincible*."

"As am I, Admiral. If only the engines in these small craft were more powerful. I'll miss seeing how this story turns out. Good luck."

Kelsey frowned. "Wait. Can't we make them more powerful? What limits their thrust?"

"Safety interlocks," Jared said. "Those grav drives might explode if pushed too hard."

"And an explosion would be worse than our current problems how?"

He followed her train of thought and decided she might have a point. It would put the pilots in grave danger, but if they volunteered…

"*Invincible*, contact the pilots. See if they're willing to take the risk."

A few moments later, the AI responded. "All are prepared to risk it, Admiral. The danger is high, though. I recommend everyone abandon ship before you put your plan into effect."

"Open a ship-wide channel. Tie in every suit com as well."

"Ready, Admiral."

"All hands, this is Admiral Mertz. We're going to try one last thing to save the ship, but we can't do it with you on board. Abandon ship. All hands abandon ship. Godspeed."

An undulating warning sounded on every speaker at maximum volume. It announced the absolute worst case for any ship.

Swarms of emergency pods jettisoned from the hull. They darted away at savage velocities, designed to carry their precious cargo clear of whatever was going to kill the ship. They all angled down toward the planet's surface, their beacons screaming for rescue.

He looked at the bridge crew. "I believe you have a pod waiting for you, too."

Zia shook her head. "I'm the captain of this ship, sir. I decline to leave her before everyone is safely away. Everyone else, you heard the Admiral."

No one moved. Kelsey put her hands on her hips. "Jared, you're wasting time. Save this ship. If it doesn't work, then we can run for our lives."

"So much for me being noble. *Invincible*, have the pilots disabled their safeties?"

"They have, Admiral. All report ready for maximum acceleration."

"Everyone strap in. This might be *very* rough. Align the ship as you see fit and go, *Invincible*."

The crew tightened their restraints. Kelsey, who couldn't use any of the seats in her armor, locked her helmet down and grabbed a console.

The increase in acceleration wasn't much, but he saw an immediate effect. Their course slowly began to change. Bit by bit, it edged closer to being enough.

Then a massive impact rocked the ship. Fresh alarms wailed.

"One of the cutters exploded, Admiral. Hull breach amidships. We're beginning to rotate. I calculate less than a fifty percent chance this vessel will rebound from the atmosphere. I recommend that you order the others to cease acceleration and abandon ship."

He nodded. "Kelsey, please accompany the bridge crew and abandon ship. I'm going to stay and try to make this work."

"We both know you can't move me, so let's save the theatrics and get on with this."

Silence reigned for a few seconds. "Well, then. One last roll of the dice. We'll know how this turns out in sixty seconds. It's been an honor, everyone."

He sent the order for the small craft to break away. This was it. Either they'd make it on their own or they wouldn't make it at all.

It didn't take long before he felt the ship punching through the upper regions of the atmosphere. Even a massive vessel like this could move in odd ways when meeting an almost fluid resistance. The exterior scanners showed quite the light show as they went deeper.

At least until the drag ripped off the exterior scanner arrays. Shortly after that, it started raising the hull temperature. That temperature change would be the only way they'd know if they made it back out of their death dive.

The gentle movements of the ship became wild bucking in a much shorter time than he'd thought possible. Kelsey had the worst time of it. The console she was holding onto broke loose and sent her tumbling.

That scared him to death, but she grabbed onto another one and braced herself under it. "I'm fine. This tumbling can't hurt me in my armor. I'm more worried about smashing one of you."

"The temperature is leveling off," *Invincible* said. "I believe we may be skipping back off the atmosphere. Much the same as a thrown stone skips across water."

"How do you even know about that?" Jared asked. "And as a warning, those sink in the end."

"The video collection in the library is quite instructive. If we are skipping out of the atmosphere, we should have enough time for *Ginnie Dare* and *New York* to arrive. They can tow us into a stable orbit."

Zia turned to face him. "The hull temperature is definitely leveling off. We're not going deeper into Harrison's World's atmosphere."

That brought a loud cheer from the rest of the bridge crew and a sigh of relief from him. "Well done, everyone. Well done."

"Thank the small craft pilots," his flag captain said. "They really saved our bacon."

"Do we have communication? Can we get them to return and help stabilize the orbit until the destroyers get here?"

Zia shook her head. "We're completely cut off. No communications, no scanners. No weapons, for that matter. The beam arrays are gone. The missile tubes are intact, but the hatches will be welded shut. We also lost our flip vanes. We're trapped in this system until we can replace them."

Kelsey climbed out from under the console she'd used as cover. She'd bent its leg columns with her grip. She pulled her helmet off and shook out her hair. "That beats the alternative. I'd rather have to wait to leave than never get out of here at all."

"Speaking of not being able to go anywhere, we need to find out what that pinnace is up to. If they think it's worth doing, we have to stop them."

Jared nodded. "We need one of the probes launched after it. Make that a priority, Zia, and find some way to get in touch with *Ginnie Dare*. I want them in pursuit as soon as possible."

Zia turned to her console. "Aye, sir. I'll send someone out a lock to look over the probe launcher and to make an estimate of our new course. They can use the suit com to get in touch with the pinnaces. One of them can relay to *Ginnie Dare*."

Jared rose to his feet. "You forget it's just us. I'll go take a look and get this rolling myself. Come on, Kelsey. You can make sure I don't fall off."

The hostile pinnace's course worried him. What could it be racing toward? Obviously, something that the enemy thought might be helpful against his ships. If it could take out *Courageous*, it was nothing to sneer at. He had to stop them.

30

Sean breathed a sigh of relief when he got word that *Invincible* had survived her near-death experience. He hadn't known the ship even existed before today, but he grasped how important something like it would be to the Empire. No matter what Captain Breckenridge thought, war with the AIs was inevitable. Hell, it was already happening. They had to have the ships and technology to win it.

New York was already in orbit and helping to get the crippled superdreadnought into a stable orbit. *Ginnie Dare* was more than halfway to the gas giant the enemy cutter was running toward. It wouldn't be able to stop them from getting there, but Captain Roche would be right on its heels.

Meanwhile, Sean had his own problems.

The ride Olivia West promised arrived on schedule. It was a fully loaded vegetable lift, packed to the gills with harvested corn. It was in large bins that they had to unload and stash in the safe house before they could go to her secret headquarters.

Frankly, if this was the most effective ride she could manage, she might be in an even worse position than he'd feared.

Half an hour later, they had the lift cleared, and everyone piled into the back. The prisoners came with them. Sean didn't want to leave them where they could cause trouble. If they escaped, they might manage to warn King that Sean was coming.

The lift deposited them all at a nondescript building. It didn't even have obvious guards outside. Inside was a different story.

Squads of armed civilians watched every approach into the building, huddled behind heavy weapons. If the security forces decided to come in here, there'd be a massacre. Of them.

Olivia West met him in a large room that they'd converted into a command center. She came over with her hand extended. "Commander Meyer. Thank you for coming so promptly."

He shook her hand gravely. "It's my pleasure, Coordinator."

"If you and your men will come this way, I have weapons and armor for all of you. A fast car from a secret facility just arrived. It couldn't carry any powered armor, but I'm given to understand none of your people could use it anyway. It requires implants."

He saw a good selection of unpowered armor and standard Old Empire weapons laid out. "This will work just fine, I'm sure." He gestured for the marines to go outfit themselves. "What have you found out about my missing people?"

She looked at his arm and the makeshift sling he was wearing. "I can't help but notice you're injured. You're also limping. Were you injured in the escape?"

"Let's just say that I had an exciting exit from a moving air car. My medic set the broken arm. He thinks the knee is only bruised."

"Then perhaps you'd like to let someone with a medical scanner confirm that, and get some medication for the pain and swelling? You're about to go back into the fight, so you'd best take advantage while you can."

Stubbornness made him want to argue, but he decided that was idiotic. He pulled up a chair and sat. "Thank you."

Coordinator West summoned a woman with a bag emblazoned with the Imperial Red Cross emblem. She set it down beside the chair and pulled out a ridiculously small medical scanner.

"Hi there," she said with a smile. "I'm Doctor Janice Hauptman. I'm an emergency specialist, so you're in good hands. Tell me what happened."

"I rolled out of a fast-moving air car and slammed into something sturdier than myself. The transfer of energy didn't work out in my favor."

"No, it didn't." She ran the scanner over his arm. "It's a clean break, well set. I'll replace the make-do splint with a spray-on that will be more comfortable and sturdier. You're not in any danger from that. Any other issues?"

"My knee's bunged up."

She scanned it. "Ah, yes. It's bruised, and you have some minor tears to the cartilage. You'll want to stay off it."

"Yeah, that's not happening. I have a hundred of my people to rescue. Do you have a shot that can help with the pain? And maybe a knee brace?"

She gave him a disapproving look. "That's not the safest course of action, but I can give you something for the pain and wrap the knee. If it goes out on you, don't blame me."

"I hereby absolve you of all responsibility regarding my health when I pull my next fool stunt."

"My, aren't we grouchy."

"It's been that kind of day."

"True enough," the doctor said. "I'd just delivered your injured compatriots to your pinnace when all hell broke loose, and the coordinator won't let me go do what I need to do."

He understood her anger. "Your day is worse than mine, and it won't be ending any time soon. Did they all get away safely?"

"I assume so. We released all but three of the worst injured. I manipulated the hospital records to show even those people were gone, but we hid them in a different wing of the hospital. They're safe."

"Was Paul Cooley with them?"

She nodded. "He's a friend of yours? He's badly injured, but I'm guardedly optimistic about his recovery."

"Thank God. When all this is over, drinks are on me."

The doctor shook her head slowly. "Things were only just over from the orbital bombardments a decade ago. Those drinks will have to wait a long time."

She finished replacing the cast and gave him a sturdier sling. Then she injected something into his knee that made it immediately feel better. She finished up by wrapping it with something stretchy.

"There you go. I suggest you follow up with one of your medical professionals to get this taken care of as soon as possible."

"Thanks, Doctor. I hope they let you do what you need to do soon."

Coordinator West shook her head from where she was standing nearby. "I wish we could, but the odds are we'll need the good doctor's services when we raid the farm or the council building. I understand that sucks, but it's necessary. Thank you, Doctor."

Once the other woman had departed, Sean gingerly stood and tested his leg. It would do.

"Have you located this farm?"

She nodded. "We think so. There are several possibilities, but one of them has extra vehicles parked nearby. My tech wasn't able to get much of a satellite scan before they locked her out of the system, but only that one agricultural area seems to have that kind of buildup.

"Your marines on the island are going to be here in a couple of hours. I suggest we go out and see for ourselves. If you feel comfortable going in and freeing your people, I'd be happy to loan you my men."

Doing something was better than sitting on his ass. "I'm in, but please tell me you have something better than a vegetable lift to sneak us up in."

"Don't you think that's appropriate? Who would notice a few more around a farm?"

He sighed. "I suppose that makes sense, but the damned things are uncomfortable, and they smell bad."

"Take it out on our mutual enemies," Coordinator West said without any apparent sympathy. "We'll have larger vehicles to come in and pick up your fellows as soon as we get them loose. If they're there. Besides, I'll be with you, so I'll be in the same situation. If you're ready, we should get moving."

* * *

KELSEY STAYED out of the way while Jared focused on stabilizing *Invincible*. William had arrived, and she kept him company as they watched *Ginnie Dare* chase down the fleeing pinnace through their implants.

The superdreadnought was still blind, but William's small ship had scanners capable of seeing what was happening at least as well as *New York*.

"They told me how big she was, but that really doesn't do her justice," he said. "Your ship is monstrously huge."

"And beat to hell," she said. "After the fight with the AI, the bomb-pumped laser, the exploding cutter, and now the dive through your atmosphere, I'm not sure that it wouldn't be quicker restoring one of the other superdreadnought derelicts."

He leaned back in his acceleration couch. "I wouldn't be too sure about that. A lot of the damage is superficial. If you can get the shipyard on Boxer Station back into operation, I think she'll be back into shape quickly."

"Where do you think they're going?"

"The pinnace? I can't say that there's ever been anything worth a damn out at that particular gas giant. If I used the Terra system as an example, it's more like Neptune than Jupiter. Cold, distant, and it doesn't even have any pretty rings. No one ever built remote stations there. I can't think of any visitation at all since the system was settled thousands of years ago."

She shook her head. "There's something there. They blew up the orbitals and ran straight for it, even knowing that we'd send a warship right on their heels. They have a weapon there, or at least some way to defend themselves. We need to be able to sneak up on them."

"Come now," the noble scoffed. "Surely that imposing destroyer of yours will be able to stop them."

"I hope so, but I wouldn't hold my breath if I were you. We need a plan B."

"Perhaps you could use the stealth ship to sneak up on them."

That wasn't a bad idea, she thought, but she rejected it. "It's too slow, and I doubt it's working so well with that massive dent in the side."

"No, and Roger isn't able to fly with the dent in his noggin, either. Too bad we didn't build two."

Perhaps now would be a good time to point out that Persephone *is mostly operational. Her stealth shielding isn't as good as the saucer, but her power plants are online, and she could make the trip, I suspect.*

Kelsey froze as she considered that. Ned was right. The Marine Raider ship was designed to sneak up on people. If things went south, it might be best to have that plan already in motion.

"The little voice in my head has an idea," she said. "Can I borrow your ship? I need to pick up some people and gear."

* * *

JARED WATCHED the scanner feed coming from *New York* through his implants. *Ginnie Dare* was almost to the gas giant. Another hour and he would be in control of the area. The rogue pinnace was already slipping around to the back of the planet.

They'd cut open the probe hatch on *Invincible* and dispatched several to look the area over, but they'd arrive about the same time as the destroyer. He left getting *Invincible* into a stable configuration to Zia while he and a hastily gathered staff kept an eye on the big picture.

He really needed to form a permanent staff. The electrons were still settling in on his promotion to flag rank and events had been occurring at a rapid pace, but he wasn't just commanding a single ship anymore. A staff would help keep him organized.

Which would be a blessing right about now. The race to the gas giant was far from the only crisis on his plate. The virtual destruction of his superdreadnought flagship, the coup on Harrison's World, the rescue operations at the nuked cities, and the repair mission at the Pentagar-bound flip point were all boiling over at the same time. He was losing track of the details.

He'd moved back to the flag bridge just to stay out of Zia's way. With all its stations, it allowed the crew members Zia had seemingly plucked at random from the crew to work all around him, theoretically only disturbing him when they had something requiring his attention.

That was not how it worked, of course. He was walking around the compartment, getting updates from each group as they happened. He needed to work on his multitasking skills.

Still, it kept him from going crazy trying to watch everything in real time.

"Admiral," one of his new staff officers called out after a bit more than an hour, "*Ginnie Dare* is approaching the gas giant."

He moved over to the man's station. "What do the probes show?"

"Nothing seems out of place. They're coming around the curve of the planet, following the path the pinnace took."

Jared used his implants to read the probes' findings for himself. *Ginnie Dare* had her weapons armed and her scanners on high. She was ready for trouble.

Just not the kind of trouble that came looking for her.

Active targeting scanners from the gas giant lit the destroyer up, and two dozen missiles came boiling out of the atmosphere almost in the destroyer's face.

Commander Roche changed course to get his ship away from the planet and started firing his antimissile railguns. He stopped maybe a quarter of them before the rest blotted his destroyer from the sky.

The probes picked up a number of distress beacons, so some of his people had escaped.

"Send a recall signal," Jared said grimly. "Get the pods moving in this general direction. There's something down there with a lot of firepower, so we can't risk coming to them."

The probes weren't seeing any large pieces of debris from the destroyer. She was gone. So was most of her crew, in all probability. That was an unexpected gut punch.

There'd be time to grieve later. "Take a probe in deeper. Put it on an automatic course to orbit the planet once. We need to see what we're facing, and it won't be able to signal us until it gets back out of the atmosphere."

"Aye, sir."

Several minutes passed while the commands made their way to the probe, and the view from the probe changed as it angled into the outer reaches of the gas giant's atmosphere. The signal faded before they saw anything. They'd just have to hope the probe survived to tell them what it found.

The emergency pods slowly began reporting in. Only twelve of them had ejected in time, none of them fully loaded. Sixty-three survivors out of hundreds. Scott Roche was not among them. The senior surviving officer was Lieutenant Angela Ellis, *Ginnie Dare*'s marine detachment commander.

Jared had known they might find trouble at the gas giant, and so had Scott Roche. He'd taken every precaution, but it hadn't made one bit of difference. Now Eliyanna Kaiser's *New York* was the only surviving ship from Breckenridge's task force. He'd send her out to recover the pods at a safe distance as soon as he could.

Half an hour later, *Invincible* reacquired the probe's signal from the other side of the gas giant.

"Incoming telemetry," the man said.

Jared focused on the detailed picture emerging from the passive scans. The probe had found a small station high in the planet's atmosphere. The station had an array of missile tubes on its upper surface, too, so it was the source of that massive salvo.

It was also transmitting a signal deeper into the atmosphere. The probe noted that and turned to follow it down.

The obscuring clouds vanished abruptly. The view was stunning. A layer of colorful clouds above and below sandwiched a sky as clear as a sunny day back home.

Floating in the middle of that was a massive space station. Mighty arms sprang out of its body and linked to four vessels on humongous grav cradles.

Each of those ships was instantly recognizable as a battlecruiser. The probe couldn't tell, but Jared was certain the bad guys were bringing them to life.

Hiding them there was brilliant. The atmospheric pressure at that depth was low enough that the large ships could maneuver without burning up like *Invincible* almost had. They could lurk just out of sight and let the station support them.

His forces, in their current condition, couldn't stand against that kind of firepower. Those ships had to be computer controlled, just like the destroyers the AI had had before they'd defeated it. Those had almost wrecked his fleet.

The firepower he was looking at now would finish the job as certainly as night followed day.

31

Olivia walked through the woods behind the Imperial Marines. They in turn trailed her scouts. It seemed they were traveling in the order of most silent to least.

The scouts were woodsmen, chosen because they knew what to look for. Things that might be out of place in the forest near the agricultural area. They were ghosts, flitting through the trees and underbrush as though they were never there.

The marines moved as a group, spearheading the assault task force. Even heavily armored and carrying a ridiculous amount of weaponry, they managed to keep the sound of their passing to the occasional rustle of leaves or swishing limb. Certainly nothing that would carry for any distance.

She, on the other hand, was the one who'd tripped over a log. *After* they'd warned her about it. She might as well go running through the woods, screaming at the top of her lungs. At least that was how she felt.

The rest of the attack force, comprised of more city-oriented members of the resistance, followed farther behind, where their lack of woodcraft kept them out of the range of sharp ears.

Sean Meyer walked beside her and was obviously staying close in case he had to make a grab for her.

The marines had given her a short lecture on things she could do and things she couldn't. That's how she knew she could speak to him softly, but not to whisper. Whispers apparently carried for long distances. That seemed counterintuitive.

She probably should avoid falling down again, too.

They'd parked the lifts some way back at another farm. The farmer in question had come out with a shotgun to see who was there. It had taken some speedy talking to get him to hear them out.

She'd left some men behind to make certain he didn't call anyone, but he didn't seem like a lookout for Abigail.

One of the scouts appeared out of the darkness almost in her face. She hoped she hadn't been about to scream when Commander Meyer clamped a hand over her mouth, but she couldn't be completely certain.

Once the officer seemed satisfied she wasn't going to do anything to give them away, he let her go.

"Thank you," she said softly. She glared at the woodsman. "For God's sake, don't try to scare me to death."

He had the grace to look mildly embarrassed. "Sorry, Coordinator. Our men are at the inside edge of the forest. The main warehouse has people inside. They're showing up clear through the walls in the gear the marines gave us. Too many to count. That building has a butt load of people stuffed inside. Hundreds."

"What about guards?" Meyer asked. Two of the marines were gathered around and listening closely.

"Three sets of them outside the building. They're using lifts to hide behind. Show up just fine on those binoculars." He nodded to the Fleet officer. "We'll be keeping those, if you don't mind."

"You get my people where we can take out the sentries and you can keep the rest of the gear, too," Meyer declared.

The man grinned. "Don't need your people to get those idiots. They're watching things on their coms. Ruined their night vision. They won't see the boys sneaking up."

"I'd appreciate you taking a few marines along," Meyer said dryly. "Just in case they need to shoot someone."

"Then we'd best be about it, before someone that knows their ass from a hole in the ground comes along."

The man led the marines off, and Olivia watched them go with some trepidation. "What exactly did you just give them?"

The Fleet officer grinned. "Nothing too bad, as long as you trust those boys. Night-vision gear, Fleet marine knives, flechette pistols, civilian stunners, and a couple of long-range flechette rifles."

"Sniper rifles? I do trust them, but I bet the game wardens won't be thanking you. If those men aren't poachers on the side, I'd be astonished."

"Then issue them a year-round hunting pass. Think of it as

motivation. They'll work super hard to be sure none of the sentries gets out a peep for that kind of swag.

"Here's what we're going to do. We'll advance until we reach the open area and stop. Once the marines take out the sentries, we'll advance slowly while they secure the exterior of the building. Once we're ready to rush, we go in. Stunners only, unless we absolutely have to kill. We don't know who the bad guys are until they open fire."

Olivia nodded. "I'll leave that in your hands. I'll also stay outside until you give the all clear."

He went off to coordinate with his people and came back a few minutes later. They had to wait about twenty minutes before the woodsman appeared again, this time making some noise to announce his presence.

"We got the guards trussed up. The marines said for you to get into the forward positions."

Meyer clapped him on the shoulder. "Good work. Tell them we'll be along directly."

All the message carrying was necessary because they weren't going to chance someone catching a stray com transmission.

He turned to Olivia once the man was gone. "I'll lead the teams into place. You stay back to the rear and keep low. You'd rather not catch a stray flechette once the party starts."

"No worries there. My security people won't let me anywhere near the fighting. Good luck, and be careful."

It took about half an hour to get everyone in position to attack the building. She prayed there weren't as many guards as the numbers suggested. That would be a disaster. It also wouldn't make any sense. Why have so many people guarding the Fleet prisoners? Most of Abigail's trusted people had to be in the council building.

Olivia never heard the signal to go, but she saw the attack begin. Small charges blew holes in the thin metal walls of the building, and the marines rushed in. Almost immediately, Olivia heard flechette pistols firing. Blue stunner beams strobed in the darkness.

She was behind a lift, but she crouched lower. Her guards watched the attack unfold and kept their weapons ready. In the dark, there really wasn't that much to see.

That is, until one of the large doors abruptly slid open and people poured out into the night. Right toward her hiding spot. Some of her people fired into the enemy with stunners, but there were far too many bad guys for them to stop.

The lead security man cursed and grabbed her shoulder. "Run for the trees. Holloway and Jennings, keep her safe while we cover your withdrawal."

The two men grabbed her and ran for the woods. Someone must've seen them. That was obvious when one of the two men pitched forward, his head a bloody mess.

The other man shoved her toward the trees. "Run!" He whirled and opened fire.

Olivia didn't hesitate. She ran as though her life depended on it.

The people behind her must've had stunners, too. She saw a blue beam snap past her and hit a tree. She threw herself to the side and rolled for cover. She didn't make it, and the world went dark.

* * *

KELSEY HAD STOPPED FEARING for her life months ago, but that didn't keep her heart from rising into her throat when Lord Hawthorne almost crashed them on the island where the people from the various life pods were gathering.

"I thought you knew how to fly," she demanded as the ship settled to the plascrete.

She saw a Fleet guide rising cautiously from behind a blast barrier where he'd thrown himself. The man watched the ship suspiciously, probably not sure it was going to stay still. Kelsey couldn't blame him.

Lord Hawthorne turned toward her. "I did train," he said more than a shade defensively. "I'm a little rusty."

"You don't say."

The people she'd called ahead for came out of a hangar near the ship at a run, Talbot in the lead. He ran up the ramp she'd lowered and made his way to the flight deck.

"That was either the worst landing I've ever seen or the most amazing recovery of a complete guidance failure in history. Which was it?"

The Rebel Empire noble gave the marine a sour look. "I can see why the two of you get along so well."

She laughed. "Tell me you have some pinnace pilots. Please."

"Two of the best," he assured her. "We're going to be stuffed to the bulkheads in this thing. It's designed for three or four dozen people. We'll be dragging along three or four times that number. With the life support gear you brought, we'll be able to make it to *Persephone*, but we won't enjoy it."

"I grabbed everything on your list," she said as she got to her feet. "*Persephone* has two stealthed pinnaces, if they're still functional. We have enough crew for the ship and marines to make an assault on that new base. We just have to get there before those ships come to life.

"I had the crew on Boxer Station send over every engineer they had. If there's a problem with the pinnaces or ship, they'll do the best they can to fix them. They can't mess with *Persephone*'s computer, but it hasn't seen fit to raise a stink about the people we had examining all the systems before now."

The pilots came in and took over for William and herself. She walked William out of the cutter and gave him a hug. The act seemed to surprise him, but he'd get over it.

"You've helped us so much. I'll leave your cutter at Boxer Station. The engineers can give it a good maintenance check while we're gone."

"Be careful, Highness. The cutter doesn't matter. It's a relic of history. You, on the other hand, matter a great deal."

"I'm surprisingly hard to kill. I'll be as careful as the situation allows. See you soon, William."

"Return to your people hale and whole, with the heads of your enemies at your feet, warrior princess." He stepped back and swept into an exquisite bow.

Kelsey was still gaping as he spun on his heel and walked off toward the hangar.

"I'm not doing that," Talbot said as she walked back up the ramp.

"I hope to God no one else is, either. Can you imagine dealing with that all the time?"

The cutter was packed with people. It was going to get smelly fast, based on what she was already sensing. With her enhanced sense of smell, that could get pretty ugly. Good thing she was going to button up in her Raider armor for the trip. She'd snagged it along with everything the marines needed for the assault.

All the equipment reduced the available space even further, but they didn't have a choice. She hoped everyone had used the bathroom. The line would be murder.

"How long for the trip out?" he asked as she got into her armor.

"Three hours with pushing the drives on this thing. One of Baxter's people said it would hold. Then we make the run from Boxer Station out to the gas giant. Call that another five or six, since we don't dare stand out. Any way you cut it, this is going to be a long drive."

She finished buttoning up and began sliding her weapons into their normal locations, including her new swords. She'd brought them along in case things got really bad.

They waited for everyone to get settled in and closed the ramp. The ship was standing room only. The cutter lifted off, and they were on their way to a fight that they had to win. If, of course, they managed to get their ride working.

* * *

JARED SOMEHOW MISSED Lord Hawthorne's cutter leaving Harrison's World. It was already halfway to Boxer Station when one of his staff gave him a status on it.

He called them and asked to speak to Kelsey. She came on a few moments later.

"Bandar here."

"Kelsey, where are you going, and what are you planning to do once you get there?"

"*Persephone*. We're bringing her online. She might be able to get close to that station before it knows we're on the way. I have Talbot and a full crew of marines at my side. If we don't take these ships out, we're all screwed anyway."

"I wish to hell you'd cleared this with me ahead of time."

"It's in the report I sent you before I left."

He brought it up and scanned it. Yes, she'd tacked her intentions at the very end. She'd obviously expected he'd skim the summary. He really needed to read every word next time.

"Remind me to explain the difference between asking permission and begging forgiveness to you at some point," he said with a sigh. "Well, it's too late to stop you now. Do you have enough people?"

"We have almost fifty. A mix of marines and crew. It'll be tight, but we'll manage. Look, you have enough on your plate. I'm going to let you go. Wish me luck."

He sighed and did so before terminating the call. It burned him up that she was rushing off to save them again and he was sitting here, unable to even shoot at anyone if they failed.

That made him pause. He couldn't control any aspect of any of the situations he was monitoring. At this point, he was useless here. That wouldn't be the case if he went out to join them.

From what he remembered of that ship, it could use a lot more crew than they could possibly stuff into that cutter. He had plenty of people to spare on the crippled superdreadnought. They'd been ferrying them up from Harrison's World for the last few hours. Marines, too.

He immediately called Zia to hold two pinnaces. He then compiled a list of crew members that would be of use on the Marine Raider ship. He sent the list to *Invincible* with instructions to summon them to marine country.

Then he called Lord Hawthorne's cutter and informed the pilots of his plan to meet them out there. He ordered them to keep that information to themselves. It was time to turn the tables on Princess Kelsey and do something to help save them.

He left for marine country at a run. He'd have time to get into unpowered armor and vacuum gear. He'd also make sure that every man and woman was as heavily armed and well protected as possible. If they got into a fight, they might need every bit of damage they could deliver.

32

I t took almost an hour for Sean to get the situation at the farm locked down. A hardcore group of fighters took some of the prisoners hostage. Eventually, he sent the marines through the roof and stunned everyone after sharpshooters took out the most fanatic of the defenders with flechettes through the wall.

They'd accounted for the missing Fleet personnel, even if some of them were a bit battered. Seeing Gina the marine holding a sobbing Fleet crewwoman was the highpoint of his week.

There were a number of other prisoners. Sean suspected they were Coordinator West's political allies. He sent some men to round her up.

They came back empty-handed.

Worried, he sent everyone he could spare to scour the area for her. They found the bodies of her guards near the forest but found no sign of the coordinator herself.

"Find me whoever was in charge of this facility," he told one of West's people.

That turned out to be a scientist of some kind. Two grim-faced guards held the man up between them. It looked as though they'd prefer to be marching him outside and shooting him.

Sean followed their lead and gave the man in the lab coat a hard look. "My name is Commander Sean Meyer. These Fleet personnel are my people. I'm told you drugged them and questioned them against their will."

The man drew himself up and stared down his nose at Sean. "I'm Doctor Paul Nelson, and you have no right to—"

"I don't care what your name is or what you object to," Sean said, cutting him off. "You're guilty of kidnapping, torture, and a host of other crimes against people under my command. I could have these men frog march you outside and shoot you in the head. No one would care, and many would thank me. If you want the opportunity of dealing with the civilian authorities instead, you'd better start cooperating. Do you understand?"

The man swallowed noisily and nodded convulsively, unaware of the grins his captors were sporting at the deception. At least Sean hoped they knew he was lying.

"What do you want to know?"

"Someone kidnapped Coordinator West," he said. "I want to know who."

"I have no idea."

"Take him outside and shoot him. Dump the body in the woods near the coordinator's guards."

"Wait!" The scientist dug in his heels as he shrieked. "Wait! Deputy Coordinator King probably took her. She left just after the fighting started and went toward the woods."

Sean held up his hand and stopped the men. "She was here? I thought she was at the council building."

"She wanted everyone to think she was there, but she came here with the political prisoners. When you attacked, her guards took her out toward the woods."

"Where were they going?"

"How should I know?"

He considered the scientist. King hadn't taken him with her, so he might be telling the truth. Maybe. Or perhaps he knew more than he suspected.

"That's not good enough. I need someone here who can lead me to her. If you're not that man, you'd better come up with someone else for me to focus my attention on before I give these boys their marching orders."

"Her personal assistant was here," the scientist said in a voice filled with desperation. "I saw him lying near the questioning equipment. I'll show you. Just don't kill me."

Sean gave the man a long, searching look. "Show me."

The scientist led them to a young man laid out with the other wounded. He'd been stunned but was coming around. Someone had bound his hands together in front of him.

Sean gave the scientist a cold look. "You'd best hope this man has the answers I'm looking for. Put the good doctor into one of the cages he kept my people in."

The guards took the scientist away while Sean knelt at the young man's side. He only had to wait a few minutes before the man was able to process his surroundings.

"What happened?" the man asked.

"I think you can guess," Sean said. "You're Deputy Coordinator King's personal assistant?"

The man blinked at him. "You obviously know that."

"I want to know where your boss is."

"If you don't already know, then I won't tell you."

Sean had heard that tone before. This man wasn't going to cooperate, even if threatened with death. Sean needed another plan.

He searched the man's pockets and found his com. It was locked, of course. "Give me the code."

"No."

Why did everything have to be so hard? He gestured for one of the guards to come over. "This man is an important prisoner. Segregate him and make sure nothing happens to him."

While that was happening, he searched out Coordinator West's tech guru and handed her the com. "Abigail King's personal assistant is here. Another prisoner says that King was here, too. I think she took your boss. Can you crack this?"

The woman took the com and plugged it into a portable computer. It took a ridiculously short amount of time for her to access its contents. "Here we go. I have his contact list, and he's thoughtfully labeled her private com code. It looks like she tried to contact him after the attack, probably to see if he'd escaped. Let's see if she left a message."

An audio-only message began playing. "If you got away, meet me back at the council building. I have West in my custody."

The message terminated without any further pleasantries.

"My, she's a friendly sort," Sean said. "Can you locate that com and confirm where she is?"

"Maybe. I used to have access to all the major planetary systems, but they've been locking me out. That one isn't high priority, so let's find out."

She worked at her computer for a few minutes and grinned. "I'm in. They blocked my original access, but I found a backdoor. Yes. The com is at the council building. It seems to be in the executive wing. I'd wager she's in Coordinator West's office."

"Do you have floor plans for the council building? It might be advantageous to get in through a less obvious route."

She shook her head. "Those kinds of plans aren't available to the general public, and they're not kept on a system I can access from here. That said, it should be possible to find or create access with the right tools. I'd have to be on site to make that happen."

"Gear up. The main force of marines will be ready to assault the building before dawn. Let's see if we can get inside before then. If need be, we can make a hole to let the marines in after we reconnoiter the place."

* * *

Kelsey was pleasantly surprised at how much work the engineering team from Boxer Station had completed on *Persephone*. They'd not only verified the grav drives were fully functional, they'd vetted the fusion plants and sealed off the damaged sections of the ship. The makeshift crew could access every functional area without vacuum suits.

They'd also moved the dead into the damaged section of the ship. That was a relief. She'd not been looking forward to moving the bodies. She could only imagine how bad that would be when they started clearing out the derelicts. There must be millions of dead on those hulks.

She stripped off her armor and put it in a handy corner. Getting out of the overcrowded cutter and being able to stretch her arms felt wonderful. Still, she wished they'd managed to stuff twice as many people into the small ship. They were going to be very undermanned for this flight.

Okay, Ned. Let's have that code. If it doesn't work, we're screwed.

The code will work. Unless, of course, I changed it and don't remember.

You're filled with positive thoughts, aren't you? The code.

He gave it to her, and she accessed the computer. It digested the code for a moment and granted her access.

"I'm in! Holy cow, I'm in! Computer, do you recognize my command authority?"

"This unit has received the appropriate codes from a qualified Marine Raider. This vessel is yours to command, Princess Kelsey Bandar."

"Kelsey is fine. I want a system status check. Is this vessel capable of in-system movement and a stealth approach to a military installation?"

"Grav drives are operating within nominal parameters. Stealth systems are in passive mode. Weapons systems are degraded. Four of six beam emplacements are not operational. Flip drives are offline.

Warning, with the hull breached, this vessel cannot withstand a high speed insertion into atmosphere."

Like the small Pentagaran ship she'd flown on, *Persephone* was capable of landing. It was significantly larger than that other vessel, but the layout of the hull had told her it was possible. No one wasted time streamlining a hull on a ship that had no need to enter atmosphere.

"*Persephone*, do you have any knowledge of how this ship was damaged or of how Captain Ned Quincy died?"

"Affirmative. This vessel attempted to escape enemy pursuit in the Valhalla system by going through a particularly heavy ring of debris orbiting a gas giant. A small, fast-moving object destroyed this vessel's flip drive and killed eight crew members.

"Major Quincy was critically injured during the ensuing rescue operations. His actions saved the lives of three engineers trapped in the wreckage. The medical officer doubted Major Quincy would survive his injuries but placed him in the stasis chamber."

Kelsey considered that. "How did you escape pursuit, and how did the crew die?"

"The pursuing vessel was significantly less fortunate in crossing the ring. Its terminal course took it deep into the atmosphere, where it was destroyed. This vessel escaped into the outer system.

"Repairs to the flip drive proved impossible. The crew used their remaining supplies over the next several months and made the determination to take their lives with drugs in their pharmacology units. Several decades passed before this vessel once more made its way into more traveled areas of the system. At that point, it was recovered and brought here."

"Why didn't you self-destruct or at least wipe your memory?"

"This unit hypothesizes that the rebels believed this vessel to be without power. They never boarded, so this unit was not obligated to wipe its memory."

That was certainly to her benefit. She doubted she'd have been lucky enough to find another one of these vessels intact.

"Warning. Unknown vessels approaching."

Kelsey tapped into the ship's passive scanners. There were two Fleet pinnaces approaching at high speed from the direction of Harrison's World.

"Open a channel to them. Unknown vessels, identify yourselves."

"Kelsey, you're in big trouble."

"Jared, I didn't expect you to chase me down."

"I'm sure you didn't. It just so happens that I have some free time, and I brought some extra Fleet personnel and marines. I assume you don't have a problem with that?"

Considering how shorthanded she was, she was ecstatic. "The more the merrier. I'll meet you at the docking area."

She considered how their arrival changed the mission. "Computer, the crewmen I have with me are not Marine Raiders. Can I authorize them to operate the ship's systems?"

"Yes, Kelsey. Marine Raider vessels are often partially crewed by Fleet officers, though always under the command of a Raider."

"Excellent. One additional question. Do you have complete specs on my implants and all Raider equipment?"

"Yes."

A thrill ran up her spine. It felt like Christmas.

"Upload them to my implants. All of them. Include any classified files you have in storage. I'll review them as time permits." She accessed her implants and granted the computer access to some memory.

"Upload complete."

Kelsey made her way to the docking area with a bounce to her step. She skimmed the implant specifications and grinned. She'd been in the dark for so long. Finally, she had the manuals. Now she wouldn't have to guess what she was capable of anymore.

If, of course, she survived the next few hours.

She transmitted copies of everything to Boxer Station, *Courageous*, and *Invincible*. This information was so difficult to come by that she couldn't chance it being lost again. She locked it down so that only someone of the rank of captain or above could access it, but only if she didn't make it back. After a moment, she added Carl Owlet and Doctor Leonard to the list.

The docking hatch slid open as she arrived. Jared and a stream of Fleet officers and marines came out. Most headed for the areas of the ship where they'd be working, but some followed Jared as he stepped up beside her.

"We're really going to have to work on our coordination," he said as she led him back toward the bridge. "If you'd simply asked me for help, I could've sent a lot more people."

"I was afraid you'd try to stop me."

He shook his head. "Not this time. One way or the other, we need to stop these bastards. If they get those battlecruisers online, we're screwed. Does this ship have weapons?"

"Not many. It comes with six beam emplacements, but only two are working. Other than that, we're ready to go. I've accessed the computer, and it has accepted me as its commander."

He smiled. "So, now you get to command in space, too. You can appoint yourself an admiral."

"That's not funny. I'll never know enough to command a ship in space. I'm happy to have you to lean on."

They arrived at the bridge, and she spoke. "Computer, I'm placing Admiral Jared Mertz in command of this vessel."

"Negative. Only a Marine Raider may command this vessel. This unit cannot accept Admiral Mertz as the commanding officer. However, you may designate him as your operational delegate."

"Well, I suppose that'll have to do. Make it so. Are you ready to move, *Persephone?*"

"Yes, Kelsey."

She turned to Jared. "The ship is yours, Admiral. Let's go take these bastards out."

He smiled grimly. "It'll be my pleasure, Captain Bandar."

33

O livia awoke with a massive headache. She'd been stunned. It took her a minute to realize that Abigail had tied her to a chair in her own office at the council building. And not the comfortable one behind the desk.

Abigail King sat in that one. The bitch looked smugly pleased with herself.

"It's about time you woke up. I've been overseeing the consolidation of the planet while you've been napping. I hope it doesn't irk you too badly that I'm savoring the moment."

Olivia's mouth tasted like something had died in it. "This is the point in the program where I tell you that you'll never get away with this and you share your clever plan with me."

"Since you'll never escape this building, I don't have a problem with that scenario. Your rebel friends have been sneaking around outside for the last hour or so. They probably don't realize that I can see them moving into place to attack, but that's okay. It's all part of my so-called clever plan."

"Not to quibble, but technically you're the rebel. We're the resistance."

"So you did know. I'd been curious." Abigail rose from behind the desk and walked around to stand in front of Olivia. "I really don't care what you and the scum like you call yourselves. You're traitors, and once we restore the Lords to power in this system, we'll root you out."

Olivia shook her head. "You know the AIs murdered trillions of people to enslave humanity. How could anyone support continuing that?"

"Because I and the other loyalists get to wear the boots on the necks of people like you. The AIs are in control, and nothing you do will ever change that. What did you hope to accomplish? Revolution? The Lords are firmly entrenched and have enough firepower to stop anything you try."

"It looks like you're the one in the building about to be overrun. In the end, it doesn't matter if I live or die. The resistance will win. You can't stop men in powered armor."

The other woman laughed. "That's the best part. I don't have to. Once the attack begins, I'll scurry out your secret exit and let them have everything. Ah! You didn't know I knew about that, did you?

"You also didn't know we made extra nuclear weapons when we built the bomb-pumped lasers that destroyed the stations and the superdreadnought. We had to, because we didn't know where we'd need to put every weapon. Besides the three that are still in place in buildings Master Calder owns, I had the spare brought here. Once I'm away, I'll blow it up. Oh, and you, too."

Olivia tried to keep the despair she felt off her face, but she doubted she'd succeeded.

* * *

JARED WAS AMAZED at how stealthy *Persephone* was. After they began moving toward the gas giant where the enemy awaited them, the computer advised going to what it called "active stealth" and increasing speed substantially.

That seemed counterintuitive, so he tried to find out what that entailed. The computer politely told him to mind his own business. It was classified, and he didn't have need to know.

Somewhat nonplussed, he kept the speed where it was and told the computer to engage active stealth. Due to the position of Boxer Station, he could communicate with it without risking the enemy receiving a transmission that tipped their hand for most of the trip out. They managed that by restricting where the communication beams went.

The staff at Boxer Station had replaced the scanner units destroyed in battle, so they had a good view of the system that didn't tell the enemy anything they didn't already know.

"Boxer Station, *Persephone*. We've gone active with stealth. How are you reading us?"

The voice of the lieutenant in charge of Boxer Station's repairs sounded shocked when she came on. *"Persephone,* we've lost you on our scanners. You were there one moment and then you were gone. We've gone to targeting scans, and we think we *might* have you ranged, but we can't be sure."

That was ridiculous. They were right in Boxer Station's lap. There was no way they could *fail* to see them. At this range, they could have seen the fighter that he loved so much, even just coasting along.

Jared shook his head and stepped over behind the helm console. "Take us up to the speed that the computer recommended."

Lieutenant Heather Brand touched her console. "Increasing speed."

"Persephone, we have you again," Boxer Station said.

"I knew it was too good to be true," he muttered. "Go ahead, Boxer Station. How clear is the reading?"

"It's spooky, Admiral. Even though we know pretty much where you are, the readings aren't firm at all, and they're getting weaker as you pull away. By the time you get to extreme missile range, we'll have lost you again. If we weren't painting you hard, we'd have already done so. Whatever stealth that little ship has, it's amazing."

This might have a chance of working after all.

* * *

SEAN COULDN'T BELIEVE he was even trying this. He had a ring of marines around the council building, entrenched with heavy weapons. At his command, they'd storm the building after pinnaces took out the defensive positions. Inside five minutes, they'd have most areas under their control.

So, instead of going with that relatively safe plan, he was sneaking through the sewers with his rag-tag team of marines and the coordinator's closest confederates. Their plan? To find a spot where they could breach an unused subbasement with a shaped plasma charge. Then they'd infiltrate the more traveled corridors and try to rescue the coordinator.

What could possibly go wrong?

The coordinator's tech wizard had a scanner of some kind and was probing the walls of the wretched tunnel. The incredible stench didn't faze the woman in the slightest.

"I think about here." She tapped the moldy, stained plascrete beside her. "This should be about three meters thick and heavily reinforced. You'll want to keep from going overboard with the blast. If you take out the wall on the other side of the room, you might bring down the level above it. That one has machinery that will be noted if it goes offline, and it might collapse this whole section of the building."

"Lovely. Everyone, spread out. If this building is so shielded, how do you know where to place the charges?"

"Power conduits," the woman said as she made her way past him, wisely retreating down the sewer. "I can see the ones feeding the area around the council building, and they give me distances."

"So, you're guessing."

The woman's eyes narrowed. "You don't have to be insulting. This is much more refined than a guess."

He raised his hands in surrender. "Have it your way."

The marine armorer carefully placed a plasma charge on the wall. They could tailor the output by regulating how much plasma it generated. That theoretically allowed them to use only the force necessary. They'd know in just a minute how good the tech lady was.

"We're ready, sir," the man said. "We need to pull back about fifty meters. I can remotely detonate it at that point."

Once they were in place, he made sure the marines were ready to charge and gave the order to go.

The explosion was more significant than he'd expected but still low key. The plasma flash was blinding, but they'd shielded their eyes. Once it was done, they rushed in. The hole through the wall was large enough for them to use but still bubbled with heat.

One look through told him that the blast had trashed the room, but it hadn't done more than blacken the far wall. The tech had called it almost precisely. Dinner was on him if they made it through this alive.

The marines tossed heat-resistant material over the shattered remnants of the wall and scrambled into the council building. They divided into teams to hit the critical areas as quickly as possible. He led his people up three levels to near where the coordinator's office was and waited for the word that everyone was in place.

One by one, the teams checked in. When the last one was ready, he gave the order. "Go. Go. Go."

* * *

KELSEY WATCHED the gas giant through *Persephone*'s passive scanners as they entered orbit. It was beautiful, in a cold, ethereal way. All pale colors in sharp bands. A darker-blue storm that was probably bigger than Avalon churned along the equator.

She and the marines were strapped into their slots on the two pinnaces the Marine Recon ship boasted. They'd had to leave

Invincible's pinnaces back at Boxer Station. They weren't stealthy enough.

They slipped past the protective station without it seeing them. Based on the way the missiles and beam emplacements were laid out, it wouldn't be able to shoot at them now. That was one less thing to worry about. She didn't know if there were other stations hidden in the planet's depths, but that was a problem for another day.

The station hosting the battlecruisers wasn't scanning, but they'd be hard to miss if anyone was looking at the area visually. Their only chance for success was to slip up completely unseen.

Persephone would stay in the clouds above the battlecruisers. The stealthed pinnaces would drop down as quickly as possible and try and land on the station before anyone saw them.

"Talbot, is everyone ready?" she asked.

The marine nodded. "Ready, Princess. Say the word and we drop down on these bastards and ruin their day."

They'd crammed almost two hundred marines into the two pinnaces, a third more than they were rated for. Yet that was a ridiculously small number of people to storm a space station and four battlecruisers. Less than forty on each team.

The only saving grace was that the enemy had to have even fewer people. Not counting any automated weapons platforms, of course. If those were active, they'd all die.

"Kelsey, we're in position," Jared said over the encrypted combat link. "They're not showing any sign they know we're up here. Once you cut free and start dropping, you'll be at the station in less than sixty seconds. Are you ready?"

"As ready as we'll ever be. Everyone, stand by for drop."

"Good luck."

The pinnaces cut loose and fell like stones into the pale clouds.

* * *

ABIGAIL HAPPENED to be pouring a drink when she felt something shake the building. Just a little. The ripples in the expensive alcohol told her she hadn't imagined it.

"Well, I think we might have some visitors," she purred at Olivia. "If so, I'd best be on my way. I wouldn't want to linger and get caught up in the blast. Do say hello to everyone for me, and pass along my heartfelt wishes for them to roast in Hell."

She sent the activation command to the warhead, and the timer went live. Fifteen minutes. Now it was unstoppable.

Olivia couldn't respond. After a while of listening to the woman rave, Abigail had gagged her. That was unexpectedly satisfying.

The former coordinator of Harrison's World glared at her replacement as Abigail made her way through the secret door behind the bar and into the small lift hidden there. It took her quickly down to an abandoned grav train station.

The massive concourse must've once served a large section of the city, but now it sat forgotten. Not empty, though. A shiny new grav train waited to whisk the coordinator away to safety in case of a dire emergency.

And it would fulfill that function. The title was hers. And the best part? Abigail could blame the explosion on her enemy. Nothing could stop her now.

34

Sean led the men and women under his command toward the coordinator's office. They had stunners out as their primary weapons because they'd rather not injure any more people than absolutely necessary.

He'd visited the Imperial Senate building back on Avalon as a kid and then later as a serving officer called to give testimony on Fleet affairs. This place one-upped that august building in snoot factor. Seriously, who put marble busts of all the former councilors in little alcoves? After five hundred years, they were *everywhere*.

Everything around them spoke of large amounts of money spent for the sole purpose of showing off wealth and power. As corrupt as some of the senators at home were—and he knew one such man very well from his association with Captain Breckenridge—they weren't in the same league as this.

Thankfully, most of the defenders were elsewhere. Probably guarding the most likely exterior approaches. All he saw at first were civilians, who wisely fled.

That changed when they arrived at the executive wing. Armed and uniformed security commanded them to halt and then opened fire with flechette pistols. His people outnumbered them, though, and their stunners carried the day. One of the coordinator's people was badly wounded in the firefight, so he detailed a few people to guard their backs and watch over her.

Sean expected the coordinator's office to be under heavy guard, but the outer office was deserted. The marines flowed into the main room and cleared it quickly. Coordinator West sat tied to a chair and gagged.

He pulled the cloth from her mouth. "Are you okay?"

"No. She has a nuclear device in the building. It's activated and on a short timer. We need to initiate an evacuation right now. We only have ten minutes."

Sean used his knife to cut her free. "Most of the people won't get clear in time. Where is it?"

The coordinator's tech woman ran behind the desk. "The computer is wiped, but the basic system controls are still intact. I think I can—"

A loud alarm began wailing outside the door. The tech looked smug. "Fire alarm. It won't get them far, but it's better than nothing."

Coordinator West rubbed her wrists and stood as soon as she was free. "Abigail used the secret escape route in this office. I know where it lets out. I need some people to get me there fast in whatever grav vehicle we can find. We might be able to get the code from her."

Sean pulled out his Fleet com. "I need a pinnace on the roof right now with two squads of marines. Eliminate the defensive positions and pick up Coordinator West. Take her wherever she wants to go. Fall back ASAP. There's an armed nuke in the building on a short timer. Ten minutes."

They reversed course and made their way back toward the rotunda. Muted explosions outside told him the marines were carrying out his orders.

The tech came up beside him. "I think I know where the bomb is. If we can get to it, I might be able to disarm it."

"What are you?" he asked. "Some kind of vid hero? How can you do all this stuff?"

"Years of hacking everything that can be hacked, and some things that supposedly can't. No matter how well shielded this thing is, there'll be radiation. If they wanted to keep that under wraps, the only place that makes sense is the vault."

"Vault? Like in a bank vault?"

She nodded. "Pretty much. It's under the rotunda."

Olivia smiled grimly. "That would be just like her." She ducked into an office and wrote something on an important-looking piece of paper. "Here's the door code."

Sean grabbed the marine armorer. "We might be able to get to the nuke. Can they be disarmed?"

The marine nodded. "If it's not too complex or booby-trapped. It's possible."

"Come with me. Everyone else, go with the coordinator."

* * *

THE PINNACES DROPPED out of the clouds right on top of the station. Kelsey could clearly see it on the visual scanners as they fell toward it. She waited for it to open fire or for one of the battlecruisers to blast them, but nothing happened.

Right before they hit the station, the pilots savagely decelerated and clamped onto the hull. The ramp went down, and a marine tossed out a magnetic breaching charge. Once the ramp was back up, they remotely detonated it.

The shock wave shook the pinnace badly but didn't dislodge them. The marines lowered the ramp again and poured out of the pinnace. They made it into the station without any problems and bypassed the closest emergency containment doors.

She expected an alarm to be sounding, but it was quiet inside. There was computer access, but it rejected her attempts to interface.

"Talbot, take your men and block access to battlecruisers one and two," she ordered. "Lieutenant Evans, you have three and four. I'll find the station command center."

"On it," Talbot said. "Keep your head down, Princess. We have unfinished business."

She grinned and led her team deeper into the station. There were no markings to indicate where anything was. She'd just have to assume that the control center was somewhere in the central shaft.

They took to the stairs to make sure no one ambushed them in the lifts. Somewhere in the distance, she heard the sound of flechette rifles firing.

"This is team three," a voice said. "We're encountering hostile fire from the docking port to battlecruiser three. Men without combat armor. We're going in."

A few moments later, teams four and one called in. They'd gained access to battlecruisers one and four without resistance. Those ships seemed to be in standby mode. Main power was offline.

Talbot called in last. "We're getting fire from battlecruiser two. Nothing serious. We're going in."

"This is team three. We're in. The battlecruiser also seems to be in standby mode. Main power offline. We're starting our sweep."

"Talbot here. Battlecruiser two is online. Main power active. We're heading for engineering."

Kelsey keyed her com. "Teams one, three, and four, if you do not encounter resistance, detach your reserves to assist team two. Lock down your engineering spaces to keep the main systems offline."

A stream of acknowledgements flowed back to her. If only one of
the battlecruisers was active, they might be able to win this even if it
got away.

"*Persephone*, this is Bandar. Three of the battlecruisers seem to be
offline. We're securing them. Be ready if the last one gets away."

"Copy," Jared said. "We're not seeing any action from the station
above us, so I'm going to leave it be. If the battlecruiser breaks away,
we'll take it out. We'd have already opened fire on it, but the station
raised battle screens as soon as you breached it. It's brought targeting
scanners online, too. That means it'll lay into us as soon as we act. Do
what you can to stop it from detaching."

"We'll do our best. Bandar out."

That was about the time that the stairwell door below them opened
and men poured in. They immediately opened fire on her.

* * *

OLIVIA RACED to the roof of the council building and met the marine
pinnace as it came roaring in for a landing. The far side of the roof was
on fire. It looked as though something had exploded. She ran up the
ramp as soon as it came down, with the rest of the infiltration team at
her heels.

"I need to talk to the pilot," she told the man with the headset. "To
show him where to go."

"This way, ma'am."

He led her through a door at the front of the pinnace and to a small
compartment where the two pilots sat.

One of them, a woman, looked over her shoulder. "Sit down at the
flight engineer's console and tell me which way to go."

There was only one seat open, so Olivia sat and looked at the map
the woman had put on display for her. "Go south. You're looking for a
warehouse near the edge of the city. I'll find it before we get there. Make
it fast. We don't have much time."

"Roger that."

The woman turned and touched the controls. The pinnace lifted
smoothly into the air and blasted forward, crushing Olivia into her seat
with acceleration. Now she knew how thrilled and terrified her driver
must've felt when he got to go fast.

She tore her attention away from the pinnace and studied the map.
Whoever had designed and installed the escape route had used one of
the city's old grav train links. The line now terminated at a warehouse.

"I have it."

"Excellent. Touch it on the screen."

Olivia touched the warehouse on the map.

The pilot was silent a moment. "I have it. There look to be two normal ways in. A cargo loading area and a personnel door."

"There's a disabled lift in the office area on the south side," Olivia said. "Only, it's not disabled. It leads down to a train station. My implants can open it and control the lift."

The pilot spoke softly, probably to the marines. Then she nodded. "Let me land the pinnace so you can approach from the street."

She brought the pinnace down, and the marine that had brought Olivia up to the flight deck escorted her back out.

The heavily armed marines surrounded her as she made her way into the building. The lift opened to her implant command. Half a dozen marines went in with her and pushed her behind them. That seemed fair. They had all that armor.

She sent the lift down to the station below. The doors opened just in time for the train carrying Abigail to pull to a stop.

The doors on the vehicle slid open and Abigail ran out, only to freeze when she saw all the weapons pointed at her.

"I'll wager this comes as a shock," Olivia said. "Don't you villains ever learn?"

"But...How could you...I left you..."

Olivia held out her hand to the nearest marine. "May I borrow your pistol?"

The man handed her a flechette pistol that she could barely get her fingers around. It felt as though it weighed a ton.

"I don't have time to blather. Give me the code to disarm the nuclear device."

"Go screw yourself."

Olivia shot her in the leg. The pistol kicked harder than she'd expected. A big splotch of blood appeared on the other woman's leg, and she fell down screaming.

"Is that enough, or shall I shoot you in the other leg?"

Abigail snarled at her. "You can go to hell. I've already killed millions, and you'll just shoot me anyway."

Olivia thought about that for a moment and nodded. "I think you're right." She raised the pistol and pointed it at the other woman's head. "I should shoot you dead, but then I'd have to live with that memory in my head. I'll just have to settle for something else."

She smashed the barrel of the weapon across Abigail's face, breaking her nose. Far less satisfying but not as cold as an on-the-spot execution.

"We need to go, ma'am," the marine said, gently taking his pistol back from her. "The LT says we only have five minutes to get clear of the area. If Commander Meyer can't stop the bomb, we don't want to be here when it goes off."

She let them hustle her and their sobbing prisoner back into the lift and prayed the commander was able to stop the looming atrocity.

35

J ared listened to the chatter between the teams with mixed emotions. They'd completely surprised the enemy, that was for sure. Three of the four battlecruisers were powered down and drawing needed resources from the station.

That was good. That was *great*.

Except for the fact that the last one was on internal power and coming to life. That was bad. *Very* bad.

The bad guys must've focused their attention on that one. It made sense. A completely functional warship of that size would have a very good chance of taking out every mobile vessel in this system. It could certainly defend this planet from all attacks while they took their time getting the other three ready to fight, especially with the armed station above it.

Kelsey and the rest had an excellent chance of taking everything else intact. All that left for him to do was figure out how to defeat a ship the size and power of *Courageous* with a damaged Marine Recon vessel. One with only two operational beam weapons and no missiles at all.

"The operational battlecruiser has detached from the station," Lieutenant Brand said. "It raised battle screens before it exited the station's cover. They appear to be opening the range from the station but are not accelerating much at all."

"Can we penetrate their screens with our beams, *Persephone*?"

"Yes, Admiral. However, the amount of damage this vessel can cause is limited, and its battle screens are significantly weaker than those of a battlecruiser. One direct salvo will likely destroy this vessel."

They needed a bigger weapon. Well, it just so happened that they had one. He opened a shipwide channel. "All hands, this is Admiral Mertz. I want all nonessential personnel to go to the rescue pods and stand by. When I give the order, the rest of you will have thirty seconds to join them. Slave all controls to the bridge. I'll eject you when the time is right. It's been an honor."

That seemed entirely too much like the speech he'd given on *Invincible* earlier.

"Lieutenant Brand, lay in a course to ram the battlecruiser in the engineering section. If we can disable their drives, it won't be a threat anymore."

"Aye, sir. I'll need to move us around to a better approach vector. It will only take a—"

She leaned forward and stared at her console. "Explosion on the battlecruiser. Something big in the engineering section."

Jared tapped into the scanner feed. It was a damned big explosion. Now there were large secondary blasts ripping the aft section of the ship into chunks. Its grav drives failed, and it began falling.

That's when he saw a pinnace detach from the hull of the doomed battlecruiser. It looked damaged, too.

"We're receiving a transmission," Brand said.

The overheads came to life. "*Persephone*, this is Talbot. We've disengaged from the battlecruiser, but we took some damage. A hand would be really nice, because our drive just failed."

The pinnace arced downward and disappeared into the clouds below the station. It didn't have the strong hull a battlecruiser did. The pressure would quickly crush it.

"Take us after it," Jared ordered. He hoped they could catch it before the pressure did their own compromised hull fatal damage. If that happened, they'd all die.

* * *

THE BOMB WAS RIGHT where the tech suspected. On any other day, he'd stare at all the art and baubles packed into the small room. Today he only had eyes for the oblong weapon set on top of an ancient, hand-carved chest.

Sean stared at the complex bundles of wires and controls on the nuclear weapon with apprehension. Especially when the armorer shook his head.

"No way," the man said. "I can't defuse that in five minutes."

The tech attached her computer to it. "Maybe we can disable the antitampering mechanisms. It's not as if we have much to lose. We can't get far enough away to survive the blast anyway."

Feeling like a third wheel, Sean watched the two of them work feverishly. The countdown clock was racing toward zero, and still time seemed to flow like molasses.

At fifty-three seconds, the tech shouted in triumph. "I've disabled the antitampering features!"

"Can you disarm it?"

The marine shook his head. "No, but I'll keep trying."

That's when the solution hit Sean. "Can we accidentally set it off?"

"No."

"Put the spare breaching charge on it and run like hell."

The man gaped at him for a second, whipped off his pack, and pulled out the spare charge. He fiddled with the controls and slid it under the bomb. "Out! We need to close the vault to maximize the damage."

That was probably going to piss off a number of wealthy and powerful people. He could live with that.

Seconds later, the three of them had the vault closed and were running for all they were worth. They made it into the stairwell just as the charge went off.

The good news was that he immediately knew the nuke had failed to explode. The bad news was that the stairs collapsed on them, and he lost consciousness in a moment bright with pain.

Kelsey hunched down and returned fire at the hostiles. They didn't have powered armor, so the exchange was very unfair.

"Make a bridgehead," she said. "Find the control room, and let's pin them down."

The marines moved ahead of her and immediately ran into heavy resistance. They kept moving forward, but the bad guys contested every centimeter. The fighters on the other side had the benefit of knowing the layout and having prepared the area for defense. They hadn't had long, but someone over there knew what they were doing.

"All teams," Kelsey said. "Send everyone you can to deck nine. Find a way in and put pressure on the defenders. Hell, make a new way in and keep them off balance. We need to end this now before someone over there gets desperate."

She got responses from everyone but Talbot.

"Talbot? Do you read?"

More ominous silence.

"Anyone from team two. Respond."

After another lengthy silence, she called Jared. "*Persephone*, do you see anything going on with battlecruiser two?"

Her brother's silence was even more frightening.

An explosion in the distance announced one of the other teams making a move. The marines in front of her used it as a cue to drive forward. There was a hail of flechettes, and then they were overrunning the defenders.

The fight trailed off rapidly from there. The defense had been very fragile. Once the marines made it in, they rapidly seized control of the deck except for the armored hatch leading to the control center.

With the ships not showing signs of resistance, and no one finding people on any other deck, she suspected the remaining enemy was on the other side of that hatch. So she needed to get inside and end this.

But she'd try to talk them into surrendering first. There were obviously things going on under the surface of Harrison's World that she'd like to settle before they had to leave.

The hatch had a communications interface, so she linked to it through her armor.

"Surely you don't expect us to just open the door?" a man asked. He sounded cultured. Refined.

"That would be the sensible thing to do," she said. "We have control of this station and the ships. This isn't going to go in your favor. Yield and you live. Resist and die. It's as simple as that."

He laughed. "After what we've already done? Don't insult my intelligence. You'll turn us over to someone on Harrison's World for trial and execution."

She had to admit he had a point. There was no chance these people wouldn't pay the ultimate penalty for their part in the nuclear explosions. No matter what she promised, that debt would need to be paid.

"True," she said. "How about a quick death after a fair and speedy trial?"

She didn't know where she'd read that, but it seemed like the appropriate brand of gallows humor.

"Thanks, but we'll just stay where we are. You're welcome to come in, but I promise you a warm welcome. Oh, and I'm sure you'd rather not destroy the controls and computer for this station. That might make things dicey when the grav drives fail. Like what happened to your ship."

Hopefully, that was a lie, but Jared's silence worried her.

She terminated the conversation and turned to the marines. "Okay, we need a plan to get into that compartment without destroying everything. Ideas?"

Lieutenant Terry Evans eyed the hatch. "That looks pretty thick. We need to figure out how large the control center is and see if there are other ways in."

"That's a good place to start," she said. "Everyone spread out and find me a way in. I'll watch the hatch."

It only took them a few minutes to make the assessment and regroup.

"It's big," Evans said. "Maybe thirty meters across. This is the only entrance on this level."

"What about above it or below?"

He shook his head. "We'd have to breach it, and that'll still wreck almost everything in there when we come in shooting."

It doesn't have to.

She listened to the voice of the dead Marine Raider. *What are you thinking, Ned?*

If you set a plasma grenade on the lowest setting, it will probably breach the compartment. I'd suggest the ceiling. The odds of something important being that high are minimal. Once you gain access, you can toss a combat remote down the hole and jump in after it.

Kelsey shook her head. *I'd still trash the compartment with flechettes. If I go for stunners, they'll shoot it up resisting me. And me too, of course.*

They'll be somewhat disoriented from the breaching. To minimize damage, I suggest you use my swords. If the marines toss in smoke, the enemy will have difficulty even seeing you. Your implants will let you see them just fine, though.

I've never used those swords in combat. I'm pretty sure I wouldn't be very effective with them. You had years of practice and training.

I could use them for you, if you permit.

She considered the plan for a moment and slowly nodded. *I'll do it. Thanks. You have my permission to control my body during the upcoming combat until the fighting is over.*

"Okay," she said. "Here's the plan."

To say they all thought it was a bad idea was an understatement. "Suicide" was the word that Evans used.

So she put her foot down. "I think the odds are a little better than that. In the end, what choice do we have? Come on. We don't have any more time to waste."

She almost dragged a couple of reluctant marines up to the next level and estimated where the control center was under them. There were some empty compartments that might have been offices on a normal space station. Leave it to an AI to include them on a station that most likely never saw a permanent staff.

Kelsey picked the compartment that was best placed and got everyone ready. One marine would toss the reduced-strength plasma grenade, another would throw a combat remote into the breach, and the rest would follow up with smoke.

She drew her swords. "Go."

Even at reduced strength, the plasma grenade sounded like the end of the world. It blasted a hole in the deck bigger than the office. The marines followed up with the remote and smoke.

Her armor processed the signals and gave her a layout of the control center. It was big, all right, and full of people staggering around as though they were drunk and firing pistols at shadows.

No time to waste.

Kelsey jumped into the compartment and gave herself over to Ned Quincy.

It was very much like when she'd allowed what was to become Ned to control her the last time. Except this time there was a lot more blood. Arms and hands seemed to be the preferred targets to her swings, though there were a few thrusts. And screams. Lots of screams.

All in all, killing everyone in the compartment didn't prove necessary, thank God. Some people were unconscious, and others chose to surrender. Those with missing hands or arms had no choice but to stop fighting or die.

Less than thirty seconds after she jumped into the compartment, the fight was over, and Ned returned control of her body to her.

She really needed to start working with these swords so that she could do that for herself. She opened the hatch, and the marines rushed in, securing the compartment and the prisoners.

While they did that, Kelsey found an active control panel and accessed the station's scanners.

The battlecruiser was far below them. It seemed to be in the process of coming apart as it fell. *Persephone* was somewhat higher but also falling. She doubted it could go much lower and survive.

* * *

JARED HAD to take *Persephone* deeper than he'd have preferred, but the able Lieutenant Brand came up with a way to save the pinnace. She flew the ship under it and slowed their descent until the pinnace was safely on top of the ship.

The marines made their way to the nearest airlock, which was on a slope, so that made getting them in trickier than it would have been in space. Then they slowly rose up until they were back in the same clear atmospheric band as the station.

As soon as they became visible, Kelsey called the ship.

"Thank God!" she said. "We thought you were gone."

"No," he said, "though getting Talbot and his men off that ship was a hell of a lot more complicated than it should've been. What's your status?"

"We've secured the station. We have injured and wounded prisoners. The station computer is being unexpectedly cooperative. The prisoners never expected us to get into the control room so quickly. I found an open console with the command overrides already entered."

She smiled at him over the link. "This fight is over."

36

Twenty-four hours later, Jared was sitting back at Lord Hawthorne's estate with Kelsey at his side, Olivia West and Commander Meyer sat across from him, and Lord Hawthorne was making drinks.

The commander was a bit worse for wear. He sported an arm that had been broken twice in one day, three broken ribs, and a shattered knee, but he was in good spirits. Things could've been worse. He didn't die in a nuclear explosion, for example.

"Are we sure that there aren't any other little surprises scattered around the system?" Lord Hawthorne asked.

Jared shrugged. "We can't tell until we examine everything more closely, but why have a second station hidden when you have something like that one?"

Olivia nodded. "That fits with what we've been able to pull from Abigail and Lord Calder. Once we authorized the use of truth drugs, they spilled their secrets readily enough. Our forces raided their secret base—the one where their single pinnace came from—and we'll be going through their secrets for quite some time. The gas giant station was there as backup for the system AI, by the way. If things got bad, it would activate the extra ships.

"Your attack on Boxer Station was so sudden and overwhelming that it didn't have time to complete the activation. After you won, the station shut the battlecruisers back down when it never received final orders from the AI."

She sighed. "That illustrates how badly outclassed we'd have been if we'd have attacked it on our own. It would have destroyed us. Thank you."

"Yet here you are," Kelsey said, "in undisputed control of this planet. With the loyalists on the run, you can consolidate your gains. And now that Doctor Leonard has repaired the malfunctioning flip jammer, we're not in deadly danger of the computer-controlled destroyers overrunning us.

"Speaking of which, he could use some help repairing the third one that was damaged in the original fight. We'd like to block Erorsi and Pentagar off from the Rebel Empire. In fact, it would be very useful if we could make more of those."

Lord Hawthorne grimaced. "We can probably repair the one unit, but we won't be building more very quickly. It took years to construct the ones we have. It requires incredibly fine tolerances in the parts and a host of rare materials. We anticipated expanding the construction later. So, no, we don't have any spares laying around. That third one is actually meant to be a spare."

"Pity," Jared said. "Still, we have time. We also can't count on that device being a panacea. Anything man can build, he can circumvent. We have to plan on that happening and not rely on being safe forever.

"We'll move the spare to Erorsi, and we'll just have to take some calculated risks when we take them offline for maintenance. We'll need the parts and manuals, of course."

The nobleman nodded. "I'll get them for you tomorrow."

"We've made arrangements for a cutter to bring the bodies we found on *Invincible* down tomorrow, too," Kelsey told Olivia. "I know they were your comrades, and they deserve to finally come home."

He could see the coordinator's eyes growing damp.

"Thank you. That means a lot to me." Olivia cleared her throat. "What do we do next? Obviously, freeing the rest of the Empire won't happen overnight, but that has to be our goal. We fix the ships we can and make our plans going forward.

"Well, so long as that's what the emperor says. We're under your authority when it comes to things like that."

"Don't you already have a lot to do here?" Sean asked. "Rescue operations and recovery from the nuclear explosions will take years. Suppressing the loyalists and keeping them from other mischief will take even longer."

"That's a good point," Kelsey said, "but we need to be working toward that goal. Here's what I propose. Our ships will need weeks of repairs. Perhaps months. That gives us time to help get things in motion.

"We'll get the shipyard at Boxer Station back online and reactivate the asteroid mines. Raw materials and finished parts will be key to getting the repairs of the derelict vessels under way. I'm more than happy to share those responsibilities with Harrison's World, with the understanding that Fleet needs to keep the system and the ships locked down. We've all seen what a few unpleasant surprises look like when they threaten to put the AIs back in control."

That brought immediate nods from everyone.

"On behalf of Harrison's World," Olivia said, "I can say we have no desire to rush things. And I don't care who overthrows the AIs, so long as it's done."

There was nothing like a near-death experience or two to get people cooperating, Jared thought. "So, we'll need to leave some people here when we go back to Avalon. Specifically, we need a senior Fleet officer to command Boxer Station."

Kelsey nodded her agreement. "I realize you have Captain Black, but he's going to have his hands full. And until I know you better, I want someone I know to be in charge."

She turned to Commander Meyer and pointed her finger at him. "Poof, you're a Commodore. Welcome to command of Boxer Station and the system space of Harrison's World."

Jared enjoyed how the newly promoted officer's eyes bugged out. It was nice to watch his sister roll over someone else for a change.

"Wait a minute!" the flabbergasted officer said. "I'm not even cleared for duty. I was relieved and charged with a whole host of crimes."

"I hereby dismiss those charges," Jared said. "The doctors will get you cleared for duty long before we're ready to go. You'll be able to get your implants done, too.

"I'll solve one of my headaches by leaving you the senior officers from *Spear* and *Shadow*. You know them best, and they won't have problems working for you. And, of course, plenty of men and women to fill out your work rosters."

Jared turned to Olivia while Meyer mentally floundered around. "Once we're certain we have all the data we can get off the system AI, we'll wipe it and rebuild the personality with uncorrupted code. It will be able to run the station and probably increase the efficiency of the construction bays in getting our ships fixed."

"I'm sure Captain Black would like a look at both the hardware and software before you do that," she said. "At some point, we may want to build more. To fight the AIs, we might need some of our own."

"Speaking of parity," Kelsey said, "I need to bring up a touchy subject. I haven't been here long, but I can see that the Rebel Empire has a well-defined caste system. That comes from the AIs, and it has to go. The built-in discrimination has to stop."

Lord Hawthorne sighed. "We know. Changing it wasn't an option before you came. Having met you has brought just how deeply ingrained it is into stark relief. We'll lean heavily on Commodore Meyer and his people to point out where we need to change and take steps. It can start with universal implants."

Olivia nodded vigorously. "First, we need to start getting people's existing implants updated before they learn what's really going on and the AI code makes them start fighting us. Then we *will* begin making civilian implants available to everyone."

"The senior military officers come first," Lord Hawthorne agreed. "Then the other council members. As we clear the top people, they'll smooth the way for doing their subordinates. By the time you're ready to return home, we should be secure. Other than Captain Black, only the people in this room know your secret."

"Then we can begin the process of making implants universally available," Olivia said. "The plans for the normal civilian models are in the computer at the Grant Research Facility. We can get production lines set up for both versions. We can have spare equipment built for you by the time your ships are ready to travel.

"We also examined the small, computer-controlled weapons platforms. They were definitely built by human beings, but not on Harrison's World."

"We actually found the construction facility," Jared said. "It's on Boxer Station. It looks as though the AI forced the Fleet engineering people to design and build them for it. Thankfully, it wasn't automated, or there might have been even more of the damned things. That said, I'm considering how we might be able to use something like them in the future. I *hate* losing marines. A wave of these up front might save a lot of lives. I'll see that you get plans for them, too."

"What about the Raider implants and equipment?" Kelsey asked. "Can Grant build those?"

"Maybe," Olivia said. "Now that you have the full specs, it's at least possible. They'd certainly help make a difference with the Marines. That's something to talk with Captain Black about. He's already made a lot of progress in mass-production of civilian-grade medical nanites. He expects to have Fleet grade ones very soon."

"Are those the same as what I have?"

Olivia shook her head. "No. He's already found the ones used by the

Raiders are significantly more advanced. More powerful and more capable. Those will take more study."

"Ned tells me they were fairly new in his time," Kelsey said. "Top-of-the-line gear."

"Captain Black thought so, too. He's adjusting the process and may very well have something worked out by the time you're ready to depart.

"Speaking of departing, when you go, I'd like to send William with you as our representative to the Imperial Senate and the head of our delegation."

Kelsey looked around, satisfied. "That sounds perfect. We don't have a crisis in sight. I'm seeing smooth sailing all the way home!"

Jared wished he shared her optimism. If the last year had been anything to go by, something else would come out of nowhere to bite them in the ass. And, of course, he'd have to deal with the fallout of what they'd done and with his homicidal half brother that was certain he was out to steal the Throne.

Well, that trouble was for another day. He stood, refilled his glass, and then topped off everyone else.

"Everyone," he said solemnly, "I give you the Empire. May she triumph over her enemies."

The rest of them climbed to their feet and raised their glasses.

MAILING LIST

Want the next book in the series? Grab *Paying the Price* today or any of Terry's other books below.

Want Terry to email you when he publishes a new book in any format or when one goes on sale? Go to TerryMixon.com/Mailing-List and sign up. Those are the only times he'll contact you. No spam.

Did you enjoy the book? Please leave a review on Amazon or Goodreads. It only takes a minute to dash off a few sentences and that kind of thing helps more than you can imagine.

You can always find the most up to date listing of Terry's titles on his Amazon Author Page.

The Empire of Bones Saga
Empire of Bones
Veil of Shadows
Command Decisions
Ghosts of Empire
Paying the Price
Reconnaissance in Force
Behind Enemy Lines
The Terran Gambit

The Empire of Bones Saga Volume 1

The Humanity Unlimited Saga
Liberty Station
Freedom Express
Tree of Liberty

The Fractured Republic Saga
Storm Divers

The Scorched Earth Saga
Scorched Earth

The Vigilante Duology with Glynn Stewart
Heart of Vengeance
Oath of Vengeance

ABOUT TERRY

#1 Bestselling Military Science Fiction author Terry Mixon served as a non-commissioned officer in the United States Army 101st Airborne Division. He later worked alongside the flight controllers in the Mission Control Center at the NASA Johnson Space Center supporting the Space Shuttle, the International Space Station, and other human spaceflight projects.

He now writes full time while living in Texas with his lovely wife and a pounce of cats.

www.TerryMixon.com
Terry@terrymixon.com

http://www.facebook.com/TerryLMixon

https://www.amazon.com/Terry-Mixon/e/B00J15TJFM

37075087R00157

Made in the USA
Lexington, KY
20 April 2019